# – Armada Wars –
# List of the Dead

## R. Curtis Venture

# – Copyright –

First published in December 2014.

ISBN-10: 1505896010
ISBN-13: 978-1505896015

Copyright © 2014 R. Curtis Venture, all rights reserved. R. Curtis Venture asserts the moral right to be identified as the author of this work and the owner of the intellectual properties within.

All characters and situations appearing in this work are fictitious. Any resemblance to real persons, living or dead, or to real events, is purely coincidental.

ArmadaWars.com

## – By the Author –

**Short Stories:**

*Kudos*

**Novels:**

*Steal from the Devil*

*List of the Dead*

*The Ravening Deep*

This is **vol. two** of Armada Wars.
Reading the books in the correct order
is highly recommended.

## — Contents —

Prologue: Splinters .................................................. 5
01 – Settling Dust ................................................... 21
02 – Survivors ....................................................... 40
03 – *Disputer* ...................................................... 56
04 – The Beast of Blacktree ...................................... 85
05 – You Don't Choose .......................................... 104
06 – Change of Plans ............................................. 114
07 – The Ashes of Lophrit ...................................... 132
08 – The Occupation of Mibes ................................ 149
09 – Boys Will Be Boys .......................................... 175
10 – The High Ground .......................................... 189
11 – Roll Out the Tanks ......................................... 214
12 – The Natives are Restless ................................. 240
13 – The List ........................................................ 268
14 – Your Mother's Son ......................................... 289
15 – These Old Scars ............................................. 304
16 – *Tenebrae* ..................................................... 319
17 – Shaeld Hratha ............................................... 340
18 – Compromised ............................................... 361
19 – A Rock and a Hard Place ................................ 384
20 – Fear the Deep ............................................... 402
Epilogue .............................................................. 416
About the Author ................................................. 424

# – Prologue –
## Splinters

Almost another full day passed before the bone-shaking quakes ceased, before the air grew still and silent. Gradually, after nearly another hour had gone by, the birds began to take up their calls once more. The electric thrum of insect life returned just as cautiously, eventually contributing to a sense that nothing was out of the ordinary whatsoever, that nothing strange had happened.

But it *had*.

Junn Delanka was still on watch. It was not that he did not trust the young couple to wake him if anything happened; Omin had shown himself to be both resourceful and brave, and Halfre was doing a remarkable job looking after the Camillion survivor. The simple fact was that since the falling had started he had not been able to tear himself away from the view.

The survivor. He should probably go and check on him; Halfre couldn't be expected to debrief the poor man when finally he regained consciousness.

Delanka scanned the landscape one last time, although he was not sure what he expected to see. There had been no movement on the ground whatsoever, and no new splinters had dropped from the sky for a long time now. Before, when they had been falling, they had come at regular intervals. He was almost certain that the phenomenon had now ended.

The splinters stared back at him impassively; brooding, silent, and enigmatic.

From the battlement wall of Camp Camillion he could see clearly across the grasslands all the way to the horizon, in the direction of the distant capital. He had come that way with Omin and Halfre, and he shuddered to think what might have happened to them had they crossed the grasslands just a few hours later.

What had once been a tranquil plain of reeds, grasses, and small shrubs, was now a technological forest of the macabre.

The splinters had dropped from the sky — presumably released by some parent craft concealed within the clouds — and they now stood motionless, for all the worlds as if they had always been there. Each one of them had grounded upright, piercing the soft surface and throwing up huge plumes of soil and plant matter. They had each embedded about half of their considerable length in the ground, and not one of them had broken apart or toppled.

Even at this distance a dense white mist was visible, curling sluggishly around the bases of the splinters and reaching out across the surrounding land. Whatever the splinters were for, and whatever they had delivered, Delanka knew instinctively that they spelled trouble for those who had survived the first assault.

He tore himself away from the vista, and carefully descended the steps to the empty space between the old outer wall and the Bremer barrier.

Marks in the ground told him, loud and clear, that the sections of the temporary wall had been moved hastily into place perhaps two days ago: the soldiers stationed at Camp Camillion had apparently been expecting a sizeable ground assault, and they had used the reinforced concrete blocks to create a kill zone within the outer perimeter. But the damage to the rest of the base suggested that when the attack had come, it had been from above.

It made sense. Attacking civilians and local barracks already softened by artillery bombardment was one thing; an assault on a live MAGA training facility was something else entirely. Without orbital support from the *Vehement*, Camp Camillion would have received no overhead cover. Only an idiot would have charged its most resilient line of defence instead of exploiting that vulnerability.

He hopped over one of the fallen Bremer sections, a T-shaped chunk of concrete longer than he was tall, and passed through the gap it had left when it was toppled from behind. He glanced down as he stepped onto the thick concrete and saw that it was blackened, cracked, and pitted with nicks and indentations. Nearby, a gaping impact crater was gouged in the earth; this section of the wall was probably knocked out of place by the force of whatever ordnance had slammed into the ground.

He picked his way carefully through the debris that littered the bare earth, and threaded a path between what remained of the shelter modules. Here was a crumpled barracks block, there the remainder of an armoury; even the reinforced walls that surrounded those structures had been torn open as though they were no more resilient than paper.

After a few minutes of carefully avoiding craters, sharp plasteel edges, and the oily smoke from smouldering wreckage, Delanka at last reached the low building which was just intact enough to serve as a temporary refuge. He took a long, slow look around, satisfied himself that nobody was watching, and ducked inside.

Halfre's voice helped him locate her before his eyes had started to adjust to the gloom.

"What's happened?"

He could just make her out, kneeling on the ground near where the others lay.

"Nothing. Nothing at all; it's all quiet out there. They haven't changed since they dropped."

"Oh." Disappointment dragged her voice down. "I was hoping you'd say help has arrived."

"I wish I could, but there's been no sign of any air traffic. Theirs or ours."

His eyes were adjusting gradually, and he could now see that Halfre was sorting through items which she had laid out on the floor in front of her. They looked like the contents of a field medical kit, and some ration blocks. She was taking inventory; good for her.

Delanka knelt down and nodded towards the unconscious corporal.

"How is he doing?"

"Okay, as far as I can tell." She pulled the blanket back carefully, exposing the corporal's shoulders and chest. "It wasn't so bad once he was cleaned up. Most of these are old injuries; he's been hit by something though."

Delanka nodded slowly, as Halfre pointed to where a large and ugly bruise had bloomed across the soldier's chest.

"Looks like he was knocked down by an explosion. Winged by flying debris, and probably banged his head when he hit the ground."

"He could be in a coma for all we know. Maybe we should try to wake him up?"

"His body is trying to limit the damage. He's not bleeding, and he can breathe, so we should leave him as he is."

Halfre looked unconvinced. "He could be bleeding internally."

"If he is, there's nothing *I* can do about it. How about you?"

She shook her head.

"We leave him then."

He could see that she was not entirely happy, but she seemed to accept there was nothing they could really do. He changed the subject.

"Omin?"

"Sound asleep." A smile crept back to her face. "He was exhausted."

"I'm not surprised. I'm more surprised that *you* aren't."

"I am," she said, "but one of us had to stay awake. He was complaining so much I thought it'd be easier to let him sleep first."

"Complaining?"

"Headaches," she said. "The slightest thing triggers them. He's been breathing in smoke and dust, not to mention all that pollen from the grasslands. I think he was probably understating how bad they were."

"Fair enough. And her?"

Halfre followed his gaze to the small pile of blankets in the corner, which rose and fell softly and ever so slightly.

"Asleep as well."

"Has she told you anything?"

"She's not said a word since we got here."

"Poor kid," Delanka said. "Probably saw things that will haunt her for the rest of her life."

"I think we all did."

Delanka nodded silently. He could well imagine that Omin and Halfre had seen terrible things during the onslaught against their town; he had seen enough himself, and combat was his business. He tried not to think about the fate of those who had been on the *Vehement* when it tumbled from orbit in a mass of burning fragments.

"How about you?"

"Hmm?"

"Your injury," she said.

He rolled his shoulder self-consciously, testing his side with slow caution.

"Just a flesh wound. I won't be much good in a fight, but I don't think I'm in any real danger."

"Do you need anything for the pain?"

"No, I'll manage. We should conserve the meds for when we really need them. I just need to make sure this doesn't get infected."

"Okay. You should change the dressing."

Halfre resumed her inventory, stacking the blocks of rations in groups of five and pushing each complete stack away from her. Delanka could see what she was doing: working out for how many days the five of them would be able to eat.

He watched while she worked. During their flight from the town they had not had much of an opportunity to get to know each other, and he had only got so far as establishing that Halfre and Omin were a couple. Dirt aside, she was a pretty young woman, and he felt a strange sense of gratification that she was involved with someone as instantly likeable as Omin. He found himself wondering who she had left behind.

"Did you... lose anyone?"

Halfre's hand paused in mid-air, hovering momentarily over one of the last few uncounted blocks. She stayed like that for a moment, then carried on.

"I can't... I'm just not ready for that."

"Okay. I'm sorry."

"It's not your fault."

There was a low moan from one of the bunks.

"He's waking up." Halfre said.

"Pass me some water." Delanka moved to the side of the corporal, and twisted the cap off the hydration pouch Halfre handed to him.

"Where—?"

"Don't try to move too much. Here, drink some of this."

Delanka lifted the corporal's head gently, and pressed the nozzle of the pouch against his lips. The corporal sipped gratefully.

"You've been out for a day or two," Delanka said. "Do you remember what happened here?"

"I remember we got our asses handed to us." The corporal's voice was hoarse and quiet. "I must have hit my head pretty hard to have been out for that long. Feel like I've been sparring with a Rodori."

Delanka smiled. "I'm Private Delanka, Second Platoon, 104th."

"Corporal Suster, Twenty Seventy-Ninth. Permanent training staff."

"What happened here, Corporal?"

"Call me Staff; everyone else does."

Suster raised himself onto his elbows, exertion and pain showing clearly in his face, then turned on to one side. He winced, but bore the pain.

"Are you okay, Staff?" Delanka said.

"Yeah, just... *really* tender. I seem to remember a wall flying towards me."

"And before that?"

"Well... word spread pretty quickly when the gate stopped responding; camp leaders were right in the middle of a training brief from Command. But nobody knew what was happening. We got a very chaotic burst from the *Vehement*, then nothing."

"They came down in flames," said Delanka.

"Shit," said Suster. "We thought they might have jumped out, seeing as we got left to fend for ourselves. Guess we were wrong on that."

"What happened next?"

"When we heard orbital strikes in the distance we knew something big was happening. We sent fighters to recce the capital, but they didn't come back. Comms were jammed at their end, and we couldn't raise them. That's when we started to prep for an attack.

"Camp Camillion is just a training base. We have a few air defence turrets, but barely any live rounds. So all we could do was build up the perimeter. We took apart the training area and used the sections to make an inner wall."

"I saw," said Delanka. "I'm guessing that was a waste of time?"

"You can say that again. Water?"

Delanka again helped the corporal to take a drink. This time, Suster was able to take in much more. He almost drained the pack.

"I could drink ten of those," he said. "Yeah, they hit us from the air. It was pretty fast. Fast, and brutal."

"What happened to everyone?" Halfre asked.

Suster looked at her as if seeing her for the first time. His quizzical gaze travelled from her to Delanka.

"This is Halfre," Delanka said. "Civilian survivor. There are two others with me."

"Well, Halfre, I'm not sure what you mean. I would have thought it was obvious."

"This is a big camp," she said. "But apart from you, we've only seen a few bodies. There should be many more, yes?"

Suster looked at Delanka again.

"I was going to leave that part until you were back on your feet," Delanka said. "But she's right. I counted eighteen, apart from you."

"*Eighteen*? We had the better part of two battalions here."

"You don't know what happened to the others?"

"No. The attack started, and there were explosions all around... I remember everyone running about, then a shell came down almost right in front of me. It hit a building dead on and I took a piece of wall in the face. Then I woke up here."

Halfre and Delanka looked at each other, and he knew what she was thinking. They had both seen the special interest that the enemy showed in those who were not killed outright.

"Speaking of which," Suster continued, "my skull feels like it's breaking apart. Do you have anything?"

"Here." Halfre handed him a couple of tablets. "These should help."

Suster took the pills gratefully, and popped them into his mouth, swigging them back with the last of the water.

"Thanks," he said.

"You should rest up," Delanka told him. "We're probably safe enough here for the moment."

The corporal nodded slightly in agreement and sank back down, his eyes closing. He raised one hand and massaged his brow gingerly.

Delanka looked across to Omin's sleeping form and sighed. "Guess I'll go back on watch."

"Are you sure? How long have you been awake now?"

"Doesn't matter. I think I'm getting my second wind."

"I could wake Omin—"

"No, let him sleep. I'm the one with the training."

"When he wakes up, I'll tell him to come and take over from you."

"Fine. In the meantime, you get some rest too. I don't think anyone here needs a round-the-clock vigil any more, and we need to be ready to move at a moment's notice."

Delanka willed his reluctant body to move, and struggled to his feet. He took one last look around before leaving the way he had come in.

Outside, the light was beginning to fade. He was still able to see unaided, and picked his way back to the fallen section of the Bremer barrier. It was not long before he had reached the outer wall, and he clambered back up the stone steps to the battlement.

At the top, he stopped and reached out with his hands to steady himself. Light-headed, he sat down carefully with his back to the stone, conscious of the risk of tumbling back down the steps. He concentrated on breathing. His body was starting to protest against his determination to stay awake.

The next time he opened his eyes, it was dark.

The air was cool and damp, and a gentle breeze wafted over the wall. For a moment he was disoriented, unable to make anything out, then he realised that he was surrounded by a thin fog. Somewhere in front of him, hidden in the vapour, the wall came to an abrupt end and gave way to empty space. He decided not to move.

There was a slight sound off to his left, and his head jerked towards it. Someone else was up here with him.

His eyes were adjusting rapidly, and he could see a figure standing a few metres away, fully exposed and staring out over the plains.

"Omin?" He whispered. There was no reaction, and he tried again, louder this time. "Omin!"

Omin stayed where he was, looking out over the surrounding grasslands. In the distance, the tops of the splinters stared back at him blankly, across the ocean of mist to which they had almost certainly contributed.

Delanka gripped the top of the wall, and hauled himself to his feet. Keeping low, he edged forward until he was next to Omin.

"Hey." He took hold of Omin's forearm.

"I can hear Him." Omin's gaze was unwavering. "I can hear the song. *Our* song."

"What are you talking about? Hey, NO!"

Delanka lost his grip on Omin's arm as the young man suddenly started forwards, placing his hands flat on the top of the wall and swinging a leg up as if to climb over the edge. Delanka grabbed, and managed to take hold of Omin's arm again, pulling it out from under him. Omin began to topple backwards, and Delanka gently but firmly pulled him down to the floor.

"He's *calling* me," said Omin. "Me!"

"You're not going anywhere." Delanka placed a knee on his chest.

"Omin? Junn?"

Halfre's voice floated through the mist, somewhere below them.

"Up here," Delanka called. "Be careful on those steps."

Moments later, Delanka saw Halfre's form emerge nearby.

"Omin... I can't find him, Junn."

"He's up here," Delanka said. "Tried to step off the edge of the wall."

"*What*? Why?"

"I don't know. He kept saying someone was calling him. Help me with him." Delanka shifted across to create space for Halfre, stepping over Omin. "We need to get him down from here, before he hurts himself."

Freed from under Delanka's knee, Omin tried to get up. Halfre took his hand and pulled his arm towards her, wrapping her own hands around his. He did not resist.

"Can't you hear it?" Omin asked her.

"I can't hear anything, Omin. Nothing. There's just silence."

"Oh, you poor thing."

Halfre looked at Delanka. Their eyes met, and Delanka knew that she was beside herself with worry.

"Let's get him back down there." He hooked his hands under Omin's arms.

Between them they managed to half carry, half guide Omin back down the steps, a much less difficult feat than Delanka had anticipated. The young man was compliant, and allowed them to direct him this way and that. Delanka did not know why, but he had been expecting Omin to bound back up the steps and leap for the edge at the first opportunity.

Together they walked him across the void between the outer wall and the Bremer barrier, the mist swirling around their legs. It was much denser nearer to the ground, but even so it was difficult to see much in front of them. All around was an eerie stillness, the night completely devoid of any sounds. Delanka searched for the gap that led into the camp.

As they came closer he saw it; an empty space in the grey barrier enclosing what remained of Camp Camillion. He manoeuvred Omin in that direction, and Halfre followed suit.

They were a few paces from the gap when he heard a soft crunching noise; the sound of feet grinding down the dirt. He stopped, and felt Halfre stop with him. Omin stood almost motionless between them, his head swaying as if he were simply intoxicated.

There it was again, up ahead. Someone — or something — was just on the other side of the barrier, slowly and quietly moving through the blankets of mist.

Delanka reached down slowly with his free hand, and quietly grasped the grip of his side-arm. The mag-tag released it with a soft *click*, which to his ears might as well have been a resounding boom.

He pulled the weapon from his thigh holster and raised it in front of him, silently thumbing off the safety. He held it close to his chest, his trigger finger resting against the guard.

Delanka checked himself just in the nick of time

when the girl stepped up onto the fallen concrete block.

"Oh!" Halfre gasped, and then began to laugh.

"Shit the bed," Delanka vented. "My nerves! I am really starting to regret coming to this planet."

"What are you doing out here?" Halfre asked. "You should be back where it's safe."

The girl stared back at them, wide-eyed and shivering. She had been walking with her arms clasped around her body, but now raised one hand to point out into the fathomless mist.

"He... left," she said.

Those were the first words Delanka had heard the girl say since they had found her in the transit hub. He looked towards Halfre, and saw that she was torn between Omin and the child.

"Go on," he said. "I've got Omin."

Halfre released her grip and went to the girl.

"What's your name?"

"Caela," she said.

"Well, Caela, we need to go back now. It's not safe out here."

"He *left* me," Caela said, her gentle voice plaintive. "I was all alone."

It did not take them long to get back to the shelter of the plasteel module. Halfre grabbed a couple of blankets from the bunks, and wrapped one around each of Caela and Omin. Suster was nowhere to be seen.

"Will you be all right if I go after him?"

Delanka was already checking his weapons, and he looked at Halfre expectantly.

"How are you going to find him out there?"

"I've a pretty good idea where he's going. Will you be okay though? With Omin, I mean."

Halfre looked at her partner, who sat on the

edge of a bunk. He rocked backwards and forwards, staring at a spot on the floor.

"He's stronger than me," she said. "If he tries to go, I won't be able to stop him."

"How would you feel about restraining him?" Delanka pulled a cable tie from a pouch.

She eyed the plastic cuffs reprovingly.

"They won't hurt him," Delanka said. "It's for his own good, anyway."

"I suppose."

Omin barely resisted when Delanka bound his wrists together; he almost seemed not to notice. When the private was done, Omin's arms encircled a metal support pillar that reached from floor to ceiling.

Delanka scooped up his helmet from where he had left it when they first arrived, and quickly checked the self-diagnostic routine.

"Please come back," Halfre said quietly.

He paused, and looked up. She gazed steadily back at him, her expression neutral, but seeing her sat there he was struck by how helpless she really was. On the one side of her was a terrified child she had snatched from the jaws of death, and for whom she had adopted responsibility. On the other, her partner; whatever his current condition signified, it was obvious that he too was now dependent on her. Without Delanka, Halfre might not be able to keep them safe. Or herself.

"I will." He donned his helmet, snapped the visor down, and a heads-up display melted into cohesion before his eyes.

Back out in the dark, Delanka felt much more comfortable with his helmet on. He mentally chided himself for not having taken it with him to the battlement wall. The damp chill of the fog was now gone, thanks to the seal, and the visor helped to enhance his vision. It marked obstacles for him, enhanced edges, and occasionally picked out the tiny heat signatures of Guathelia's nocturnal animals.

If Suster had started behaving like Omin, then judging by the way the younger man had been moving, Delanka guessed that the corporal would be ambling along at a relaxed pace. He set off at a jog, estimating that he would cover twice as much ground as Suster in the same time.

He aimed directly for the forest of splinters.

## – 01 –
## Settling Dust

Elm Caden was both powerful and ineffectual. He was fearsome and reluctant. He burned with fury and was chilled by fear.

The Emptiness had left him to deal with a whirling morass of contradicting thoughts. Only it *hadn't* left him; not really. It had finally grown beyond its boundaries — the ones which Caden had imposed on it since childhood. It had shattered its constraints, and forced him to integrate all the negative emotions he had banished within it over the years. It had been a frighteningly noisy chaos at first, followed by a deep and abiding silence.

Silence.

*Fill the silence*, Amarist Naeb had told him. One of the strange people on Aldava had said the same thing. Exactly the same. What silence? *His* silence?

Coincidence: the contemporary occurrence of incidents of a similar nature. In his line of work it was a concept he regularly fell back on. Today though its comfort was lacking, and the mere word struggled to satisfy him.

He looked out along a deep, smouldering furrow carved through the remains of an already dead city, and sighed.

The battleship *ICS Hammer* had been shot down over Woe Tantalum while buying him time to complete his mission. A victim of her own tactics, she had been pummelled by the planet's orbital quarantine platforms and eventually slammed into the ground. It was likely that few aboard had survived, if any.

And what had he achieved?

He had found a mere handful of the weapons stolen from Gemen Station. The others were gone already, and he knew not where. His only lead had been Medran Morlum, and that unfortunate wretch was no longer in a position to answer questions.

Caden instantly remembered his behaviour, how he had forced Morlum — at gunpoint, no less — to reveal information that would obviously cost him his life.

And Throam. Loyal, dependable Rendir Throam. Caden had spoken to Throam as if he no longer trusted him. He struggled to think of any way he might have cut his faithful counterpart more deeply.

"Fuck!"

He shouted it into his helmet's faceplate. Again, drawing it out this time, as loud as he could manage. It was all he could really do to vent the sense of shame.

Woe Tantalum did not care. The winds continued, and the planet still turned.

After a while, finally realising that Corporal Daxon was trying to contact him, Caden un-muted his link and trudged back towards the others.

○ ○ ○

Rendir Throam worked tirelessly and without complaint — as he always did — hauling crates of kit from the storage compartments of the lander Eilentes had piloted. The dropship had somehow landed under fire, without exploding around them, but there was simply no way it was going to fly again.

When the *ICS Hammer* had come down, the small shuttle Caden had borrowed from Fleet Command was still in her hangar, and everything they had left stored in it was destroyed along with the ship. Throam felt it prudent to recover every piece of inventory he could from this other damaged vessel while he still had the chance.

He hissed through clenched teeth as he lifted one of the plasteel containers, remembering how much time he had invested in loading their kit aboard that requisitioned shuttle back on *Hammer*. Nobody had thanked him, either. It would not have felt so futile a task had they used more of the gear. He was glad the weapon cases had come with them when they dropped to the surface with Bravo Company: most of the other equipment they could easily replace, but there were not many places he would find a working Lancillon Industries compact mini-gun. Not any more.

The winds of Woe Tantalum gave no respite, and he breathed hard in the confines of his closed helmet. The visor was incredibly resistant to misting up, but he could still smell his own musk in the filtered air. Sweat was held inside the helmet by the same foam lining that cushioned his head; there was no getting around it. Even with a dehumidifier shunt built into his respirator, he felt clammy and unclean. The little machine could only draw so much moisture out of his helmet, and Throam — who often sweated just through the huge effort of holding his body upright — was almost panting.

"I know you want to get down there and help, but you're just not equipped for it."

Caden's voice came over the group channel. Throam looked up, and saw the Shard talking to Corporal Daxon and Private Norskine.

"Let the search and rescue teams from *Disputer* handle that detail themselves."

"More hands are always appreciated," Daxon said. "They'll be thankful for the leg up; *Hammer* is a big ship, and the sooner they search the wreck the better."

Caden's reply was terse. "If you think your combat armour will protect you against radiation leaks and pressurised fires, be my guest. Don't say I didn't warn you."

Daxon mumbled something in reply which — even through his link — Throam could not quite make out.

Caden was completely right, of course: *Hammer* lay burning on the ground, and what remained of the battleship was undoubtedly a death trap. There was no way of telling what damage had been done to the fuel lines, reactors, or superstructure, to say nothing of the ordnance bays. Best to leave that detail to the Life and Rescue specialists *ICS Disputer* had sent down to the surface.

But Caden's tone was off. Before, on Echo — and later on Aldava — he had bonded effortlessly with the troops of Bravo Company. Ever since they had fought their way through the ruins of Woe Tantalum, and confronted Medran Morlum in his makeshift staging area, the Shard's whole attitude seemed to have changed.

And what was it Caden had said to Throam, right after that encounter with Morlum? Oh yes: *I*

*really need to know that you're in my corner.*
What in the worlds was that all about?

∘ ∘ ∘

Even the turbulent, bruised skies of Woe Tantalum looked beautiful to Aker Santani, when at long last a square piece of the outer bulkhead fell inwards and clanged heavily on the deck. After being stuck in the dark for nearly two hours, utterly reliant on a respirator and unable to move, she welcomed natural light of any sort, or of any feeble strength.

"Captain Santani?"

The blinding white beam of a flash-light settled on her face. Wisps of smoke curled lazily through the beam, and settling dust shone brightly where the light caught it.

"I'm alive," she said, squinting. She brought up her free hand to shield her eyes. "But I can't move."

"We'll have you out in no time."

"I'll be fine; I don't think I'm bleeding — just pinned. Check the others first. I've not heard anything from some of them for a while now."

The brilliant beam swept around what remained of the command deck, hovering momentarily over each of several slumped forms. Santani followed the beam with her eyes as best she could, craning her neck to see. The emergency lighting had failed shortly after their impact with the ground, and this was the first time she had seen the full extent of the damage.

A limp, grimy hand raised into the air shakily, accompanied by a raspy, gurgling cough. The beam landed on it and stayed there, wobbling as the owner of the torch wriggled through the still-glowing hole that had been cut from the hull.

"Klade," Santani said. "Is he... is he going to

make it?"

The rescue worker knelt down by Santani's executive officer, and pressed a sensor paddle against his chest.

"If we get him out of here quickly. Cyanotic, apex beat is in the wrong place, and he's got a right rattle going: looks like a perforated lung. He's probably only alive because of how he's positioned."

More rescue workers were coming in now, blocking out the planet's meagre daylight as they stepped carefully through the orange-rimmed hole.

The one by Klade signalled to another. "Priority."

The second approached Klade, opened a medical kit, and went to work. The first crept cautiously around the tilted deck, moving from person to person.

"Dead: mark for recovery. Concussion: low priority. Fractured ulna and two broken ribs: stabilise. Dead: mark for recovery."

She knew it was an essential process, triaging the crew who lay injured and dying about her, but Santani could not help but wince at the cold descriptions of her fallen crew members' injuries. There was a sharp stabbing sensation deep in her gut.

Trapped beneath the cross-beam that had collapsed on her command station, unable to help her own crew members, she lay in the dark silently and felt warm tears run down her cold cheeks.

○ ○ ○

Euryce Eilentes had found yet another group, this one — like the others before them — standing inert amidst the ruins. She flagged the location on her rifle's scope, copied it to her holo, and then sent it to Volkas via her link.

"Enjoy," she murmured to herself. She raised the scope back to her eye. "Plenty more where they came from, it seems."

They had located a few such groups since securing the derelict chemical works where Morlum and his comrades had guarded the stolen Imperial warheads. Here and there, spread out around the long-destroyed town, were small teams of humans and Viskr. The ones who had somehow escaped being cut down when Caden's team swept through the city on their way to Morlum.

Eilentes would have called them pockets of resistance, only... they offered no resistance. It was as if someone had pushed a button and put them all on standby.

The individuals from the chemical works — who had been still as statues when Caden and Bravo Company found them — were now corralled in the broken courtyard below Eilentes' position, penned in by some of the ground troops deployed from *Disputer*. Not that they appeared likely to run: each of them was as docile as Amarist Naeb had been, when Caden and Throam had first brought her out of Gemen Station.

Worlds! That seemed like so long ago.

As she scanned the buildings systematically for other enemy positions, Eilentes set a part of her brain to work on what she had seen so far. Throam had told her what Morlum said before he died; that the 'Rasas' had nobody to tell them what to do, and that those in charge of them must have been killed already.

As far as she knew no enemy commanders had yet been identified, whether living or dead. Whoever or whatever it was that directed the actions of these Rasas was nowhere to be found.

Her scope passed over the smouldering trench that *Hammer* had sliced through the town, when the great ship had slammed her belly into the ground and barrelled gracelessly towards her final resting place.

What if *Hammer* had demolished an enemy command post?

The timing would have been about right, and all evidence would have been utterly destroyed; crushed into oblivion.

She made a mental note to run it by Caden later on; the Shard might even have come to the same conclusion.

○ ○ ○

Santani insisted on staying by the smoking hulk of *Hammer*, watching the search and rescue teams bring her crew, one by one, from the open belly of her lifeless ship.

First there were stretchers; the most critically wounded personnel were rushed to receive field care in a surgical module dropped by *Disputer*. After that came those with minor injuries, almost all of them helping each other. Finally there came the body bags.

By the time she had started to count double figures, she had to look away. She leaned painfully on a long piece of plasteel shrapnel, trying to take the weight off her right leg. A field medic had hurriedly applied a basic brace, but she would need more definitive intervention before she was able to stand fully on those bones again.

"Ma'am, you should come away from the wreck and move to the recovery area. It's not safe to be here. We have no idea what condition the reactors are in."

She turned her head to look at the speaker, and saw it was a woman. Through the glow of the holographic overlay in the helmet visor, Santani could make out young, pretty eyes. Even in this tortured place, standing next to what would doubtless become a tomb for those who could not be recovered, those eyes sparkled with life.

"I can't leave yet," she said. "Not until they bring the last one out."

"Yes, Ma'am... sorry Ma'am."

The young woman went back to her work, and Santani watched her leave with a deep sense of vicarious foreboding. How long before that one was herself being pulled from the dead husk of a ship? How long did *anyone* really have?

She looked back along the hull, and forced herself to watch them bring out the body bags. Nihilism, she thought, is solely a privilege of the living. Respect will be the courtesy I extend to the dead.

○ ○ ○

Elm Caden seemed to be having one stupid conversation after another. First Daxon had wanted to take his fire team into the toxic inferno of *Hammer*'s corpse. It was well-intentioned, but really not very prudent. After a few minutes of tiresome debate, Caden had palmed the corporal off onto Kohoi Chun: after all, the welfare of the troops *was* the sergeant's responsibility.

Then it had been Volkas, asking for Caden's casualty report. Casualty report? Your job, Volkas, not mine. I don't even know what half of your people are called.

Now, it was the Executive Officer from the *ICS Disputer* who was giving him problems. The man seriously needed to work the stick free from his ass.

"We will not be accommodating your prisoners in the brig aboard *Disputer*, Shard Caden. It's simply too dangerous. They cannot be allowed even the remotest chance of gaining access to this ship's systems."

"Dangerous? They're vegetables, Yuellen."

"You haven't been told, have you?"

Caden sighed to himself. "Told what?"

"About Fort Kosling."

"What about Fort Kosling?" It was like pulling teeth.

"All but destroyed. That one you found on Herros; Amarist Naeb. She managed to cripple the entire fortress."

Caden was silent for a moment. It hardly seemed possible. "How? Last time I saw her she was off in her own little world."

"Well, it didn't last. I'm sure Captain Thande will be giving you a comprehensive briefing after you leave the surface."

Caden groaned inwardly at the reminder. Captain Thande! Her reputation as a stern and humourless officer preceded her.

"I'll look forward to that."

He closed the private channel, rejoined the group channel that the ground parties were using, and set off across the charred landscape in the direction of the prisoners.

As he came closer to the courtyard, he saw that Bruiser was standing guard. Apparently not satisfied that half a platoon of other MAGA troops kept watch already, the Rodori was leaning against what remained of a stone wall, his cherished machine gun in hand.

"Anything to report?" Caden asked.

"Nothing," Bruiser rumbled. "These people don't move."

"Stay vigilant, guys. Apparently they aren't as harmless as we thought."

Bruiser moved his head forwards, angling his face down to maintain eye contact. Perhaps an expression of curiosity? Caden would have to see what the Imperial databases had to say about Rodori body language.

"These people are a threat to us?"

"Possibly. While we've been gone, Amarist Naeb somehow managed to take out Fort Kosling."

Bruiser's head jerked back again. Surprise maybe?

"Huh. That is one tough human."

"You don't say. Listen, I'm not sure what's happening with these prisoners yet. The XO on *Disputer* doesn't want them on his precious command carrier. Keep a close eye on them until I know where they're going, will you?"

"Not a problem."

Caden gave a thumbs-up, and walked away.

"One woman versus a fortress," he heard the Rodori say. "My kinda gig."

o o o

Santani picked her way carefully through the littered masonry and metal scrap, trying to keep out of the way as best she could whenever corpsmen and field medics hurried by. It was not easy to move aside quickly, not with a probably broken leg and the dubious assistance of her makeshift crutch. Twice, in her haste, she almost sent herself tumbling to the ground.

The entrance to the field surgery loomed ominously before her; the screams and groans of the injured were audible even through the double-doored airlock, even above the howling atmosphere of Woe Tantalum. It was as if she had discovered a portal to the hell of the old world, and could hear the lamentations of the damned trapped within.

She forced herself to enter.

Inside, the noise was horrific. Men and women alike shouted, shrieked, begged, pleaded, threatened, calling out to anyone they thought able to help them escape their agony. The whine of powered surgical tools sliced and grated through the clamour without warning, and she shuddered involuntarily every time she heard those sounds and the inevitable accompanying screams.

She pulled off her respirator and hobbled between the cots, dodging the frenetic medics as best she could, careful not to trip over the equipment that punctuated the orderly aisles. Everywhere she looked she saw the misery of injury; torn clothing, charred flesh, exposed bone.

The denizens of the module were a mixture of her crew, and the soldiers who had already been on the surface when *Hammer* came down. She passed by several MAGA troopers with missing limbs; those lucky few who had suffered only glancing blows from the razor-edged rings of skulkers. Blood pooled around some of the cots, and the smell of it hung thick in the air, mixing with the stringent scent of antiseptics and the burned-rubber stench of coagulant foam.

Then she saw Klade.

Her first officer was laying on his side, bare from the waist up, with a mask strapped over his face. His chest was bruised darkly, and at the centre of the ugly discolouration a dressing was already wicking blood from the wound it covered. His eyes were wide; bright holes in a mask of dried blood and grime. They moved, found hers staring back at him, and tried to share a smile with his mouth.

"Klade," she said. "I'm so sorry."

"He's going to prep," said a medic, and hastily checked the tubes connecting Klade's mask to a machine. He hooked the machine on the rail surrounding the trolley.

"You will pull through," Santani said.

The medic kicked off the brake, and began to pull the trolley into the aisle. Klade raised his hand weakly, as if to wave Santani off; the only way he could communicate with her. She raised her hand in reply.

"You *will* pull through," she whispered.

∘ ∘ ∘

"Why is it you always tip up when I'm just about finished?"

"Good timing I suppose," said Caden. "We have a problem."

Throam grunted, and sat down heavily on one of the crates he had recovered. "Don't we always? Go on."

"*Disputer* says they won't accept our prisoners in their brig. But we can't very well leave them here."

"Why not? They're welcome to this shit-hole."

"For one thing, they're undeclared enemies of the Empire. We need to find out as much as we can about them."

"We could do that here."

"That's hardly optimal, is it?"

"Suppose not."

"There's something else, too. I'm told Amarist

Naeb all but destroyed Fort Kosling."

"You're kidding?"

"No, seriously. The XO told me. These people aren't the drooling idiots they appear to be. There's a lot more to them than that."

"I can see why he doesn't want them on the *Disputer*."

"He does have a point. But we can't just walk away. They could be rejoining their forces and feeding back intel within hours."

Throam stopped what he was doing, straightened up slowly, and looked Caden directly in the eye.

"You're not suggesting we kill them all?"

"I wasn't 'suggesting' anything." Caden shrugged.

"You thought it though."

"It *is* an option."

"They're our prisoners."

"I know."

There was an awkward silence, and Throam found himself wondering if Caden wanted to be talked out of it, or given license to act. It was not a question he appreciated, in either case; decisions like that were firmly and undeniably in the remit of Shards, not their counterparts.

He changed the subject. "Think there's a connection between these people and what we saw on Aldava?"

Caden tilted his head slightly, as if wordlessly questioning the change of topic. But he replied nonetheless. "It seems likely. I think we might have witnessed the early stages of... whatever it is that's affecting them."

"They were all around you."

Caden remained silent for a moment. "So?"

"Any idea why?"

"You're talking about the plaza, right? Before the Kodiak came for us? I just assumed it was because I was the first of us to get in amongst them."

"Sure about that?"

"No, of course I'm not sure. Could have been that, but it might have been something else entirely. I don't know what was going on any more than you do."

Truth be told, Throam had no idea what he was expecting to hear. But what he *did* know was that in all the time he had known Caden, he had never seen him throw away another's life as casually and as consciously as he discarded that of Medran Morlum. And now Throam stopped to think about things, he also realised that Caden had never before told him to do something as vindictive as kicking Joarn Kages through a window. Something was different for sure, and it was a recent change.

"It's just that you've been... I mean, you haven't been yourself for a few days now." He paused as Caden raised an eyebrow, but no reply came. "You know it, I know it... pretty sure Euryce has picked up on it too, and she basically only just met you."

"Yes, and I'm really interested in what your new squeeze thinks of me." The Shard was muttering, looking to the side, as if he were no longer in the conversation.

Throam reeled. "My new *squeeze*? This is exactly what I'm talking about. This isn't you. You're hostile, Elm. Aggressive. I don't get it. Aggression is *my* job."

Caden started, looking for all the worlds as if he had surprised himself.

"You're right, I'm sorry." He looked suitably ashamed. "Don't tell Eilentes I called her your squeeze, will you?"

"Are you kidding? She'd take your balls as trophies."

"Exactly."

There was another awkward silence.

"You *have* changed though," Throam said. It was too risky to let it go now; if he knew Caden at all, he knew that the Shard would not make it easy to come back to this conversation once it was over. "And the timing is, like... pretty convenient. I'm just saying."

"*What* are you saying, Throam? Convenient for what? You'd better clarify, because it sounds very much like you think I'm connected to that lot." He jerked his head vaguely in the direction of the corral, where Bruiser and the other soldiers still guarded the prisoners.

Throam folded his arms across his chest. "Suppose I am."

"Oh, this had better be good."

"Not impossible, is it? They probably started acting all fucked-up too, before they ended up like that."

Caden raised his hand to his forehead habitually, as if his patience were wearing thin, and his glove clonked against his visor.

"Listen, I know I've been out of sorts lately, but I'm not one of them" — again, he jerked his head towards the prisoners — "and I'm not about to pull an Amarist Naeb on you."

"Would you even know if you were?"

"Okay, point taken. I *am* going through some stuff, as you have so keenly noticed and helpfully pointed out, but it's not *that*. For one thing, it predates all this Rasa business by some considerable margin."

"What then?"

"I really don't think this is the time or the place, Throam."

"Right, well you need to make the time later on."

"Oh, do I?"

"Yes, you do," Throam said, patiently. "Because I can't do my job right if I don't know where your fucking head's at from one moment to the next."

"Fine. Yeah... no that's fine, I'll schedule you in." Caden jabbed and prodded at his holo without looking. "Happy?"

"Don't forget."

"I won't."

"And don't 'forget', either," Throam intoned.

"I won't."

"Good. I'm just worried about you, you do know that right?"

"Yeah, I'm touched. Listen, we still have to come up with a plan for those Rasa goons."

"Think I might have an idea about that," said Throam. "I'm going to need Bruiser down here... and some of that kit they're using on what's left of the *Hammer*."

○ ○ ○

Santani left the field hospital, and struggled gracelessly along what had once been a stone boulevard. The crowded module, filled as it was with the chaos of suffering and the stench of the dead and dying, had been too much for her.

She hobbled along, away from the corpse of the *ICS Hammer*, and headed for Bravo Company's position.

The wind tugged at her flight suit pants, ruffled her captain's tunic, clawed at her loose hair. Her respirator covered much of her face, but she could still feel the icy chill of Woe Tantalum's atmosphere. She balled her empty hand into a fist, tightened the grip of the other around her makeshift crutch.

Someone is going to pay for this, she thought. My crew deserved better than to die out here.

From what she had seen in the triage area, some sixty of her people were either being worked on, or waiting for treatment. That meant that she had potentially lost over ten times as many.

Worlds! To have been on the lower decks when they hit the ground.

Her heart sank, and she felt tears visit the corners of her eyes once more. She wanted to pull away the mask and wipe her face, wipe away the guilt and the pain. As much as it might allow her to breathe, the respirator was also suffocating her; trapping her in with her sorrow.

No, not yet. You've got to keep it together for a little while longer.

Step by awkward step, she made her way towards Eilentes' crash site. Eventually, through the broken walls and mounds of frozen slag, she saw the hull of the downed lander. As she picked a safe path across the uneven ground, panting hard now with the exertion, she saw people in the opening of the rear hatch. She flicked her holo, and her link found and joined the group channel.

"That should do the trick," one of the figures was saying. "One temporary brig, for all your custody needs."

She rounded the outside of the craft, and the interior space of the rear lock came into view. A towering Rodori was lumbering down the deck, arc welder in hand, grinning that impossibly wide grin that made members of his species look so maniacal. He caught sight of her and tilted his head, and the pair on the ground turned to follow his line of sight.

"Captain Santani." It was Caden's voice. The least enormous of the three armoured figures motioned with his hand. "It's good to see you alive. I'm so sorry that *Hammer* came down, and for your crew of course."

Santani came to a halt. "She was a dependable ship, and they were a dedicated crew—"

"They were indeed," Caden said.

"—But I would have given them all up if it meant never having to bring you here."

"Oh."

"Was it worth it?" She asked.

"I would say—"

"Spare me. You're hardly going to say 'no', are you?"

## – 02 –
### SURVIVORS

Occre Brant jolted awake, feeling as though he had just fallen from a great height. His face was pressed against someone else. Twisting his neck, he looked up into the overly satisfied eyes of Peras Tirrano.

"Welcome back, Sleepy."

He sat upright slowly, as naturally as he could make it seem, pulling away from her shoulder. Her arm slid from around him reluctantly.

"What's happening?" He asked groggily.

"Rescue ship just snagged us," she said. "About frigging time too."

"How long was I out?"

"Six hours, give or take. I wasn't really counting. You seemed like you needed that, anyway."

"You're not wrong."

Brant stretched off his limbs in an attempt to relieve the muscular fatigue that went with sleeping under straps in a weightless environment. The survival shelter which had ejected them from Fort Kosling had no artificial gravity of its own, but the borrowed force from whatever ship had just captured them was beginning to make his blood vessels tingle happily.

As his head cleared, he became aware of the

others around them; the murmuring and the hushed conversations. Even after they had spent so many hours drifting in space, he could tell that some of the other survivors were still shocked at the sudden and unexpected demise of their fortress.

"Any idea how many made it off the station?" He asked.

"Rescue have been broadcasting updates. Last one said they had counted virtually all survival shelters as successful launches."

"That's great news."

"Doesn't mean all the people are on them though."

"Yeah, I guess not. Still; let's hope for the best, right?"

"That seems a bit naïve," she said, flatly.

Brant didn't reply. He knew what would happen next if he tried to argue with her: she would get louder and more difficult, until everyone aboard the cramped lifeboat was convinced that most of their friends and colleagues had been left behind to perish in fire or vacuum.

A muffled thumping sound travelled through the hull, and then nothing for a few moments more. Then the seal indicators around the circular egress hatch turned green all at once, and the hatch itself popped open with a reassuring puff of air exchange.

"How many we got in 'ere then?"

A woman in full hazmat kit stood in the opening, peering into the survival shelter. She did a quick headcount, jabbing her finger in the air as she tallied the occupants, and then tapped regally at a holo before disappearing out of view.

"Charming welcome," Brant said.

"They probably just forgot where they left their red carpet, but if you can wait I'll go and help them find it."

"Funny."

"It'll be a support vessel. Hauler, salvager; something like that."

"Yeah, I figured. Come on, let's find out what the deal is."

They both released their safety harnesses, and climbed cautiously to their feet. Tirrano stumbled on the first step, and leaned against Brant.

"Careful," he said.

They joined the short queue of survivors who clambered slowly from the lifeboat, and eventually found themselves on a scruffy deck that somehow seemed as though it were physically too small to contain such a large piece of cargo.

"You're aboard the *Pride of Jeddis*," a loud but slightly disinterested voice came from ahead of them, floating over the heads of the small crowd. "I am First Mate Akari. If you fine ladies and gentlemen would follow me to the mess, there's food waiting."

Tirrano grabbed Brant's arm and pulled him in the direction of the voice. As the other people milled in the general direction of the passage connecting the cargo bay to the rest of the ship, she forced her way through until she found Akari.

"Wait just a second," she said imperiously.

Akari was not quite what she had expected from the depth of his voice. He was a short man, shorter than her at any rate, and incredibly wiry. He had a full, black beard which was almost obsessively neat in contrast with his dangerously unkempt hair. He smiled faintly as he waited for her to speak.

"What do you mean, food? Surely you can have us on the ground in less than an hour?"

"We're not putting down in the Kosling system," Akari said. "We're under orders, lady; all the ships taking part in the rescue effort."

"What orders?"

"From Eyes and Ears, and Fleet Command. Collect as many staff from Fort Kosling as possible, and ferry them immediately to the emergency command post being set up at Fort Laeara."

"We're going to the Perseus arm?"

"Damned straight you are."

"Well shit," said Brant. "They're sending us practically all the way to the front line."

○ ○ ○

Despite the bitterness he carried in every fibre of his being, Maber Castigon had to admit a simple truth: the decadent, self-indulgent citizens of the Imperial Combine sure knew how to entertain themselves.

A swelling, jubilant roar from the spectator stands signalled that something incredible had happened in the arena below. He glanced down, curious to know exactly what kind of violence had people leaping from their seats on this occasion.

One of the players was laid out on the ground, face down in a small puddle of blood. He was just outside a scoring zone. The other four were chasing after the ball as it rolled away from him; two running it down separately, and the other pair struggling to follow even as they pummelled each other's faces with their gloved fists.

Maulball Mini-League. Five players, one goal, virtually anything goes. If only people realised how closely this game is modelled on life itself, he thought.

The one on the ground moved his arms, gradually propped himself up, and seemed to shake off whatever brain injury had knocked him out. Just as well, since nobody would be coming to help him. Not that Castigon gave a damn about a random maulball player's health.

He tore himself away from the oddly engrossing action. Whatever happened down there in the arena, it was not his concern. He had come here to deal with his next target, not to get swept up in tournament fever. And he had come too far now to blow it all by allowing himself to be distracted.

Even if the distractions *were* attractively violent.

A long, long time ago he had been an ardent fan. He followed his local league with zeal, obsessing over team stacking and iconic plays and injury bonuses, from his teens far into his twenties. He had even found time to keep abreast of the majors while at the Imperial War College, where personal time was horribly short and communication links infamously expensive.

But that was all before Urx and its subterranean prison. Long before! Worlds, it felt as though it had been in a different lifetime. Only a decade had passed — ten Solars — but his recollection of prison was more like an actual reality than any of the memories preceding it.

Except the ones pertaining to the fallout from Ottomas, of course. Those were emblazoned in his mind, his heart, and whatever that ragged, threadbare thing was that people insisted he should call his soul.

He had done his level best, he told himself once more. He had done his best to bring the Trinity Crisis to a swift conclusion, and everyone he had trusted to have his back — every single one of them — had stuck a knife in it, and then twisted the blade.

The two runners lunged for the ball together, and it was knocked away as they landed heavily and fought to launch themselves back after it. Neither would let the other rise from the ground, now that they were down, and the crowds encouraged them boisterously.

He made his way along the sweaty corridor that ran behind the stands, ignoring the elevators, moving swiftly towards one of many staircases which could take him up to the next tier. Only three more levels, and he would be within spitting distance of his quarry.

Down below, in the arena, a bone snapped. The sound managed somehow to reach every part of the stadium, but the roar of the crowd drowned whatever scream surely followed.

Castigon kept his head down as he passed under the cameras. Admittedly they were fairly primitive models, and probably not even working given the dilapidated state of the stadium's back areas. And he was wearing a disruptor prosthetic, which in theory would shift his features and stop recogniser holos from identifying him. But he was not one for taking big risks. He still remembered some of the lessons he had learned in his time baby-sitting Shards, and 'leave nothing important to chance' was a firm favourite.

Up, up, up the stairs, two at a time.

Castigon had found over the past few days that he *really* liked stairs, and it had taken him a while to realise why such a small thing should give him any enjoyment at all. In all those Solars he spent at the Empress's pleasure in Correctional Compound One, he had never gone up or down. Everything he did, everywhere he went, it was all contained on a single level. Forwards, backwards, left and right. Beneath the surface of Urx there were no steps, and no ledges. Not even ramps.

Stairs, it seemed, were a privilege to be savoured only by the free. As weird as it might have sounded to anyone else, he was happy for any opportunity to steal enjoyment from the Imperial Combine, even if it was something as trivial as ascending a flight of stairs while unlawfully at large.

So fuck the elevators. He would only get trapped in them anyway, if something went wrong.

One of the players was slammed heavily into the arena wall, still holding the ball over his head. The ball glowed brightly, signalling that he had his thumb placed correctly in its single hole. As long as he had custody in a scoring zone, he was accumulating points with every passing second. He stretched his arm as far and as high as he could while flailing with the other at the two players who punched his body eagerly. A fourth limped towards them. The fifth was noticeable only by his absence; the broken bone must have been one he could not manage without.

A vicious gut-punch folded the player with custody in half, and the ball was snatched away from him, flung hard across the ground towards the central goal, and immediately chased by the small rabble of players.

Castigon had almost reached the stairway up to the next tier, and despite his earlier caution he found himself pausing to watch this new development.

It really *is* a compressed version of life, he thought. Take what they've got, and try to keep it for as long as possible, to stop anyone else from taking it until you've turned it into something that can't be stolen away. Every man for himself.

He flattered himself that he could have, no... *should* have, been a philosopher.

○ ○ ○

Gordl Branathes was the last person Brant would have expected to welcome them to the Laeara system. But, as it so happened, there he was.

Brant and Tirrano had passed through Arrivals without incident, and walked out of the debarkation area with no real clue as to where they should go next. Although Fort Laeara was almost certainly laid out in exactly the same way as Fort Kosling, neither of them had the faintest idea what they were supposed to be doing there.

"Thank goodness you both made it!"

Branathes pushed his way through the other refugees until he reached them.

"I don't think your particular manifest was actually passed to Life and Rescue. There was some debate as to whether we should show you as missing in action, or killed."

"Oh," said Brant. "I honestly don't know how to respond to that."

"Which was it?" Tirrano asked.

"MIA, of course. I won."

Tirrano looked at Brant and smiled with the very corners of her mouth. "At least someone thinks I got action."

"Well, let's not stand about. Lots to be done!" Branathes waved them both towards one of many passageways, oblivious to Brant's prickling and Tirrano's mischievous grin.

Brant tried to ignore his colleague. "What exactly are we here for, Sir?"

"Information scraping," Branathes said. "Assisting the war effort. Operation Seawall is not going well. Fleet appear to have really riled the Viskr Junta, and they're hitting us back just as hard as we're hitting them, if not harder."

"How bad has it got?"

"At the moment it's entirely restricted to fleet warfare, but Commander Operations agrees with Eyes and Ears: it's only a matter of time before some damned idiot nukes a colony."

"The Perseus conflict, all over again."

"Exactly. Our job, as ever, is to collect, collate, and coordinate information. That will go a lot faster and smoother if we're closer to the front lines. Hence, here we are at Laeara."

"If I can be honest, Sir, I'm not really happy about being so close to the fighting."

"Nonsense Occre. Fort Laeara is the safest place on the Perseus arm. Last time the Viskr attacked this system, it damned near cost them their entire armada."

Brant knew at the intellectual level that his senior was correct: the Viskr had indeed been turned away from Laeara robustly, when their siege engine broke so spectacularly against the Imperial defences. Somehow that information failed to make him feel any safer. The primitive part of his brain wanted him to turn tail and run.

"Do we know exactly what happened yet?" Tirrano asked. "At Fort Kosling, I mean."

Branathes was now walking between them, and Brant assumed that Tirrano had grown bored with trying to get a rise from him.

"You don't know? It's been all over the E&E channels. It's all anyone has been speaking about for half a day."

"Sorry Sir, we were a little preoccupied floating about the Kosling system in a raft."

"That Rasa of yours escaped. She sabotaged the environmental control systems, set fires, then shot her way out of the station in a stolen ship."

"No shit? Told you so, Brant."

"Indeed. 'No shit', as you say. We don't know where she went, or why she chose that moment to leave, and — thanks to her handiwork — we've lost all the data Doctor Laekan collected on her condition."

"Laekan," Brant said. "Has she come aboard yet?"

"Not as far as I'm aware. I have her marked down as KIA for the moment."

"Why not MIA?" Tirrano asked.

"Because she's probably dead. I doubt that Rasa left Laekan alone to stand and watch while she sabotaged the station."

"Huh. That would be a dreadful shame. I liked her."

Tirrano glared at Brant behind Branathes' back. "You only knew her for five minutes."

"Still wouldn't want her to be dead, Peras. And in any case, she was the only person who got to examine Amarist Naeb in detail. We could have done with that information."

"Maybe when you get around to extracting Doctor Bel-Ures, you'll take better care of that one. You know; now you've had a practice run."

"Bel-Ures?" Branathes stopped dead, and they both took a couple of steps farther before they too halted and turned back toward him. "Doctor *Danil* Bel-Ures?"

"That's the one," Brant said slowly. "You know her?"

"Well not personally, of course, but she was — if I am not mistaken — one of the people working on Herros."

"The very same," said Tirrano.

"And you say she needs extraction?"

"Yeah. According to transit records, she went home to the Meccrace system shortly before Gemen Station was breached."

"We're hoping she will know how we can best defend against the weapons that were stolen," Brant added. "Not to mention the fact that she might have an idea what happened there."

"Of course, of course. Yes... it's absolutely vital that she is located immediately."

"Do you want us to sort that out before we get swept up in all the heady excitement of information scraping?"

"No Occre, that's fine, thank you. I'll get you inducted here, then I will go and see to it personally. It's simply too important to let anything go wrong. Not that I think you'd mess it up."

"Right," Brant said.

"Even though you definitely *would*," Tirrano whispered behind his back.

o o o

Castigon had long ago come to believe that one could always rely on the sloppiness of others, and he was rarely disappointed. It still amazed him though that the rule seemed to be as true for Imperial Shards as it was for everyone else.

The Shard who was guarding the proconsul's private box, and the counterpart who was guarding the Shard, were themselves inside the box. There was only the one entrance.

What a pair of complacent morons.

With the door being closed, there was for the

moment no prospect of anyone inside the box spotting him. The proconsul and his guests would be watching the match, and the Shard and counterpart were unlikely to look in Castigon's direction long enough to recognise him, especially with all the obstructions between them.

He took a moment to ensure that he had his bearings, that he knew which was the best route out of the stadium. Once he had done what he came here to do, he would need to make a quick exit. But he would still need to avoid the cameras if he wanted to make it off this planet again. And his timing would be critical.

Another roar erupted from the endless ranks of spectators, and the commentator announced a perfect delivery. One of the players must have caught the ball as it re-entered play, and kept custody of it until they could slam it back into the goal. Castigon almost regretted the fact that he had missed how that had been done, given how violent these players had been so far.

There was no set time for a maulball match: the game would run until only one player could physically go on, at which point the competition would be deemed ended.

He waited.

Eventually, the winner was decided. While the team out of Cebris City had a player who stood unopposed, it was the Veralla City team whose player had accrued the most points when time was called.

The Cebris survivor yelled at the referee with colour and vigour, claiming that Veralla had put himself out of the running at that particular moment only so that the points she was gaining in the scoring zone would be discounted. The referee shook his head slowly, ignoring her curses and her protest.

The crowd disagreed noisily with the verdict. Cebris stormed from the arena, shoving a ground marshal out of her way. Someone was making a futile effort to help the victor to his one good foot, even as food, cups and programmes began to rain down into the arena.

It could hardly have been more perfect.

On the tiers, the restless crowds were beginning to move. Different groups formed, shifted, and broke apart again. People milled about, filling the corridors and stairwells. Angry shouts came from some, disappointed murmurs from others. Castigon watched the motion of the crowd carefully as he waited near the short access ramp which led directly to the private box.

Presently, as he had expected, the door clicked. It began to open. Quickly, in one deft movement, he unclipped a chunky metal disc from somewhere inside his jacket, pressed down a stud in the centre of the lid, and slid it across the floor. It skittered across the threshold, and through the widening doorway of the box.

"What the— *down!*"

The shout had been a female's voice, and he guessed it was the counterpart.

There was a powdery *thud*, and thick brown smoke began to pour from the open doorway.

Castigon drew his pistol, made sure the dampener was engaged, and advanced. Figures stumbled from the smoky room, blinded, coughing, and spitting up mucus, but he ignored them all. He was only looking for one person in particular, and these others were no threat.

The Shard collapsed out of the doorway, half-carried by his counterpart, and retched as he fell towards the floor. Tears streamed down his face, cutting streaks through the dirty residue from the smoke grenade.

Castigon abbreviated the Shard's misery with a couple of very quiet bullets, and cracked the counterpart around the back of the head. No need to give her the opportunity to come after him.

He re-holstered his weapon, turned from the scene, and walked casually back down the ramp. Within seconds the heaving crowd had absorbed him, and Maber Castigon was carried away by the tide, blending into the liquid mass of faces.

○ ○ ○

"Welcome to Central Operations," said Branathes. "Let me show you to your stations."

"Impressive." Brant whistled.

"Very impressive," Tirrano agreed.

"I'm glad you approve," Branathes said. "Because we could be here until this is all done with."

Brant took a moment to look around carefully, taking in as much of the busy compartment as he could. The overhead had been removed from the two decks above the one they were on, so the circular space was three stories tall. It was dominated by a central holographic map which displayed a representation of the entire Perseus arm. As Brant watched, operators standing in front of it zoomed the whole map in to a single star system, then farther still, isolating an Imperial task force.

"Is that real-time?"

"That particular bit, yes," Branathes glanced up at the displayed ships. "Unfortunately not all of it is though. Our listening posts aren't close enough to provide that kind of telemetry on the inner Viskr systems, and we haven't cracked their comms network yet. Much of our information is coming from logs, conventional reports, databursts when we can get them, and good old gate echoes. We have to compile and confirm everything."

"Shame." Brant continued to look around. Holos lined the walls, and people were moving between them with swift purpose. He wondered if his assigned fate involved learning how to do whatever it was they were doing.

"Peras," Branathes said. "You'll take over from me. Casualty recording and projection. I'm not saying it's too menial for me, because it's important work. It's just that it frees me up for work which is even more important."

"Of course," she said. "Which station?"

"Right there." Branathes pointed to the holo behind her. "You'll be passed the data on ships and facilities which are missing or downed as it comes in. You're already familiar with the List, so you just need to tabulate what's given to you."

"Yep, definitely not menial at all."

"If things really heat up — which they probably will — you'll be projecting our losses too. That function will be crucial."

Peras did not look convinced, but Branathes continued on his way without trying to persuade her any further.

"Occre, I have something different for you to sink your teeth into."

"Wait a second," Tirrano said.

"What is it?" Branathes walked back to her, and Brant followed.

"This shows all the known survivors from Kosling," Tirrano said. "Someone must have updated it while you were fetching us. Look, right here: Doctor Vella Laekan. She was logged fifteen minutes ago."

"Where is she?" Brant asked.

"Medical, surprisingly enough." There was a note of mockery in Tirrano's voice, which evaporated as she continued to read. "Oh... it goes on to say she's in a critical condition. They've had to induce coma."

"Shit," Brant said quietly.

"Probably for the best," Branathes offered.

They both turned to look at him.

"I mean, obviously that's been done for a reason, yes? To give her the best chance of survival?"

"Guess so." Tirrano said.

"I sure hope she pulls through." Brant added.

"Of course you do. We all do. I'm sure she'll be fine; Fort Laeara has some of the best surgeons available. Anyway Occre, come with me. I'll show you to your station."

As his supervisor led him away, Brant did something he had never, ever thought he would do. He craned his neck over his shoulder, locked eyes with Tirrano, and mouthed a message to her.

*'We need to talk.'*

# – 03 –
## DISPUTER

It was in her voice. It was in her posture. It was in her gestures, her gaze, and the slight curl of her thin lips. Everything about Captain Helia Thande gave the impression that she had just presided over one execution, and was impatient to get a move on with the next.

Caden could almost feel the hostility radiating from her, particularly in Santani's direction, and he wondered exactly what it was that had provoked such a strong reaction.

"When a ship goes down in a time of war, it traditionally does so during combat with the enemy. How exactly did this happen?"

Caden flicked his eyes across to Santani, and saw her fidget. She had one hand under the table, presumably in her lap or on her leg, and with the other she tapped the polished black surface without rhythm. She stared, but didn't see.

"Captain...?"

Santani looked up from beneath her fringe. "We *were* in combat."

"The fight is taking place on the Perseus arm," Thande said. "Woe Tantalum is not a defence priority. It literally could not rank lower."

Santani looked towards Caden.

"Captain Thande," he said, "*Hammer* was operating under my instructions, at the behest of the Throne. I don't think it's fair to—"

"I'll ask for your contribution when I am ready for it."

Caden stopped dead, his mouth hanging open for a second. Thande's voice was cold, measured, and steady. Few people who knew what a Shard was, and what a Shard did, ever spoke to him as she did now.

"Santani," she continued. "Explain to me why you saw fit to ground a battleship, killing almost half your crew."

"You're not my senior. Why should I explain it to you, when Command will be debriefing me anyway?"

"I have to file a report of my own, you know. I will have to justify my decision to bring an entire battle group out here, while a major military operation was being conducted elsewhere. I'd like to be able to corroborate the reasons why I thought that decision was correct."

Caden imagined he felt the air thaw slightly. In truth, he thought, it would be difficult to argue that Helia Thande had not helped them out a great deal. Certainly many of the surviving crew from *Hammer* owed their very lives to her.

"Woe Tantalum was a staging area," Santani said. "There's some kind of new alliance forming between Viskr, humans, and we think a third party. They were making preparations for a large scale attack."

"If you were trying to use the *Hammer* as a weapon, you missed entirely."

"No, that's not what happened at all."

"Perhaps you should start at the beginning."

"Fine," Santani said. "I was tasked with assisting Shard Caden in the recovery of stolen weapons. The trail led to Woe Tantalum. When we arrived, we were faced with a mixed fleet of Imperial and Viskr ships; all of them hostile. The quarantine network was compromised, and there was traffic moving between the ships and the surface.

"Caden and his team went to the surface, while *Hammer* engaged the hostile ships to keep them busy. I don't know who was commanding them, but they were a pushover. We almost had the upper hand when another ship arrived.

"That thing was huge. I've never seen anything like it; it was armed and armoured like a dreadnought, only... only it was *massive*. I can't even make you understand the scale just with words. We didn't stand a chance fighting it, and we couldn't abandon the people on the surface, so we tried to hide in the atmosphere.

"Unfortunately it followed us in, and we weren't as well hidden as we thought we would be. The only way we could fight back was to order the quarantine network to come back online. That's what shot us down, and you know the rest after that." There was a slight catch in her voice. "As for the dread... ship, I presume either it was destroyed or it fled."

Thande had been staring at Santani throughout her account, and her face gave no hint of her impressions. She continued to stare for a few silent, uncomfortable moments, then turned her head towards Caden.

"Did you see this 'massive' enemy ship, Shard Caden?"

"No," he said. "I was on the surface at the time.

We were a little occupied."

"You didn't see it in the atmosphere?"

"I did not."

"It was in the high atmosphere when it engaged us," Santani offered. "It wouldn't have been visible from the ground."

"It would have been if the platforms shot it down. If it was as big as you said."

"I... suppose it would have."

"No such vessel was detected fleeing the system when *Disputer* arrived to bail you out, Captain Santani. There was a handful of Viskr and Imperial ships, as you described, which fled together into the Deep Shadows. But no sign of your 'dread ship'."

"Our sensors were recording constantly."

"The same sensors which feed into storage modules that currently lie smashed across the surface of a planet? Those sensors?"

Santani remained silent.

"You had best prepare a list of your dead, Captain. I think we can safely say that there will be an inquiry."

Caden looked across to Santani while Thande flipped their preliminary reports across her holo. Their eyes met briefly.

"Shard Caden," Thande said, thumbing off the holo. "What can you tell me about events on the surface?"

"We took fire from the ground on the way down, as you know. Unfortunately we lost Captain Pinsetti and one of his MAGA platoons. When we got to the surface I had two of the remaining platoons take out the surface-to-air turrets, and the last platoon went with me.

"There was resistance from a mix of humans

59

and Viskr, accompanied by a few skulkers. I'd call it light resistance though — we had much the same experience that Captain Santani had with the ships. They seemed incompetent.

"Eventually we located their base, for want of a better word, and that's where I found the missing assets. Well, some of them."

Thande waited until she was sure he had finished. "That might even be a less impressive story."

"I didn't realise we were in competition."

"Oh you aren't. But I expected something more... *significant*-sounding, seeing as it cost us a battleship and a great many lives."

"I'm not going into any more detail. With respect, Captain, I don't know you. I don't know what level of clearance you've got with respect to my mission. The fact that nobody has mentioned it suggests you have no clearance at all. So sorry, but I won't be sharing anything more with you until I've conferred with Eyes and Ears."

Caden kept his gaze level with Thande's, and he was peripherally aware that Santani was watching them both intently.

"Very well," Thande said. "I certainly wouldn't want you to compromise security on my account."

"Good," said Caden. "Now you'll have to forgive me, but it's been a really long day. I'm tired, I've been shot at quite a lot, and to be blunt I would very much like to end this meeting. I urgently need to speak to Command before I retire. I trust you'll be extending the usual courtesies?"

"Of course. Quarters have been prepared. Captain Santani, Commander Yuellen will show you to yours now. I'd like to speak to Shard Caden on his own for a moment."

Santani rose slowly to her feet, gave Caden the slightest of nods, and walked towards the doors of the wardroom with her head held high. Caden was not surprised to see that she failed to pay any respect to her fellow captain.

"One thing." Santani turned back to look at Thande. "How did you disable the quarantine network? I ordered my XO to have the access codes scrambled."

"Commanding officers from three different ships can order the network to shut down, even without the codes. As long as they can also supply a handshake signal from Fleet."

"Oh, I didn't know that."

"You would have known had you bothered to complete the latest training package, Captain. It went out to all COs several months ago."

Santani's eyes narrowed. "I see. I'll leave you both to it then."

When the doors closed behind her, Thande appeared to relax. But only in the most marginal way that Caden could detect.

"What's your view of this 'dread ship' she's blaming for driving *Hammer* into Woe Tantalum's atmosphere?"

"I wasn't there," said Caden, "but I have no reason to think Captain Santani would exaggerate something like that. I'm fairly certain her bridge officers will confirm what she said."

"Won't they just." Thande's tone told Caden she would mistrust those assurances just as certainly as she expected them.

"They didn't strike me as liars."

Thande regarded him with that still, inexpressive gaze of hers, a gaze which betrayed nothing.

"I was instructed to inform you that Operation

Seawall has essentially failed," she said. "The Viskr armada is larger than we thought, and not so disorganised."

"I'd heard something along those lines. What's the damage?"

"Hard to say. We still have fleets engaged all along their border, and Command are scrambling to reinforce our lines without compromising planetary defence forces. Viskr counter-offensives are now threatening some of our Perseus arm colonies."

"Brilliant," said Caden.

"I am given to understand it was Eyes and Ears who advised Fleet Command on the need to strike first," Thande said. "I am also given to understand that they did this based on information you yourself gave them."

"In a way. If you're suggesting that Operation Seawall is my fault, I reject that entirely."

"I wasn't, actually. Commander Operations can make his own decisions, and if anyone is going to take heat for this débâcle it will probably be Admiral Betombe. I just think you might want to keep your head down for a while."

"Noted. What do you know about this situation at Fort Kosling?"

"Well... that woman they're calling the 'Rasa'? Apparently she escaped, although from what I hear she wasn't even under guard, which I have to say is bizarre to me. She stole a ship from drydock and used its weaponry to slag the station from the inside."

"Survivors?"

"Almost everyone. Core systems were very heavily damaged, but virtually all of the emergency shelters were launched. Recovery was already underway when we jumped here."

"Good," said Caden. He found himself thinking about Occre Brant. Him, and even Tirrano.

"That one *was* basically down to you."

"I think I might have to take that bullet, yes. Although to be fair I wasn't the one looking after Naeb."

"Which brings us to the next topic: those prisoners you brought aboard."

"I thought you might mention that."

"I'm not really very impressed that you undermined my XO."

Caden could not help but smile slightly. "He said you wouldn't have the prisoners in your brig. They aren't in *your* brig; they're in mine."

"While I am fairly impressed at your counterpart's imaginative use for a lander's hull, I think you might have asked me before using Life and Rescue's recovery haulers to lift it aboard my ship."

Caden opened his mouth to reply, but she continued. "And I don't think those prisoners are any more secure in that thing than they would be in proper custody facilities."

"We've left two platoons from Bullseye on the cargo deck to guard them. A third platoon is bedded down. They'll rotate so everyone gets some rack time."

"Bullseye?"

"Bravo Company, from the 951st. Same thing."

"Right. And you think that will be enough?"

"Probably. Even if all of those prisoners somehow escape, they'll be gunned down. There are enough troopers down there to start a new colony."

Thande sighed. Caden realised it was the first

time he had heard the woman breathe.

"Very well. I'll defer to your experience with these... people. But, as I said, I'm not happy that you undermined my first officer. I realise I can't give you orders, but could you please at least make an effort at professional courtesy while you're aboard my ship."

"I think I can manage that."

"Good. We've been ordered to deliver Bravo Company back to Admiral Pensh, so we're going to be heading to the Laeara System. Is there anything you need to know about *Disputer* before you're shown to your quarters?"

"I'll manage. I am curious about one thing though."

"What's that?"

"Why were you so much more frosty towards Captain Santani than you are towards me?"

Thande hesitated for a moment, regarding Caden with a searching expression. She seemed to come to a decision, relaxed a bit more, and sat back in her chair.

"Santani is very much of the Old Guard. Cocktails on the quarterdeck, drinking stories that involve a rear admiral, internal loyalties put before the chain of command: that sort of thing. She's stuck in her ways. Her attitude might have been good enough during the slugging matches of the Perseus conflict, but times have changed."

"But still, she was just doing her job."

"If she had kept herself fully up-to-date with current operating procedures she might still have a ship. As things are, Command is now going to have to furnish the Second Fleet with a replacement ship and crew. Not to mention sending out a couple of hundred death notices."

"That is very unfortunate, and I regret my role in it. But in her defence our presence at Woe Tantalum *was* sanctioned by the Chamberlain."

"Are you for real?" Thande sputtered. "The Chamberlain? He knows even less about fleet procedure than Santani does. Hell, even this table knows more than that useless sycophant."

"Point taken."

"The fleets are commanded by Fleet Command. Clue's in the name!"

"Again, Captain; point taken."

Thande seemed to realise she was ranting, and calmed down quickly. "They've been trying to yank her into the modern era for a long time, and she's just handed them their opportunity. Even if she isn't punished for destroying *Hammer*, Captain Santani will be flying a desk for the rest of her career. I personally don't want her to see me as an ally in any inquiry that comes out of all this, just because I turned up to bail her out."

"So you're making sure that comes across loud and clear."

"Exactly."

"Well, that seems fair."

"Oh, don't feel left out." Thande gave him a thin smile. "I don't generally have any fondness for Shards either. Never have done. Put a foot wrong in *my* ship, and I will do everything I can to snap it off."

Caden returned the smile, as thinly as he could. "Nobody is ever pleased to see me."

○ ○ ○

Although both Throam and Eilentes had served on a Glory-class carrier before, Throam did not recall ever seeing one quite as literally ship-shape as Thande's *ICS Disputer*. She was everything *Ham-*

*mer* was not, and not just because that unfortunate battleship had crashed into a planet.

*Disputer* was trim, organised, and almost unbearably clean. Crew walked briskly along her passageways, not wasting any time in idle chat. The loudest thing on some decks was the steady thrum of the air cyclers, and the processed atmosphere reeked of sterile formality. It was as if the entire vessel were a reflection of her captain's personality.

In some ways it was chilling.

Throam arrived at a single-width hatch, checked the plate on the bulkhead next to it — twice, just to be sure he was about to enter the right cabin — and slapped the entry panel gratefully. His link pulsed silently as the panel queried it.

The hatch popped open, and he stepped through the opening to see Eilentes perched on the edge of the bunk. She looked up from her work.

"Cool, right place. I was sure I'd got turned around out there," he said.

"You did serve on the *Embolden* for an entire Solar; it can't be that different."

"Used to find my way around by all the different crap people left stacked up in the passageways. They're too fucking clean here; everywhere looks the same."

"You'll get used to it," Eilentes said. She went back to her work.

"You're cleaning your rifle again?"

"Gotta be ready, just in case Caden ever gets around to asking me to do something actually worthwhile. Anyway, Woe Tantalum was a punishing environment. Ambrast doesn't like being dirty."

"Ambrast? That's a new one."

"Sure is, brand new. Ambrast, the Moachim X50-S Pointseeker. Definitely my favourite boy."

Throam sniggered before he could stop himself, and Eilentes stopped cleaning. She placed the scope down carefully in her lap.

"What?"

"Nothing, just never got used to you seeing them as your 'boys'."

She resumed her task. "It's a sharp-shooter thing. You know this already. Our rifles are our friends. More than that; they have to be utterly trustworthy. More so than people."

"Why 'Ambrast'?"

"He's the guy who single-handedly took down the *Trysk Morsilivan*."

"Oh yeah. History's greatest exaggeration."

"It was witnessed by an entire regiment."

"Bullshit. No fucker does stuff like that in real life — don't matter how good you are."

"Whatever; I'm not his advocate. You asked why the rifle is called Ambrast, and that's your answer."

Throam grinned inwardly at Eilentes' tone, and watched her for a moment as she dedicated her entire attention to cleaning the weapon. She was trying hard to not look at him at all.

"So, you know... while you're messing about with dirty old Ambrast over there, you're kinda missing out."

She replied flatly, without looking up. "Oh, how's that?"

"Because you could be messing about with dirty old me in here." He stepped through the inner hatch to the wash enclosure.

The enclosure was much better than the basic

facilities they had had on *Hammer*. It was a bigger space for a start, and actually closed off from the rest of the quarters. The shower cubicle was full size. More importantly, the toilet was full size as well. Luxury! Later on he would thoroughly enjoy breaking that in.

A faintly illuminated green strip surrounded the curved door of the cubicle, indicating that it was safe to use liquid water. He opened the door and turned on the flow.

Now that it knew a hot shower was in its future, his body began to tell him about the cost of the trip to Woe Tantalum's surface. Aches and pains sprang up all over. He peeled off his under-layer gingerly, and dropped it on the floor.

The water temperature must have risen almost immediately, because the mirrored wall of the enclosure was already steaming up. He examined his body quickly, before the opportunity went away.

His left forearm felt like it was made of iron. He folded the arm, as far as he could with his biceps muscle in the way, and lifted it above his shoulder. Sure enough, there was a faint bruise around the elbow. His skin was naturally dusky, but there was no mistaking that area of dull red-brown. Soon it would be purple, then black and yellow.

His back stung, and he twisted at the waist, craning his neck over his right shoulder to try and look in the mirror. For most people the manoeuvre would have been a simple one; for Throam, his wide neck almost immediately came up against a thick wedge of trapezius muscle. He tried to drop his shoulder on that side.

It was difficult to find, thanks to the ungainly angle, his tattoos, and the gradually misting mirror, but it was definitely there: almost camouflaged by the pattern of his back-piece, a long, thin gash ran across the top of his right lat. How the hell had *that* happened? He made a mental note to check his outer armour, extra carefully.

It was becoming difficult to see anything in the mirror now, despite the moisture reclamation system, and he decided to get in the shower. He was sure that if there were any other injuries which needed attention, the hot water would reveal them. It usually worked.

Throam sang to himself while he lathered up, not caring that he was off key. He had always been of the opinion that sheer volume counted for a lot more than being in tune.

When he was halfway through brutally murdering the second verse, the door of the cubicle juddered. The sound was accompanied by a burst of cold air. The soap meant he could not open his eyes, but he smiled anyway: the intrusion could only really mean one thing.

"Hey," he said.

"Hey," came the reply.

Her left hand landed on his hip; the other over his own hand, the one in which he held a body scrubber, and Eilentes moved it around in small circles on his chest. She brought their hips together, and his smile broke into a grin as he felt an erect nipple slide lightly across the top of his abdomen. He pulled her lithe body in with his empty hand, and felt her standing on tip-toes to kiss his lips. He craned his neck downwards, lowering his mouth towards hers.

Eilentes let go of his hand, moving hers down to assist the other in cradling his buttocks. A surge began to rise, and he looped his now freed arm around her and pulled her in tight. Her breasts squashed up under the overhang of his pecs, and he turned towards the bulkhead, taking her with him. Water cascaded over his head as they moved into the flow, rinsing the foam out of his hair and down his face. It washed over them both, some trickling down his cleavage and pooling in hers.

They were still kissing, and Eilentes pulled his hips farther in towards her, harder, rubbing herself against the front of his thighs. Her body was athletic — always had been — and he could feel her slick abdominals tensing and undulating against his crotch. The surge rose, fell, rose higher, became a throb, throb, throb, and swelled between them. He grabbed her neck with one hand, his thumb under her jaw, and kissed harder. Each breath was forced through his nostrils, heavy and raggedly uncontrolled.

She broke her mouth away with a jerk, panting.

"Tell me what you're going to do," she breathed urgently.

Throam backed her against the wet bulkhead, used both hands to slide her whole body up it, and pushed his pelvis between her thighs. She wrapped her legs around his waist, and he held her up on one arm. The other hand went back to her neck. She turned her head, twisting her throat into his grip, then took his wrist with one hand, grabbed his shoulder with the other, and arched her back as he planted his feet wide and pushed up inside her.

"Gonna fuck your fucking snatch off."

"So romantic!" She gasped.

o o o

Two decks up, and seven compartments across, Caden and Santani had intercourse of a very different sort.

"Condescending bitch!" Santani fumed. "Doesn't she realise I just lost half my crew?"

Caden decided to give her a moment before replying. After leaving Thande he had immediately sought out Santani's quarters, and found her — despite the awkwardness of her injured leg and its rigid casing — pacing back and forth in a rage. There was a comical air to her wobbly venting which Caden tried very hard not to react to.

"I mean, not even 'I'm sorry for your losses, I've arranged for your survivors to see the bereavement counsellor'. Straight in with the recriminations."

"Look at it from her point of view," Caden said. "She gets a reinforcement request, jumps across the galaxy, and finds the captain who called her up has already crashed her own ship into a planet. That's going to surprise and annoy anyone."

"I really don't care how she feels about it. What was I supposed to do? Stay in orbit and get ripped to pieces? Flee, and leave you all down there?"

"I know, Aker. I know."

"Now that miserable twat is deciding how many ways I went wrong, and she'll be passing that along to Command."

"Don't get hung up on that." Caden raised his palms. "Yes, there will be an inquiry. But they'll only really be interested in her sensor logs and statements of fact. They don't need her opinions; they can form their own."

Santani looked at him with an incredulous expression, and sneered. "Oh yeah, because that's how it works."

Can't really argue with that, thought Caden. But then maybe you *want* to stay angry, because you can't face up to what you've just done. You selfish bitc— *No!* Get a grip. That's not how I see her. That's *not* what I think. That's the Emptiness talking.

He realised she was waiting for him to say something, and decided on a change of tack.

"How is Commander Klade?"

Santani stopped pacing and turned to face him, pivoting on her healthy leg. She hesitated, the anger slowly melting away, and eventually sat down.

"Better. Stable. He was brought up to *Disputer* and moved to sickbay."

"Good to hear."

"Thank you for asking."

He hesitated. "I'm... not blind to the fact that this happened largely because of me."

She didn't reply.

"Before, on Woe Tantalum, you asked me if it was worth it."

"I'm sorry about the way I spoke to you. I was in a bit of a state."

"Yes, I realise that; don't worry about it. I can't imagine what it's like for you to lose so many people, to feel responsible. But it wasn't in vain, Aker. You know that. You heard what Brant said about those weapons; because of us whole worlds will be spared a miserable fate.

"A lot has happened in the past few days. A lot of strange things. Now we know that the Empire has undeclared enemies, and we have some idea of what they're capable of. If it hadn't been for *Hammer*, we'd all be dead, and the Empire would be none the wiser about what's happening."

"The cost was too high," she said.

"I don't mean to trivialise what you're going through, but that remains to be seen. Don't forget there are still plenty of those weapons out there. We won't know the scale of what we've prevented until they're used. And for all we know right now, that's the least of our worries."

Santani wiped her eyes quickly, as if she didn't want him to notice. "Do you think the Viskr are behind all this?"

"I did, but I'm not so sure since we found Morlum. He said the Viskr don't control the Rasas. The ones we tangled with weren't using typical Viskr tactics, and they weren't anywhere near as capable as they should have been, either. Also let's not forget there were plenty of Viskr in amongst those Rasas we killed and captured. The Junta has troops on tap; why would it need to zombify its own people?"

"So someone else is behind the Rasas."

"I'd bet anything that whoever controls that dreadship of yours is pulling the strings. Somehow using Viskr and humans as if they're puppets, and taking our ships."

"You think they have the Empire's weapons, too?"

"It would be a safe assumption."

"If that's all true, then Amarist Naeb would be one of their agents."

"And she has fled. That would imply either that they wanted her back badly, or she had some kind of objective to complete at Fort Kosling."

"I doubt it's the latter," Santani said. "How could anyone have predicted you'd turn up? That you'd move her to that particular fortress?"

"So the questions are... what's so damned important about Amarist Naeb, and how exactly was she recalled?"

∘ ∘ ∘

Throam had just about stopped short of being true to his word. He was usually an animal in the bedroom, but this time he had been much more primal than that. Not just a mere animal, but a beast: demanding, aggressive... almost frenzied.

Eilentes took her time in the wash enclosure, cleaning and soothing herself carefully. On the one hand, she had needed that for a good long while now. But on the other hand... she might not actually be able to walk from here to the bunk without wobbling.

She stepped through the hatch into the main compartment, grabbed the bulkhead for support, and almost winced.

Throam was laying on his back with his hands behind his head, completely naked and spread-eagled across the entire bunk. She watched his chest and stomach rise and fall rapidly, saw the bumped ridges of veins embossed on his shoulders and arms, distorting the flow of his tattoos. He was *still* pumped up.

He raised his head at the sound of her movements, and gave her a smile that mixed triumph with deep satisfaction.

Don't you look pleased with yourself, she thought.

"How'd you like *that*?" He asked.

"That was... something else," she said, starting to towel-dry her jet-black hair.

He watched her slender frame as she dried off. "Fuck yeah."

"You're still juicing, right?"

"I might be."

"A proper cycle?"

"You could say that."

"I did see the marks. You're obviously injecting

on top of your orals."

"Fine, yes; I'm injecting again."

"You're not just using steroids, are you?"

"I upped my doses."

"Rendir, please. I've seen what you're like on high doses. You've never been like that before. What else are you taking?"

Throam rolled his eyes at her.

"Are you mixing in some stims? Little bit of White Thunder? What? Come on, you can tell me."

"Just a heavy cycle."

"No, it's more than that. You were pretty rough in there."

"What can I say? I guess I'm just an unstoppable fuck-machine. Sorry if you didn't like it."

"I didn't say I didn't *like* it." She giggled. "It's just that I... probably won't be able to, er, take a hammering like that very often."

"You think that was a hammering? Imagine getting stuck underneath that Bruiser."

She knew he was changing the subject, but decided to let it go. He was one of the most stubborn men she knew. Well fine; if he was going to change the subject then he could have some mockery instead.

"Is that what you've been thinking about out here? Getting stuck under Bruiser?"

"Not like *that*." He stuck his middle finger up at her. "I heard he's so dedicated he turns his link off before he even steps foot in the gym. Know what that means for him? No translations. He literally can't be distracted from lifting. They say he presses seven hundred kilos. Imagine *him* thrusting away on top of you."

"I get it now," Eilentes said. "Someone's feeling

inadequate since the bigger, stronger guy turned up. Is this because Caden and I started calling you 'Tiny' back on Echo?"

"No it fucking isn't." He pushed himself up onto his knees. "Inadequate? Fuck off. This is your big, strong guy right here; come and find out if he's tiny or not."

Eilentes looked at him holding his semi-hard cock in his hand, with an indignant yet hopeful look on his face, and she could not help but burst out laughing.

"Oh, you kill me. You really do."

"I'm serious. I need to fuck."

"Already? You really want to go again, right now?"

"I'm building up to it pretty fast. You think I can't?"

"No, I'm sure you're bursting with testosterone. And I know damned well you're anything but tiny. But I really can't manage it again, Rendir. Not yet."

"I'll smash your back doors in this time."

She grimaced. "It's still going to hurt, you big idiot."

"Fuck's sake." He dropped heavily onto his back again.

She grabbed the edge of the bedding, hauled it out from under his legs, and climbed onto the bunk. The bedding contracted back into its default shape, gently holding their bodies against the mattress.

"There's no way I'll sleep with that fucking thing over me," Throam said. "I'll cook."

"That's your problem for being so freakishly hot."

"If I cook, you cook too."

"Good point."

Eilentes pulled the memory bedding back again, until its rigid end cap clicked back over the foot of the bunk. It didn't try to return. She slid her hand along under the bunk until she found the usual cubby hole, and pulled out a rolled-up cotton sheet.

"You know, if the gravity goes while we're asleep, we'll float off without the safety covers."

"Not as bad as it sounds," said Throam. "Happened to me twice now."

He pulled an arm out from under the sheet, and raised it over the pillows. Eilentes lifted her head and neck, and he slid the arm under her.

She rested her head on his upper arm, felt herself rise momentarily as he tensed, and turned her face towards him. Even with the height she gained by laying on his biceps, she felt as though she were much lower down. Between her eyes and his, a steep slope of chest muscle and thick shoulder became her horizon. He had always been a big man, but in the time they had spent apart the man had become a mountain.

"There's something I wanted to say," she said. "I didn't get a chance before."

"Hmmm?" Throam rumbled. She felt the sound through his side.

"I wanted to say sorry. Sorry for having a go at you about Gendin. I honestly didn't know."

"It's okay."

"Really though, I hope I didn't upset you."

"It's okay, Euryce."

"If you want to talk about it at all, you just let me know, yeah?"

He turned his head, and peered down at her over the horizon. "Seriously, it's okay. I don't want to talk about it, right?"

"Sorry, I just thought you might want—"

"All I want now," he said, "all I can *think* about, is that I really need to come again. I am fucking rampant."

"I told you, I can't take another round of that."

"There's more than one way you can get me off." He pushed her head under the sheet.

The reply was muffled and indignant. "You dick!"

"Yep!"

o o o

Caden was tired, mentally and physically, but this was a conversation that simply could not wait. He wished sincerely it could have been one he need not have at all.

"I'm sorry," Fleet Admiral Bel-Messari was saying, "but I don't really see what you expect from Command."

Caden sighed to himself, and tried again. "Eyes and Ears knows fine well that there have been blackouts other than Herros and Echo. You need to follow up on them, right now. Don't leave it to local patrols to deal with: treat this as an Empire-wide crisis."

"But... why?"

"You have listened to what I've said, yes?"

"I have indeed, Shard Caden. But I have not heard anything that I could use to justify taking resources away from Commander Operations during a time of war. He would have my scalp for that."

"It's your responsibility!" Caden sputtered.

The hologram of Silane Creid chose that moment to make a deft intervention. "If I may? It's not that we aren't taking this situation seriously,

Shard Caden. It's just that the renewed offensive against the Viskr obviously takes precedence right now."

"Oh don't give me that." Caden felt the pressure building behind his eyes, between his shoulders. His gut felt like it was floating. "Don't you even *dare*. You know damned well that the whole reason we're in this mess is because of what Fleet, and Eyes and Ears" — he jabbed his finger at Bel-Messari's hologram, then Creid's — "were cooking up at Gemen Station."

Creid smiled gently. "And what was that exactly? Do tell us."

"You were building weapons of mass destruction. In peace time!"

"But of course we were," Bel-Messari said. "Do you think for a moment that our enemies aren't? That our potential enemies aren't?"

"I'm sure they are," Caden said, in a tone which could have cut glass. "But they probably take adequate steps to make sure their facilities remain secure."

He spat out the word 'secure' as if it tasted of dead bodies. In a way, it did.

Bel-Messari's holographic form looked down briefly, and Caden switched his attention to Creid just in time to see him look up. The invigilator had most likely just tapped out a private message to the Admiral.

"As difficult as it is to admit this, you are probably correct on that count. We're still no closer to understanding how our forces were overcome."

"Then Admiral, for the sake of the people we have already lost — and their families — devote some resources to finding out."

"I told you; Commander Operations will not divert the ships at this time. Believe me, I know how his mind works."

"At least try a universal handshake," Caden said. "Check every registered gate will respond, and request an up-to-date databurst from every ship, station, and facility."

Creid answered first. "That will be incredibly damaging to the economy. The down-time alone —"

"Fuck the economy. This needs to be done."

Bel-Messari frowned. "Please keep a civil tongue, Shard Caden. I don't care who you think you are; neither of us are going to accept being berated by *you*."

"If I have to come to Command in person to get your cooperation, admiral or not, I will do much more than fucking berate you."

Bel-Messari shook his head slowly, and his hologram fizzled out of existence.

"Well," said Creid. "How... persuasive."

"Invigilator Creid," Caden began again, trying to force some degree of control back into his voice. "Surely you of all people realise the need for us to gather information at this point? There are far, *far* too many unanswered questions."

"Such as?"

"Well for one thing, who exactly is behind this new alliance which is apparently running amok in our territory. Who took those weapons of yours, and what do they plan to do with them. And also — this is just an example, stop me if you don't think it's important — what in the many worlds has been done to those people we found, and why did one of them try to blow a fortress to pieces just to escape one of our doctors?"

"Well now, that last one is something we might

be able to get to the bottom of." Creid steepled his fingers and leaned forwards. "The *Vavilov* is equipped to answer all manner of questions about these so-called 'Rasas' of yours. I'll have it diverted to take them off your hands. You're not really that far from each other."

"That at least would be something," Caden said. A thought occurred. "You're not proposing... experimenting on them? Most of them are humans. Imperial humans."

"Experimenting? No, of course not. The *Vavilov* is purely a research ship. There are no secret torture labs on *our* vessels."

"I'll have to take your word for that."

"I can assure you, it's perfectly true. As for this 'new alliance' you mentioned, you'll have to forgive our scepticism. It's perfectly obvious that the Viskr are manipulating our citizens. We might not know how just yet, but we will find out."

"And the mystery vessel Captain Santani fled from? This 'dreadship" which she says was probably in the Herros system too?"

"Utter rubbish," Creid sneered. "She doesn't want to admit a straight defeat at Woe Tantalum, and she concocted that story to explain why victory was never within her grasp."

"And then convinced her entire command crew to go along with the scheme?"

"Naturally."

"You've never served, have you?"

"I don't really see what that has to do with anything, Shard Caden."

Caden leaned in close to the holo, and barely kept the anger and contempt from his voice. "That's exactly my point, Invigilator Creid."

Creid stared at Caden for a few seconds, and

then his holographic image also vanished.

"You were a lot of help," Caden said.

The Chamberlain's hologram smiled.

"If you think they were difficult to convince, you should try speaking in front of the Home Council."

"I don't believe it's my role to convince anyone. It would have been useful if you had stepped in, instead of sitting there in silence."

"Fleet Command will have their own plans for chasing up on those blackouts, I'm sure of it," the Chamberlain said. "Indeed I think it's entirely possible to worry too much about that sort of thing."

"You sound very relaxed about it."

"Naturally there are things going on behind the scenes which you are not privy to."

Caden closed his eyes momentarily, and sighed. "Of course. I should have known there would be. And Eyes and Ears?"

"Eyes and Ears, I suspect, are just covering their embarrassment. Oh, they become more like politicians every day."

"I suppose you have nothing to contribute to that situation either?"

"They have their mandate and they have their means. It is certainly not up to me to do their thinking for them. If they fail the Empress, they will answer for it."

"I don't think the many worlds of the Imperial Combine should fall into chaos, just because of a lack of cooperation." Caden drummed his fingers on the desktop, staring at the Chamberlain. He tilted his head slightly. "I'd like to request audience."

"I will of course ask, but as you would expect the current crisis is taking up much of Her Radiant

Majesty's time."

"Please do. It's been far too long."

"Indeed I shall. And I will pass on your concerns regarding the apparent lack of action from Fleet."

"I would appreciate that. Ever since this started, I've felt like I'm coming up against a brick wall every five minutes. I don't seem to recall ever meeting such resistance from ships' captains before. It's just not right."

"Some might say that's for you to deal with. Assert your authority, Shard Caden."

"I can't help but feel that perhaps matters might be different if people were reminded of Her Majesty's existence more frequently. After all, when they tell me 'no', they tell Her too."

"I will pass that along also."

"Thank you."

"There is some other business. As I recall, you asked to be sent after the renegade Maber Castigon once you returned from Woe Tantalum."

"I did. I remember it vividly."

"You have your wish. After conferring with Correction and Probation, and the Chamber of Justice, the court of Her Radiant Majesty the Empress formally orders you to hunt down the fugitive Castigon, and authorises you to exercise summary justice."

"He's to be killed?"

"Indeed. Assassinated, like the Shards he murdered. Good riddance, I say."

"He has certainly earned it."

"Earned it, oh yes."

"I still have a few loose ends to tie up. Those missing weapons are still out there, as are the people who took them. And there's someone I need to find who might be able to tell us more."

"Oh, you should do what you need to do, of course. But Maber Castigon is a priority."

"Nobody wants to put a bullet in his chest more than I do, but is he really that important at the moment? Considering we're at war?"

"We are indeed at war, yes, and he is killing Shards. He is proving to be quite adept at it, and we cannot afford to lose such valuable resources at this time."

"I see. Well, it's certainly nice to feel wanted for a change."

# – 04 –
## The Beast of Blacktree

As it was in the beginning, so shall it be in the end. All shall crumble. All shall become dust, and then vapour, and then energy, until — when the very last sparks of the cosmos have faded to nothing, when the links between subatomic particles are stretched so far that they simply disappear, when the tenuous fabric of reality is as lost as the memory of the beings which once inhabited it — there will be only void: a timeless, empty nothing. We are but embers in the wind.

The old mantra tumbled around in Groath Betombe's head, crashing heavily within the chaotic chimera assembled from his dreams and his senses; each intonation every bit as real as the dust and the fire, the shrapnel and the screaming, the clamorous whirlwind of images and the sounds his unconscious mind fabricated.

Darkness came, and with it a snatched instant of quiet. Then a vivid light that burned to his very core. Then darkness again.

"Admiral?"

A sensation of motion, of travelling backwards, black fabric sweeping around him and blotting out all else, before pulling back to reveal the world; all light again.

"Can you open your eyes for me? Open your eyes, Admiral."

"Too bright," Betombe croaked. His eyelids parted tremulously.

The corpsman turned the head of a surgical lamp away from them, pushed it until it swung over the admiral and came slowly to rest facing the bulkhead.

"You're going to be fine," he said. "I have to admit though, you did have me worried for a short while."

"Condition?" Betombe said.

"Very minor injuries on the whole. You were thrown clear across the command deck, so expect some pain and bruising. You hit your head pretty hard, from what I'm told, but I've not seen any evidence of haemorrhage."

"I meant the ship."

There was a pause.

"Umm... I'm afraid I wouldn't know." The lights flickered as he spoke; once, twice, then back to full brightness. A rumbling growl travelled through a nearby passageway. "But we did take some damage at Gousk, obviously."

"I need to get back to the command deck."

Betombe raised himself on his elbows, then his hands, and swung his legs off the side of the bed.

"I really wouldn't recommend that, Admiral. You need to stay in sickbay for the moment."

"You said very minor injuries. I *need* to be on the bridge."

"I did, yes, but you might still be concussed. In any case, the command deck is no longer habitable. The ship is being run from auxiliary command."

"Then that's where I have to go."

"You need to be observed."

"Well then, you'll just have to come with me, won't you?"

The corpsman sighed deeply, as if resigning himself to the excursion, and reached for a medical kit. He shouted hurried instructions to some of the other medical staff.

Betombe's feet touched the cold deck plates, and he rose cautiously from the bed. Swaying, he put his hand out to steady himself, and waited for his vision to stop swimming.

"Are you okay?"

"I just need a minute."

"I really think it would be much better if you stayed here."

"You made that quite clear. I appreciate your concern and your most remarkable insistence, but I can't very well sit this out."

"As you wish, Admiral."

"Where are we, anyway?"

"The Hujjur system, Sir."

"Makes sense," said Betombe, pushing his arm through a sleeve of his tunic. "Closest Imperial system to Gousk."

"Here, let me help," the corpsman said. "You've got the wrong arm there."

Betombe looked down. Sure enough, he was putting his tunic on backwards.

"I can manage," he said, pulling his arm free of the sleeve. "This says nothing about my condition, you understand."

"Hmmm."

"Hmmm, *Sir*."

Another rumbling, banging sound moved along the passageway outside. A harsh judder was transmitted through the deck, seemingly chasing after the noise. *Love Tap* was complaining about his own injuries.

"I'll sort it out on the way," Betombe said. "Come on."

The corpsman followed him obediently into the passageway, turned left after him, and halted in his tracks. "Auxiliary command is this way, Admiral."

Betombe turned on his heel, and felt his brow gingerly. "Perhaps you had better lead the way."

They set off again, the corpsman in front this time.

"How did we end up here?" Betombe asked, as they hurried through the ship.

"From what I've been told, our fleets retreated here from Gousk shortly after you were knocked out of action. When we arrived, we picked up more Viskr forces."

"They were already in the system?"

"That's what I hear."

"For what reason?"

"I have no idea, Admiral. I've only been given a few scraps of information while I've been patching people up."

"Did we lose many?"

"There are three on ice. Two others I don't expect will pull through."

Betombe grimaced. "And on the other ships?"

"I'm afraid there hasn't been time for me to confer with the other medical officers."

"I see."

Betombe stayed silent for the rest of the way, musing on the small amount of information he had gleaned. The last thing he remembered from Gousk was seeing Viskr ships burst from a chain of wormholes, barrel past their damaged siblings, and hurl themselves viciously at the Fourth and Sixth fleets of the Imperial Navy.

After that part he was a little hazy on the details.

Whatever had happened to his beloved ship, it must have been a heavy blow indeed to reach deep inside the body of *Love Tap* and so decisively damage the command deck. The dreadnought was not exactly what he would call a soft target.

Then of course, there was the question of how the Viskr were able to bring in such effective reinforcements in the first place. Operation Seawall, planned around the latest information from the Perseus arm listening posts, was supposed to have accounted for all enemy naval movements near the border. Each and every one of the Viskr fleets within range was meant to have been kept occupied by an Imperial force of equal or greater strength. But at Gousk...

He realised they had arrived at auxiliary control.

"Admiral on the deck," came a call from inside the cramped compartment. The crew stiffened.

"As you were," Betombe said. "Who has the conn?"

COMOP was the first to answer. "The XO, Sir."

"I'll take it from here, Commander Laselle. Thank you."

"Aye, Sir. You have the conn." She turned to the woman at the COMOP station. "Let the ship's log show that the Admiral is back in command."

"Bring me up to the present moment, Commander."

"Sir. Shortly after the Viskr reinforcements arrived at Gousk, *Love Tap* took a glancing blow from a cutter. The starboard hull was breached, resulting in the explosion of a primary power coupling under the command deck and a substantial loss of atmosphere.

"You were knocked unconscious, so I made the decision to retreat to the nearest friendly system. We therefore jumped to Hujjur, which is our present location."

"I'm aware of our location," Betombe said. "I need to know our *situation*."

"Shafted, Sir."

He raised an eyebrow. "Explain."

"The gate wasn't responding, so we were forced to jump to the system periphery. When we arrived we briefly detected Viskr ships in orbit of Blacktree. We tried to make a short jump to reinforce the planet's defence cordon, but our coils stalled."

"Someone's interdicting?"

"Yes, Sir. No outgoing wormholes. We can't jump in towards the planet, we can't jump back out of the system, and we can't call in reinforcements."

"Any reinforcements already coming?"

"Nobody knows we're here."

He placed a hand to his brow. "What have we lost?"

"Another three ships went down after the *Gorgon*, and five more are no longer in any condition to fight. We've taken some moderate damage ourselves; you probably already felt the results."

"I certainly did," he said. "It's been a while since I was in this neighbourhood. Refresh my memory: what are the system assets?"

"Blacktree is the only populated planet in the system. It has a small number of orbital platforms, and a cordon comprising three battle groups; mixed cruisers and destroyers, if memory serves."

"Have you made contact?"

"That's another problem," Laselle said. "The gate appears to have been either disabled or destroyed. The system's nexus is now so unstable that comms are suffering significant lag."

"And no doubt hampering our sensors?"

"Exactly. Data on enemy movements is becoming less reliable by the minute. We just have fragments, and they aren't very clear. All we can be sure of is that there's a battle going on in the system interior."

Betombe went silent for a moment, putting the information in order.

"You made the right choice, leaving Gousk. How long to get to Blacktree at best speed?"

"Under conventional thrust, factoring in acceleration: just under two days."

"Ouch. How long to get *out* of the system?"

"Six hours. The battle could be over by then."

"Shafted, as you said."

Betombe bit his lower lip thoughtfully, and picked his way through the cramped compartment until he reached the central command station. Sitting down, he activated the station's holo and identified himself to it.

"Do you have orders for the crew, Sir?" Laselle asked.

He looked at her for a moment, a frown of concentration on his face. "Not yet. Put together a battle map. Use the sensor readings you think are the most reliable, then apply the most likely movements the enemy will have made since the data was gathered."

COMOP interrupted. "Admiral, *Hydra* Actual states she has taken too much secondary damage after the battle at Gousk. Fire in main engineering, apparently. She will have to bow out from any engagement in this system."

"Instruct *Hydra* to leave the system at best speed, along with any other ships that aren't battle-worthy. As soon as they are able to open a wormhole, I expect them to retreat back to Laeara."

"Sir."

"The battle map is ready, Admiral."

Betombe rotated his chair to look at the holographic volume his executive officer was manipulating.

"Based on the last good sensor reads we were able to get, there is most likely a Viskr battle group moving along this path."

She traced out a short arc with her finger: close to the distant planet, moving away from the position of *Love Tap* in sympathy with Blacktree's orbit of the Hujjur star.

Betombe leaned forwards. "Then the interdiction radius will be receding with them, away from us."

"It should be, yes. But it could take hours for the edge of the field to pass us by."

"True, however with this data you can work out the optimal route to get us beyond the interdiction field. It's not much, but it will shave off some time."

"I'll start on that right away, Sir."

"Once you have a navigation solution, pass it to the rest of the fleet. Including *Hydra* and her group."

"Understood."

While his XO returned to her work, Betombe sat back in his chair heavily. He had not realised that he was leaning forward, that he was holding his body tense. Fatigue overcame him without warning, and a dull pain turned his forehead to frozen stone.

"Are you all right, Sir?"

Betombe looked to the side, his eyes half closed, and he saw the corpsman standing beside his chair. He had completely forgotten the man was still with him.

"For the moment," the admiral replied.

"If there's nothing more to be done here, Sir, I'd like you to return to sickbay."

"I can't do that, Doc," said Betombe. "I have hours of logs to review."

○ ○ ○

Betombe's body jerked, and he realised he had been adrift in a sea of thought. Exactly what he had been thinking about, however, he could not quite remember.

"Back with us, Sir?"

He looked up and saw the corpsman still standing over his command station, pointing a sensor at him. "I think I lost my concentration there for a moment."

"You did. Have you ever been diagnosed with any kind of apnoea, Admiral?"

"No. Why?"

"Your breathing slowed considerably. I'd like to run a few quick tests, in case it's related to that bang on the head."

Betombe was about to respond when COMOP interrupted. Good old COMOP.

"Incoming wormhole, right on top of us... point of origin is outside the system."

Betombe waved the corpsman away. "Tactical, stand ready."

"Message from *Hydra*. They've crossed out of

the interdiction zone, and opened this wormhole for the rest of us to join them."

"Excellent! Team-player points for *Hydra* Actual. Have the rest of the fleet jump to join her, and make sure they're battle-ready. We'll jump back in again immediately, and join the fight at Blacktree."

"There's still the problem with the gate." Commander Laselle spoke softly as she stepped in towards Betombe, not wanting the others to hear. "Without a gate to target our arrival precisely, we run the risk of enmeshment."

"Don't worry," the admiral said. "We used to do this all the time towards the end of the Perseus conflict. We'll open a wormhole as close to the battle as we can and send a probe through first. It'll be fine."

"If you say so, Admiral."

"And I do."

"We're ready to jump, Sir."

"Take us out of the system, Helm."

*Love Tap* entered the wormhole, and immediately dropped out again. The Hujjur star was now almost indistinguishable from the rest of the firmament.

"All ships reporting successful jumps," said COMOP.

"Good. Helm, calculate for the vicinity of the battle. Commander Laselle already extrapolated the likely movements of the ships; take their positions relative to the planet's orbit into account, and try to get us ahead of them. That should minimise the chances of running into debris."

The Helm officer stared back blankly.

"Here, let me help." Laselle leaned over to share the holo at his station. "He doesn't ask for much, does he?"

"No, Ma'am."

"It's not pretty, but it will get us there," Laselle said, finalising her calculation.

Far outside the reach of the interdiction field, *Love Tap* was free to open a wormhole safely. His huge gravity needle generator thrummed into life, rapidly built up a store of power, and plucked a passage out of the nothingness of the universe.

"Launch a probe," Laselle ordered.

COMOP nodded and tapped at her controls. The moments crawled by as a solitary probe streaked through the event horizon and started to send back data.

"Measurable debris is at relatively low levels," COMOP said eventually. "Combat is about two light-milliseconds away, as far as I can tell from this data."

"Good enough," Laselle said.

"Ready?" Betombe asked.

"Ready." She returned to her station and opened a channel across the ship. "All crew to general quarters; this is not a drill. Prepare for immediate combat jump."

"COMOP, signal the rest of the fleet. Helm, take us to Blacktree."

The ships moved forward as one, and transited through the wormhole in a brief flickering of twisted light.

"We've lost *Dragon*... enmeshment." Tactical was shouting immediately, the moment *Love Tap* emerged in high orbit of Blacktree. The hull was already ringing with the sounds of low-energy impacts. "More small debris than the probe suggested."

Betombe stared at the battle map intently, his eyes darting left and right, taking in the data as quickly as he could. At the leading edge of his battle group, the icon representing the *ICS Dragon* had turned yellow. He took it all in, his eyes skipped away to the next data-point, and then—

"What in the darkest Deep is *that*?"

"Unknown vessel," COMOP replied. "Configuration not recorded. They're not flying colours, Sir, and there's no transponder I can identify."

"Look at the *size* of it!" Laselle gasped.

Betombe stretched out the holographic glyph, and switched it across to enhanced view. A vessel snapped into focus, visible light imagery annotated with edge overlays and data readings.

The ship was vast. As a dreadnought, *Love Tap* was big. But the unknown vessel dwarfed his hulking frame. Oriented almost at right angles to the other ships, carving through the outer atmosphere of Blacktree, it spat out missile after missile from launch tubes which riddled its entire length.

"Thirty kilometres," Betombe breathed. "It's over thirty klicks long! Is it a ship, or a station? What a beast!"

"Admiral," Tactical said. "The other ships — ours, and Viskr too — they're all firing on that thing."

"Time to range at hard burn?"

"Four minutes."

As he watched, a group of three Viskr frigates dropped almost into the same plane as the unknown vessel, slicing vertically through the atmosphere and unleashing multiple salvoes against the flank of the intruder. But the missiles streaked away, became smaller and smaller, dwindled to points, and finally all but disappeared. Betombe's stomach knotted itself when he saw the faint specks of explosions spattering uselessly against a dark expanse of irregular, onyx hull.

The unknown was like nothing he had ever seen, in both form and construction. Oddly shaped, according to a design plan he could not even guess at, its colours were suggestive of materials other than simple plates of metal; the nearest fit he could imagine was that the hull was something like polished basalt. The nature of the lurid orange glow from what appeared to be reaction engines was a mystery, as was the purpose behind them being mounted in a helical arrangement around what he assumed to be the blunt forward end of the vessel. Where he would have expected to see the main drives, to the stern end, was an asymmetrical and forking tail of tapered shafts. He could only guess at their function, and came up empty.

Betombe became aware that the frigates were now tumbling through the atmosphere in pieces. A battleship which had followed them in tried to turn away, slowly and painfully fleeing a barrage of return fire that looked as though it had already done its work.

He balled his fists and squeezed until they were white. "Analyse all the remaining assets."

Tactical and COMOP pushed their holos together, and worked side by side. They swiped and tapped quickly, flowing around each other's movements.

"Imperial forces all identify positively as Blacktree defence cordon," COMOP said. "Seven ships left, all destroyers. Every cruiser is gone. The Viskr have a large-frame capital ship drawing most of the bogey's fire, at bearing zero-three-five, elevation negative zero-one-one. Looking at these readings it's almost all they have left now."

"Defence platforms are gone too," Tactical added. "There's debris everywhere in the low orbital range."

"Small amount of chatter going on out there," COMOP continued. "Imperial and Viskr. Looks like there's some kind of temporary alliance. There are several jamming signals. Message fragment from one of our cordon ships: just says '...the big one'."

"Who's interdicting?"

"I think it's the Viskr, Sir. Hard to tell."

"I'm reading possible e-warfare signatures. Countermeasures are running on our sensor palettes and comm systems."

"One minute to range, Admiral."

"Inform all commands: we're going to join the fight. Weapons free; ships will target the unknown vessel and fire at will. We'll worry about who they are later."

"Forward auto-cannons primed," Tactical said. "I have a firing solution."

"Target with all rails as well," Betombe ordered. "Don't just use flash lasers to blind them; you see anything that looks like a sensor palette, you hit it with something solid."

"Yes Sir."

"What's our drone complement?"

"Forty-six remaining."

"Launch them all. Same for the rest of the fleet."

"Effective targeting range reached."

"Then you may indulge yourself. Full salvo."

Tired and battered from their struggle at Gousk, the remains of Betombe's battle group released what munitions they could at the intruder. Slugs and missiles rained across its hull, for all the worlds appearing ineffectual. Even the forward cannons of *Love Tap* failed to pierce the beast's thick hide.

"We're taking return fire," Tactical said. "Slugs and flechettes. Turrets are holding up so far, but that's mainly because the gravity well is working for us."

"I've lost the transponder signals for *Satyr* and *Friendly Crack*," COMOP warned. "Status unknown."

"Keep firing," Betombe muttered.

"Sir, we're going to lose more ships."

"KEEP FIRING!"

COMOP and Tactical exchanged worried glances.

"Turrets are five percent over-capacity; we're starting to lose flak coverage."

"Here come the missiles!"

"I see them. Laser interceptors are firing free."

"The last destroyer from Blacktree just went down."

"Most of the Viskr ships are gone," said COMOP. "It's just their cruiser, and a handful of support vessels."

Laselle bent down towards Betombe, and spoke as quietly as she could over the noise. "Sir, we can't stay here. That thing is going to be the end of us all."

"Tactical, what's the status of the unknown?"

"A lot of our ordnance is getting through, Admiral," he said, "but it's having little effect on that armour. Our ship-to-surface missiles would probably do some real damage, but I'm afraid at this range they're too slow to get past its defences."

"Helm, back us off," Betombe conceded. "COMOP, please tell our other ships to back off too."

"Shall I cease fire?" Tactical asked.

"Yes. Divert any non-essential power to charge the main beam capacitors."

Laselle looked startled. "If we use the cutter against this thing, and it doesn't work, we'll be a sitting duck."

"Seems to me this kind of situation is exactly why we have the damned thing in the first place," Betombe said.

"But Sir—"

"We don't have much choice, Commander. I do not intend to allow that craft to finish whatever it was doing in Blacktree's atmosphere."

"We don't even know what that was... why it's here."

"It's clearly hostile. Blacktree's own ships were firing on it when we arrived."

The lights on the command deck dimmed by more than half, and Helm's holo darkened until only the basic thruster controls and positional grid were lit. The main reactors were channelling all their energy output away from the engines and non-critical systems.

Tactical broke the expectant silence. "We're still taking fire. Defences are down to minimal power; those shots are going to start getting through."

"Employ the same trick we used at Gousk; have the rest of our ships provide a flak barrier for us."

"The bogey has cleared the atmosphere; making for high orbit," said COMOP. "It's more of a threat to us now."

"Capacitors are ready for main beam."

Laselle placed a hand on Betombe's arm. "Are you sure you want to do this?"

"I don't see any alternative. Tactical: target whatever area you think is most vulnerable, and fire."

"Firing main beam."

In an almost silent instant, the only sounds were the ringing of the hull and the *whir-thump-thump* of the defensive turrets, tracking and firing on incoming ordnance.

Outside the ship an almost invisible beam of intense energy strobed on and off. *Love Tap* poured the entire collective output of his reactors straight forwards, burning into the intruder in a rapid series of searing pulses.

"Their hull is breached; I'm seeing internal explosions. I estimate less than one percent structural damage... but they *are* moving off."

"Interdiction has stopped," Laselle said. "Must have been them after all. They're opening a wormhole for themselves. Fleeing."

"What's our condition?"

"GNG has stalled, and main conventional drives are down." COMOP swept through his systems overview. "We're not going anywhere, but we can still manoeuvre on reaction thrusters. C-MADS are offline, as are the forward auto-cannons. We have enough power to run a handful of gauss guns and missile tubes, and there's enough residual energy in the capacitors for another brief burst."

"I think we might need it," said Tactical.

"Explain," Betombe snapped.

"The Viskr capital ship, Admiral. It's turning back towards Blacktree."

"I'm seeing a radiological spike," Laselle added. "Their ship-to-surface missiles just went hot."

"They've launched!"

"Take them out! Take them out *NOW!*"

Betombe was on his feet, standing behind Tactical. He watched helplessly as the missiles streaked away from the Viskr cruiser and arced towards Blacktree's atmosphere.

*Love Tap* opened fire with a barrage of tungsten slugs and missiles of his own, as did his remaining companions. One by one the Viskr missiles exploded.

"Too slow." Betombe watched fiery impacts bloom against the already ruined hull of the capital ship. "Reorient us for main beam. We're going to bleed those capacitors dry."

"They've launched a second volley. The ship is moving to block our intercept solutions."

"Fire the damned cutter!"

"Still five seconds before we're pointing at them."

"Two missiles have gone atmospheric," Laselle said. "We can't stop them from here."

"Does Blacktree have any surface-to-air?"

"I don't know, Sir."

"Cutter on target, Admiral."

"Fire then! For goodness' sake fire!"

*Love Tap* emptied his capacitors into the undefended Viskr cruiser, carving a chain of molten holes through bulkhead after bulkhead in the space of a few seconds. Explosions rocked the capital ship's frame, and it began to list.

Tactical looked up from his holo, his face grim. "Impact detected. I'm sorry Sir, but the first missile... no, *both* missiles have hit. Nuclear detonation at a single site."

Betombe felt the way back to his station, eyes fixed on the battle map, and sat down wearily.

"Worlds, what have they done?"

"They're going up in flames," COMOP said. "We must have breached their reactors."

"How many of the enemy ships remain?"

Betombe's voice was hollow.

"Two. Light vessels; not jump-capable."

"Order our escorts to run them down."

Laselle was still poring over the sensor readings from the planet. "Admiral, they've actually missed every single one of the major cities."

"Thank the worlds for that!"

"I don't think it was an accident," she said. "If they'd wanted to nuke a major population centre, those missiles couldn't have been farther off course."

"Then what did they hit?"

"From records, looks like it was an area of arable land at the outskirts of a small agricultural town."

"So they *did* hit a population centre?"

"I don't think so. I think the town itself was collateral damage."

"Well... what were they aiming to hit?"

"Crops? Livestock? I'm afraid I have no idea. Why would anyone nuke fields?"

"Can we—" Betombe managed to say, right before his vision wobbled and everything went black.

# – 05 –
# You Don't Choose

Rendir Throam's mothers had exposed him to the *Fiesta de San Pedrito* every single year of his life so far, but he remembered no occasion further back than his sixth Solar amongst the living. The year 3714 — by the Earth Legacy Calendar — was for him a period of many first memories.

It was the third day of the festival. His parents were not taking him to school, even though this particular morning was the beginning of a beautiful Friday. Not that Rendir had noticed there was anything terribly amiss; school was a phenomenon of which he had thus far sampled only a few months, and the experience had not yet wormed its way into his consciousness as a new reality. He did not feel responsible enough for his own whereabouts to consider himself missing, nor did he yet grasp the concept of public holidays.

Walking between Peshal and Lamis, holding one of their hands in each of his, Rendir beamed back at the glorious sun. Only a couple of hours ago it had been beneath the horizon; already it had climbed almost half as high as it would be when the day climaxed.

He strained to see the thin sliver of moon the house holo had told him was also somewhere up there, but from this particular part of space it was too thin and too close to the overpowering radiance of Sol to be seen.

Rendir recognised the avenue they were strolling down, and smiled to himself. Straining against his mothers' hands, challenging their faux reluctance, he dragged them towards the East-230 observation platform.

They always let him go right to the outer wall, pretending with wide mouths and scared eyes that he was hanging precariously over the edge of the city. He also pretended; pretended not to know. Even at his young age he was perfectly well aware that there was a safety barrier hidden beneath him.

Today felt different though, and when he released their hands he simply ran to the wall and peered over it, standing on his tip-toes.

The light glanced off the calm waters of the Bay of Chimbote, forcing him to squint. He held up his hand in front of his face until his eyes adjusted a little. Far beneath him a scattering of leisure skiffs and streamlined yachts were mere specks on the water.

The sun had already burned away the thick oceanic fog that wreathed the land throughout most of the night. Even on the ocean-facing side of the city, hidden as it was in the vast shadow of the tower, altitude and air movement had driven away the damp from every nook and cranny. Only the garden foliage and deliberately sheltered gauze traps now held back reserves of the pre-dawn moisture. Between the sun and the air, and the ducting, light channels, and passageways which honeycombed each floor of the structure, the rest was lost forever.

Rendir did not care about that. He saw nothing

inconvenient about a month which was cool enough for comfort yet threatened no rain whatsoever. To him, it just *was*. Worrying about what *was* and what *is* and what *could happen* he left to the adults.

"Come on Ren, let's keep going. You've seen this view a hundred times."

Rendir knew that Lamis was sometimes called his Canal Mother, though not by friends of the family. He knew not what it meant, nor that it related to his own person.

She took his hand and turned back towards Peshal. Peshal smiled at them both, a serene and loving expression, as she caught them unawares with her holo.

"Oh. Oh, I wasn't ready!" Lamis said.

"It looks more natural. Unposed."

"Still, I prefer some warning. *And* I've not put my face on yet."

"You don't need to," said Peshal. "You're beautiful just the way you are."

Lamis smiled coyly. She pulled a stray strand of dark hair back over her ear.

"But..." Peshal prodded her holo with a hopeful finger. "It's not really worked."

Lamis and Rendir looked at the image that she held out to them. The holo had exposed the sky wonderfully, in a thoroughly believable shade of blue. Their solid black silhouettes rather spoiled the uniformity.

"Oh, that *is* a shame," said Lamis. "Come along Ren; we're fleeing your mother."

"One day you'll wish we had more images of the family," Peshal called, as Lamis made a mock effort to run away with their son.

○ ○ ○

Before she went after them, Peshal stole a last glance out over the bay, across to the archaeological site that was the silent heart of old Chimbote. Not for the first time she thanked Lamis for convincing her to relocate to Earth. She had never felt so much at home as she did in the towering City of Peru.

As a place to live it had truly contradicted all of her expectations, as well as challenging her misgivings. She hated heights. She hated being around large numbers of people. She hated being on or near open water. It was fair to say that she had dreaded what it might be like. And yet here she was living a kilometre and a half above the shallows of a major ocean, along with fifteen million other inhabitants... and loving every second of her new life.

Peshal had been a third-generation native of Shuul before she defied social convention by coming to live permanently on the homeworld. For someone with her colonial experiences, the unique cultural melting pot of one of Earth's gargantuan tower cities was breathtaking.

Amongst Peru's fifteen hundred habitable levels lived a passionately swirling mixture of people. One could always hear Hispo or sometimes even old Spanish when out in public. Some still spoke Quechua, although Peshal could only just recognise it. Once she had heard an utterly unfamiliar tongue and was told it was Shuara, a language spoken by a tiny minority of the Ecuadorian folks taken in by Peru.

And the food! She had never tasted anything like it. For centuries, Chimbote had made its name by redistributing the bounty of the ocean. These days, now that the Restoration Project had finally turned around the great ecological slumps of the past, that bounty more or less met the protein needs of all Peru. The marine life on Shuul, on the other hand, she had found just as unpalatable as it was visually repellent.

She had learned to cope with the bustling nature of the city. Sometimes, it did not seem busy at all. Even with Peru being occupied almost to capacity, there was plenty of room for comfort. Green space and recreational facilities were built in by design, as were open areas sculpted with cunning to seem much larger than they really were.

The ocean no longer bothered her. Her brain had realised after a while that she was just as far from it up here as she would be if she lived more than a mile inland. So all she had to worry about was the height, and it was perfectly possible to wander around Level 230 all day without coming anywhere close to the outer wall.

Except for occasions like this, on which she was prepared to allow Rendir's exploratory tendencies to rank above her own admittedly irrational fears. At times like this, she took the opportunity to challenge her fear; a little each time.

Still at the outer wall, she forced herself to look down into the bay. Her fingers tightened around the guard rail until the blood was squeezed from them.

After a moment longer, she left to catch up with her family.

o o o

Lamis and Rendir strolled through the plaza, holding hands, taking in the sights and sounds. The central concourse was lined by people; men and women alike, sitting in a huge ring while they made preparations for the latter half of the festival.

Rendir stopped in front of a group who were chopping limes in half, squeezing out the juice, and throwing the rinds into huge tubs destined for the organic reclamation bins. He stood and stared until a woman smiled up at him, and she handed him half a fruit. The flesh glistened in the morning sun, and he pressed his lips and tongue against it. His face screwed up instantly, and the woman laughed.

Lamis was standing behind him, and laughed with her. "Be careful what people hand you, Ren."

He dropped the lime into the nearest tub, disgusted, and the woman continued with her work; chop, squeeze, toss.

"Do you know what all this is for?" Lamis asked.

Rendir looked up at her with a blank expression. He was far too young to know.

"The juice will be used to make cerviche," she said. "Cooking without cooking."

Rendir contorted his face again. He knew with the certainty of youth that he was not fond of cerviche.

Lamis began talking to the woman who had handed him the offensive fruit, and Rendir lasted a few minutes before he became restless. Eventually his tugging at her hand became too persistent, and she followed his gaze to a group of children playing on the other side of the plaza.

"Go on then," she said. "I'll call you in a little while."

He ran off to join them, and Lamis sat cross-legged on the floor. She scooped limes towards herself and joined in with the group effort.

Chop, squeeze, toss.

The festival was one of the highlights of her year. For as long as she could remember, the City of Peru had celebrated the patron saint of Chimbote, even though the vast majority of the population had no real ancestral connection to that ghost town. But celebrate they did, and every year the city was festooned with decorations, the air thick with fragrance, and the open spaces resonant with laughter and music.

She could spare a few minutes to help with the preparations, no matter how small the contribution. You get back what you put in, her parents had taught her.

Lamis had lost track of all time when Peshal caught up with her. Something about the repetitive task of slicing and juicing the fruit had sent her into a sort of semi-conscious trance, and her mind had wandered far.

"Where's Little Man?" Peshal asked as she sat down next to her.

"Playing with some other children." Lamis gestured towards them. She leaned towards Peshal and kissed her on the lips.

Peshal smiled, and began gathering some limes towards herself from the piles that were stacked around seemingly bottomless hoppers. She placed them on her skirt, in the hollow between her folded legs. Someone handed her a knife, and she went to work.

"Ahh, this takes me back," she said.

"How far?" Lamis said, with a faint smile.

"About a Solar."

Lamis had known what the punchline would be before it arrived, but she still chuckled to herself.

"Such wonderful memories," she said, the sarcasm so subtle that a casual listener might have believed she really was lost in nostalgia.

Peshal rested her head on Lamis's shoulder as they worked. The angle made the chore slightly more awkward, but the contentment more than made up for it.

They carried on in silence for a while, and Lamis had again lost track of time when she first became aware of a growing commotion. She stopped, turned her body, and Peshal was roused from a daydream of her own. She looked as though she too had been adrift in thought.

Across the concourse, some of the other men and women had stood up. They were all looking towards the outer edge of the plaza, where a frenzied knot of children was being prised apart by adults.

"Little Man," Peshal said. She stood up, and limes rained from her skirts.

They both ran towards the fray. Lamis saw Rendir being pulled away from an older, larger boy, and went straight to him.

"Ren," she said. "What happened?"

His lip was split, and his clothing pulled out of place, but he was relatively unscathed compared to his opponent. The bigger child had blood streaming from his nose, and an eye that was already puffing up.

Rendir blurted it out in an angry screech. "He called you sick. He said I was a dirty bastard creation."

Lamis saw Peshal's jaw drop, and the welling of angry tears in Rendir's eyes. She took their hands and led them both a short distance away from the crowd.

"What a little horror," Peshal said. "I hope his parents are proud."

"I doubt it." Lamis dabbed gently at the tiny trickle of blood that oozed from Rendir's lip. "Got his comeuppance though, hey Ren?"

"I hate it," Rendir said. "I hate it!"

"Of course you do Ren; it's a horrible thing. But some kids really think that rubbish when they're still young."

"No, I hate being like *this*."

Lamis and Peshal looked at each other.

"What do you mean?" Peshal asked him, crouching down to his eye level.

"Having two mums," he said.

Peshal stood up again, and turned away from him. Lamis could see Peshal was holding her hands over her mouth.

"Lots of people have two mums, Rendir. Or two dads. Some little boys and girls even have more than two."

"I don't like it," he insisted. "They always make fun of me."

"That will stop; I promise. One day soon those children will be taught the Principles, and they'll begin to understand where they have gone wrong. Why they can't always trust their instincts. They'll stop."

"But I don't like it *now*."

Lamis sighed to herself, wishing that this conversation could have waited just a couple more Solars before it came up. Waited until he understood emotions a little more clearly.

"You don't choose your family, Ren."

"You did."

"That's different. You'll understand when you're older."

"You always say that."

Lamis resisted the temptation to snap at him,

and leaned away to take Peshal's hand. She pulled her wife close, and they both crouched down to Rendir.

"Ren, listen," Lamis said. "Your family will always be there for you. You look out for one another, and you love each other without conditions. Do you understand what I mean?"

He stared at her sullenly, but he didn't answer back.

"As you get older, you'll meet people who you love dearly, and they'll become part of your family too. And you always, always, always protect your family. But what you don't do is choose them, Ren. You don't choose."

Rendir stared into the middle distance, as if not willing to commit to saying he understood.

But Peshal squeezed her hand just a little bit tighter.

## – 06 –
## CHANGE OF PLANS

The *Vavilov* was within a mere hundred metres when it came to a relative stop alongside *Disputer*. Caden leaned on a polished rail in one of the carrier's pristine observation passageways, looking out over the research vessel and wondering what its last mission had been.

Next to him, also staring out at the bulky ship, Santani was in a world of her own. If her gaze could have bored through metal, the *Vavilov* would have been in real trouble.

"Worst case scenario," Caden started slowly, "is that you are discharged, right?"

Santani took a moment to answer, as if she were gathering her thoughts back from the depths of space before she spoke. "Assuming they don't think I was criminally negligent, yes. However if they *do*, I could end up in prison."

"I really don't think it will come to that," Caden said. "You can justify your actions. It might be that some desk-flying admirals will disagree with those actions, but you were acting with the Empire's best interests at heart. Not to mention those of your colleagues."

She looked at him with an expression that he had come to learn meant 'you don't know how these things really work, do you?'

"But even if they convict you, the Empress can intervene in sentencing matters. She'd make them commute it."

She managed a smile. "I don't think the Empress would know who I am, never mind do something like that for me."

"Really She would be doing it for me."

"Ah."

"Of course that would probably just mean house arrest instead of prison, but it's a start."

"I thought you came here to cheer me up?"

"That was the plan, yes. Sorry."

Her smile faded quickly, and he could almost feel the abiding sadness in her.

"Maybe it was a mistake to visit sickbay so soon."

"How could I not?" She said. "They're my crew. My people."

"Yes, I suppose you're right."

Before she could answer, the ship's comm system whistled, and a message was passed out summoning Santani to the command deck.

"What does she want with me now?" Santani said.

"Probably seen you walking around in an unfleetly fashion."

"Would you mind coming with me? I can't take another dose of her right now, not on my own."

"No problem."

They started walking along the passageway, back towards the hatch that would take them to the deck interior. Santani still limped on her injured leg.

Outside, in the darkness, *Vavilov* accepted a transfer umbilicus from *Disputer*.

They walked in silence to the command deck, occasionally passing crew who hurried by quietly on their own business. It was the first shift — early morning by ship's time — and most people looked to be thoroughly preoccupied, doubtless wrapped up in planning their daily duties.

Until boarding this ship, Caden had not realised just how comfortable and welcoming the atmosphere in *Hammer* had been. Here, those few people who even acknowledged them did so only to query their identities.

At least they're security-conscious, he thought.

On the command deck, the XO waved them through to the wardroom without so much as a greeting. Thande was already seated behind the desk, and she rose as they entered the compartment. Caden saw immediately that there was bad news written in her face.

"Please, take a seat," Thande said. "I'm afraid this is not going to be easy."

Caden noted that she was directing her attention mostly towards Santani as she spoke.

"What's happened?" Santani asked.

"We just received word from the Seawall operations team at Laeara. I regret to inform you that the *Stiletto* went down in battle."

Santani stifled a gasp. "The Admiral?"

"Admiral Pensh is officially listed as KIA."

Caden could almost feel the grief sinking into Santani. The wardroom seemed darker somehow.

"I'm sorry to be the bearer of this news, Aker. I know you've worked with Admiral Pensh for a long time."

There was a long silence, and Caden felt as though nobody knew what to say. Had Santani received this news on any other day, matters might have been different, but after losing her own ship... it was tragedy piled on tragedy. Words seemed insufficient.

"Thank you for letting me know," Santani managed eventually.

"Obviously this does change things a little," Thande said quietly. "The 951st Battalion were assigned to *Stiletto*, so we have nowhere to return Bravo Company to."

Santani remained silent, and Caden could tell that the words were drifting over her.

"What's the plan?"

"The Second Fleet is now being commanded temporarily from the *Yatagan*. Until there's a clearer picture of how the remaining ships will re-organise, and until they come clear of the combat zone, Bullseye can disembark at Laeara with Captain Santani and her crew. Call it unscheduled shore leave."

"I'm sure they'll appreciate that. For my part, I've received orders to go after a fugiti—"

Thande's link chimed and, without waiting for Caden to finish, she tapped it to accept the channel. "No, it's fine, Commander Yuellen. Go ahead."

Caden watched her face fall, and wondered how that was possible given that her expression had already been as grave as any he had seen before. The XO's message clearly carried bad tidings.

"I see. Send it to my holo."

Thande tapped at the panel in front of her, and her eyes flicked rapidly over reports and charts.

"More bad news?"

"The Viskr have attacked Mibes," Thande said. "They have a blockade in high orbit, and may already have armour on the ground."

"Shit."

"We're being diverted to join the counter-offensive, so there's no time to take anyone to Laeara now. I'm afraid, Captain Santani, that you will have to bear with me for a little while longer."

"I understand, Captain Thande. Mibes clearly takes priority."

"There's a databurst for your eyes only, Shard Caden. I'm forwarding it to you now."

Caden opened the packet on his own holo, and skimmed across the text.

– DIVERSION –
Travel to Mibes.
Extract listed personnel.
Resume Castigon mission on completion.
– PRIORITY ONE –
[Restricted Data]

Caden read the brief message, bit his lip, and read it again. He had not expected to be turned away from his manhunt so soon, given the tone with which the Chamberlain had delivered the order, but with Caden already being present on *Disputer* the diversion did make logistical sense.

The restricted data that was attached to the message was short, direct, and listed in bullet points. Not too taxing, he thought.

"Nothing worrisome, I trust?" Thande said.

Caden looked up, and smiled.

"It looks like you'll be bearing with me as well, Captain. For a little while longer."

o o o

For once, Throam woke first. He opened his eyes to see the blank, grey bulkhead staring lovelessly back at him, and rolled over to face Eilentes.

She was facing him, breathing softly, with her eyes closed. Hair trailed across her face and spread over the pillow; black rivulets on an Arctic canvas.

He brushed the hair back gently, and she sighed. Then, slowly, her eyes opened.

"Hey," Throam said.

"Hey. What time is it?"

"Early. First shift just came on."

"Shit. I'm supposed to be meeting Norskine down on the range."

Eilentes kissed him quickly on the forehead, then lifted the sheet away as she rolled over. Swinging her legs off the bunk, she dropped it behind her.

"Didn't know you two were getting all pally," Throam said as she walked away.

"Well, us gun girls have to stick together," she said. "Not jealous are you?"

"Little bit, yeah. Was hoping you'd stick together with me a bit more."

She smiled awkwardly as she disappeared behind the wash enclosure door. He heard her sitting down, than calling out to him. Loudly, to mask her noises. She had always kept some modesty for herself.

"You'll get time enough later, babe."

"Can't Norskine wait a bit longer? It's not like she'll have nothing to do. It *is* a range."

"Oh Rendir, come on. That's rude. You wouldn't want to be stood up, would you?"

"You wouldn't stand me up," he said. "I'm too damned hot to stand up."

She laughed, and there was the sound of water flowing through the basin. Splashes.

"Yeah, keep telling yourself that."

"You don't think I'm hot?"

"You know I do."

"So you mean you'd stand me up?"

"No." She reappeared in the cabin, towelling her face, neck and arms as she spoke. "I wouldn't put myself in a position where I was supposed to meet you, but made you wait while I fucked about with someone else."

"She won't mind. She's a trooper. Leave her to it and fuck about with this hot, sexy-ass someone else."

"Okay, you're starting to annoy me now." She gestured towards him with the towel, a frown creasing her forehead. "I made an arrangement and I mean to keep it."

She tossed the towel back into the enclosure, and started pulling clothes out of the kit bag she had not yet bothered to unpack.

Throam watched her dress. She was yanking the clothes onto her body, silent, avoiding looking at him. He waited, laying on his side, fully expecting the next thing he heard to be '—and another thing.'

But she stayed silent, and the sweaty air started to feel thin and frigid. He wondered what it was exactly that was so terrible about wanting to spend more time in bed with someone, and came up blank. Most of the time when he had sex with people, or said he wanted to, they didn't tend to grumble about it. He was accustomed to a certain level of giddy enthusiasm.

Eilentes was on her way to the hatch before Throam decided one of them had to break the deadlock.

"So I'll see you soon then?"

"And another thing," she said, turning back towards him, "I'm not just some fuck-bucket you can hold onto because it's easy. Learn to have a conversation, for fuck's sake."

He sat up on the bunk. "Where in the Deep did that come from?"

There was a flash of realisation across her face, the angry mask slipping for a second. Whatever she had been stewing over, Throam knew her well enough to see that she had not actually planned to bring it up now.

"Well, I tried to say the other night. But it kind of got superseded by the whole Gendin thing."

"Getting back together? That?"

"Yeah, Rendir. That."

"That thing you said you were sorry to bring up?"

Eilentes leaned against the hatch, sighed deeply, and sank down slowly until she was sat on the deck with her feet planted in front of her.

She spoke first. "I didn't, Rendir. I said I was sorry to have a go at you about Gendin. Look, the whole thing with your son is your business, but it's important for me to know where I stand, yeah?"

"You're gonna be late for Norskine." Throam rolled back towards the bulkhead. "Don't want you blaming me for it."

"I'll tell her I need an hour."

Throam heard Eilentes tapping out a quick message on her holo. Moments ago he had just wanted her back in bed with him; now, nothing would please him more than if she hurried off to nail some targets with Norskine.

"So... what exactly is this?" She said.

He succumbed to the inevitable, and rolled onto his back so he could look at her. "How do you mean?"

"You and me. Are we back together, or are we just sharing a bunk?"

"Same thing, isn't it?"

He gathered from the look on her face that it definitely wasn't.

"Seriously... I don't know what you want me to say."

"I want you to say what you feel."

"I like shagging you?"

"Rendir..."

"I *really* like shagging you? What? Throw me a bone here."

"Oh my worlds. Come on, you can do better than that. At least try."

Throam tried to imagine what he would say in her position. Thanks for fucking me so good, big boy. No, that probably wasn't right; he knew that much.

"Okay, this isn't going to go anywhere. I'll just ask you. Where do you see this going? Sex on tap, until one of us gets transferred or killed? Or do you think it's destined to turn into something more?"

"Suppose it might—"

"You suppose? What about... what about what you *want* to happen?"

"I've not really thought about it."

"Maybe you should. I'd really like it if you did. I don't like uncertainty, Rendir. I need to know where this is going."

Throam turned the question over in his mind: what did he want? Truth be told, he had not spent any time thinking about his own future for a long while now, never mind his future with anyone else. Euryce had popped back into his world, and bunking up with her again had simply felt right.

Maybe that was the point.

"See, here's my problem," Eilentes continued. "We were seeing each other for almost an entire Solar when you were assigned to the *Embolden*. It was just like this is now: duties, sex, training, sex. We never took it anywhere. Then you left and... and I hardly heard anything from you."

"I thought you liked it like that—"

"I spent a long time wondering if it had really meant anything, Rendir. A long time. Now we've met up again it's like we were never apart, and I... well I mean it's not *bad* exactly, but it's like we're back to square one, you know? And now you tell me you went off after you left me and... and had a kid with someone else, just like that. So I have to answer my own question, see? Did it mean anything to you? Did *I* mean anything to you? It looks like the answer to that is 'no' Ren, it really does."

She stopped, as if she needed to let the statement hang in the air. Throam waited for a second, taking it all in. He had known this conversation was inevitable, and that it could only have run along these rails.

And that was what he had been afraid of.

○ ○ ○

Caden glanced up from the charts, looking towards the wardroom entrance. The XO met his eyes, nodded curtly as he entered, and went to his captain's side.

"We'll arrive at Mibes in four hours, Captain. I thought you'd want to know."

"Thank you, Commander Yuellen. Carry on."

"Yes Ma'am."

He turned on his heel to leave the wardroom, eyeing their work area, and Caden found himself wondering why Yuellen could not have simply used the comm instead of interrupting them with his physical presence.

He carried on from where he had paused when the XO entered.

"Captain Santani would have been hard-pressed to support the Woe Tantalum landing without the loan of Bravo Company. They were only just enough, and I don't want a repeat of that. What assets can you send to the surface?"

"This is a Glory-class heavy carrier, not a piddling battleship," said Thande. "Our role profile is to support ground as well as fleet. So we're carrying pretty much everything, including a full MAGA battalion."

"Everything?"

"You name it, we can supply it. Polybots, area denial systems, swarmers, gunships, Kodiak transports, Gorilla platforms... take your pick."

"I'd bet Throam would love to take you up on that."

"He's welcome to indulge himself at the expense of the Viskr occupation."

"I'd rather he kept things low key, seeing as he'll be with me. But thanks for the offer."

"Define 'low key'."

"A small, quiet team, with a modest support unit. Barely noticeable against the backdrop of a counter-invasion."

"I get the feeling you've planned your side of this operation already."

"More or less. To be honest the objective they've given me is fairly straightforward. I'll take Bullseye with me; they're essentially orphaned, and it will make your commanders' jobs easier."

"As you wish."

"I will need to borrow landers, as well as some

bits and pieces from your armouries."

"My XO will arrange all that for you."

"Aren't you going to ask me what my orders are?"

Caden watched Thande's face, looking for any small signs of the curiosity he suspected was snaking around beneath the surface. Santani would have been trying to pry the details out of him by now. But Thande was not Santani.

Still waters run deep, he thought. And these waters are damned still.

"I don't really need to know," Thande answered. "Just tell me what areas you will be working in, on the off chance it becomes necessary to fire on the surface."

"I've already flagged them up on your mapping system. I need to be in the civic heart of the capital. Naddur, it's called; after the general."

"Noted. I'll try not to bombard it."

"That would be appreciated."

Thande smiled her thin smile.

"What about the orbital side?" Caden asked. "Are you getting much from Command?"

"We know the Third Fleet has mustered in the system. They're standing off for now, gathering information. We're going to rendezvous with them there, and join up with the rest of the Fifth. Third will be taking the lead for this operation."

"Any idea yet on enemy numbers?"

"Basically equivalent to our two fleets."

"Equivalent to? Not less than? Doesn't that concern you?"

"If it were up to me, we'd roll in with half the armada and smash them to pieces. But it's not up to me. Commander Operations is calling the shots, and whatever resources travel to Mibes will be the

125

ones that he deems necessary and available."

Caden sensed a certain defensive fragility in her tone. "Okay, I didn't mean to get your back up."

"You didn't exactly. I just don't like being patronised."

"I didn't mean to do that either."

"It won't be my first battle, Shard Caden. Please try to remember that this is what we in the fleet do. Look after your own mission, and let me worry about what happens in orbit. I'll keep my own counsel on what I need to be concerned with."

"That's absolutely fine by me," Caden said. "Please let me assure you that I didn't mean any offence. It was just a question."

"Very well."

Not for the first time since boarding *Disputer*, Caden found himself wondering if there were maybe some magic formula for keeping her captain happy.

Probably not, he decided.

○ ○ ○

Eilentes waited. She could almost see the rusty cogs grinding slowly against each other in Throam's head, and wished that for once in his life he would connect that giant melon to his heart. Between the two organs he ought to have been able to cobble together a healthy emotional dialogue. Worlds knew they were both big enough.

"Any thoughts?"

"Sorry, Euryce. I don't have the answer you're looking for. I've honestly not thought about it."

"Great." Her body seemed to deflate beneath her.

"But I can kind of see where you're coming from," he added. "Really."

She looked up again, hopeful that he might be about to have a personal breakthrough. His face was sincere, she knew that much. Whatever was going through his big head right now, he was going to be honest with her. Which, along with his apologetic tone, actually sort of helped.

"When I left the *Embolden*, it was because they'd paired me with Caden. Not because I was leaving you."

"I know."

"I'd been out of the Academy for over four Solars, right? The first thing that happened was I got a month's refresher. That shit was intensive. I didn't have a lot of time for anyone else, but I did *try* to keep in touch."

"You did," she said softly. "Once or twice. I remember, believe me."

"Then I was actually on duty with Caden, and you honestly would not believe how hard it was at first. I know we make it look easy now, but it *has* been ten Solars. We know each other inside out. Right at the beginning, we were learning each other on the move. Mission to mission. I don't know how we even stayed alive that long, to be honest. Between him always trying to do everything himself, and me breaking whatever I touch, we should have been dead a long time ago."

Eilentes smiled to herself, imagining a comically inept version of the pair bumbling around the galaxy and leaving a trail of destruction in their wake. It wasn't so drastically far-removed from the reality.

"And then when I met Ephisia, it was just... well she was there, she was amazing, and it felt like it was good timing."

"Ephisia?"

"Gendin's mother."

"Oh."

"It wasn't good timing at all. It was a horrible mistake."

"Really?"

"Put it this way: I don't call her Ephisia any more."

"What do you call her?"

"Thundercunt."

Eilentes roared with laughter. "Oh! Oh Rendir, you've had it bad. Thundercunt! Oh my worlds, she must have fucked you over big-time to earn a name like that."

"She did."

Eilentes forced herself to calm down. "Do you want to tell me this? It wasn't an idea you favoured before."

"Might as well. It's all connected, right?"

"Go on."

"Ephisia was like a dream come true at first. She was stationed with us, on the same rotation, and was she ever beautiful and warm."

Eilentes had never heard Throam describe anyone as 'warm' before, not even herself, and she fought back a small, sharp jab of envy.

"Then her rotation changed, and suddenly we were crossing over more often instead of being free at the same times. It got pretty hard to spend time together. It wasn't long before she wanted me to drop things like special training and the gym, to make things easier."

"Oh dear." Eilentes could see as plain as day where the other woman had first gone wrong. "Big mistake."

"Yeah, you know it," Throam said. "Trying to force me out of the gym? Crazy. Should really have been my first clue."

"So what happened?"

"She convinced me we should start a family. Still don't really know how that happened. I mean, I'm a counterpart. That kind of thing is not recommended at all. But she was on about it for a long time, getting in my head until I thought it was a good idea too. Or maybe I just wanted her to stop asking."

"Oh, Rendir." Eilentes moved closer to the bunk. "What were you thinking?"

"I don't know. I don't think I was. And then it was there, it was happening, she was pregnant. And you know what? I was actually glad. Despite all the misgivings, I was so glad I actually told myself it would work. I wanted it to work, badly."

"But it didn't?"

"No, it was a nightmare. Don't get me wrong; I loved Gendin the moment I saw him come into the world, but it just wasn't to be. Me, her, and him... at the time I wanted to be the family man, I really did. But I didn't want to stop being a counterpart. The best counterpart anyone could ever be. That's what did it for my family in the end."

"What happened?"

"She left me. No warning, just upped and went when I was on a training exercise with Caden. Note was half a page long, Euryce. Half a page."

She found that somehow she had reached the bunk, and she sat down on the edge of it. She reached out and touched his warm shoulder, and realised when she did so that he was shaking slightly. She had never seen him cry, and wondered if this would be that moment.

It wasn't.

"Thunder*cunt*!" He shouted it without warning.

"She fucking used me."

"It's okay, Rendir. I so get that name now. Where did they go?"

"Some shithole of a backwater planet on the core-ward fringe."

"If you knew where they went, why didn't you try to get them back?"

"I didn't want *her* back," he said. "And what kind of life would the boy have had living with me? No. There was a time when I wanted to steam in there and take my son away from her, but it didn't last long. They kept us running missions.

"Caden held me together. He said he would go with me if I wanted him to. For support, you know? But the chance didn't come for a long time. And when it did come around I'd cooled off. I'd thought about it for too long. I knew it wouldn't be the right thing to do. For me, maybe, but not for him. Not for Gendin."

"I think that was the right decision."

"It's his ninth birthday soon," Throam said, sitting up. "I count them off. Count towards the day he can make his own choices."

"Oh, Ren." She wrapped her arms around him.

They stayed like that for a while, until Eilentes' link began to chirrup incessantly. She tried to mute it without making the movement too obvious.

"If that's Norskine, you should go," Throam said. "You don't want to keep her waiting forever."

"Will you be all right?"

"Hey... it's me."

Eilentes kissed the top of his head, and stood up. On the way to the hatch she paused, and turned back towards him.

"I think that was the most I've ever heard you say in one go."

He smiled as she stepped through the hatch, and she waited until it had closed fully before she started walking down the sterile passageway.

She stopped, mid-step, and nearly lost her balance.

Some part of her mind had been processing the conversation, rapidly shuttling through it on endless replay, and it had just put her whole brain on alert.

Throam had pulled the old bait-and-switch on her. He had guided her towards having the conversation about Gendin because it was preferable to answering her original question, and he knew she would be unable to resist hearing the tale. He had never had any intention of talking about where their maybe-relationship was going, and he had said nothing which would have constituted an answer.

The sneaky son-of-a-whore. Or, as he had so rightly corrected her previously, son-of-two-whores.

She looked back towards the hatch, then forwards in the direction of the waiting Norskine.

In the end, she chose Norskine. At this point, she felt as though she had little more to give if it came to another argument. She had said all she could, explained how she felt. If he could not bring himself to give her a proper answer, then it was obviously not that important to him, which was sort of an answer in its own right.

For now, she forced it out of her mind.

## – 07 –
## THE ASHES OF LOPHRIT

Captain Kabis Borreto was finally beginning to accept the reality of the situation. His brain knew that his eyes were showing him the evidence which explained everything; it just didn't want to believe them.

Lophrit was a wasteland.

The civilian hauler *Leo Fortune* had touched down in the space between several of the craters pitting what remained of a pad at the capital's starport. It was only the sheer size of the concrete expanse that allowed there to be an unspoiled area big enough to accommodate the modest ship.

Borreto stood at the top of the hauler's open cargo ramp, and sucked air over his clenched teeth. He stared, and stared, and stared, yet nothing out there obliged him by moving. The silence was almost painful.

"Boss?"

He turned back towards the cargo bay.

"Boss, what in the many worlds happened here?"

"Fucked if I know, Prayer."

Prayer Monsul had her hands shoved inside the front of her grimy overalls, resting on the top of her chest. She came to stand by his side, and she too gazed out at what had once been a rapidly growing town.

"Shit. Someone did a right fuckin' number on this place."

"You said it."

"Gonna call it in?"

"Not yet. We're not exactly here on official business. Let's find out how bad it is first."

"How bad it is? Boss, it's bad enough. We know that already."

He stared straight ahead.

"Boss... seriously. The gate's missing, the orbital defences are gone, and the capital is fuckin' rubble. How much worse does it have to be?"

"If there are survivors here, we have to stay. If they're all dead, we fuck off quick as we can, and send an anonymous burst to the network."

"We 'have to stay'? Says who?"

"The universal moral imperative."

"You're a right fuckin' idiot sometimes."

Borreto ignored her, and walked back into the cargo bay. He punched the comm to call the cockpit.

"Sayad. Arm yourself and meet me on the ground. Bring our passenger."

"You got it."

Borreto came back to stand next to Prayer, and spat over the side of the ramp. "Who the fuck did this?"

"Think it was the Gomlic?" Prayer asked. "They're the closest major power."

"Doubt it," Borreto said. "They don't like confrontation. I read they seek non-aggression treaties with everyone they meet. Pretty sure they have one with us."

"Yeah, I suppose it's not really their style at all.

I don't know what to think."

"Neither do I, Prayer. Neither do I."

The cargo elevator started up at the rear of the bay, its gears squealing in protest. At some point, he thought, I really need to grease those up properly. Before they catch fire.

He turned to watch the wide platform as it descended slowly from the main deck, revealing two figures centimetre by centimetre.

The one on the left was Sayad Idiri, easily identified by his bright red flight suit. The one on the right then could only be the passenger.

In his many Solars as a hauler, Borreto had sourced plenty of paying fares from the Backwaters. But this was the first one he had almost instantly regretted picking up. There was something wrong about the man, something in the way he spoke and the cold, dead look in his eyes. He made Borreto's skin crawl.

The platform came to a grinding halt, juddering when it hit the deck of the bay. Sayad and the passenger stepped off, and picked their way through the cargo crates on their way towards the rear ramp.

"What's up, Boss?" Sayad asked.

"You know how sometimes our job means we deliver more than just cargo? How sometimes it's humanitarian aid?"

"Yeah?"

"This is one of those times."

"Is that why you told him to arm himself, Captain?" It was the passenger who asked.

There was a short silence.

"No," Borreto said. "That's because of you."

Without being told, Sayad stepped subtly away from the passenger.

"No offence, buddy, but I don't know you. I don't know your problems. What I do know is you needed to use the Backwaters to catch a ride, and in situations like this that kind of extra complication makes me... nervous."

"I completely understand," said Castigon, "and you're right to take precautions."

Prayer cut right through the awkward moment, in that way she had which was blunt but somehow also managed to be as sharp as a razor. It was one of the reasons Borreto liked to have her around.

"You got any experience with disaster relief? First aid? Anything like that?"

"You could say that. I can turn my hand to most things."

"Good. Pass me that, would you?"

Castigon looked to the side, and saw the metal box Prayer pointed to. He unlatched it from the deck and picked it up.

"Heavy. What is this?"

"PRAISE unit."

"A what?"

"Penvos Robotics Autonomous Intelligent Sensory Equipment. Basically a robot sniffer dog. They all think it's funny to have me run it, because of my name."

"It *is* funny," said Sayad.

"Fuck off, fly-boy."

"Stow it," said Borreto. "We've got work to do. Come on down."

Sayad and Castigon followed Prayer and the captain off the ramp, then stepped away quickly when it began to fold up against the cargo bay opening.

"Here," Castigon said, and handed Prayer the box.

She took it, placed it on the ground, and activated the controls on the top surface. The box clicked, hummed, and opened out, unfolding and twisting until the entire thing had reshaped into a metal quadruped. Small sensor arrays folded out from the front end and the underbelly.

"Off you go, boy." Prayer tapped her holo, and the PRAISE unit loped away with a fluid, rhythmic bounding motion.

"It's a polybot?" Castigon asked.

"Not exactly. It's more like the kind of machine that inspired polybot design. Earlier model. Cheaper."

Borreto was impatient to get moving. "Let's get after him, before he gets out of range."

"All right," said Prayer. "You're the fuckin' boss."

They walked as a loose group, Borreto and Sayad allowing Castigon to go ahead with Prayer. Borreto was not exactly thrilled to see his engineer so close to the wild card passenger, but there was not much he could do about it, short of tying the man up and making him walk at the end of a length of rope. That kind of thing tended to attract negative customer feedback.

"You think the same thing went down at Ophriam?" Sayad asked.

"Why would I think that?"

"It'd explain why the gate wouldn't respond to us," Sayad suggested.

Borreto thought about it. They had wasted two days waiting for passage to Ophriam, before giving it up as a bad job and placing the goods in storage. Without the destination gate they would never have made it all the way there; the *Leo Fortune* was far too small to survive a lengthy, turbulent wormhole.

He had had neither the nerve nor the patience to make a series of jumps through other star systems — each leg of the journey would have increased the chances of a patrol yanking them out of the queue to inspect their cargo. The merchandise had still not been collected since, and the buyer had not been in touch. Given the nature of the transaction, he suspected they would never call.

All the better for us, he thought. Gave us default rights to those goods, and the time to fulfil another contract.

Although this job was not exactly going as planned either.

"I suppose it's possible," he replied at last. "But there are plenty of other explanations. Gate might have just been malfunctioning."

"I guess." Sayad lapsed into silence.

The town seemed to look flatter the closer they got. Borreto sniffed the air, and smelled the stale, dry odour of burned homes. There was woodsmoke in it, and a plastic tang that caught in the back of his throat, but something seemed to be missing.

"Smell is wrong," he said. "There's no decay."

"There is," said Prayer. "Just... nowhere fuckin' near enough."

She pointed to her holo, and Borreto peered over her shoulder to see what the robot was sending back to her.

"He's been over five blocks already. Well, you know... what's left of them. Building density suggests there would have been over three hundred residents in that area alone. PRAISE has sniffed out enough residual organics for about six bodies."

"Six?"

"Yeah, I know. Concentration suggests they're buried beneath the rubble. Nobody on the surface at all."

"Keep at it."

Borreto left Sayad with Prayer, and wandered over to where Castigon was standing. The passenger was staring out over the ruins with a completely neutral expression, his empty face betraying nothing.

"You had someone here?" Borreto asked.

"No."

"Why'd you come then?"

"I thought confidentiality was one of your unique selling points?"

"Just curious is all. Don't say if you don't want to."

Castigon filled his lungs with the still, dead air, and slowly exhaled.

"To be honest, Captain Borreto, I think my presence here is completely redundant. The person I came to find is probably dead."

o o o

Brant met Tirrano in the commissary, half an hour earlier than usual. She nodded to him, but continued to eat, pretending that she had no particular interest in his presence.

Nice touch, he thought.

He placed his tray on the table and sat down opposite her. She continued to give the food her undivided attention.

"No way to know if anyone is listening in on us." He murmured it softly while he unwrapped cutlery from a paper napkin.

"Just have to hope for the best," she said.

"They'll call it sedition."

Tirrano shovelled food into her mouth, shrugged as she swallowed, then dabbed at her lips with a napkin of her own.

"It's not like we're planning to kill someone," she said. "We're just hypothesising."

"Right."

"Right. So go on."

"Branathes," said Brant. "He's... wrong."

"Wrong how?"

"I don't know. I noticed it back on Fort Kosling. He seemed, well, blasé about everything that was going on. And he was practically beating the war drums himself over the Viskr situation."

"That makes him an incompetent and an idiot, nothing more. We knew that already."

"True, that's why I didn't really say anything before. But then there was yesterday."

"What about yesterday? Come on love, spill it."

"Didn't you think it was odd that he argued with people to show us as MIA instead of KIA, yet he was certain — with no evidence at all — that Doctor Laekan was dead? About which, I'd point out, he was flat-out wrong."

"A bit, yes. But he's always been an opinionated oddball."

"And then when we told him that Danil Bel-Ures is alive and well, and could possibly tell us more about what's going on, he literally stopped in his tracks and told us to forget it."

Tirrano's hand stopped on the way back up to her mouth. "I have to admit, I did think that was a strange thing to say."

"Yes, because it *was*."

Tirrano's fork continued on its way, and she chewed thoughtfully.

"Amarist Naeb," she said when she was finished. "She started off in medical."

"Yes, that's right."

"But she left in the *ICS Hector*."

"Yeah. What about it?"

"On a fortress, there are literally dozens of pressure hatches between medical and the nearest access to the docks. Half of them are opened from remote security stations."

"You're right. Fuck me, who was opening them for her?"

Tirrano placed her cutlery down on the table. "Could it really have been Branathes?"

"Think about it. We believe the whole reason we found Naeb was because she was part of a force which penetrated a secure research station. We now know she wasn't a blank slate after all; she was able to act independently, and she escaped against all the odds. What if there are more Rasas out there? What if they are more like sleeper agents than mindless blanks? What if it wasn't even Naeb who disabled fire containment at Kosling?"

"Like you said, fuck me."

"Sorry, but it just sounds wrong when you say it."

"Never say never, right?"

"Let's stay on topic."

Tirrano smirked at him.

"Seriously Peras, this is important. The whole fortress could be at risk. Shit, the whole Empire."

"Fine, go on."

"If we're right, then we can easily predict his next move."

"We can?"

"Isn't it obvious? He thought Laekan was dead. He made a point of telling us her data on Naeb was lost with Fort Kosling."

"You don't think—"

"I do, Peras. I do think that. Logically, the next thing he would have to do to protect himself is get rid of Doctor Laekan."

"Fuck me."

○ ○ ○

The sun was almost kissing the horizon when Borreto asked Prayer to call it a day. Thankful for the reprieve, as late as it arrived, Castigon came back to join the others as they trudged dejectedly from the ruined town.

"I can't fuckin' believe it," Prayer was saying. "Where are they all?"

"Where are who?" Castigon asked.

"Last time we were here," Borreto said, "this was a thriving city. The capital, right? Population of about a hundred and sixty thousand."

"So?"

Prayer answered for the captain. "PRAISE reckons there are about two hundred dead under all that rubble."

"So few?" Castigon said. He was genuinely surprised.

"I know, right?" Said Prayer. "Nobody on the ground, and no survivors."

Castigon fell silent. It was the first time since leaving Correctional Compound One he had been faced with a problem that didn't somehow revolve around reaching and killing particular Shards of the Empress.

A whole city levelled, and cleared out almost completely. It was unprecedented. He figured there must have been an initial bombardment to kill the surface-to-air defences and comm towers, then a ground operation of some sort, then the town would have been pounded fiercely to flush out those who had managed to hide.

But who would do such a thing? Who could? Like most of the more remote Imperial worlds, this planet had orbital platforms that could punch right through a large-frame cruiser. The remains of those shattered platforms were now adrift in and around their orbits. Why would someone invest in breaching those defences, just to disappear a bunch of civilians from the surface of a world as boring as this one?

The humanitarian in you is resurfacing, he thought. Put an end to that shit, right now.

He made a conscious effort to shove the woes of Lophrit aside in his mind, and concentrated on his own problems. In a way, the trip had not been wasted. The Shard he had tracked to this world was almost certainly dead, or it might be that she soon would be, depending on what had happened to the people who were unaccounted for.

It had saved him a little time, and a lot of risk. He could move on to his next target.

"What are you planning to do about this, Captain Borreto?"

"Nothing," the captain said. "There's nobody here we can help. We dust off and leave. We'll send a message to the network to let them know what's happened here, and the proper authorities can handle it."

"Do you really want to draw that kind of attention to yourself?"

"It's not a problem. We'll send anonymously."

"There really is no such thing as a truly anonymous message, Borreto. If they want to identify the sender, they will."

"Well, Prayer can work wonders with a comm

system."

"It won't be enough. You might as well just hand yourself in."

Borreto stopped walking, and turned to look Castigon in the eye. "You mean I might as well hand *you* in, don't you?"

"Am I that transparent?"

Borreto supplanted the question with one of his own. "How much danger are you putting me and mine in?"

Castigon noted the captain had crossed his arms, and was now tilting his head and squinting slightly. His posture was defensive, his gaze betrayed the fact that he was re-assessing Castigon as a potential threat.

"No more danger than you would be in carrying anyone else," Castigon said. "Unless you send that fucking message, then you've got real problems."

"You want to stay right here, son? Here with all the fucking ghosts? I'll waive your fare if you do. You carry on like that with me, and you'll be hitching your next ride with whoever comes to investigate."

Castigon weighed up the options. He could easily put Borreto down, he was confident of that. But the pilot and the woman had continued walking and were nearly at the ship. If he was going to commandeer it for himself, he would have to reach them across open ground. The chances of doing that without being shot were pretty damned slim.

He still had a lot to do. He chose to bite his tongue and play the long game.

"Forgive me, Captain. That was disrespectful of me. How about you double my fare instead, and take me where I need to go next?"

Borreto frowned, and Castigon figured from the barely perceptible twitches of his eyes and facial muscles that he was weighing up options of his own.

"Triple."

"Triple, and you don't tell anyone about this fucking graveyard until we part ways. You do, and you'll get nothing."

"Done. Where do you want to go next?"

"Serrofus Major."

"Really? With all the unrest that's going on there right now?"

"I won't be on the surface for long," Castigon said. "Believe me."

"Should have gone for more than triple," Borreto muttered.

"Too late now. If anything goes wrong, I'll compensate you accordingly. How's that?"

"Guess it'll have to do."

Borreto turned and walked away from Castigon, back towards the ship.

Castigon smiled. It was a long time since he had been part of a team, even if the team was really just being paid to ferry him about, and probably wanted rid of him at the first opportunity.

He looked back across the quiet, still ruins before he carried on to the landing pad. The absolute extent of the capital's unexplained death was strangely eerie. For the first time in an age, he shuddered involuntarily.

○ ○ ○

Brant felt his scalp contracting with a cold, tight sensation, and he wondered if this had been a good idea after all. He sneaked a glance sideways, the smallest possible motion he could manage, and saw Tirrano was staring ahead fixedly. She looked perfectly calm and collected, and he wondered how she always managed to appear unruffled when being dressed down.

"It's not that you went ahead and did it without telling anyone," Branathes was saying. "It's the fact that you didn't ask *me* that's so disappointing. In case you two have forgotten, I am your supervising officer."

"We assumed you would concur with our reasoning," Tirrano said flatly.

"Did you now?"

"We just thought," said Brant, "when you mentioned that we had lost all of Doctor Laekan's data at Kosling, that you might approve of certain safeguards. She is, after all, the only person who has examined a Rasa."

Branathes glared back at Brant with a cold glint in his eyes. He held the gaze for far too long, and Brant began to feel that he was being scrutinised by someone who had never met him before. Something invisible with many legs crawled across his skin, everywhere at once.

"I don't suppose it occurred to either of you that putting an armed guard around Doctor Laekan's medbay draws attention to her?"

Brant saw Tirrano move, and looked across to her. She was looking back at him.

"Honestly, Sir, that's irrelevant." Tirrano continued to look at Brant until she had already begun to reply to Branathes, then shifted her attention back across to their supervisor. "The threat to Laekan will come from people who want to silence her, and they would already know she poses a risk. Wouldn't they, Sir?"

"Don't be insolent, Peras. It doesn't look good

on you at all."

Brant spotted the deflection immediately. He felt the rise of bile in his throat for a second.

"It's not insolence, Sir. She's right. There probably is a threat to Laekan, and she needs to be protected. Having that protection there when it's needed is much more important than worrying about what it looks like—"

"Enough," Branathes said. "I've heard enough of this. The armed guard goes."

"With respect, Sir, that's weapons-grade bullshit."

Brant's jaw dropped, and he turned his whole head and shoulders to look at Tirrano. This had not been part of their strategy.

"I'm going to pretend I didn't hear that, Tirrano. I'm going to pretend I didn't hear it, and give you a moment to think of a more appropriate reply."

"Sir," Tirrano said. "You are so far off the mark on this you might as well just go and kill her yourself."

"Operator Tirrano, you are mere words away from being relieved of your duties and escorted to your quarters."

"Fat chance."

Brant felt as though he were adrift on the ocean. His life raft was whirling and tipping over the swell, and every so often he caught a glimpse of his cresting oar as it floated farther and farther away.

"Peras, what are you doi—"

"Here's the thing, Sir." The pitch of Tirrano's voice was rising. Brant could see her body tensing, could almost feel her chest and throat tightening himself. "If she gets rubbed out, after we have put a guard around her then taken it off again, it won't be you who takes the fall. It'll be us. You'll say we failed to convince you, that we didn't do our jobs right. You know you will. I mean let's be frank here; we all know how much you love keeping your job."

Branathes was silent. Brant could not decide if that was a good sign, or a bad one.

"So I'm sorry you didn't like us acting on our own initiative, and trying to ensure the safety of a colleague and fellow human being, but if you want those guards taken off her medbay then you can issue that order yourself. Sir."

Branathes remained silent for a long and uncomfortable moment. Brant shifted in his seat, waiting for judgement.

"Very well," the monitor said. "If that's how you feel, I will do it myself. But this is not over. You are both on report, and I will let you know later on what the consequences will be for your outrageous lack of respect."

"Yes Sir," they said together.

"Now get out, and go back to your work."

Brant and Tirrano stood in silence, and walked out of the office. As soon as the compartment doors closed behind them, and they were walking down the corridor, Tirrano forced out a deep breath.

"Oh, what a *prick*. Rasa or not, that man needs a wrench taking to his head."

"Cool it, Peras. What the hell was that in there?"

"He was going to manoeuvre us into doing his dirty work for him," Tirrano said. "Surely you picked up on that?"

"I really couldn't tell if he was being a prick because he is one, or because he's actually an enemy agent. We should have just let him try to whack Laekan, then intervened when he was beyond any reasonable explanation."

"There's no way we could do that. It would look a bit odd, don't you think? Hanging around medical when we have duties to see to? And it's not like we can tell anyone else about this."

"But we're back to square one. He's going to remove the guards."

"Cameras. We'll catch him."

"We don't just want to catch him though, do we? Laekan actually does need to survive."

"How do we stop him then?"

"Remember those weird structures in Naeb's brain? Bit of a giveaway. We could somehow contrive to get him under a scanner."

"He'll know. There's no way he would willingly go through with that."

"We could always knock him out and tell medical he fell on his head."

"That's a lovely idea."

Tirrano fell silent, and they continued walking for a few minutes before a new thought occurred to Brant.

"What if..." he began.

"What?"

"What if he's not the only Rasa on Fort Laeara?"

"Oh my fucking worlds, Brant," Tirrano said. "You sure like finding problems."

## – 08 –
## THE OCCUPATION OF MIBES

*Disputer* soared smoothly from the dark heart of a bound wormhole, followed closely by her companions. Spread out before her, against the dazzlingly bright backdrop of Mibes, dozens of Imperial starships were already waiting in high orbit of the planet.

"Jump successful," said Helm. "Local stellar locks confirmed. Slight discrepancy on pulsar locks, but it's well within limits."

"I'm hand-shaking with the Third Fleet," said COMOP. "Transponders verified."

"Sound general quarters, and get Shard Caden up here immediately," Thande said. "Signal *Stoic* Actual; find out where he wants us."

"Already receiving a data packet from the Third's flagship, Captain. Deployment details have been sent to the helm station, and objectives with contingencies have been sent to Tactical and yourself."

"No time to talk then?" Thande murmured. "Fair enough. Let's take a look."

She tapped the data package that had appeared on her holo, and skimmed through the contents.

Tactical was already updating the central battle map. "Viskr ships are holding position, Captain.

They're in defensive formations, blockading the planet. Looks like your classic stand-off."

"Noted. Anyone talking to us from the surface, COMOP?"

"No, Ma'am. Most frequencies are being jammed. I'm just getting static on the traffic control, defence, and governmental channels."

"It says here that the Viskr were deploying ships to the surface when the Third Fleet arrived. What can you tell me about that, Tactical?"

Tactical returned to her station. "We have direct line of sight to six cities. I'm reading enemy landers and gunships in and around five of them, and at least seven of their destroyers have gone atmospheric."

"That's all we need," Thande said. "This is going to have to be quick, or it'll turn into a hostage situation."

"More enemy ships arriving." There was a note of alarm clearly audible in Tactical's voice. "They're shoring up their lines."

"Let them come," said Thande. "We just have a few more minutes to wait until we make our opening gambit."

"What's *Stoic* got planned, Captain?" COMOP asked.

"You'll know it when you see it."

Thande looked across to Tactical, who had received the same data packet as her, and they shared a knowing smile.

"Captain, Shard Caden has arrived at the command deck," said the XO.

"Well then, Commander Yuellen; you may let him in."

Heavy security hatches isolating the command deck from the rest of the ship rumbled aside, and

Caden stepped onto the bridge. Before they had even reached their stops, the thick metal blast doors began to close after him.

"Welcome to the command deck, Shard Caden," said Thande. "I thought you might want to see a naval operation being executed properly."

"Interesting. I would have thought you'd want Captain Santani up here, given your words of advice to her."

Thande leaned sideways in her chair, conspiratorially. "She was less than cooperative when I suggested it to her earlier."

"How odd."

Thande could not decide if the Shard was simply being dry, or making some kind of sardonic comment at her expense.

"Sarcasm?"

"It hardly matters. You didn't bring me to the command deck to gain my approval, did you. What have we got?"

Thande waved her hand lazily at the holographic layers of the main battle map.

"It seems the Viskr were able to get boots on the ground before the Third Fleet arrived, after all. Given the number of vehicles we can see from up here, the probable strength of arms and armour they have on the surface suggests a full-on occupation of the planet."

"Then this border conflict has been formalised as a true war at last."

"Indeed. Now we're here to assist the Third, our combined fleets are evenly matched with the Viskr... more or less."

"What's the play?"

"I'm glad you asked." Thande smiled. "We're going to try to pull off the old 'metal rain' routine while we get boots of our own down there."

"Risky," said Caden, and he grimaced.

"It's better than trying to duke it out in high orbit. By the time we were to rout their fleets, their ground forces could have levelled a few cities. We have to get down there and physically kick them off the planet, and we can't do that without enforcing orbital cover."

"Speaking of which, please don't crash *Disputer* into the planet while I'm down there."

Thande opened her mouth to reply, uncertain whether the remark was intended to be amusing or insulting, but she was interrupted before she could think what to say.

"Micro-wormhole detected, Captain," said COMOP. "It's forwarding a coded signal. I'm told additional assets have arrived at the system periphery. Receiving their final destination co-ordinates now."

"It's about to begin," Thande said, half to Caden and half to the command deck at large. "Expect to take heavy fire for a short period, but if all goes well we will gain a shooting advantage very quickly."

"That sounds like my cue to disappear," said Caden.

"Wait a moment," Thande said. "You'll want to see this. Don't worry; you'll have time to get ready."

She pointed towards the battle map, switched in the visible sensor feed, and a panoramic view of Mibes appeared as an inlay in the holographic volume. The view point was close enough to the planet that the texture of the cloud systems was just starting to become apparent.

"Be ready to drop our orbit rapidly, Helm."

For a moment, nothing happened. Then, almost simultaneously, dozens of wormholes began to form. Shimmering in the highest reaches of the atmosphere they appeared as discs; dark, starry wells that reached away to depths unknown.

And then they evicted their travellers.

"What a sight!" Thande said.

Guardian Shields arose from the dark pools one by one, already oriented with their crudely curved dishes facing the Viskr fleet. Dangling towards Mibes, slender drive stems pushing constantly against the pull of the planet's mass, they drifted slowly away from one another, forming islands of refuge.

Tactical broke the awed silence that had fallen across the bridge. "The Viskr lines are opening fire. Massive incoming. Looks like they've guessed what we're going to do."

The XO issued orders in rapid succession, standing near the centre of the command deck, hands clasped behind his back.

"Turrets and lasers, Tactical. You know the drill. Helm, take us down to the nearest Guardian's flak shadow. Don't stop for anything."

"Yes, Sir!" Helm sounded for all the worlds as though she were excited.

"You've seen the good bit," Thande told Caden. "If the ship is destroyed before you can get yourself ready for your part, you'll know this operation went straight to hell."

"Don't hit the planet," Caden warned her again.

He turned on his heel. COMOP opened the hatch for him to leave, before Thande could find an answer.

○ ○ ○

Throam and Eilentes were waiting for Caden

when he reached the flight deck, already dressed for battle. Eilentes stayed silent, but Throam gave him a knowing smile and flicked his eyes downwards. Caden followed the counterpart's gaze down to his forearm, and saw he was wearing the gauntlet that matched the compact mini-gun he was so proud of owning.

"Oh boy," Caden said. "I said 'low key'. Why is nobody getting this?"

Throam's smile became a wicked grin.

"Better to have it and not need it..."

"Fine, whatever. Just don't take your own legs off. Or mine."

Caden swept his gaze across the flight deck while he clipped his armour over his base layers. Across the cavernous space, he could see dozens of landers being prepared hurriedly by a mixture of MAGA troopers and navy flight staff.

"Did Volkas say anything about who we're dropping with?" Eilentes asked, addressing Caden. He noticed her arms were folded, and wondered why she looked so put out.

"We'll be going in with Sergeant Chun again," said Caden. "I doubt Volkas will have much to say about that."

"I don't know," she said. "I got the impression he thinks we're a bad influence on Daxon and his mates."

"Yeah, well... we are."

"They were already fuck-ups when we met them," Throam said.

Eilentes gave him no response, and Caden felt the overwhelming urge to fill the silence.

"Actually, I meant he's going to be pretty upset about the rest of their battalion being killed. The *Stiletto* went down."

"Shit," Eilentes said. "When did you find that out?"

"Couple of hours ago."

"That'll be why Norskine was off her aim on the range."

"I'd guess so."

"She didn't say a word about it."

Caden finished dressing and took the rifle Throam offered him. He slung it over his shoulder and heard the familiar *shunk* of a mag-tag locking the weapon in place.

The deck juddered, and far above them he heard the sounds of glancing impacts booming through the upper compartments.

"We're taking fire," Eilentes said. "That's going to mean a rough descent."

"We won't launch until we're in the shadow of a Guardian Shield," said Caden.

"Even so, the lower we drop the less cover we'll have. And we'll be dropping real fast."

"The cruisers that stay up here will be providing a flak barrier. Anyway, MAGA are deploying an entire expeditionary force to this fight. The Viskr can't possibly shoot down that many landers."

"I'm pretty sure this drop will still come at a high price."

"That's why you'll be flying our lander," said Caden. "Try not to break this one."

"You think I didn't try last time?"

"I'm kidding, Eilentes."

"I know, just... well you haven't exactly complimented me yet, have you?"

Caden glanced up from the zadaqtan blades he was pushing into his webbing, and caught the tail end of an expression that flickered across Throam's face. It was a look that said 'Really? *Now*?' He looked across to Eilentes, confused.

"What's that?" He asked.

"You stuck me with looking after the shuttle on Herros, and left me out of the loop entirely at Fort Kosling. I feel like I'm not getting the opportunity to do anything really useful."

"You're a pilot and a sharp-shooter. You've dropped us safely to Echo, Aldava, and Woe Tantalum, and you did a bang-up job of covering us from up high on that last trip."

"Not really what you'd call massive contributions though, hey? I don't mean to sound ungrateful, but I'm really not feeling part of the team here. Tell him, Rendir."

"Oh man, don't get me involved in this."

"Clearly you *are* involved," Caden said to him. "Tell me what?"

"I'm not 'involved'," Throam said, "I'm just the one who gets to hear the complaints."

"Hey!" Eilentes placed her hands on her hips, and stuck out her chin. "It wouldn't fucking kill you to support me once in a while. Caden, it's this simple: I *can* do more and I *want* to do more."

"Fine." Caden sighed inwardly. "Whatever you want. Be a big mother-fucking heavy hitter. Pull a crazy stunt and get shot. Wouldn't want you to get bored doing your job, would we?"

Eilentes was running down the deck towards one of the landers before he had finished talking. "Knew you'd see it my way!"

"That's not how she screamed it before," Throam said, as he and Caden set off after the pilot.

"Screamed it?"

"Screamed, yelled. Same thing."

"When did all this happen?"

"The minute we arrived on *Disputer*. Euryce doesn't keep her opinions to herself. Not for long, anyway."

"How come you didn't tell me about this sooner?"

"Didn't get the chance. You've been off playing counsellor to Captain Santani and trying to find the humanity in that Thande creature. Anyway, kind of got distracted by all the other shit."

"What other shit? I feel like I've missed out on something here."

"She kept trying to dig up Ephisia and Gendin."

"Oh, right. How you feeling about that?"

"Well in the end I just told her the story. It was easier that way."

"So what's the problem?"

"She's got a malfunction going about our relationship as well. It's doing my head in. I'm not in the right place to talk about that at the moment."

"Okay, well I hope you're in the right place for a fight. You do have your head in this game, don't you?"

"Course I do, Caden. Do you?"

"What do you mean?"

"You're still off, and we still need to have that talk. Before one of us gets hurt."

Caden stopped and held Throam's gaze for a moment, wanting to put his counterpart in his place. But he knew that if he did, he might say something he would always regret.

"I'll be fine," he said. "We'll both be fine. Don't worry, Tiny."

○ ○ ○

It was fortunate that *Disputer* was such a large and

hardy ship. As swiftly as she plummeted towards the safety of the nearest Guardian Shield, the incessant rain of metal and fire from the Viskr lines moved many times faster.

"We're closing on cover," Helm said.

"Ma'am, *Requiem* is abaft of us. She's taking heavy hits. I don't think she's moving under her own power any more."

"Show me," Thande said.

*Requiem* appeared on the battle map, racing towards the flak shadow of the same Guardian Shield that *Disputer* was headed for. The two ships followed the same heading, but even as Thande watched *Requiem* following them in, the burning aft end of the light battleship began to swing out to port. Slowly, dreadfully, *Requiem* was entering a spin.

There was a moment of tense silence on the command deck, the clatter of impacting decoy flechettes seeming to fade away to nothing. On the battle map, the handful of life boats that *Requiem* managed to launch were flung away violently from her tumbling frame. The battleship was spinning around her own centre of mass, pushed by enemy munitions and surface explosions into a roll she was unable to correct. The momentum her engines had provided before they failed her now carried her fatefully onwards.

Still firing, her C-MADS turrets were twitching fitfully as they tried to differentiate between incoming fire and hull debris. Her entire length was peppered by shots from the Viskr gauss guns even as she lost altitude, slowly and inexorably sinking below the Guardians and continuing on past their fields of cover.

"She's sent out a distress call," COMOP said

quietly.

"There's nothing we can do for them," the XO said, just as quietly.

"We're in the flak shadow, Captain."

Thande snapped out of her morbid trance and forced her head to clear.

"Identify best-fit solutions for flak barriers."

"Already on it," Tactical said. "I'm seeing a number of trajectories we can cover. Locking in the most useful ones now."

"Whenever you're ready."

Tactical punched in the commands, and *Disputer* re-purposed her defences. Sheltering beneath the vast metal and stone umbrella of a Guardian Shield, she was now able to direct her interception fire out at an angle, protecting other ships and Guardians from the continuous stream of enemy ordnance.

"Their cruisers are launching missiles already," she said. "Reading multiple spikes. They must be sick of trying to chip away at us with rail guns."

"Well then; have our turrets prioritise missile targets."

"Ma'am."

Thande watched the battle map intently, noting the names of the few ships which, like *Requiem*, had not made it to safety. It was regrettable that there had been several losses, but the gambit appeared so far to be paying off. The Viskr fleet was now stuck in high orbit, with their forces on the ground cut off from any support. As long as the Guardians held out, the enemy fleet would not be able to get any more drop ships through to the surface.

Or, for that matter, their nukes.

"*Stoic* and his battle group are firing into the atmosphere," COMOP said. "Looks like they're going after those destroyers the Viskr sent down there."

"Excellent," Thande said. "That should make life much easier for our ground teams."

"Captain," Tactical said, "I've been analysing the Viskr fleet. There are one or two newer ships, but the bulk of their forces are really old models. The kind of medium-frame rigs we'd have been fighting at Chion over two decades ago. In fact it looks like their only capital ship is the *Nakrikhul Srabir*, which I believe actually was in that battle."

"Seriously?

"Yes Ma'am. Unless it's been decked out with new offensive systems during the past twenty Solars, it's not much of an opponent."

Commander Yuellen stepped up to the tactical station, and bent down to look at the holos. "Have they got anything up there that *does* present a serious threat?"

"As I said, a few ships which appear new. Classes we haven't seen before. If they were considerably more powerful than the rest of the Viskr ships though I suspect we'd know it by now. No, I think the only real threat comes from their numbers and their position up the gravity well. The ships themselves are relics."

"They're... desperate?" Thande asked the question under her breath.

"Flight decks one through four all report drop-ready, Captain."

"Send them a go, COMOP," said Thande. "And let's hope they all reach the surface alive."

o o o

Eilentes fought with the controls, fought for stabilisation, fought for deceleration, fought for evasion, but mostly she fought for sanity.

The lander screamed through the atmosphere, nose almost straight down, hurtling and rolling and shaking in the midst of a loose wing of identical craft, and shadowed by decoy drones. It was threatened occasionally by the few enemy shots that managed to penetrate the cover provided by the fleets sheltering high above. Kilometres away from them, in every direction, other groups of landers were making the same terrifyingly rapid descent from their parent ships.

A crimson alarm winked at her from the tactical holo, then became a swathe of red when she failed to respond immediately. Cursing, she slapped a tile and fired a burst of flechettes directly into the path of a razor-tooth missile that streaked up from the surface.

"Incoming!" She yelled into the comm. "Surface-to-air. All landing craft, be ready to deploy countermeasures."

There was a quick round of acknowledgement from the rest of the drop squadron, yet still she saw a brief burst of orange-black as a lander ahead of them took a direct hit.

She gritted her teeth, and tried not to scream with frustration.

"This is Bullseye Actual. We have eyes on the el-zee. All landers, track to my beacon."

Eilentes flicked her eyes rapidly between her descent manager and the landing zone marker that Volkas had sent to her mapping system. She swore under her breath when she saw how far off the mark she was.

"Everyone back there had better be strapped in," she muttered, and slammed the lander into a tight curve.

More missile warnings erupted in front of her, and she fired off burst after burst of countermeasures. When tracers flashed past the forward canopy, her scalp tightened and the skin on her face and arms prickled and flushed in a white hot instant. She hoped this descent would not end like the one on Woe Tantalum. With this entry angle, and at this air speed, they would definitely not survive a crash landing.

She realised Volkas was speaking again over the squadron's channel. "—already picking up a number of enemy units on the ground. Be ready for a hot landing."

"Damn it Volkas," she said to herself. *"We're supposed to be coming down in a quiet spot."*

The terrain below expanded rapidly, details becoming clearer with each passing second. She could see the entire sprawl of the city of Naddur, and even as she watched the swelling vista her eyes began to resolve thin columns of black smoke rising from the buildings amongst the outskirts.

And from the buildings which fringed their landing zone, grey smoke and flashes of light.

"Great!" She hissed through clenched teeth, then hit the comm again. "Bullseye Actual from Lima Bravo One; that landing zone is crawling with hostiles."

"I see them, Bravo One." Volkas's voice crackled with interference. "We don't have time to relocate. We're going to come in fast, and release the swarm directly over them. I'm tasking our decoys to assist."

"Acknowledged." Eilentes closed the channel.

The ground and buildings were rushing towards her, expanding faster and faster, and her hands ached to hit the controls and pull up the nose of the craft. But not yet. Not yet. Not until Volkas sends the word to—

"Release swarms."

Eilentes' hands jabbed at the controls, and the lander slowed its descent rapidly, lifting its nose as the powerful vertical lift engines started air braking. She hit tiles on the tactical holo, and the lander's mission pods popped open.

Two at a time, the lander jettisoned a cloud of area clearance drones. The swarm dropped towards the ground, each drone kicked in its own turbines with less than fifty metres to go, and they burst outwards to sweep the area around the landing zone.

The lander came down over flat parkland, near to the civic district. Short, bulbous native trees lined the avenues, and Eilentes made sure she touched down in an area that was screened off by as many of them as possible. The building line was on the far side of one of the nearby avenues, and when the engines began to power down she could already hear the sound of weapons fire even through the thick canopy. The swarming drones — those from the other landers as well as from their own — circled the zone at high speed, firing off short, vicious bursts of small-calibre rounds each time they picked up enemy movement.

Eilentes popped the exterior hatch and climbed down quickly, delaying her exit only to grab two rifles from the rack behind the piloting seat.

On the ground, she saw that the rear hatch had already been opened. MAGA troops were spilling out, taking up defensive positions in a perimeter around the dropship. Other landers were coming down around them — the remains of their particular drop squadron — and spilling out soldiers of their own.

She spotted Caden and Throam and headed over to them. As she approached, she prompted her amour to skinprint to the same urban design that they were already wearing, and her outer layer mimicked the environment automatically.

Caden was pointing out a terrain feature on Sergeant Chun's holo when she arrived.

"I need to be here," Caden was saying. "Eyes and Ears have positively located their staff at the emergency bunker beneath the commerce hall, and it's likely they have secured the Proconsul there too. From our descent it looks like there's not much conflict around that area, but getting there might be a problem."

"Why the commerce hall?" Chun asked.

"Secondary fall-back," Caden said. "The Viskr assumption will be that people of significance or status will remain near their posts. They would never think to check such a mundane building."

"What do you need me to do?"

"Hold this position. The swarm is doing a pretty good job of sterilising the perimeter, but that won't last. Once the Viskr notice a dead zone behind their lines they'll move more squads in."

"How long?"

"Say a couple of hours? Chances are we'll be cut off from you very quickly. If we don't come back in five, pick up everything and fall back to a more defensible position."

"You want Daxon's team again?"

"If you can spare them."

"Spare them? Fuck Caden, please take them off my hands. Seriously — keep them."

"You ever worry that you might start believing your own joke?"

"Nope."

"Fair enough."

There was a rushing noise above them, and Eilentes found herself dropping towards the ground instinctively. She looked up in time to see a wing of Viskr fighters streak across the sky, chased by the roar of their engines.

"Enemy tac-fighters," she called out to Caden and Chun. "They've probably pegged the landing zone."

"They'll be coming around for another pass," Caden said. "Any air support?"

"Not yet," said Chun. "The Viskr have their own anti-air down here, and we think they now control the city's air defences too. The main expeditionary force needs to grind them down before Fleet will even risk going for air superiority."

"That's going to be a problem."

"Yeah. But it's my problem, not yours. We're unloading our Gorillas now, which will help. You should get going before they hit us."

Eilentes fell in with Caden and Throam, and jogged back towards Daxon and his fire team. The soldiers were waiting patiently, standing around one of the Kodiak armoured transports that had rolled from their lander.

"Eilent–es." Norskine dragged out the last syllable. "Ready to make use of all that practice, sister?"

"You know it," she said. "Ambrast is all warmed up, and ready to go."

"Ambrast..." Throam chuckled. Eilentes shot him a look, and he stopped at once.

"Taliam, I'm sorry about... you know. The 951st Battalion."

Norskine looked at Eilentes with misty eyes,

but smiled weakly. "War is hell, right?"

"All aboard that's coming aboard." Daxon dragged back the Kodiak's sliding side door.

"No, we go on foot," said Caden.

"You sure about that?" Daxon asked. He kept his hand on the side of the vehicle.

"I realise we'll lose the armour, but we'll gain discretion. The Kodiak is far too visible from the air. Without a Gorilla to cover our asses, it would just take one good hit to kill us all."

Eilentes grimaced. "Wouldn't call that a good hit, exactly."

"You know what I mean."

"Okay troops, you heard the man. We go on foot. Bruiser, you take point."

Bruiser nodded at Daxon, and pulled his GPMG from the mag-tag on his armour. Eilentes had never known anyone else even attempt to stow such a heavy weapon across their back; not even Tankers were proud or stubborn enough to try. The Rodori made it look as though the effort were truly trivial, but she knew that a general purpose machine gun was anything but lightweight.

As the team moved off, Caden fell in beside Daxon, followed by Throam. Eilentes took up her customary position a short way off the flank of everyone else, watching the far building lines and rooftops for the slightest signs of trouble. But she could still hear the hushed conversation through her link, even over the nearby popping and thumping of gunfire and bombardment.

"Our main force is going to be engaging the Viskr barricades on the south bridge and the west gate, both of which lead to the civic centre," Caden was telling Daxon. "That should draw the bulk of their resistance, but they won't leave their rear unguarded. We'll take the most direct route we can along the eastern edge, then cut in towards the commerce hall. I expect we'll find trouble, but it shouldn't be anything we can't handle."

They hurried quickly across the park, through rows of the squat trees, and soon arrived at a gravelled boulevard that divided the edge of the park from a continuous row of tall buildings. Expanses of blue-black glass fronted most of the white stone buildings, and double doors a storey tall were set into many of them. From the look of them, Eilentes guessed they were at the edge of the financial district.

The group moved off east towards the nearest junction, hurrying along the boulevard right at the foot of the building line. When they reached the end of the row of buildings, Bruiser dipped his head around the corner quickly, then pulled back.

"Looks clear," he said. "Wait."

Bruiser dashed into the north arm of the junction, and took cover. Nothing happened.

Eilentes moved up with Caden and Throam, and peered down the road. Everything was still, despite the sounds of battle that seemed to ricochet from the streets all around them. Other than a few shattered windows on the first couple of floors, and a barely visible veil of drifting dust, the fighting seemed to have passed this street over.

Bruiser was crouched behind a large stone planter. A row of identical planters ran down the central reservation of the road, placed at intervals, and each one contained a taller, thinner version of the stubby trees from the park. The street itself was paved with the white stone favoured by Imperial town planners, with raised kerbs which looked as though they held back a flood of glossy black gravel. As soon as she stepped on one, Eilentes realised it was a continuous, fused surface.

Bruiser broke cover and moved farther in, ducking down again behind the next planter. The others followed, by ones and twos, while Eilentes stayed glued to the building line. She was perhaps more exposed than the others, but as they moved down the street, bit by bit, she had every chance of covering most of the hiding places they passed.

A trio of fighters screamed over them, headed back the way the group had come. Eilentes ducked into cover along with everyone else, even though her experience told her the pilots would never have noticed people in the street below. Not when they were zeroing in on another target at such high speeds.

"You know they'll probably have set down skulkers all around the city," Daxon said. "Those horrible bastards are perfect for ambushes in these urban spaces."

"I can do without all that nonsense again."

"You and me both, Caden. You and me both."

Despite her gritted teeth and steely glare, Eilentes found that her stomach knotted itself at the mere mention of skulkers. Just the thought of the vicious, brutal devices made the tiny hairs on the back of her neck stand up, made her skin flush cold.

If anything suddenly whirred into life as they approached it, or began tumbling and rattling across the ground towards them, threshing at the air with razor-edged rings of cold metal, she was afraid her scream would bring all the enemy's forces straight to them.

"Word up." Bro was right behind her. "FOB's been established. I've got accurate coordinates for the lines of engagement."

"We all good?" Caden asked.

"Yeah, they're a good ways off. Shit..."

"What is it?"

"Kinda sorry we're missing it. It sounds seriously brutal!"

"All in good time, Bro," said Daxon. "We got a job to do here for the moment."

"Hold it guys," Eilentes said. "Bruiser's stopped."

She peered at the Rodori, wondering why he had dropped to one knee behind one of the stone planters. There was a cross-roads ahead, with buildings forming blind corners, but he was nowhere near close enough to have seen a threat off to either side.

"What's the problem, Biggun?" Caden asked.

"Mines, I think."

"You sure? I'm not seeing anything."

"That's because you don't see heat."

Caden pulled down his helmet visor, and Eilentes did the same. Sure enough, there were faint spots of heat on the ground ahead. They were barely warmer than the ambient temperature, but far too uniform and regularly spaced to be random fluctuations.

"What sort of shitty-ass mine glows with IR?" Norskine said, snorting.

"One with a core that can blow a crater the size of our lander," Caden replied grimly.

"Visors, everyone," Daxon said. "Don't get anywhere near those hotspots."

"Don't need to tell me twice," Bro said.

"Bruiser, Norskine; take the junction."

Bruiser waited while Norskine moved forward cautiously. When she had caught up, he moved to the left building line. She mirrored him on the other side of the road, hugging the right wall, and they advanced together. They inched forwards, sneaking quick glances into the road which crossed theirs, then peering out more slowly. They each scrutinised the stretch of road opposite their own position, for the widest possible view.

"Forty metres, no obstructions. No hostiles; right clear," said Bruiser.

Norskine followed up. "Seventy metres, obstruction fifty metres. No hostiles; left clear."

"Move up," said Daxon.

Bruiser held his machine gun in both hands, hunched over it as if that would somehow make his huge frame smaller, and jogged through the intersection to the other side. He threaded his way through the hotspots, coming no closer to them than was absolutely necessary.

Daxon moved up to replace him at the junction, keeping watch for any Viskr or their machines.

"Caden; go," said Daxon.

Eilentes watched Caden follow in Bruiser's footsteps, with Throam just metres behind him. The counterpart would shadow him wherever he went. She wished for a moment that he would do that for her, then squashed the thought down.

"Norskine, after me."

Daxon bolted across the space, and Bro moved up to replace him. The private gestured to Eilentes.

"You and Norskine go next, yeah? I'll bring up the rear."

"Okay."

Eilentes saw Daxon reach the far side, and before she knew it Bro was hissing "Go!"

Norskine had set off at a jog and was a quarter

of the way into the crossroads before Eilentes even began moving. She hunkered down low, following Norskine's path, wondering how the hell the soldier could keep up that pace and still make out the faint heat readings on her visor.

Eilentes heard a sharp crack, and saw Norskine's head and neck jerk to one side. The trooper stumbled sideways, landing on the ground in the middle of the junction and rolling onto her front. She didn't move.

"Sniper!" Daxon hissed into the group channel.

Eilentes dropped onto one hand, kicked her feet in a circular motion, and scrambled back to cover with Bro.

Another crack, and a plume of stone dust sprang from the ground near Norskine's motionless body.

"Norskine!" Bro was shouting into his link. "Yo Taliam, you still with us?"

There was no reply.

"I see them," Daxon said from across the way. "Eilentes, they're on your left side. Three hostiles at about forty metres. Behind partial cover on the wall nearest you."

"You'll have to take them," Caden said. "We pop out of cover long enough to get the shot, they'll have us."

"Give me a moment," Eilentes said. She steeled herself, getting her nerves under control, then stole a brief glance around the corner. "That's fifty metres, Daxon."

"Fifty, forty: same thing."

Eilentes realised with a start that the cover was probably the same obstruction Norskine had noted just before declaring the junction clear. The street they were crossing was heavily damaged down near the Viskr position, with rough chunks of masonry littered across the flagstones. The cover itself looked as though it had been the entire ground floor frontage of a building, which had somehow sloughed off and collapsed — mostly intact — across the pavement and half of the road.

She dropped to one knee. "Give me a distraction."

Bruiser ducked out of cover and fired a quick burst into the street. Three geysers of powdered mortar burst from the wall behind him, a split-second after he began moving back.

Eilentes was already in action. In one movement she leaned out of cover, brought Ambrast from an upright carry almost to horizontal, fired off a single round, and ducked back.

"One," she said.

Several rounds raked the ground at the mouth of Eilentes' junction. There was a pause, then another shot hit the ground near Norskine. Eilentes could not tell if the shooter lacked a clear line of sight to where Norskine had fallen, or if the potshots were taunts.

"Doubt they'll fall for that again," Daxon said.

Eilentes agreed silently, and she turned to face Bro. "I need you to be a decoy."

"You aren't serious?"

"Listen, I know it's a risk. But Norskine is laying there possibly bleeding out, so don't take too long agreeing."

"Fuck. Yeah, you're right."

"And don't forget the mines."

"Oh shit, yeah."

"Ready?"

"Ready. No, wait! Yeah... ready."

"Go on, Bro! Go!"

Bro dashed into the junction, zigzagging around the hotspots, and was leaping over Norskine before the first shot split the air behind him.

Eilentes slipped into her own space and time. She was aware of every sound that moved the thick air. She heard Bro's heavy footfalls on the ground, lengthened into crackling forevers. She knew without looking that the Viskr shot was a miss, even while she took aim herself, and smiled at the stretched *thachhhht* of the sniper's round hitting a building. Her scope brought the enemy closer to her, intimately close, so close she might whisper a secret, and she ended him.

This time, there was no return fire.

"Two."

"Third one's gone to ground," Caden said.

"Fucking hell," Bro panted. "That was not cool."

"You see Taliam?" Daxon asked. "Is she still alive?"

"Didn't really get the chance, Dax," Bro said. "Everything was a blur."

"Fuck."

Eilentes was back in full cover, staring across at them. "Am I clear or not?"

"Can't really tell," Daxon said, ducking out quickly. "I've lost line of sight— Oh shit, he's got backup. Three more of those ugly fuckers just appeared from nowhere."

"Eilentes—" Caden said.

"You're going to have to cover me again."

"EILENTES!"

"Caden, what?!"

"I don't mean to rush you," said Caden, "but you've got company."

Eilentes glanced across at the others. Caden and

Throam gestured frantically, pointing straight back at her.

She turned around to look back down the way they had come, and her heart made a mad bid for freedom through her open mouth.

Skulkers were coming.

## – 09 –
## BOYS WILL BE BOYS

Fog this thick was always a double-edged sword. Rendir moved stealthily through the damp oceanic air, trying to make as little noise as possible, straining to hear the slightest sound that might give away the enemy's location. He squinted into the drifting, white-grey morass, knowing that the advantages it gave him were also being bestowed on the other side.

He could not let them win. And he was the last man standing.

Masel and Nidri had been mown down by gunfire, during the first assault by the Viskr on his landing party. Corporal Ichen had been pulped by a skulker that lurched at him from the wet-wreathed shadows. Hitami — sweet, bold Hitami — had blown herself apart with a grenade, in a desperate bid to cripple the enemy's armoured column. They were all of them gone.

His last chance to end the occupation was to reach the Viskr command centre, and blow it to the Deep. If he failed, then this world was doomed to slave under the yoke of oppression for the rest of time.

Rendir stole his way through a long passageway, clinging to the wall, leaping across the openings that led off to invisible chambers. It was a straight run, but he could not yet see the other end; could not yet see what lay in wait for him in the veiled depths up ahead.

He went on regardless. Cowardice was a foreign concept to him.

When the trap was sprung, the threat came from behind. Too late he heard boots clomping on the ground, quickly coming up behind him. He whirled around and saw a dark shape emerging from the mist, already pointing at his chest.

Rendir collapsed against the wall, his whole body jerking and his hands flailing. He sank to the ground and slumped onto his side, tongue lolling out of his mouth, eyes rolled back in his head, and shuddered out his cooperatively dramatic death throes.

"Peow-eow-eow! I *got* you!"

"Geerrrghh–ghh–ghhhhh!" He said.

"I GOT HIM!"

More shapes moved towards them, stepping out of the fog.

"The Viskr Junta wins again," Josué declared. "You guys give up yet?"

"NEVERRRR!" Rendir yelled it from the ground, throwing up his arms and casting off any pretence at being dead.

"Are we playing again?" A smaller boy stepped towards Josué. He was at least a Solar younger than the others.

"Of course we are, stupid," said Josué.

"Can I be on your side?"

"Don't be so *stupid*. We're playing with the same teams, Elías."

"You're not supposed to call me stupid, Jos. I'm gonna tell mama!"

Rendir got to his feet.

"No you won't," Josué said. "If you do, you can't play with us any more."

Elías stuck out his lip, but remained obediently silent. His position in their fraternal dictatorship had been made quite clear.

"What do you want to play next?"

Josué turned his gaze towards Rendir, and considered the question out loud. "We've done the Battle of Kemrik, the Massacre at Rinnow's Point, and the Occupation of Baujaan — twice. Those are all the good ones."

"Najila fell last week," said Rendir. "I saw it on our house holo. We could do that."

"Doesn't that mean the Viskr are supposed to lose?" Josué's face was the very picture of disapproval.

"Maybe this time they won't." Rendir waggled his eyebrows, as if that might entice Josué to accept being on the doomed side of a conflict.

"I'm a bit sick of playing as the Crusties," Josué said. "Shall we all swap sides?"

Rendir shrugged. It was easier than having an argument with Josué; much easier.

"How does it go, Ren?"

Rendir looked behind him, and saw that his crack assault force had returned from the dead. Hitami was looking at him expectantly. He felt his cheeks go hot, and hoped the mist was enough to hide any blushing.

"We went to Najila to blow up their ship factories," he said. "But the ones in space were only where they put them together. They were making the engines and the guns on the ground."

Josué frowned. "So... we just pretend to fly about and shoot at a planet? Lame game!"

"No, we went down to the planet too. We wanted to take their strilli... their zetrill—"

"Their xtryllium?" Josué formed the word carefully, with a barely hidden smirk. Rendir might have been the group's resident Perseus conflict expert, memorising every news report he saw and turning each one into a game, but Josué was far, far better with the difficult words to which their sport exposed them. He never missed a chance to remind everyone of that.

"Yeah, to get their *xtryll*-ium." Rendir aped Josué's pronunciation clumsily, and the other boy's face adopted the satisfaction of a harsh critic.

"*Xtryllium*. It's just capture the flag all over again. Bor-ring."

"I think it sounds fun," said Hitami.

"Nobody asked *you*," Josué said.

Rendir bristled.

"So?" Hitami said. "Nobody asked Roima Gotharom to blow up that big Viskr ship, but she still did it."

"Well my dad says she's just a jumped-up crowd-pleaser with a flagpole stuck all the way up her bottom."

"Your dad's an idiot then."

Josué stepped towards her. "Say that again, I dare you. I *double*-dare you."

Hitami stood her ground. "Your. Dad's. An. Idiot."

"I'm going to knock you on your ass!"

Rendir was between them in an instant, his face right in front of Josué's. He was the taller of the two by half a head, and broader, but Josué puffed his skinny chest out as if that would somehow compensate.

"Back off, Jos."

"What's it to you, Rendir? Is she your girlfriend?"

Josué laughed, and his friends laughed with him.

"Rendir's got a *girl*friend. Ooh, please don't hurt my girlfriend."

Rendir counted to five, as Peshal had taught him. Be the reed, she always said. Be the reed that bends in the wind but never breaks.

"Stop being a kid," he said. "I have to go in soon. So do you. We're just wasting time."

"Yeah, Josué. I'm getting bored," said Nidri.

"*Am* I on your side?"

Josué made it look as though he were backing off from Rendir to speak with his brother, nothing more.

"I already told you; yes."

"I don't think I *want* to be on your side now," said Elías.

"Fine, go be a filthy Crusty with these losers. You know they all get killed? But maybe this way you'll get a girlfriend before you die."

Rendir's friends had all moved over to one side, and Elías went to join them.

"Soldiers of the Imperial Combine, with ME!"

Josué shouted the order and dashed back down the passageway, followed closely by his entourage. Rendir watched them disappear into the fog, bounding away with whoops and whistles, in search of a corner that would serve as a landing zone.

"I don't like your brother very much," Hitami said.

"I don't like him very much either."

Hitami smiled at Elías. "You're okay though."

Elías went bright red.

"Guess we should find ourselves a good place for a factory," said Rendir.

Ichen's face lit up. "What about the solarium? It'll be empty in this weather."

"Oh, good idea," said Hitami. "And it's only open at the front. Easy to stop them sneaking up on us!"

They ran across Level 230, not bothering to shout and holler as Josué's side had. The longer it took the others to find them, the better their chances were. Few of Josué's friends had any real patience.

"Sentries, there and there," Rendir said. "Give me a spotter up high!"

The others scrambled to follow the orders. When it came to military manoeuvres they obeyed Rendir without question. Not one of them had seen anywhere near as much footage from the front lines as he had.

Elías climbed onto the wall surrounding the terrace of the solarium, and then up onto the roof of a permanent awning built into one corner. Even with the fog, it was the ideal spot from which to see without being seen.

"I think we should have some things for them to try and *capture*," said Hitami. "You know, like parts. They can't win if they don't get them."

"But we don't have anything," said Masel.

"Yes we do," Hitami said. She walked to the edge of the solarium, took hold of a potted plant, and dragged it to the centre of the terrace. Masel and Ichen looked at each other, then followed her lead. Before long, there were four neat rows of them in the middle of the tiled floor.

"There. Weapons factory."

Rendir gave Hitami a thumbs-up. "Nice work,

Private."

She beamed back at him.

Time passed slowly in the cold, damp gloom of the early evening, and Rendir began to wonder if perhaps they had gone too far across the level. Josué and his friends might even be too lazy to scour every corner for them. It was, after all, a lot of ground to cover.

Once or twice passers-by moved quietly through the fog, going about their business. Rendir tensed every time they appeared, expecting an attack, until he was sure that the dark shapes were adults and not children.

Eventually, the intrusion came.

It was one advance scout, running through the fog quickly and quietly. She galloped along the broad avenue in front of the solarium, realised she had missed quite a large opening, and doubled back. She saw Masel in the same moment that he saw her.

"HERE!" She shouted.

"Peow-eow!" Masel's fingers riddled her with imaginary bullets. "Down you go!"

"Ack-ack-ARGH!" She collapsed to the ground, shaking violently.

"Weapons free," Rendir said. He wiped the back of his hand across his mouth, a gesture copied from one of the many holo clips he had pored over.

The others came swiftly towards their comrade's death cries.

Masel gave as good as he got, falling at the same time as the boy he gunned down. Two more ran at the entrance to the solarium, with Josué following closely behind them, and passed between Ichen and Nidri.

Josué spied the deliberately misplaced rows of potted plants, understood, and shouted to his troops. "Seize those weapons!"

The two Viskr sentries riddled his vanguard with bullets. As he passed between his fallen soldiers, Josué opened his arms wide and pointed a finger of each hand at Ichen and Nidri.

"Pow, pow!"

They fell obligingly to the floor.

"Brack-ack-ack!" Shouted Hitami.

Josué ignored her, and grabbed for one of the pot plants.

"Hey, I got you."

Josué continued to pay no attention to her, and took the rim of another pot in his free hand.

"I *got* you," she insisted, and took his arm.

He shrugged her off aggressively. "No, stupid. You missed."

"I didn't, that's not fair."

Hitami tried to pull one of the plants back, and he pushed her away.

"Get off, I'm taking them. I'm seizing this factory in the name of the Empress."

She pushed him back.

Rendir was back between them just before Josué's hand reached her face. The boy had swung it hard towards her, but from so far back that the wide, arcing strike took forever to complete. The hand slapped against Rendir's upper arm, and stopped dead.

Rendir pushed Josué; one hand in the middle of his chest.

"Oh, come to save your girlfriend?"

"You're dead. She shot you."

"No she didn't!"

Josué emphasised the word 'didn't' with a hard

shove of his own, pushing Rendir with both hands.

*Be the reed.*

As Rendir took a step back, he grabbed Josué's wrists and turned. The other boy was put off balance, half-stepping and half-falling forwards, and began to struggle with him.

Rendir tried to keep hold. Josué was moving more quickly, and it felt to Rendir as though he wanted to get his hands free so he could strike out again. They turned around and around, stumbling together towards the edge of the solarium, and Rendir kept having to tilt his face away to avoid being clawed by Josué's flailing hands.

Rendir saw Ichen and Nidri, watching with open mouths. Elías, climbing down from the awning back onto the outer wall. Hitami, looking as though she were tired of watching boys fight. Masel, silently placing a mental wager.

They banged against the wall, and Rendir felt his back collide with something else. Something much softer than stone or metal.

"REN!"

Hitami shrieked so loudly that the world itself seemed to stop. Both Rendir and Josué looked towards her.

"Elías! He fell! He fell off the edge!"

The boys released each other at the same time, and stood on tip-toes to look over the wall. Neither could see down the far side, so they both hauled themselves up onto it.

Two metres below them, just visible through the drift, Elías was laid across the taut metal cables of the safety barrier.

Josué dropped back down from the wall, and ran wailing into the fog.

○ ○ ○

Rendir was led home by Father Cabrera, and he had the good sense to hang his head in shame for the benefit of the priest.

Warned ahead of time, Peshal was waiting at the door of their home. She looked at Rendir as though she would have many things to say once Cabrera had left them alone.

"I think this belongs to you," Father Cabrera said.

Peshal ignored her son. "How is he?"

"He broke his arm across one of the cables, but he should be fine."

"Father, I'm so very sorry this happened," she said. "Rendir should have known better."

"Boys will be boys," he said.

"I don't think we'll be letting him off quite that easily."

"Don't be too hard on him," said Cabrera. "Elías *did* have his brother with him. I'll be having words with my dear first-born when I get home; Josué should be the one looking out for Elías, not Rendir."

Peshal finally looked at Rendir. It was as though she had pierced him with her eyes.

"What was it this time?"

"Frontline," he said quietly.

"I can't hear you, Little Man. What was it this time?"

"Frontline," he said. "We were playing Frontline."

"Those damned news feeds." She turned her attention back to the priest. "He won't stop watching them."

"War coverage is perhaps not the best diversion for a young mind," said Cabrera.

"I know."

"I can think of better things he might be doing."

"I can think of some too. There's a whole room back there that needs repainting, Little Man."

"I was thinking of something along more theological lines," said Cabrera. "Many of the youths of Level 230 were in and out of trouble before their parents brought them to me."

"Brought them to you...?"

"Yes, at the church. Humanity Redeemed."

Lamis appeared at the doorway.

"Go inside, Ren," she said.

Rendir obeyed, his eyes fixed on the fascinating ground. He went into the house and sat down in a chair, then looked up again. He could still see and hear the adults talking on the doorstep.

"What are you proposing, exactly?"

"Just that you let him come along to my lessons," Cabrera said. "It's after the service. Think of it as Sunday school for adolescents."

"I really don't think he would be interested in that," Lamis said. Rendir could hear a familiar edge in her voice, and he could see that Cabrera was oblivious to it.

"Well, none of them are interested at first. But after a while, the simple lessons of our One Saviour—"

"No, thank you."

"Surely there is room in your boy's life for a little faith? For the teachings of one of the last great religions?"

"You don't want to know her views on religion," Peshal said.

Rendir knew them well, and braced himself accordingly. Across the room, he could feel Peshal doing the same thing.

"Oh, surely you can't be that opposed to a little bit of religion?"

Peshal placed her hands over her ears and closed her eyes.

Lamis smiled pleasantly. "Organised religion is what you get when egos masturbate in unison."

She slammed the door.

Peshal opened one eye. "Is it over?"

Lamis smiled demurely at her, and Peshal uncovered her ears.

"Which one was it?"

"Masturbation."

"Oh my worlds." Peshal began to giggle. "You didn't? Oh, love! We'll be hearing more about this."

Lamis looked across to Rendir. "And you, you little bugger. You didn't hear a word of that, did you?"

"No Ma'am."

"Good."

Peshal was managing to get herself back under control. "Little Man, you need to stop watching those news feeds. The war is not for young eyes."

"But mum..."

"No buts, child. What in the many worlds will happen next? What if your friend had fallen over the barrier?"

He looked at his shoes.

"He'd be dead, Little Man. Dead. Do you know what a fall of a kilometre and a half does? It's not like in the holofilms, child. Even over water, you go splat."

He looked up at her.

"SPLAT!"

Rendir jerked upright in his seat when she shouted, startled by the outburst.

"I think he gets it," Lamis chuckled.

"I've got a meal to prepare," said Peshal. "You want to finish the lecture?"

"You know me," Lamis said. "Always up for delivering a good lecture."

Rendir screwed his face up, and kicked the chair with his heels. When he opened his eyes fully, Lamis was watching him with an amused smile on her face.

"So go on then," she said. "What's the real story?"

Rendir told her everything. How they had been playing Frontline; how mean Josué had been to his younger, less intelligent brother; how Josué had threatened Hitami and tried to hit her; how Rendir had bent in the wind like Lamis's reed, and in doing so had knocked Elías off-balance.

He finished, and waited for Lamis to tell him off for all the various mistakes he imagined must have been dotted throughout his afternoon.

"Why didn't you punch that little bastard right in his spiteful face?"

He was stunned. Lamis had always been the more direct of his mothers, but he had never, ever heard her advocate violence, much less encourage it in him.

"What—?"

"If some jumped-up little snot was squaring up to Peshal, I'd send him home with a bloody nose."

"But mum, Peshal says I should be like the reed—"

"I know what she says, Ren, but there's a time and a place for holding hands and singing in harmony. When people are threatening you, or threatening your friends, you make them stop. Otherwise, they'll keep right on doing it."

He looked towards the kitchen door, then back again.

"Trust me, son. Your life will be a lot easier if people know not to mess with you."

"But—"

"Don't be the reed, Ren. The reed has no will. Be the damned wind."

– 10 –
## THE HIGH GROUND

Caden felt his stomach flip the moment he caught sight of light glinting off the sharp, whirring edges of bladed rings. It was a problem too far, and a vicious one at that.

He saw Eilentes standing alone on the far side of the junction, directly in the path of the oncoming skulkers. The machines skittered and jostled, rolling towards her along the road, looking for all the worlds as if they each wanted to reach her first.

Suppressing fire came from the right. The Viskr behind the barricade of rubble knew there was still someone left behind at the intersection, and they clearly wanted to make life difficult, if not altogether impossible.

Norskine still lay on the ground, for all practical purposes in the centre of the open space, completely vulnerable. She had not yet moved a muscle.

Caden felt someone barge past from behind him. Throam stepped forward, reached over his own shoulder, and pulled his most beloved weapon from its mag-tag. He inserted his left fist through the rotor ring, clipped the shock mount to its gauntlet, and gripped the fire control bar.

"Caden, give me a hand."

Caden moved in to help. "There," he said. "You got it?"

Throam's hand found the feed chute that Caden had pulled out for him, and he linked the ammo can on his back to the compact mini-gun.

"Better stand back." He said it to nobody in particular. "This is going to get messy."

Before Caden had time to say 'I've got a better idea,' Throam stepped partially out of cover and began to douse the Viskr position.

Spent casings sailed from the rotor ring. The Viskr cover started to crumble immediately, gouts of plaster and dust bursting from it along with pieces of stone and mortar. The ringing metal hail and the incessant hammering of the gun itself combined to a deafening level.

Caden bellowed at Eilentes through the link. "It's now or never, Euryce!"

She was still looking back at the oncoming skulkers, Ambrast now mag-tagged to her back. Her stubbier assault rifle was raised, and shell casings bounced around her feet. The centre skulker looked as though it had snagged up inside, and came to a grating halt. The other two knocked it aside and continued to roll towards her.

"NOW, Euryce!"

Eilentes turned and ran for the intersection, slinging her rifle onto her back as she moved.

"Mines!" Caden reminded her.

She gave no reply still, but he could see from the way she was already moving to one side that she remembered to avoid the first hotspot.

Throam's mini-gun roared as it sprayed the disintegrating enemy position with bullets. He roared along with it. Caden felt the anger there, and glee alongside it.

Eilentes dashed to one side, back again, reached Norskine.

"Get up, you lazy cow!" She grabbed Norskine's arm and hauled her torso up. The soldier was limp, a dead weight, and Caden could see that Eilentes was struggling to lift her unaided.

Bruiser was already sprinting back towards them, weaving around the mines. Had he not seen it with his own eyes, Caden would never have guessed the Rodori could move so quickly, or with such agility.

Bruiser grabbed Norskine's other arm and hauled her up, taking all of her weight with ease, and — still dodging hotspots — both he and Eilentes ran as hard as they could back towards Caden.

"The mines!" Caden shouted.

"I... KNOW!" Eilentes was panting the words into her helmet.

"No, *look*."

Caden pointed past them, back to the skulkers. Eilentes looked over her shoulder as they reached cover, and saw what he meant.

The skulkers showed no signs at all that they were going to stop at the edge of the crossroads.

"Throam — time to go!" Caden yelled. "I think you got them all, big man."

Throam's mini-gun whirred and clanked to a halt, and he whirled around with a boyish grin on his face. The last standing corner of the barricade collapsed to the ground behind him.

"Three, four, five, six," he said, finishing Eilentes' body count.

"Run please."

Daxon and Bro had already taken Norskine, and set off again up the road with her between them, following after Bruiser.

Caden pulled Eilentes' arm firmly, and she immediately fell in beside him, running after the others. Caden did not need to look to know Throam was following. He could feel the heavy footsteps, and heard the chuckling that went with his counterpart's appreciation of his own handiwork.

The first explosion came when they were halfway down the road. The others followed straight away, in a near-instantaneous chain of bangs.

Caden was pushed forwards when the shockfront hit them, and he felt Eilentes stumble too. He pulled her in to the building line, hunkering down next to the stone as debris and dust plumed past them like a gritty fist. A split-second later he felt Throam land against his back, dropping to his knees and placing his whole body between them and the threat.

Pieces of sharp metal rained down on the street, clanging as they hit. A curved section fell through one of the slender trees, severing limbs as it went. Fat, waxy leaves and pieces of rubbery-looking wood came down with it.

"Fuck me," Throam said. "They really aren't smart at all, are they?"

"Guess not," said Caden.

They stood up, dusted themselves off.

"Norskine," Eilentes said. "I couldn't tell if she was alive or not."

"She's breathing," Daxon said through the link. "Round clipped her visor; broke it and knocked her clean out. But she's alive."

"Close call," Eilentes breathed.

"Good job you had a bad-ass hero on hand to save you all," said Throam.

Caden winced when he saw Eilentes' expression. All the tension of the fight and the relief of hearing that Norskine was still alive seemed to evacuate from her face, heading for safety somewhere else. She put her hands on her hips and looked Throam right in the eye.

"You're seriously going to play the hero card now?"

Throam hesitated before he replied. "Did just cover you all while you got the fuck out of that sticky mess, right?"

"Any of us could have done that, Tiny." She stomped off after the others.

"Don't call me Tiny."

Caden smiled to himself. Throam had said it really, really quietly.

"You're definitely in the dog-house." He was careful to ensure he used his private channel to Throam.

"Don't I know it," said Throam. "Shit man, and they wonder why we don't want to commit to anything."

Caden laughed to himself. "Oh yeah; you've got it real bad. Rendir, if she wasn't bothered about you she wouldn't be angry. I'll bet you anything she's sleeping in your bunk when we get back to *Disputer*."

"You're on."

"Are you two dicks coming?" Eilentes' voice carried an unmistakable tone of annoyance across the group channel.

"Right behind you," said Caden.

Throam turned to go after the others, and as he did so Caden grabbed his arm.

"Worlds... you came close there, mate."
"What is it?"

"Piece of a skulker embedded in your back."

"No way."

"It's right in the middle of your ammo can."

"Good job I was using the old 10/W then, yeah? And you didn't want me to bring it."

"Whatever. Don't try and make out like you can claim credit for that."

Caden grabbed the non-lethal side of the metal fragment, and pulled. Even through his gloves he could feel it was still hot.

The piece of skulker came free with a metallic *screech*, and he dropped it to the ground. An ugly rent was left behind in the thin plasteel shell of the ammo can.

"Don't know if that will have jammed the feed chute," said Caden.

"Better fucking not have done; these things are hard to find. Lancillon Industries isn't in business any more."

"But you're alive, that's what matters."

"Yeah, I guess."

"Say it like you mean it," Caden said.

"You know that thing would've gone right through you if I wasn't there, yeah?"

"Good job there was a bad-ass hero on hand to save me, right?"

Throam just grinned.

They hurried over to the others. Bro was holding Norskine's damaged helmet, while Daxon checked her eyes. The corporal held up one eyelid, then the other, shining a small light at the pupils. Bruiser sneaked the occasional look back from his position a few metres up ahead. Eilentes went to kneel down next to her friend.

"We can't stay here long," Caden said. "How is she?"

"Banged up a little," said Daxon. "Just from the fall I think. Impact bowled her over, and probably knocked her out too."

Caden paused for a moment while he considered the tactical implications. "Is she going to be combat-effective?"

"Don't know yet. She might be concussed."

"You asking 'can she fight', Caden? Is that really your priority?" Eilentes said. There was an edge to the question.

"I'm not indifferent to her injuries, Eilentes," he said. "But whatever we do now, her condition is going to affect us all. We can't leave her here. We can't spare anyone to take her back. If we run into trouble, we'll need to be sure she's capable. If not, we'll need to look out for her as well as ourselves."

"You're right, that doesn't sound like indifference at all."

For a moment, Caden let the comment wash over him. But something in her voice, the informality of her casual sarcasm, made him tense up. His skin prickled under her criticism, and he began to sense the first seething rise of anger.

"I know you're pissed at Throam, but I won't have you dumping that shit on me too. My priority is the mission."

A silence fell across the group. After a moment, Eilentes stood up and walked away.

"Get your head back in the game," said Caden.

"Give her a minute," Throam said. "Trust me on that. Give yourself a minute, too."

"Fine." Caden forced himself to find his calm. "Daxon, we probably won't have long before the Viskr swarm this position. Chances are those commandos called in for reinforcements before Throam took them apart."

"Seems likely."

"You're the field medic here. So what's the prognosis?"

"Can't say for certain. She looks all right, sure. I'd like to see a scan of her skull, but obviously that ain't happening."

"So what do you suggest?"

"I can give her a couple of shots. Wake her up, kill any pain, give her some focus."

"Going to have to be that, I think," Caden said. "Doesn't seem like we have many options."

"Agreed."

Daxon popped open one of the pouches on his armour, and pulled vials from within. He started loading a compression injector.

"Get her arm bared, would you Bro?"

Bro placed Norskine's helmet on the ground reverently, as if it were a holy relic, and moved in to help. He released the outer armour from her forearm, unsealed the join between her glove and her sleeve, and tugged the material back up to her elbow.

"Knew I'd get your clothes off eventually," he joked.

"Okay," Daxon said. "That wasn't creepy at all."

Daxon found the vein with expert speed, swabbed Norskine's arm with a sterilising pad, and pushed the nozzle of the injector against the skin. One press of the trigger, and he was rolling her sleeve back down again.

Norskine's eyes fluttered open straight away.

"Welcome back, sleepy. You okay?"

"I feel like shit," she said.

"Where does it hurt?" Daxon asked.

"Fucking everywhere."

"Where does it hurt most?"

"I just told you. Everywhere."

"So nowhere in particular; excellent."

Norskine put out her arms as if to steady herself, and tried to rise. Bro helped her to her feet, and she began to look herself over.

"I can't find my tail," she said. "Guys, where's my tail?"

Caden watched, bemused, as Bro appeared to actually help her look for it. "Daxon, what exactly did you give her just then?"

"Just a quick shot of pain meds and, er, a sort of amphetamine."

"Amphetamine?"

"It *is* part of the med-kit."

"Well... she's up and about. I guess that's something."

"I think I can hear colours," said Norskine.

○ ○ ○

Eilentes was still fuming, but she was not sure exactly why.

The team had moved on, making good time through the empty streets and not running into any further trouble. Once or twice they had all ducked close to the building line while aircraft thundered overhead, and they had once been forced to take cover while a group of the Viskr equivalent of polybots loped across a junction up ahead of them, but they had seen no more ground troops and — thankfully — no more skulkers.

Even to Eilentes' untrained ear, the echoing sounds of the ongoing battle had changed. The thumping of anti-aircraft turrets had been virtually continuous when they had first arrived, while the landers were still coming down through the atmosphere. Now, they sounded only occasionally.

Whatever the MAGA troops were doing on the ground, it sounded as though they had either won back the city's air defences, or destroyed them.

Frequently now she heard a heavy clanking, followed invariably by a resonant *thud* and the sharp, staccato rattling of large-calibre chain guns. She recognised the sound from one of the simulated scenarios she had been subjected to in basic training; it was the sound of Gorilla ground superiority platforms, planting their fists like anchors and hammering the enemy with a barrage of firepower.

All of these sounds of battle surrounded her, and yet she could not shake off the feeling of being annoyed. She chided herself mentally for stewing over the half-arguments she had had, unwilling to admit to herself that she was subconsciously keeping her attention off the fighting and the prospect of a sudden and violent death.

A Viskr tactical fighter collided heavily with the top edge of a building almost directly overhead, and flipped engines over cockpit. It sailed across the street, black smoke pouring from the engine housings, and embedded itself in the building opposite. Falling stone and glass smashed on the pavement below, and pieces of burning material dripped and crawled down the wall. The wreck creaked and shifted, then settled in place.

"Shit," Daxon said. "That was a bit too close."

"No time to stop and stare," said Caden. "We need to keep moving. We're almost right on top of it."

Eilentes could see that Norskine was beginning to recover — both from her fall, and from the medication Daxon had dosed her with. The round that had knocked her off her feet had left a groove in the otherwise smooth surface of her visor, and the surrounding material had turned a crackly, opaque white. With the visor down over her face she would not be able to see a thing, and the internal data overlay was broken anyway. With the visor flipped up, however, Eilentes could see Norskine's face, framed by the front opening of her helmet. She looked nauseated, as if she might hurl at any moment, but at no point did she let it hold her back. The private kept steadfastly on, her jaw set with grim determination.

Be like Norskine, Eilentes thought. Get back up off the ground. Don't let anything slow you down.

"Okay, the commerce building is on the other side of this row." Caden pointed to the buildings directly ahead of them. "Eilentes, I want you up high. Keep an eye on our entry point: I don't want to come back out and find the position over-run."

"You got it," she said.

"You good for this job?"

"I am, yes. Trust me."

"I do, Eilentes. I really do."

She saw in his face that the sentiment was genuine, and her cheeks and the back of her neck burned with shame. She almost forgot why she had even been annoyed with him.

"Norskine," said Daxon. "Want to go with Eilentes?"

"Trying to cut out the dead wood, Corp?"

"No, I just think you'd be better off up high. And I don't want anyone going off on their own."

"Fair enough." She turned to Eilentes. "You and me, sister."

Eilentes smiled back at her. Norskine was regaining her composure minute by minute, and Eilentes had no misgivings about trusting the private to watch her back.

"Let's do it," she said.

They had reached the end of the road, a T-junction running west and east. The sound of the fighting was loudest to the west, somewhere beyond a wide plaza that was visible a hundred metres or so down the road. Even as they hurried across to the foot of the buildings opposite, a heavy bombardment turned the paved area into a cratered dead zone.

"Need a way in," Eilentes said.

Norskine answered by smashing a window with the butt of her rifle. She stood back, away from the falling glass, and knocked away more of the pane to make a hole that was large enough to be safe.

"That'll do it," said Eilentes.

"Don't forget to check in," said Caden. "Hopefully this won't take long, but if we're gone more than half an hour you might want to start worrying."

"Oh yeah, I'll worry all right."

Eilentes ducked through the broken window and into the gloom. Outside, the others moved off towards the east end of the road.

Eilentes looked around, and saw the room was an open-plan office of some sort. Whoever had been working here had left in a hurry; there were private holos still in standby mode, personal effects and clothing left behind, even half-eaten food at some of the work stations.

"This way," Norskine said. "Stairs and elevators."

"Oh please, let the elevators be working," said Eilentes. "I can do without climbing eight storeys."

Five minutes later, after failing to have her wish

granted, she emerged from the roof access door. Huffing and puffing, she clasped her hands behind her neck and sucked the air into her lungs.

"Thought I was fitter than that, too," Norskine panted.

"Stairs..." Eilentes gasped. "Flat ground, I can go on forever. Stairs? Fuck right off."

"You two in position yet?"

Caden's voice came over their links without any warning, and Eilentes realised the channel had been open the whole time.

"Yep," said Eilentes. "And thanks for that, by the way."

"Wasn't me who killed the power grid."

Eilentes imagined Caden and the others having a good chuckle at their expense, and rolled her eyes at Norskine.

She went to the edge of the roof and glanced over the parapet that ran along it. Below them was a large public square, dotted with utilitarian stone benches and the ubiquitous native trees. The central feature of the square was the domed commerce hall, no different — as far as she could tell — from the commerce hall of any other Imperial world. She imagined the square would be full of kiosks and marquees on trading days.

"You look clear from up here," she said. "Nothing moving at all. There's some armour standing at the western edge of the square, but nobody with it. Looks like Viskr artillery."

"Keep an eye on that, Norskine," Daxon's voice said. "If it looks like it's going to be moved into play, light it up with a targeting laser. Bro says our air support is now being deployed by Fleet."

"Roger that."

"We're going in," said Caden.

While Eilentes set herself up, Norskine looked over the edge to watch the small figures below running towards the commerce hall. Eilentes kept her attention on what she was doing; the last thing she wanted now was a misfire at a critical moment.

She popped a small, matte-black tripod from the clips on her thigh guard, flicked out the legs, and set it down atop the small wall at the edge of the roof. Then she rested Ambrast on the tripod, marrying up the screw thread with the socket in the rifle. She tightened the nut as much as she felt necessary, and pressed the stud that told the rifle to skinprint. Ambrast's outer layer shifted until it closely matched the hue and texture of the wall, then locked in the pattern.

There was not much she could do to blend her own silhouette into the surroundings, so she took a scrim from one of her pouches and strung it up behind her, between two comms antennae. From the ground, it would hopefully look like miscellaneous rooftop junk. It was not exactly ideal, but as long as she was not visible from below as a distinct head and shoulders she was happy with that.

A good ten minutes had passed before movement to the west caught her attention. She lifted a spotting scope to her eye, and took a closer look.

Down on the ground, a group of Viskr had entered the square on foot. They were close to the armoured transport that carried artillery on its back, but as far as she could see they were not trying to move or use it.

She zoomed in for a closer look.

It was the clearest view she had had of Viskr in the flesh. Of course she had seen holo footage and images in training, and there had been those few times where she had seen blurred glimpses during combat and from her hide site on Woe Tantalum, but the only Viskr she had seen up close and personal had been the desiccated, ragged corpses left behind on Echo.

These Viskr were not half-degraded, in a crowd with humans, or darting quickly in and out of cover. They were alive, away from the fighting, and moving casually.

She studied one of them carefully. She remembered being taught that the old enemy had two genders, like humans, but she could not tell if it was a male or female she was looking at.

The Viskr had coppery skin, rough and deeply fissured as if it were made from old bark or thick, dried mud. Its head was a flattened diamond, the front side the deepest. The long axis of its skull was parallel with the shoulders, and its black eyes were placed only slightly above the line of a narrow mouth. On top of the head, two bony ridges ran from each brow to the back of the neck, bowed outwards. She could make out smaller crenelations and bumps arrayed in rows between them.

It reminded her of a fantastical cartoon character she recalled vaguely from childhood; a man with a pastry for a head. Only it had a gun, which it held in clawed hands. The pastry man, whatever he had been called, had never had a gun. Or claws.

She realised it was the general humanoid shape of the creature which made it look so strange to her; without evolutionary context, her mind tried its best to reconcile this unearthly biped with its model of humankind, and found the differences repellent. But it was not a relative or an off-shoot or a distant cousin. It had evolved somewhere else entirely, without any biological contact with man.

She wondered if that was what made the Viskr so easy to hate.

The Viskr's head and torso moved out of her view, and she dialled back the zoom to recapture it. When she did so, she saw the odd configuration of the leg bones. The ankles were much longer than they were in humans, giving the impression the alien might lurch forward at any moment, pouncing or springing into a run. It made the figure look predatory.

"Should maybe light them up?" Norskine was tapping a thin targeting laser against the palm of her gloved left hand.

"They don't look like much of a threat at the moment," said Eilentes. "If we call in a strike, it might just draw more of their buddies here."

Norskine nodded towards Ambrast. "You could take them out."

Eilentes considered the idea. The risk was that there might be others out of her line of sight who could make her position and sound the alarm. The benefit was that... well, she couldn't think of anything in particular.

"I think we should leave them to it for now. They're not enough of a threat to make us draw unwanted attention."

"If you say so," said Norskine. "So... anyway: what's the deal with you and Throam?"

"I wish I knew." Eilentes looked away, and continued to survey the square below. Every few seconds she cast her eyes back to check on the small squad of Viskr.

"You *are* sleeping with him, right?"

"I was. Not sure if I want to carry on with that, if I'm honest."

"Are you sure? He's one sexy man-beast."

"Oh, he is. But I know him from way back, and he's not changed at all."

"How do you mean?"

"We were together on the *Embolden*, for near enough a whole Solar. Turns out it was just sex to him. He left me to go work with Caden and didn't look back."

"Ouch, that's gotta hurt. Why are you back sleeping with him now then?"

"I don't know, Taliam. I guess because" — she paused momentarily, realisation dawning on her — "I guess because it's *easy*."

"So it is just sex then."

"I suppose. I do love him, I think. But it doesn't feel like it goes both ways."

"Get rid, Hon. Bro is free."

"I thought you two were—"

Norskine snorted. "He wishes!"

"You know, I think he does."

"Really?"

"You work together. How could you not know?"

"I just don't look at him that way. He's my bro, you know?"

"Clever."

"Thought it up all by myself."

"Well maybe— Hey, check it out."

Eilentes grabbed to the side for Norskine, caught her sleeve, and pulled her low and close.

"Where?"

"Over there." Eilentes pointed to the eastern corner of the square.

Another squad of Viskr were marching hurriedly from the end of a road, passing through a row of bollards and entering the square itself. A gangling polybot came after them, its movements mechanical yet sinuous.

"This place is starting to get crowded," Norskine whispered. "Crusty central."

Eilentes closed her eyes for a brief moment, considering the tactical situation below.

"Okay, we light up the armour."

"You sure?"

"If anything, it will keep them occupied. Caden will be coming back out of that hall any minute now, and the last thing we want is for his team to end up stuck between two lines of fire."

"What if they make our position?"

"We'll have to cross that bridge when we come to it."

"Seems like we'll already have burned it by then."

"Cute. You've got the laser. Do the honours?"

Norskine leaned against the inside of the wall, and shone the targeting laser at the artillery. She managed to splash it across the top of the armour, where the troops on the ground would have no view.

"Guess we wait?" Eilentes said.

"Yep."

The wait was not a long one. Eilentes heard a muffled roaring sound build steadily behind them, then suddenly a MAGA atmospheric gunship was directly overhead, its vertical lift turbines blasting hot air down onto the rooftop. It hovered for a moment, moved over the square, then tilted forward and sideways, circling the armour nose-first.

The Viskr to the east ran to cover. Those by the armour scrambled for cover too, one of them loosing a rocket first. The rocket made it just half way to the gunship before it was shot down.

The gunship pulled back, lifted its nose, and

fired off a missile of its own.

Even their rooftop trembled with the force of the explosion below, and a column of smoke billowed from the crater which remained.

"Yes!" Norskine shouted.

The gunship hovered for a moment more before heading north, strafing its chain guns along a street beyond their view.

"—I say again: Eilentes, report."

Eilentes tapped her link. "Caden; Eilentes. MAGA just took out that armour. There are some Viskr in the square now, but nothing we can't handle from up here."

"Glad to hear it. We're coming up now. Be advised we have non-combatants with us."

"Understood." She closed the channel. "They're coming back out. We need to start clearing that square."

"Finally," said Norskine.

They both leaned on the wall, peering over the top. Eilentes took hold of Ambrast, placed her eye to the scope, and found her first target.

"One," she said. In the square below, a Viskr soldier dropped from his inadequate cover and sprawled on the ground.

"Two." Another Viskr dropped dead.

"Three—"

"Hey, we got a new problem," Norskine said, tapping her shoulder.

"What...?"

Eilentes followed Norskine's gaze, and saw immediately what that problem was.

The best part of a platoon was rolling into the square from the north road, accompanied by a column of crawlers. The commandos marched alongside the vehicles, not one of them as tall as the crawlers' oversized wheels.

On the west corner, skulkers had rolled up to the crater and rattled around it as if quizzical about what had occurred there. The polybot that had arrived with the smaller squad gambolled across to them, rummaging through the mangled debris and chattering to itself.

"Okay," said Norskine. "*Now* it's Crusty central."

Eilentes hit her link. "Caden, you might want to hold your position for a moment. Either that, or hurry the fuck up."

"What's the problem?"

"You're about to have company. Lots of company."

Norskine pointed again, and Eilentes looked down. Caden and his group were already emerging from the commerce hall.

"Location and disposition?"

"Other side of the commerce hall, coming into the square now. They do seem to be focused on the crater we just made."

"Brilliant."

"Can you get into our building from down there?"

"I think so. There are doors this side."

"They may well be insecure. When we came through the building, it looked like the work force had left in a hurry."

"Okay. So we run for it."

"Got you covered."

Eilentes looked down, and saw Caden, Throam, and the others. Civilians in rich-looking fabrics ran with them, guided along by Daxon and Bro. Bruiser was now in the rear, watching warily for any opposition.

They ran out of her line of sight, and there was a moment in which she was sure something must have gone wrong.

"We're in," Caden said. "Going to get off the ground floor. Keep eyes on the square, and don't be seen."

"Bit too late for that," said Norskine.

From below, Eilentes heard a horrible noise, somewhere between the wailing of a distressed baby and the honking of a proximity alarm. She looked towards the source of the sound and saw the polybot bounding across the open space of the square. It was making a beeline right for them.

"Can those things climb?" She asked.

"Yes," said Norskine. "And it will kill us if it gets up here."

"They're starting to look this way," Eilentes said. "Looking to see what it's screaming about."

"Fuck 'em," said Norskine. "We've got the high ground."

"You're right." Eilentes wasted no more time. She was back at the wall again, cradling Ambrast, taking shot after shot.

"Four. Five. Six."

"Leave some for me!"

"Seven. You have to kill that damned robot. Eight. Nine."

"Oh fuck, yeah."

Eilentes was peripherally aware of Norskine moving away from the edge, and heard her stand. Then moving off down the roof, towards the west end of their edge. Out of the corner of her eye, she saw Norskine lean over the wall, with her assault rifle held in front of her.

"I see it," Norskine said. "It's reached the wall."

Eilentes scanned the square quickly, made sure

the Viskr below were still in disarray, and risked sticking her head over the edge to glance down.

The polybot was below, already climbing the wall halfway between her and Norskine. It twittered and honked angrily, smashing its own footholds into the stone with the ends of its six appendages. Eilentes imagined it could do much worse to a soft human body.

Norskine opened up, and the robot's front right leg snapped back from the wall. The last section of the limb fell away, tumbling back to the ground, and the polybot jerked its small, angular head towards the private.

"Oh balls," said Norskine.

The polybot came faster, turning towards her and marching steadily up the sheer face of the building with an iron will.

Eilentes let go of Ambrast, leaving the long range rifle on the tripod, and popped her assault rifle off its mag-tag. She fired on the polybot.

This time, its two front left limbs took the brunt of the damage. They remained intact, but were clearly disabled. They dangled limply down, the middle one banging against the rear leg.

The polybot paused its ascent, snapped its head towards Eilentes, and screeched.

She ducked back behind the wall as rounds from below began to pepper the building. Norskine had retreated to cover too, and the pair of them looked at each other.

"Fall back?" Eilentes shouted.

"Fucking yes we fall back!"

They crawled forward a few metres until they were out of the line of sight from the ground, then ran for the opposite wall.

She heard the polybot crash over the edge of

the roof before they had reached the far side, and brought her rifle up as she whirled around to face it.

The polybot looked as angry as any machine she had ever seen. It reared on its hind legs, taller than a person, and waved the remains of its other limbs in an intimidating display. Eilentes wondered if it had been programmed to scare the shit out of its enemies, or if this was something it had come up with all by itself.

Norskine opened up on it, and Eilentes followed her lead.

The polybot dropped flat, limbs out wide, and scuttled towards them. Most of the shots missed, slicing the air above it, and it was almost on them before it reared up again. The sharp, broken end of a front limb slashed past — a hair's breadth from Norskine's face — and Eilentes backed away until her legs hit the wall behind her.

Then the polybot seemed to get smaller and more distant.

Bruiser heaved, tugging on one of the polybot's rear limbs, swung it around his body once, twice, and let go.

The polybot sailed through the air, spinning around in a clumsy cartwheel, and disappeared over the edge of the roof. Seconds later, the unmistakeable sound of breaking things came from the square far below.

Eilentes stowed her assault rifle, found her empty hands were trembling, and clasped them together.

"You okay?"

It was Caden's voice. She looked around, and realised the others had all come to the roof.

"Just about." She went to recover Ambrast.

"So. Many. *Stairs.*" Bro was wheezing, his hands on his knees.

"Told you before; get in the fucking gym," Norskine said. But she still went over and placed her hand on his shoulder.

Throam nudged Caden's arm. "We can't stay here. It's a death-trap. Even if they don't follow us up, they'll be arranging an air-strike."

"I know, let's get mov—"

The square rang with the rattle of large-calibre chain guns, and within seconds everyone on the roof was covering their ears.

Eilentes was already at the edge of the roof, and looked out across the space.

In the corner of the square where the Viskr had been waiting with their artillery, a Gorilla platform was filling the entire intersection. Beneath one of its huge metal fists were the shattered remains of a skulker. The Viskr machine — so capable of reducing a human to mincemeat in seconds — was nothing but scrap metal beneath the weight of the autonomous MAGA vehicle.

The platform dropped its shoulders and reoriented its chain guns. Eilentes covered her ears again, just in time to muffle the sound of thousands of rounds per minute, and watched the impacts rake through the platoon near the commerce hall. The Viskr crawlers tried to manoeuvre amongst their own troops, unable to retreat quickly enough, and one was shredded right before her eyes when the Gorilla's rounds tore through it.

Eilentes felt the rooftop tremble beneath her feet, and looked to the east. Another Gorilla platform was entering the square, lumbering on its front arms and shorter, stockier rear drive limbs.

The Viskr were being hemmed in.

The second Gorilla straightened its arms, raising its body, and fired off a series of shots from its ventral cannon. The rest of the crawlers were blown to pieces, knocking down their accompanying soldiers.

"Oh yeah, we've got the high ground all right," she heard herself say.

– 11 –
## Roll Out the Tanks

They were almost back on the ground floor when the entire building rattled with the force of a series of explosions. Dust fell through the stairwell, and beyond its thin walls Caden heard the shattering of a thousand window panes.

"What the hell was that?"

"Sounded like shelling," said Daxon. "Almost on top of us."

They hurried downwards, Bro's voice the only sound on the group channel. He cursed each flight of stairs they descended.

"Oh hell," said Caden, as he emerged cautiously from the stairwell on the ground floor.

Around him, he could see that all the windows had been blown in on the one side of the building facing out into the square. Most of the glass on the other side had been broken outwards by the force of the blast. The air hung thick with dust and smoke.

Partitions and desks were strewn across the floor, and he could see several small fires in amongst them. Flaming debris had been carried in by the explosion. Two of the pillar walls between the windows had collapsed inwards, spilling chunks of concrete on the ground, and the tall double doors were now smouldering fragments.

"Tell our passengers to go back up a few floors while we check this out," Caden said.

He waited while the message was passed back to the civilians from the commerce hall. Despite half of them being Eyes and Ears operatives, and the other half the leaders of the city, not one of them had thought to rescue a link of their own before fleeing to their shelter.

"What a mess," said Eilentes.

"I'm more worried about *that*."

Caden pointed out into the square. In the far left corner, where the Viskr armour had stood just a half hour before, five polybots picked over the twisted wreck of a Gorilla platform. Smoking craters pitted the ground around it.

"They shelled the square," said Daxon. "Making the most of their losses."

Norskine moved up next to them. "Where's the other Gorilla? There were two."

"MAGA must have pulled it back," said Caden. "No point losing two assets."

"We should get out of here before those polybots hear us," said Throam. "Don't fancy being torn limb from limb today."

"I hear that," said Caden. He moved back to join the others.

Bro was straining to hear the expeditionary comm through his link. "Sounds like we've taken some heavy fire all around," he said. "But air support is starting to turn the tide in our favour."

"Still good on the el-zee?" Caden asked.

"Yeah, I'm pretty sure the landers are right where we left them."

"Okay, then we go back the way we came. Simplest and quickest route. Someone go up and get the—"

"Think again," Throam shouted, and pushed over a desk. "Cover!"

Caden saw the counterpart was already crouching behind the desk, with the top of it between his body and the windows which faced away from the square. He looked out through the broken panes and saw movement in the street beyond.

Caden had his back pressed against a concrete pillar just before the bullets started flying.

He risked a very brief glance, and instantly absorbed the situation. The street they had come down — the same one they were in when the fighter had crashed above them — was filled with Viskr ground troops. Over their heads, he had seen the shiny, circular rings of skulkers bringing up the rear.

"More problems here," shouted Bruiser.

Caden looked straight out of the square-facing windows, the same windows to which he was completely exposed by his cover, and saw the polybots bounding towards the building.

"Oh *fuck*."

"Contacts, both sides," shouted Daxon. "Bruiser: facing rear. Take those polybots down. Everyone else: eyes front. Viskr have ranged weapons, take them first. Skulkers can wait."

Ambrast was already loosing rounds, and Caden saw one Viskr after another falling to the ground. He could not even say where Eilentes was shooting from — she had found a hide somewhere without him even noticing she had moved away.

"Eilentes," he said into his link. "Where *are* you?"

"Upstairs with your friends." Another Viskr fell. "Five. Someone needs to look after them, right?"

Bruiser's GPMG rattled continuously. The Rodori held it in both hands, lumbering casually out to the square through the empty doorway. One of the polybots collapsed before it was even a quarter of the way across the square. It tried to continue towards him, crawling on broken limbs, then shuddered and stopped moving.

"We need to keep them back from the junction," shouted Daxon. "Keep it a sterile area. They get to this road in front of us, they can spread out."

"Keep them in the funnel. Gotcha," shouted Caden.

"Heads up," Throam yelled. "Rocket."

Caden ducked behind his pillar and watched as a rocket-propelled grenade whooshed past him and flew out into the square. It exploded low, against the side of the commerce hall.

Ambrast barked, and the soldier carrying the launcher went down.

Caden could see Bruiser outside the building, still firing at the remaining polybots. They were trying to outflank him, splitting into two groups, and he lost valuable time feeding in a fresh ammo belt.

"Bruiser, you good?" Caden shouted into his link.

"These polybots will reach me before I take them down," he growled.

"Throam. Bruiser needs a hand."

"You got it," Throam said. He crawled towards the back windows, keeping low, ensuring he could not be seen from the street out front.

"Norskine," Daxon said. "Take up the slack."

Throam got to his feet, hunkered down, and

went outside to join Bruiser.

"Best out of five," he said.

"I already have one," said the Rodori.

"I like a challenge," said Throam. He mounted his mini-gun on its gauntlet, and gripped the firing bar. "Let's play."

Caden was deafened by a loud bang. He saw Throam being thrown forwards onto his face, and something sharp whizzed past Caden's head and bit deep into the pillar.

∘ ∘ ∘

"Another group of fighters, aft starboard."

"Hold it together, Tactical," said the XO. "They'll give up with that soon. It's simply not going to work."

Thande watched the Viskr fighters blip out of existence on the main battle map, chewed up by the turrets on *Disputer* and the other ships which shared the flak shadow of her Guardian Shield. It was clear to her that the Viskr commanders were trying any mad scheme their battle computers suggested in their efforts to break through the Navy blockade.

How the tables have turned, she thought.

"What lines of sight do we have?"

Tactical smiled to herself. "Two frigates, three corvettes, one mid-frame cruiser."

"Anyone local to us with the same lines?"

"Yes Ma'am, I believe both *Fugue* and *Chivalrous* will also have firing solutions."

"COMOP; invite them to join us in a bombardment of that cruiser."

"Yes Captain... they're standing by."

"Tactical: lasers on their point defence sensors, and hit them with our gauss guns."

"Lighting them up, firing on rails."

Thande felt the soft, almost gentle repercussive thumps of the port-side rail guns firing over and over. She knew that out in the black, the other two Imperial ships were doing exactly the same thing.

On the battle map, the hologram of the enemy cruiser began to pull to one side. The ship rolled its long axis, trying to narrow its profile to protect itself from damage.

Good luck with that, thought Thande. You've got incoming on three trajectories.

"Status on their turrets?"

"Over-capacity, Captain. They're struggling to knock out our slugs."

"Maintain salvoes, and fire off a ship-to-ship."

An audible alert pipped twice, and she knew that several decks below them a missile had been loosed from a launch tube.

Seconds passed, then the holographic ship turned yellow. A data bracket around the cruiser showed it as an inert contact.

"Excellent work, Tactical. Now let's hit those frigates."

"Already working on it, Ma'am."

"Captain," said COMOP. "Message *Stoic* Actual. All enemy destroyers in the atmosphere have been shot down."

"Excellent news. Air support will be much easier without those guns to worry about."

"Incoming wreck!" Tactical shouted.

Thande snapped her attention back to the battle map and saw the danger immediately. The ruined hulk of a Viskr corvette barrelled straight towards the outer rim of their Guardian Shield.

"Helm, ready on evasive manoeuvres."

"Ready Ma'am."

"Impact in five seconds," said Tactical.

The battle map showed the collision in real-time. It was soundless, and disregarded the inevitable debris, but Thande got a sense of the energy of the collision. The corvette concertinaed against the solid umbrella of the Shield, and she imagined it spraying out plumes of burning plasma and catapulting buckled hull plates into the darkness.

The great dish started to tip.

"Now, Helm! Move us now."

"Evasive manoeuvres," Helm said. "Yaw minus ten, pitch minus thirty-five, full reverse."

"*Arbiter* reports contact with the stem," said COMOP. "Minor hull damage for them, but the Shield might not be able to reorient itself."

"We're clear, Captain. Still got eighty-five percent cover, not in danger of a collision."

"What about the *Arbiter*?"

"They're still fully in the flak shadow. I'm afraid we lost our firing solutions on those frigates."

"Status of the Guardian Shield?" Asked Yuellen.

"It's struggling to get back into position," Tactical said. "It will get there, but we're going to be vulnerable for a while. Down to fourteen percent exposure now."

"Can you get us any better than that?"

"The ship is too big, Commander. One way or another, we're going to have an end sticking out from the flak shadow."

Thande was about to swear when the first hits struck them. The curse turned into a shout of alarm, and she tracked the shots back on the battle map.

"Targets here and here; they know our cover is compromised. Prioritise them."

"Yes Ma'am. Locking what guns we have out

there on them now."

"The *Chivalrous* knows our situation, Captain," said COMOP. "They're firing on the targets too."

"It's not enough," Tactical said. "They're knocking our slugs down."

"I'm requesting any other unit with a firing solution to come to our aid."

"Usable turrets are at capacity," said Tactical.

"They fire off a missile now, and we're in trouble," said Thande. "COMOP, where the hell is our support?"

"I'm trying, Captain. Everyone has problems of their own right now."

"I have a spike!" Tactical shouted. "They've launched!"

"Helm, move us NOW!"

The helm officer had her hands at the controls, as if she had already decided to pull the same trick, and she fired a long burst from the ship's conventional drives. *Disputer* crawled into the flack shadow, her stern disappearing beneath the angled dish of the Shield, and her prow emerging into the danger zone on the other side.

"Another spike," Tactical said. "They're onto us. First missile is a miss. Repeat, first missile is a miss."

"Ready on turrets," said Thande.

"First missile is doubling back." Tactical's hands flashed across her holo. Sweat began to bead on her forehead. "It's a seeker."

"It's now within our defensive sphere," said the XO. "Take it down."

"Interceptors firing," said Tactical.

"*Arbiter* has taken out the second missile, Captain," COMOP said. "They're telling me we have multiple incoming on our blind side."

Thande considered this for a split second. Positioned as they were, there was no way the ship would be able to take down multiple missiles coming from the blind side of the Shield. It simply could not be done.

"Helm, reorient us to match the Shield's stem," said Thande. "We won't be able to contribute much, but we'll be even less useful if we're all dead."

"Aye Captain, moving us now."

The ship turned, angling itself into the shadow of the dish, taking up a position parallel to the Guardian's drive stem.

Five missiles appeared at various points along the out-tilted edge of the dish, curving towards *Disputer*. They sailed through the space where the ship had been, then their trajectories began to bend back into the flak shadow.

"Turrets are locking on," said Tactical. "This is going to be close."

"*Arbiter* also has firing solutions," said COMOP.

"Firing interceptors."

One by one, the missiles vanished from the battle map. The last one was within a kilometre before it blinked out. Thande bit her lip.

Helm looked up from her holo. "Ma'am, the Shield has reoriented. We're back in full shadow."

"Thank goodness for that. Get us back into the fight."

"Yes Captain. I'm moving us back to our original position."

"Captain?"

"Go on, COMOP."

"I'm... I'm getting some alarming reports from other ships. They say the *Nakrikhul Srabir* is heavily damaged, but it's now on the move."

"Why is that alarming?"

"Because they've turned their prow towards the planet," said COMOP. "They've turned towards the planet, and they're accelerating at hard burn."

○ ○ ○

Caden's ears were still ringing, but at least now he could hear the urgent yelling on the group channel.

He could see Throam moving on the ground, trying to get up. Bruiser was standing in front of him, spraying the polybots on his right with rounds. They skittered and leapt, one of them managing to avoid the fire, the other one taking it right in the face.

The other two were still coming, unopposed.

"Throam's down," he shouted. "Bruiser needs help."

"You stop firing forwards, we're gonna lose this position," Daxon said.

"Then you'd better get ready to retreat."

Caden dashed out through the rear doorway, into the square. He ran to Throam, and saw the back plate of his ammo can had been blown out. Black scorch marks covered the edges of a jagged hole in the plasteel casing, where something had forced open the incision left behind by the skulker fragment.

"You okay?"

"Winded," said Throam. "What the fuck was that?"

"Your ammo can," Caden said. "Looks like a round exploded inside it."

He dropped to one knee by Throam's side, raised his assault rifle, and fired several short bursts at the polybots on the left. The lead 'bot lost a front leg, continued regardless, lost another leg. Throam threw a grenade in front of them, and the damaged one was taken apart. The second 'bot was able to change direction in time, and it scuttled forwards more cautiously.

"Help me with this," said Throam.

Caden unclipped the ammo can from Throam's back armour plate, and the counterpart shrugged off the shoulder straps. The damaged can dropped to the ground.

Throam grabbed hold of the feed chute, and ripped it out of the can.

"This baby should still fire," he said.

He opened up with the mini-gun, and tore the cautious polybot to shreds. He kept firing until the rounds had been leached from the chute and the barrels of the gun rattled empty.

"Bruiser," said Caden.

He whirled around to assist the Rodori, but it was too late. The last polybot was already within striking range, and Bruiser was in the line of fire. The polybot reared up, and launched itself at Bruiser.

Caden was up and running before he had even decided what he would do.

Bruiser smashed one heavy fist into the polybot's head, knocking it sideways, but the 'bot stayed upright on four of its legs. The other two limbs slashed across each other, one slicing Bruiser's armour and the flesh of his forearm. The Rodori took a reflexive step backwards, pulled back his injured arm, and then launched himself forwards again.

Bruiser grabbed the 'bot around its body with both arms, pushing his whole weight forwards until it fell back against its hind legs. He tumbled to the ground with its long forelimbs wrapped uselessly around him, the sharp-tooled ends too far away to cause him harm. He grabbed its head in both hands, and twisted it clean off the body.

The polybot tried to get up at the same time as him, still lashing out with its limbs.

Caden riddled it with bullets. "Guess the control centre isn't in the head."

"We're getting pasted up here," Daxon shouted.

"Come on," said Throam.

Bruiser dropped the head, scooped his GPMG from the ground in one huge hand, and fell in beside Caden.

"You okay?"

"Just a scratch," said Bruiser.

"It's more than that, Biggun."

"But I will live."

They passed back into the building, and Caden leapt for cover. The Viskr in the street opposite looked as though they had gained numbers, not lost them.

"Reinforcements are on the way," Bro said. "We just need to hold out for few more minutes."

Daxon's voice came over the link. "What chumps are going to invite themselves to this party?"

Bro sounded amused. "Crazy ones."

Caden moved forwards to gain a better position. With their rear no longer at risk of being taken apart by the polybots, his pillar was no longer a prime spot.

He dipped out of cover and fired, alternating randomly with Norskine and Daxon, then with Bro and Throam.

The Viskr were unwilling to give up the street. Some of them were firing from behind mounds of their fallen comrades, others had almost reached the junction. The skulkers rolled forwards in stages. With their flesh allies keeping to cover on each side of the street, they would have a clear run to the building when they finally decided to advance.

"This is not good," said Daxon. "Bro, where the fuck is our backup?"

"I think that might be it behind them."

Caden risked a slightly longer moment out of cover to peer through his scope, timing matters so that Norskine and Daxon were both firing.

A man he could only describe as a grizzly great monster was behind the skulker line, brazenly jogging towards the killers as if they were only large toys. He was carrying something in his hand. Caden caught a glimpse of what looked like a metal rebar, before it was whirled around, brought up in a two-handed grip above the man's head, and driven like a stake through the heart of one of the machines.

The skulker's rings were immobilised, and it tipped over — uncontrolled — until the end of the rebar caught the ground and sent the machine wobbling helplessly towards a wall.

Caden ducked back into cover.

"What in the worlds did I just see?"

"That was Bear Mtenga."

"You know him?"

"Beardy black guy the size of a house, taking on skulkers hand-to-hand? Could only be him," said Daxon. "Guy's a fucking legend."

Caden realised the patter of bullets ripping through the walls and furnishings around their cover had ceased. He could still hear gunfire — in fact there was more of it now — but it was not aimed at them.

A new battle had started out in the streets.

○ ○ ○

Captain Thande watched with building horror as the huge, battered hull of the *Nakrikhul Srabir* hurtled past their Guardian Shield, headed straight towards Mibes.

"Impact point?"

"Ground Zero will be the city of Naddur, Captain," said Tactical. "It'll be rubbed off the map."

"Helm; lay in a pursuit course. Full burn."

"Aye Ma'am."

"What are you hoping to achieve?" Commander Yuellen stepped to Thande's side, his expression quizzical. "If we missile them, the capital will be pelted with radioactive debris."

"We're not going to use missiles," said Thande.

"Engines are at capacity, Captain," Helm called. "But they've got too big a lead. We're losing them."

"Keep going Helm. COMOP, have the other ships cover us. We absolutely have to survive the next few minutes."

"Aye. Sending now."

"Helm, what's the gap?"

"One hundred klicks, Ma'am, and widening."

"That ship looks like it's lost," said Thande. "I think we should give them a hand finding their way."

"Captain?"

"Spool up the GNGs. Make ready to open a wormhole right in front of them."

"Oh... *yes* Ma'am."

The helm officer smiled, her fingers dancing across her holo.

"Opening a wormhole at full burn?" The XO

looked both shocked and impressed. "That's pretty desperate, if you don't mind me saying so."

"I don't mind at all, Commander. It *is* desperate."

"GNGs are ready Captain. Where should I send them?"

"I don't really care," said Thande.

"I hear the Tithian Nebula is worth a visit," said Yuellen.

"Works for me, Commander. Helm; the Tithian Nebula it is."

"Yes Captain," Helm chuckled. "Opening wormhole."

On the battle map, Thande opened a pane to show the real-time view from the forward sensors. She saw the aft end of the *Nakrikhul Srabir* moving away from her, its engines flaring brightly, pushing it hard towards the planet.

Ahead of the Viskr capital ship, just visible around the edges of its hull, she could make out the familiar spatial disturbances which heralded the formation of a new wormhole.

"They're trying to turn," said Tactical. "Too much velocity; they won't make it."

Thande watched as the wormhole's aperture expanded, throwing out the apparent disc of its event horizon. The *Srabir* fired its starboard manoeuvring thrusters, killed its port engines, and — Thande figured — was probably firing its forward retro engines as well. The ship began to turn, slowly, but continued to hurtle straight into the wormhole's waiting maw.

"They've clipped it," shouted Tactical.

Most of the *Srabir* vanished into the horizon of the wormhole, and was catapulted across the galaxy. But the prow — with its sensor arrays and cannons and blocky armour — was sliced clean off where it hit the conceptual edge of the event horizon.

The front end of the ship tumbled off to one side, spinning away from *Disputer* and leaving a trail of debris and fading plasma fires behind it. Orange-rimmed lines were plainly visible to Thande as she watched it roll; the edges of bulkheads and decks which had been melted through by direct exposure to an energy boundary bordering on the infinite.

A cheer filled the command deck, and she sat back heavily in her chair.

"Tactical; what's the level of threat from that piece?"

"Negligible, Captain. It's lost all armour integrity, being open at one end like that. And it's now on a trajectory that will see it burn up in the atmosphere."

"Excellent."

"New updates from the fleet, Ma'am," said CO-MOP. "Viskr forces are disengaging. Looks like they're abandoning the fight now they've lost their capital ship."

"And abandoning their ground forces?"

"It certainly seems that way."

"Also excellent."

○ ○ ○

Mayhem was the only word Eilentes could think of to describe the scene in front of her. Absolute mayhem.

The Viskr were now being pushed back from the building that sheltered Caden and his companions, pushed back by what Eilentes could only describe as a wall of fury. A platoon of Tankers seemed to have come from nowhere.

"Holy shit," she shouted. "Look at those guys go! Bro, why didn't you tell us they were gonna roll out the tanks?"

Eilentes knew of Tanker Regiment, of course. But wherever this unit had popped up from, she had had no idea any of their kind had been deployed to the surface.

She felt almost sorry for the Viskr.

Outside in the street, the second Gorilla from the square had also turned up. It trudged slowly but steadily toward the junction, chain guns sterilising the ground ahead of it, its head and shoulders almost level with her window.

Opposite the Gorilla, on the far side of the junction, Tankers already occupied the first two floors of the buildings on either side of the road. The Viskr who were fool enough to try and retreat that way were shot from the windows and doorways.

Across the junction from Eilentes, in the street where the skulkers had mustered, the majority of the Viskr unit was now trapped. The Tanker who Daxon had identified as Bear Mtenga was back with friends, and they had cut off any hope of retreat to the rear. The last of the skulkers whirred around in a panic, throwing up from the ground the broken remains of those which had already been smashed by grenades and rockets.

"That is fucking beautiful," she heard Throam say.

She watched as the massive soldiers took the Viskr unit apart piece by piece. She had to agree; as brutal as it looked, it was certainly a sight to admire.

Everyone beneath her downstairs had stopped firing. But then, with the armour-plated, musclebound fist of the Empire fighting on their side in the street, there was not much more that they could contribute other than wasting ammunition.

She heard Caden's voice over the group channel. "Hey, Throam."

"Yeah?"

"Remember when I said you looked tiny next to Bruiser, and you said non-humans didn't count?"

"Yeah...?"

"*Those* guys make you look tiny."

"Go fuck yourself," she heard Throam say.

She smiled before she could stop herself.

Her face fell again when she heard a shrieking whine cross from right to left.

"Blitzer!" Someone shouted from below.

She caught a glimpse of a triangular wedge hurtling by, swooping low between the buildings, then in less than a second the drone was gone from her view. She popped her head cautiously out of an empty window frame and peered after it.

Down the street, the drone finished its pass and stopped dead. It rotated, hovered for a second, then accelerated hard back down the street, the guns on its three points raking the ground and scattering the Tankers below. Eilentes saw three of the giant soldiers fall to the ground.

"It's going to cut them to pieces," said Bro. "Those things look for organic bodies."

"What can we do?" That was Caden.

"Too fast for rockets." Daxon.

"What about the Gorilla?" Throam.

"Again, too fast."

Eilentes cradled Ambrast close to her chest, and patted the metal with her free hand.

"Time to earn your name," she said.

○ ○ ○

Throam saw Caden's jaw drop, and the Shard

pointed up past the top edge of the window frame.

Throam followed his gaze. "Is that... Eilentes?"

Caden nodded. "Uh huh."

"Did she just jump out of the building?"

"Uh huh."

"What the hell is she doing?"

"Just hitching a ride," Eilentes said over his link. "Need a long, straight shot to take this thing down."

"She's gone mad," said Caden.

This time it was Throam who nodded. He craned his neck, now losing sight of Eilentes as she clambered into position atop the Gorilla.

"Actually, I think she'll be okay," said Daxon. "That Blitzer should ignore her, just as long as it thinks she's part of the Gorilla platform."

"Are you sure about that?" Throam asked.

"Well..."

"Daxon!"

"Reasonably sure?"

Throam looked back to the Gorilla, and saw Ambrast's long barrel appear over the top of its head. The Gorilla was still advancing, very slowly, and the barrel waved from side to side in time with the gentle rolling and lurching motion.

"Can you make the shot, Eilentes?" Caden asked.

"Just... a matter... of timing," she replied.

The drone screeched down the street again, passing over the Gorilla. Tankers fired futilely after it, their shots all missing. The Blitzer was far too fast for them. It reached the far end of the road, turned in a tight vertical loop, flipped over, and soared back for another pass.

"Any moment now..." Eilentes' voice came through the link. "Wait for it..."

The drone reached the other end of the street, looped, and—

Ambrast barked.

"It's a miss," Eilentes shouted. "It's coming back for another sweep."

The drone shrieked back again, reached the intersection, and again stopped dead. It hovered in the air, turned, then headed down the street opposite Throam and the others, searching for new targets.

Throam leaped from the building, knocking fragments of broken glass from the window frame as he went, and landed on the street in front of the Gorilla.

"Bruiser!" He shouted. The Rodori scrambled after him.

He heard Caden shout. "What are you doing?"

The drone was still heading away from them, battering the street with rounds. Throam ignored Caden and ran into the road, over to the fallen Tankers. He grabbed the nearest one under the arms, started to pull him back towards the building, and at once regretted picking the closest one instead of the smallest one.

Bruiser grabbed a wrist of each of the others, and hauled them across the ground unceremoniously.

"Careful, Bruiser," Throam said.

"They have armour."

"Hurry it up down there, you idiots," Eilentes said. "It's heading back again."

The whine of the Blitzer's turbines was growing louder and louder, and Throam pulled with all his might. The heavy Tanker's legs dragged along the ground, his armour catching on debris and making him even harder to move.

Throam pushed himself beyond his limits.

He collapsed through the window, and Daxon, Bro and Caden came to help. Between them they almost lifted the Tanker, dragging him off Throam and into the relative safety of the room.

"Good job," said Caden.

"Heads up," Eilentes said. "It's nearly on you."

"Take cover," Daxon said.

Throam hid like the others as the Blitzer approached the building. It disappeared out of view, too high up to be seen from inside the ground floor, and he heard the change in pitch as it looped and flipped.

"It's off again," Eilentes said.

She went quiet.

"Euryce...?" Throam asked.

He heard a *crack*, and the drone jerked to one side. It rolled over and over, flipping as it sailed towards the ground, then hit the stone flags with a hollow crash.

"Got you, you little bastard," said Eilentes.

"You beauty!" Daxon shouted.

"Man, that is one hell of a woman you have there Throam," said Bro.

Throam smiled back at him. "It sure is."

"It's looking clear from up here," Eilentes said. "Think we're good for the moment."

"Come on down," said Caden. "I keep thinking you're going to fall off that thing."

It was a good few minutes before she found a way to climb down safely and made it to the ground. By the time she was standing back with Caden and Throam some Tankers had gathered with them around the front of the Gorilla, and others were tending to their injured squad mates. They cheered her as she hopped off the machine.

One of them stepped towards her.

"Lady, that was some nice shooting."

"It wasn't anything special," she said.

"Listen: I've seen some crazy shit in my time, and that was outstanding."

"It was an exceptional shot," Caden assured her.

"That made me horny," said Throam.

All eyes turned to him.

"Just saying."

"I'm Sergeant Zolyn Feior." The Tanker continued as if Throam had never spoken. "And this bunch of apes is Downfall One-Four."

Daxon gave them all a sloppy salute, and they stared back at him. Throam decided they were not the saluting type.

"Where you folks headed?"

"We're on our way back to our el-zee," said Caden. "I have some important people I need to get off the surface real quick."

"Seeing as how you guys pulled our buddies out of harm's way, and took care of that fucking horror for us, it'd be a pleasure to see you safely back to your landers."

"Where's the Bear?" Daxon asked. "I want to meet that guy."

"Bear Mtenga don't stop for nobody," said one of the Tankers, and he spat on the ground.

"He'll be off finding more Crusties to gut," said Feior. "Can't get enough of it, the crazy bastard."

"Well, anyone willing to go up against a skulker armed only with a metal bar is okay in my book," said Daxon.

Throam caught sight of movement behind the wall of troopers, and nudged Bruiser.

"Check it out, big guy. They have one of you."

A Rodori was bringing up the rear, trudging towards them with the last stragglers from the Tanker squad, carrying a heavy flame unit with the same casual ease as Bruiser.

"What's your name?" Caden asked.

"I am *The Burning Flash of Envy's Escape*," said the Rodori.

Caden turned to Feior instead. "What's his name?"

"We just call him Burner. It suits him."

Throam watched as Burner trundled past the humans and walked straight up to Bruiser. They faced each other, silent, and Throam began to wonder if they were about to settle some old score.

Bruiser said something, and his link either declined to translate, or it was not able to.

Burner said something back, and his link remained silent too.

Throam murmured to Caden. "What was that about?"

"No idea."

"Never mind that," said Eilentes. "Let's get the hell out of here."

"Sergeant," said Caden. "Just give me a minute to round up my guests, and we'll be right with you."

"Take your time," said Feior. "Word is the Crusties are falling back all over the city."

"Two minutes," said Caden. He headed back into the building, towards the stairwell.

Throam went over to Eilentes, wrapped an arm around her, and squeezed her to him gently.

"That was amazing," he said.

She looked up at him and smiled coldly.

"Now who's the bad-ass hero?"

"You are," he said.

"Size isn't everything then."

She pulled away from him, pushing his arm off her, and headed after Caden.

"Where you going?"

"Left some kit up there," she said.

"Size isn't everything?"

Throam looked over his shoulder and saw one of the Tankers staring at him, a pained expression on his face.

"She knows it is really," Throam joked.

"I don't know fella, sounded like she meant it to me."

"Well... it still is."

"Damned right," said the Tanker. "Don't be telling me my whole fucking life has been a waste."

"No, man. You're a machine."

Throam meant it. Like most of his unit, the Tanker was taller even than he, and his armour looked as though it were straining to contain his body. Throam could feel heat radiating from him, and for once he imagined what it must be like for Eilentes when she was close to him.

"Ragnar Otkellsson," said the Tanker. "They call me Overkill."

"Rendir Throam."

"What do you bench, Throam?"

"Four-ten kilos at one gravity."

Otkellsson smiled. "Four-ten. What you using?"

"Just the usual. Dianabol, test, tren."

"That it?"

"That's it."

"Child's things," said Otkellsson. "If you don't burn, your muscles won't learn."

He fished in a pouch, and tossed Throam a

sealed plastic bag.

"What is it?"

"The missing piece of the puzzle. Use that when you train and you might just push five-hundred. You can thank me later."

○ ○ ○

"The Viskr have fled the system," said Thande. "Not only that, but the reports we're getting from Laeara suggest they're pulling back from most of the border conflicts too."

Caden clasped his hands together, and felt his face adopt a smile before he could stop it.

"That is the best news I've had all day."

"Glad I could cheer you up. I take it everything went well down there?"

"Well enough. I met my objectives, in any case. I'm afraid the city is in a bit of a mess though."

"Hardly your fault."

"True. The remaining Viskr ground forces have surrendered, so hopefully there won't be much more damage. You know: once the fires go out."

"We'll have a full debriefing when you dock."

Caden decided not to tell her what he thought about having a debrief instead of a hot shower. But he had to admit, the thought of being back in the clean cocoon of *Disputer* was actually quite appealing.

"I'll let you get on," she said. "I'm sure you're eager to leave the battlefield behind."

"You're not wrong, Captain," said Caden. "I'm pretty much sick of Mibes now, and I have lost time to make up for."

"Is there somewhere you'd like us to drop you?"

He thought about all the different places Maber Castigon might have found to hide. All the many,

many worlds.

"That's the problem. I have no idea where I'm going next."

## – 12 –
# THE NATIVES ARE RESTLESS

Jidian Tarrow wanted to bang her head against the stupidly ornate desk. No, even better: she wanted very much to bang the proconsul's head against his stupidly ornate desk. That might actually provoke a useful reaction.

"If I might make a suggestion...?"

The proconsul's aide fixed her with a look that radiated contempt.

"Shard Tarrow, you were ordered only to protect the governing body from any threat posed by our disaffected citizens. If the proconsul wants your opinion, he will certainly ask for it."

Proconsul Kalistine did not bother to look up from his holo. He allowed his underling to swat the nuisance Shard back down.

Very well, she thought. It *is* your problem, after all.

She went back over to where Crathus was standing, and looked out through the panes of the closed balcony doors. At the gates directly across from them, safely outside the perimeter of the House of Governance, she could see an angry crowd gesturing aggressively and mouthing what she guessed were impolite protestations. She saw very few humans amongst them.

"More keep coming," said Crathus. "This will get much worse before it gets better."

Tarrow placed her hand on the counterpart's shoulder, and they looked at each other.

"That's how we like it."

Miall Crathus smiled.

"The new Serrofite representative has made a demand, Sir," the aide said.

Tarrow turned her back on the view.

Kalistine sounded aggrieved, as though the news were encroaching on his time. "They don't take hints, these people. What is it this time?"

"They are now calling themselves the Indigenous Peoples' Alliance, and state that they require an immediate cessation of all land clearance in the meadows."

"Ha!" Kalistine looked up from his holo, a smirk stretched across his face. "I suppose they want to move into the capital as well?"

"It would not surprise me at all, Sir."

The aide's smirk was a nastier reflection of Kalistine's.

"Kindly remind the representative of this 'Alliance' that my office will not hear Ordinary civilians. Like everyone else, if they wish to be heard they must petition one of the Raised to speak on their behalf."

"Of course, Proconsul."

And good luck finding a human of consequence who will stick their neck out for you, thought Tarrow.

"If they don't leave the vicinity of the House of Governance within one minute of being given this free advice, take stern measures to encourage them."

The aide bowed slightly before leaving the

room, wearing her satisfaction like a mask.

"You had something to say, Shard?"

Tarrow started. Proconsul Kalistine had not once asked to hear her thoughts since she had arrived with Crathus; not even to enquire what measures she wanted to put in place to ensure his own protection.

"I don't pretend to understand the fine details of this situation," she said. "But I have to wonder: why not give them back the territories they're asking for?"

"It's perfectly simple. They ceded the land to us when they accepted Imperial rule. This world is a protectorate now, and they are the subjects of Her Imperial Majesty. They'll do as they are told."

"It's a big planet. They don't seem to be asking for much of it back."

Kalistine inhaled deeply and sat back in his chair. He placed both hands on the edge of the desk, wide apart, and looked directly at Tarrow.

"Serrofus Major is already one of the most self-reliant worlds in the entire Empire," he said. "I want it to become *the* most successful, within my lifetime. Within my term. I want Maidre Shalleon and Ramm Stallahad and Damastion to look at us and wonder how we did it. Production is everything."

"So screw the natives, is that it?"

Kalistine smiled. "I wouldn't put it quite like that. They are perfectly entitled — under the laws they agreed to live by — to raise their objections through the proper channels."

Crathus snorted. Tarrow and Kalistine looked at the same time, and Tarrow saw that her counterpart was still gazing out through the windows, her back to the office.

"Your counterpart has something to say, perhaps?"

"Just clearing my throat, Proconsul," said Crathus.

Kalistine gave Tarrow a look which suggested she might like to keep her subordinate on a tighter leash in the future.

"These territories they want were being wasted," he said. "Do you know what they grow? The only thing they seem to grow? Weeds. Vast areas of the same weed, in endless monoculture. It's useless, yet they give great tracts of fertile land over to it."

"It's my understanding that it's not useless to them."

"Oh no, not at all. They hardly seem to be able to grow enough of it to burn up in all their barbaric little rituals. But of course what I mean is that it is not of any use to the Empire, and in this office *that* is what matters."

"So I gather."

Tarrow found herself liking the proconsul less and less with every passing second, and wondered how much trouble she might attract if her competence happened to slip just when his very life were at stake.

"Was that your suggestion then? To give them back the land?"

"Actually no. I was going to suggest it might be easier to resolve this if you simply raised one of the Serrofites."

This time, it was Kalistine who snorted.

∘ ∘ ∘

Castigon knew that something was wrong, he just could not say what it was.

Captain Borreto's warning about the unrest on

Serrofus Major had been the first Castigon had heard of it; he was not particularly interested in the political movements of the Empire these days. But he had seen plenty of civil discord in his time, and he knew instinctively that something different was happening here.

The people in the capital were not just dissatisfied. They were... well if there was a particular word for it, he did not know what that word was.

Whatever was going on it had so far worked to his advantage. Civic Security were being stripped away from their normal postings and redeployed to maintain order throughout the city. It had made his life so much easier, and he was not going to be ungrateful about that. Getting from the starport to the streets had seemed in his mind like it might be nigh on impossible. He had wasted hours on the journey from Lophrit thinking about how it might be accomplished, only to find the question barely had any meaning once he actually arrived.

He hurried through the streets, a hood pulled over his head and down almost to his eyes.

Castigon had heard of the Serrofites long ago, when he was still on active duty as a counterpart. The creatures' societies had been pre-industrial when the first human colony ships landed on their soil, but they were an intelligent, adaptable species, and they had quickly established meaningful communication with the settlers.

Clearly a lot had changed since then.

As he hurried through the town, he saw shops and other businesses run by Serrofite proprietors, with dual script on their signage and displays. Many of them were dark, the doors bolted and the window shades closed.

There were plenty of people out on foot — humans, for the most part — and they brushed past him often. They were quiet, hurried, and afraid. Whispers met his ears from the darker corners.

*Mastalekt*, that was what the natives called themselves. But only them. Everyone else called them Serrofites, reducing their culture to a geographical marker. The Imperial way made them a thing, which might one day be scooped up and placed where it was more convenient for that thing to be.

So had it been with him.

He reached the public square in the civic centre, and found it empty. He crossed straight through the space, not bothering to keep to the edges, hurried under the peristyle on the far side, and passed out through an arched exit. Ahead lay the House of Governance.

Now, he clung to the walls and the shadows they cast across the street. There was a crowd up ahead, congregated around the closed gates of the proconsul's compound. There would be many eyes watching from within.

The crowd was made up almost entirely of Serrofites. They teetered back and forth, looking as though their long, slender bodies were unstable on their double-footed legs. Many shades of blue and blue-grey skin combined to form a small, turbulent sea around the gates.

"*Ooracht!*" They shouted, again and again.

'Restitution,' his link informed him. The sentiment was certainly one Castigon could get on board with.

As he watched, the crowd began to simmer down. Someone was approaching from the main building, walking with slow dignity. The woman was tall and immaculately clad, her face impassive and features immobile. A bob of blonde hair framed her face.

She reached the gate, waited for the nearest thing to silence she would get, and called out across the crowd.

"His Excellency, the Proconsul of Serrofus Major, reminds you that Ordinary civilians may not petition his office—"

Anger rose from the crowd, the noise building up again. She held up one hand, and it dropped back down.

"The proper order of business, as I have told you before, is to address your concerns to a Raised citizen who will then negotiate terms on your behalf."

This time, the response was a wall of fury. It was almost a full minute before any single voice could be heard over the choir of dissent.

"There *is* none who would speak for us!"

Even through his link, the Serrofite's voice was like hot gravel dropping on cold glass.

"The same rules govern us all," the woman shouted back. "None will be favoured."

"No Ordinary will be favoured," the Serrofite retorted. "Favour is only for the Raised. And no *Mastalekt* shall ever be Raised."

The woman took a step back, and signalled to someone out of Castigon's line of sight. He had already guessed who that might be by the time a troupe of civic guards filed across in front of her.

"You have been given the only answer you will receive on this day," she shouted. "Return to your homes and your families, and consider well what your lives are worth."

"To you, they are worth nothing!" It was the same spokesman. "All we ask is that you stop burning the Sacred Meadows."

The woman, standing behind a pair of gates and a line of armed guards, stifled a snort of derision.

"You have one minute to leave peacefully," she called out.

Castigon noticed movement in the centre of the face of the House, and looked up. The balcony doors over the main entrance were open, and three figures had emerged into the light from the dark room beyond the threshold.

*She* was one of them.

The male was without doubt the proconsul of this world, dressed as he was in such finery. To his right stood two women; one a combative-looking counterpart, the other a Shard whose career he had once saved. So much for that.

"Thirty seconds."

Serrofites were beginning to leave, some grabbing on to others in attempts to convince them to make a stand.

"Twenty."

Here and there small scuffles broke out as the Serrofites disagreed violently on how best to make their point before the deadline.

"Ten seconds."

The guards brought up their rifles as one, and stepped back onto their right feet.

"Five, four, three, two, *one*."

Those who had stayed scrabbled for cover, fleeing the gates. The guards fired token shots into the ground, sending up plumes of dust. Not one Serrofite stood in defiance.

Castigon supposed idly that this display was exactly why they were no longer the masters of their own world.

The blonde woman clasped her hands behind her back, smiled a cold, satisfied smile, and turned on her heel. Castigon watched her walk back towards the House, and by the time he looked back to the balcony the doors were closing.

The whole compound, then, was on high alert already. He would need Tarrow to come to him.

○ ○ ○

Brant wandered casually to Tirrano's work station and tapped her gently on the arm. He was already walking away before she turned to look, suspended her holo, and went after him. She found him waiting in the agreed spot: an alcove on a barely-used corridor.

"A clandestine meeting," she said. "How romantic you've become."

"This is serious, Peras," he said. "Try to keep yourself under control."

"What is it now? Did he finally kill her?"

"No, I checked the feed just a few minutes ago. She's still in a coma, still just laying there."

"Then what's the problem?"

Brant hesitated. "Branathes is missing."

"Missing?"

"Yep. Can't find him anywhere."

"Did you check with admin?"

"Of course. He's not in Central Operations or his quarters, and he hasn't signed in or out of any other section for hours."

"People don't just suddenly disappear from a fortress," Tirrano said. "I mean we *are* in space."

"Amarist Naeb disappeared."

"Yeah, but she did it in a way nobody could possibly miss. She didn't simply vanish."

Brant shrugged, as if he could think of nothing to say to that.

"You think he knows we're onto him?" Tirrano asked.

"Could be."

"If he was going to flee, why would he not just finish her off on his way out the door?"

"Maybe he didn't flee," said Brant. "Maybe he left for another reason, and didn't want to draw attention by leaving a body behind. You know what he said before about drawing attention to her; it could be that was really his own anxiety talking."

Tirrano fell silent, her eyes flicking to and fro as she considered the idea. She looked up.

"Doctor Bel-Ures."

"Shit, I'd almost forgotten. Would he really go after her himself?"

"We have no idea how they work," Tirrano said. "For all we know it's only him and Naeb out there."

"What can we do about it?"

"Warn her of course. There must be someone we know in the Eyes and Ears centre on Meccrace Prime."

"But can we trust them? We don't know how far this thing extends."

"Okay, let's think this through. If he is an agent — a Rasa, like Naeb — then he is taking orders from someone. If they had other agents in the Meccrace system, surely they would just have one of *them* find her."

"Makes sense."

"But if he is going after her, then perhaps they don't have anyone there. We should inform E&E on Meccrace Prime. They can pick her up, get her family somewhere safe, and capture him when he arrives."

"Good idea. So what exactly are we going to tell

them?"

"The truth of course," Tirrano said. "Everyone needs to know about this."

"I meant in a way that doesn't make us look bored and crazy."

"Easy," she said. "Get that Shard to do it."

"The one who told us to make her safe in the first place, which we haven't done yet?"

"No... which *you* haven't done yet. I wasn't there."

"Thanks. Nice teamwork."

"It'll sound better coming from him. He's not so lowly as us. His role in this thing isn't quite so menial."

"Fine. I'll bite the bullet."

"We'd best get back," said Tirrano. "I don't know about you, but I have new data coming out of my arse."

∘ ∘ ∘

The sound of a dozen conversations dipped when Castigon entered the tavern, then rose again when the patrons had eyed him up and turned back to their own business.

He kept his hood up, looked around slowly, and walked to an empty spot at the bar.

The tavern was typical of city centre dives, the kind of establishment where he might meet people who could get things done. It was the sort of place in which he would have expected to find Kulik Molcomb obliterating his senses, back in the day. Way back before Castigon had killed the old drunkard on a dilapidated Low Cerin rooftop.

There seemed to be far too many dingy corners for the shape of the room, and a cloying drift of smoke and stim vapour hung in the air. Like Castigon, many of the customers had their heads or faces covered. Discretion appeared to be the normal order of business.

"First one's on the house," said the barkeep. He slammed a short tumbler down in front of Castigon, and filled it halfway from an unlabelled bottle.

"To your good health," said Castigon. He drained the glass, and regretted it immediately.

"Not local?"

He looked to his side, and saw that the man next to him was staring amusedly at Castigon's empty tumbler.

"Can't be, or you would have refused that piss. Arnaum: two proper drinks, if you would."

The barkeep came back, an entertained look about him, and poured out two shots from a less murky bottle.

"Health," they both said.

"So what's a fine outsider like yourself doing in a shit-hole like this?"

"Hey!" Arnaum said. The man shot him a look, and the barkeep wandered off muttering to himself.

"Just passing through on business," said Castigon.

"Aren't we all," said the man. "Name's Collis. I own an irrigation company. You might have seen the holo-ads?"

"Nope," said Castigon.

"You really aren't from around here. Well I'm just here to oversee, anyway. Try to get the lads back on schedule. Those fucking Serrofites are holding everything up, and it's costing me a fortune."

"Yeah, what's with that?"

"They always want the same thing. Ancestral

land back, more territory for growing their junk crops. Just seem to be getting a bit more bold this time. That Proconsul up on the hill should think about swatting a few of them back down to their proper level."

"It sounds like that would really help."

Castigon almost jumped from his stool when he realised a second figure was standing on his other side, uncomfortably close to him. The newcomer had a strangely intense look in his eyes, and a smile that could have hidden half a dozen meanings within itself.

"Worlds! You want to be careful who you sneak up on, friend."

"Apologies, Sir," said the newcomer. "I did not mean to startle you. My name is Pammon. Herik Pammon."

"What can I do for you, Herik Pammon?"

"Well, it's more a case of what I can do for Mister Collis here." Pammon aimed his distressingly frozen smile at Collis. "I couldn't help but overhear his complaints."

"You're talking about the Serrofites," Collis said.

"Yes I am, Mister Collis. My... *friends* and I are very interested in the Serrofite situation. Very interested indeed."

Castigon felt his skin crawl, as if all of it were flowing around his torso in search of a hiding spot. Somehow his body knew to be repulsed by Pammon. His mind could only wonder why.

Pammon was older than Castigon, and his eyes had a twinkle to them. Others would perhaps have called it a mischievous sparkle, but Castigon was not so naïve. He knew a fellow killer when he saw one.

"Your friends?"

"We are — how would you say it? — 'new players'."

"Players?" Castigon asked. "Players in what game?"

"Why, the only game."

Castigon looked at Collis, who raised his eyebrows and shrugged.

"And do you play this game well?" Collis asked.

Pammon looked as though his shoulders and chest and diaphragm were trying to chuckle, but his smile stayed firmly in place.

"Oh, Mister Collis. We *do* play it well. We play it very well indeed."

Castigon found Pammon's tone a little too confident. The man had an agenda, that much was clear, and it seemed as though it would be one of which Castigon wanted no knowledge.

He looked up, feeling eyes on him. Across the room, in an alcove lined by benches on all three sides, two men rested their elbows on an empty table. Their conversation had paused, and they looked back at him.

No, not at him; at Pammon and Collis. And they were both wearing the same rigid smiles.

Someone in the tavern was humming a strange, mournful refrain. He stole a quick glance around himself, and saw at least three others in amongst the tavern's patrons. Standing or sitting, talking or silent; they all watched Pammon and Collis with expressions which might have been contemptuous had they not suggested that quite so much gloating was going on behind the eyes.

Castigon's guts turned, and he felt an urgent need to leave and never come back.

Collis seemed oblivious to it all. "What exactly did you have in mind?"

"Well, it seems to me that these Serrofites are dangerously close already to alienating our good-willed human citizenry," said Pammon. "If they lose support from us, they won't be able to hold back human interests any more. All it would take is a little push, and the wedge will be driven too deep to remove."

"I'm listening," said Collis.

Pammon's horrible smile deepened at the corners finally, and Castigon fought back the urge to walk straight out of the tavern's door. Whoever Pammon was, whatever it was he and his 'friends' wanted, it was beginning to sound like it might be exactly the thing Castigon had come in here to find.

Once it had served his purpose, he would be back on the *Leo Fortune* and away from Pammon as fast as the hauler could carry him. And Maber Castigon — trained to fight, happy to kill — would hope never to meet that man again.

○ ○ ○

"What the...?"

Tarrow snapped awake and grabbed at the wrists of the hands that shook her.

"It's me," said Crathus. "Get up, quickly."

"What is it?" Tarrow was alert the moment she heard the urgent tone.

"Some kind of disturbance in the city," Crathus said. "Shit, might be a full-blown uprising for all I know."

"The Serrofites?"

"I'd guess so."

Tarrow rolled off the bed and began to pull on her clothes. Crathus handed her a bandolier and her holsters.

"Stupid cunt should've at least looked as though he would negotiate with them."

"Well, that's not our business," said Tarrow. "I mean I agree, yeah, but it's up to him."

"You've actually got quite a strong opinion about that, haven't you?"

"You fucking bet I have. Weapons check."

Crathus went through the motions while Tarrow checked her own gear methodically.

"You hear from his people yet?"

"No," Crathus said. "Came straight here."

"Right. We go find Kalistine first. Top priority."

"We need certainty on the perimeter," Crathus reminded her.

"Yes. You do that, then come get me."

Crathus looked at her reproachfully.

"It's fine. I'll be okay. Go on; like you said, we need certainty."

They went to the door, and Crathus gave her another reproachful look.

"Miall, don't make me make it an order."

Crathus headed off down the corridor, towards the stairs.

Tarrow drew one of her pistols and held it close to her chest in a two-handed grip. She stayed glued to the wall, moving swiftly down the corridor in the opposite direction to Crathus.

The high chambers are not far, she told herself. Crathus is just downstairs.

Within the same minute she was at the doors of the chamber, unlocking them with her link's verified security pass.

"Wake up, Sir. Proconsul, you need to wake up."

"What in the many worlds—?"

"There's something going on outside the compound," Tarrow said. "I need to get you to safety."

"What exactly is happening?" Kalistine sat up in bed, rubbing his bleary eyes with the backs of his hands.

"Well... I don't know *exactly*."

"Perhaps you should have found out before you came bursting in here." He flopped back down and rolled over.

"Oh no, don't you go back to sleep," Tarrow snapped.

The proconsul sat up again, and looked annoyed. "Did you just tell—?"

"Look, Sir. You made it quite clear earlier I wasn't to tell you how to do your job. So let's make that a two-way street for the moment, and you can yell at me later if you really feel that it's necessary."

"What if I just stay here in bed?"

"You probably won't want to when I burn the fucker down."

"Point taken."

He arose reluctantly and began to dress. Tarrow tapped her foot, amazed at the complexity of the outfit he was putting together.

"I'd suggest only bringing what you need," she said pointedly.

"I'd suggest you keep those ideas to yourself, Shard. I've agreed to come with you, not to take your orders."

"There may be a time limit involved here."

"Yes, there 'may be'. As you said yourself, you don't know exactly."

Tarrow opened her mouth to respond, but she was interrupted before she could waste the breath.

"It's the Serrofites," Crathus said from the doorway. "They're rebelling. People are fighting with them in the streets."

"Rebelling?" Kalistine looked puzzled. "They don't have it in them."

"Well, they seem to have got it from somewhere. The fires are spreading."

"Fires?"

"Yes, fires. I'm told hundreds of bundles of burning weed have been shoved in places they shouldn't be."

Kalistine's jaw dropped.

"The Serrofites are *burning the city* with weed?"

"That's what it looks like, Sir. Symbolic, don't you think?"

"I don't believe it. They wouldn't dare."

"Come on," Tarrow said. "We can agree you're wrong later. Right now we need to get you somewhere more secure than your bedroom—"

Tarrow felt the building shake, and down the hall she heard the sound of breaking glass. The windows on the north corridor must have been blown in.

"That was an explosion," Crathus said.

"Check it out, quickly. We'll head for the south wing."

She grabbed the proconsul, and as Crathus ran away from her once more, she propelled him out of the doors and down the corridor.

"They wouldn't dare," he kept saying.

Tarrow's link chirruped. "Go," she said.

"Outer wall's breached on the south side of the compound," Crathus said. "People are coming in — lots of them. Guards are falling back already. We're going to lose this building."

"Okay. Get back here and we'll find a way out."

"Don't need to tell me twice."

Tarrow yanked the proconsul's arm, trying to break through his anxious gibbering.

"Where is this House's emergency exit?"

"On... on the west wing. There's a tunnel to the commerce hall."

"Of course there is," said Tarrow. "Isn't there always? Where's the entrance?"

"In the main kitchen."

She tapped her link.

"Crathus... west wing. Find the main kitchen; I'll meet you there."

"Got it."

Tarrow hurried along the corridors, spurred on by more sounds of breaking glass and the intensifying smell of smoke. From beneath them, on all sides of the building, she could hear angry voices shouting. Not all of them were human.

"Down here," said Kalistine, pointing to a wide, curving staircase.

"Not on your life," Tarrow said. "That will be flooded with intruders in a few minutes. Is there a servants' entrance?"

"You are joking?" Said the proconsul.

"No, Sir. I am most definitely not."

"That way," he said.

Tarrow found the entrance to the servants' staircase, and bundled Kalistine down it ahead of her. She waited until she was certain nobody had watched them enter the stairwell, then pushed ahead of him.

"Keep up or stay behind," she said.

"Your constant insolence is being noted for the inevitable disciplinary hearing."

"Good for you, Sir."

They emerged in a large, square room with double doors at either end. Tarrow saw wheeled tables arrayed along one wall, and huge hampers along the other. She surmised it was a utility area between the kitchens and the rest of the ground floor.

"That way," Kalistine said.

Tarrow pushed open one of the swinging doors, quietly and slowly, and poked her head through, close to the ground. The kitchens were silent and dark. Only the faint red glow of standby lights fell across the counters, steel basins, and tiled walls.

"Looks clear," she said. "Lead the way."

She followed after him to the end of a row of counters, and he knelt down by the side of a metal cabinet against the far wall. He disappeared inside all the way up to his shoulder, looked as though he was straining, and then there was a metallic *clong*.

He pulled back his arm and shuffled aside as the cabinet swung away from the wall. A puff of dusty air hit Tarrow in the face, and she saw a square of gaping black before her.

She switched on a small torch and pointed the beam into the tunnel. The space went into the wall for about a metre, then ended. She could see there was a drop right in front of them.

"Okay," she said. "Let's get you in there, and I'll join you when Crathus arrives."

○ ○ ○

It was not the first time Castigon had sat and waited in darkness; not by a long shot.

Even through the thick outer walls, he could hear the chaos of fighting and vandalism going on outside. Pammon and Collis had done exactly what they had planned together, once Castigon had spent a short while convincing Collis that the idea was a good one. It had almost been too easy. The friction between the human and Serrofite citizens had been enough to ensure the latter group was blamed for the damage that Collis and his employees had caused under Pammon's direction.

He wondered what exactly Pammon and his friends were getting out of it, then decided it was not something he really cared about. As long as he never had to look at Pammon again, he was happy with that. The strange little man had given him the creeps, and Maber Castigon was not a man who was easily creeped out.

He sat and watched his doorway, waiting in silence.

There were eight doorways like it, locked from the inside and arranged at intervals around the inner core of the building. He had no idea which one would be used, so he had just picked one at random. It had as much chance as any of the others at being the correct door.

He heard a soft scraping noise, very faint, coming from somewhere off to his left. A door opening. Quiet footsteps. Someone shushing someone else, far too loudly.

Castigon drew his pistol, and sneaked down the corridor towards the corner.

"Now what?" Came a tired voice. "We're still in the city."

"Yes, but nobody will be looking for you here, Sir."

It was *her*. The second voice. That doubtless meant her counterpart would be nearby.

Castigon rounded the corner.

Tarrow saw him first, and froze up for a second. She came to her senses, grabbed her gun, and realised before she could even raise it that he had her in his sights already.

"Put it down, Jidian," said Castigon. "Put it down, or I kill them both."

The counterpart and the other man — he looked like a proconsul — both spun around at the sound of Castigon's voice. The counterpart raised her gun too. The proconsul took a step backwards to make sure the two women were between him and the bit the bullets came out of.

"Tell her," said Castigon.

"Miall," Tarrow said quietly. "Back off."

"Jid, no," said the counterpart.

"He'll kill you. Believe me; he *will* kill you."

"You know this man?" The proconsul said.

"Oh, she knows me all right," said Castigon. "We go way back, don't we 'Jid'?"

Tarrow stayed silent.

"You know, out of all of them, I really thought you would be the one who came through for me."

"Maber..." she said.

"After all I did for you, you went and sold me out."

"That's not true. I didn't say what they wanted me to say, Maber. I'm... happy to see you again."

"Happy?"

"Yes, truly."

"You do know I've killed half your old friends, right?"

"I had heard... I knew you'd find me eventually."

"Don't make me laugh; you were going for your gun just then."

"You startled me. There's an uprising going on out there."

"Yeah, well don't expect me to believe for one minute that you want to skip off into the sunset with me. 'Happy', what a crock of shit."

"Jid, please," said the counterpart. "My job means getting between you and—"

"Shut her up."

"Miall, it's okay. We're... old friends."

"Old friends," Castigon said. "But friends have each other's backs, right Jid? Didn't have my back, did you?"

The counterpart shifted her stance, and Castigon trained his weapon on her instead of the Shard.

Tarrow looked sad. "I never wanted them to send you away," she said. "If I could have stopped them, I would have done."

"Really. Tell me what you would have said."

Tarrow opened her mouth to reply.

"In fact don't. You've already had far more time than any of the others."

He shot her in the chest.

The counterpart screamed, dropped her weapon, and tried to catch Tarrow as she fell.

Tarrow landed on her back, the counterpart's hands under her shoulders, and her head hit the ground.

"Oh my worlds," said the proconsul. "Oh, oh no!"

"Jid, Jid, don't you fucking leave me."

Castigon started to step backwards.

"Jid, *please*," the counterpart said.

Castigon reached the corner.

"Stop where you are, Sir," the proconsul shouted. There was a note of authority in his voice that took Castigon by surprise.

The counterpart's head jerked up, her eyes narrowed, and she leapt to her feet.

"You!"

Somehow, she was inside Castigon's firing arc before he could react. She was much faster than he had expected, and — as he discovered when she struck him square in the chest with the heel of her palm — much stronger.

He stumbled backwards, tripped, and fell to the ground.

The counterpart was on him immediately, straddling his abdomen, punching him in the face. First one fist, then the other.

Castigon reeled under the blows. Somewhere in the recesses of his mind, he remembered he was still holding a pistol.

"Fuck... off," he said, and shot her up through the ribs.

The counterpart slumped to one side, and he pushed her over farther until she toppled off him and landed on the floor.

"Worlds..." said the proconsul.

Castigon was already on his feet, and his gun flew up at the sound of the other man's voice. He looked through the sights at the trembling proconsul.

"Don't..."

"I'm not going to kill you," said Castigon. "No reason to. Besides, you've got enough problems. The natives are fucking restless."

○ ○ ○

"Occre Brant," said Caden. "To what do I owe this pleasure?"

Brant smiled into the holo. He had never thought he would hear a Shard of the Empress saying it was a pleasure to see him.

"I have a sort of confession to make," he said.

"You didn't let Tirrano have her wicked way with you?"

"No," he laughed. "Nothing that bad."

"So what's the problem?"

"That doctor you wanted extracting from the Meccrace system; Danil Bel-Ures."

"What about her?"

"I kind of... didn't get around to it yet."

"Brant, I asked you to do that ages ago."

"I know, but Naeb escaped, then Fort Kosling blew up, and I kind of got side-tracked with all that."

"Right. Well you'd better get on with it then, pretty damned sharpish."

"Oh, there's more."

"Why do I have a sinking feeling?"

"We — that is, Tirrano and I — we suspect Gordl Branathes might be a Rasa."

"Branathes... as in, your *boss* Branathes?"

"Yes. He's been acting strangely, and he vanished earlier today. We think he might be going after Doctor Bel-Ures."

"I'd really like to act on that, but I'm under orders. I have an assass— I have a meeting to arrange. A really important meeting."

"Two men enter, one man leaves? That kind of meeting?"

Caden shrugged ruefully. "My job is rarely glamorous, Brant. Can you not just task this out to Eyes and Ears in the Meccrace system? That *was* the original plan."

"There's a question mark over who can be trusted," Brant said. "We don't know how many Rasas exist, or where they are."

"You have a point there," said Caden. "I have it on good authority that there are lots of them. Everywhere."

Brant's whole body flushed cold.

"You... you're sure?"

"I found that Morlum guy on Woe Tantalum," Caden said. "He was messed up, but I believe him. The Rasas are watching us."

"I don't know what to say. I mean, I sort of suspected there had to be more of them, but never—"

"Listen, it's too far above your pay grade for you to be dying of worry. You let me wring my hands over the implications, yes?"

"I guess."

"Now concentrate on Bel-Ures. Consider her a vital asset in a war we are already losing."

"A war..."

Brant was confused for a moment, not making the connection between the doctor and the fight against the Viskr. Unless...

"You mean, war against the Rasas? Not the Viskr?"

"Of course. Their war against *us*. The confrontation with the Viskr is probably all down to a ruse. Someone manoeuvred us into that conflict, and it's time it ended."

"Rasas did all that?"

"I doubt it was them alone. I think they're like drones, or... no, like tools. Pretty soon I'll figure out what kind of tools they are, what their job is. And when you know what a tool is for, you can make a good guess at who might be using it."

"I had no idea," Brant murmured.

"Nobody did," said Caden. "That's their strength. Unfortunately, our glorious leaders have still got their heads in the sand."

"What are we going to do?"

"As I said, I'm on mission. I can't do anything about Bel-Ures in person until that's finished with. But there might be something you can do to speed things up."

"Anything. You just let me know."

"I'm looking for someone. There's been a series of murders, and I need to track the person responsible."

"Just tell me what you need to know."

Caden glanced down suddenly, peering at the lower segment of his holo's display.

"Hold on," he said. "I'm getting another call. And I'm not sure I believe what I'm seeing."

○ ○ ○

"That wasn't quick at all," said Captain Borreto, eyeing Castigon disapprovingly.

"Unexpected complications," Castigon replied.

"Yeah, I can see that by the state of your face."

Castigon wiped blood from where it had trickled out of his nose. Borreto could see there was still a smear left behind, but he said nothing.

"We good to lift off?"

"Yes, 'we' are. Port authority granted us clearance already; we were just waiting for you."

"I'm touched."

"Don't be," said Borreto. "I just want to get paid."

"Ever the opportunist. Well there's still more money to be made in this adventure, if you're interested."

"Just tell me where you want to go."

"Altakanti Station," said Castigon.

"That's a military installation."

"Don't worry about it. They tend to look far, not close."

"Still, I'm really not happy about getting up close and personal with an Imperial listening post."

"It'll be fine."

"What assurances do I get?"

"Let's just say I really know what I'm doing. It won't be the first time I've flown so literally under the radar."

"You're the customer," Borreto said.

"I am. Now please, get me off this fucking planet."

"After you."

Borreto allowed Castigon to pass him on the ramp, and watched as he walked into the cargo hold.

You are going to cause me a lot of trouble, he thought. I can feel it coming.

Not for the first time since taking this passenger aboard, he wondered if the trouble would be worthwhile.

## – 13 –
## The List

Everything swam in a hot sea, a sea that flowed around Throam, enveloped his senses, permeated his body. He felt more alive now than he had on the surface of Mibes, stronger than he had been when he dragged a giant Tanker across the ground. He was a burning pillar, his own will manifested.

Metal crashed heavily on metal, echoing loudly around the gym compartment. He saw the other people looking at him, exchanging glances, and simply did not care.

Otkellsson had been right.

Throam had never moved so much mass so many times. *Never.* He felt as though nothing in the worlds could stop him.

He dropped the weights, stood up, and grunted. Standing with his feet apart, he balled his fists in front of his hips, and tensed his arms and chest.

"YES!" He shouted.

More of the other gym users looked up from their own routines, but none said a word.

He paced back and forth, watching himself in the deck-to-overhead mirrors. Steam curled from his skin in thin sheets.

The greatest session he had ever had, he owed to White Thunder. Why he had never tried it before he had no idea. None whatsoever.

"Oh, yes."

Something in his head told him he had been there long enough. After so many thousands of hours in the gym it was a difficult habit to ignore, even with chemical assistance.

He grabbed his things and headed for the hatch, thinking of Euryce Eilentes and the spectacular stunt she had pulled off, just like Caden had sarcastically told her to.

His body felt solid around him, hard, and it moved as if it still had massive stores of energy which it needed to release.

He thought of Eilentes sat astride the Gorilla, and became harder still.

"YES!"

○ ○ ○

Eilentes had managed to delay her return for hours now. She had accompanied Norskine to sickbay while the private got herself checked over, tolerating the overly sterile compartment and a corpsman with a serious personality deficit just to kill some time. She had been to the range and punished forty targets. She had even spent an hour pushing dismal navy food around her bowl in the galley.

In short, she had run out of things to do.

She stood in the passageway, resting her forehead on the outside of the hatch. Technically, they were her quarters. Just like the old days; he was crashing in her bunk.

She bashed her head on the metal, gently but firmly.

"Works better if you open it." Throam's loud

voice came from the other side of the bulkhead.

She opened the hatch.

"What took you so long?" He asked.

I don't want to have the next conversation, she thought.

He seemed not to notice her silence. "Got bored waiting, so I've been to the gym already," he said. "And hoo-boy, am I horny now."

He was only wearing pants and socks.

"That was some awesome shit you pulled on Mibes, Euryce. Didn't know you had it in you."

He was closer now. Much closer.

"It made me so *hot*."

He put his hand around the back of her head, and moved in to kiss her on the mouth. She ducked away and turned her head to the side, so he kissed her on the neck instead.

"Ren—"

"Ride me like you rode that Gorilla."

"For fuck's sake..."

She pushed at his shoulders, but couldn't move him. She never could. He backed her up against the wall. He smelled of sweat and heat and lust.

"Come on, Euryce. Let's go wild."

"Ren, stop it. I'm really not in the mood for this."

"Don't be stupid. You're always in the mood for Throam."

"Not right now I'm not."

"Yes you are."

She looked at his face, at his eyes. They were wide yet glazed. He was breathing through his mouth. She could feel his blood pumping beneath her hands.

"What have you taken?"

"Just the usual."

"Like fuck is it the usual, Ren. Tell me."

"Afterwards."

"No, not 'afterwards', I'm outta—"

The next thing she knew, she was flying towards the bunk, and he was flying with her. She had never suspected either of them could fly. He landed across her, and the wind was knocked out of her in a heavy instant.

"Ren..." she coughed.

He had her wrists in his hands, and kissed her neck again. She felt the sharpness of his stubble scraping her skin.

"So fucking hot."

He sat up on his knees, straddling her hips, and grabbed the waistband of her trousers.

"No," she said, and reached to one side.

She had her combat knife out of the sheath on her thigh before she knew what she was doing. Even on a testosterone and adrenaline and who-knew-what-else high, he recognised the danger.

"Get. The fuck. Off."

He tipped himself off her, and crouched on the bunk; a patient animal.

Eilentes rolled off the edge, hooked her kit bag from the floor on her way to the hatch, and stepped out into the passageway.

She didn't look back.

∘ ∘ ∘

Caden was surprised to see the resentful face that stared back at him from the holo, a face that was waiting patiently for him to make the proper response to the offered greeting.

"Joarn Kages? This is not a call I was expecting. Have you missed me?"

"I truly doubt, Sir, that you can fathom precisely how difficult it was for me to bring myself to contact you."

"Clearly it was not quite difficult enough," Caden said.

"How very droll," Kages replied. "Were it not for doors being slammed in my face everywhere else I turn, I would have been quite happy never talking to you again."

"That would have suited me just fine. Are you going to get around to telling me what this is about?"

"Absolutely. But first, I would like you to know that I deeply resented being defenestrated by that big brute of yours. That was not in the least bit sporting, and I am *still* in considerable pain."

"Consider it a reminder that sharing is not always the right thing to do."

"I shall certainly remember that lesson in future, but I think you will find it is not always true. Are you aware of the current state of affairs on Aldava?"

"Not specifically. After we left you, I found the population of Barrabas Fled to be a bit peculiar. I was told that was being looked in to."

"Were you, were you really? And by 'looked in to', you mean what exactly?"

"I didn't ask. I've had no involvement at all; my business lay elsewhere."

"Didn't ask, you say. Would you like to know what 'looked in to' apparently means? Would you like me to *share* that with you?"

"Go on. Clearly you're going to anyway."

"It apparently means — and I find it extraordinary that you would claim total ignorance of this kind of treachery — that no ship may leave Aldava. It means that a quarantine network is being constructed in orbit, and that the communication links between the world and the network at large are being iteratively blocked."

"What? What are you talking about?"

"The entire planet is being quarantined, Shard Caden. Isolated. Cut off from the galaxy. It's only because of my contacts and knowledge of gate relay protocols that I was able to open this channel."

"What's going on, Kages?"

"Your guess is as good as mine. Well, probably not quite as good, but better than most I would imagine. With all the increasing insanity amongst the locals, I have been cloistered away in my private emergency shelter since the day you left me flat on my back in my own courtyard. I've been monitoring the system nexus from here."

"I presume you're telling me all of this for a reason?"

"Of course. It's quite simple really: I need you to come back to Aldava and pick me up, before this whole place goes to the Deep."

"I'm on a priority mission right now. Why in the worlds would I divert to help you?"

"Because I have something you simply cannot do without."

Kages wore his satisfaction like it was a medal, and Caden raised his eyebrows. With the start of the conversation being the way it was, he had not expected the information broker to start bargaining. He figured that guilt was supposed to be part of the negotiation process.

"Okay, Kages; you have my ear. If you want to keep me on the line, I suggest you start at the beginning."

"After you left, I became curious about what you were up to at Woe Tantalum. What Morlum might have been up to. I know you won't approve of me poking around in your business, but I'm sure you can appreciate that for someone in my line of work it was truly irresistible."

"I can imagine."

"Well... even for me, Fleet signals are difficult to crack. So I went for the information I knew would be easy to unwrap. I lifted the tables for Woe Tantalum from the central database's List of the Dead. I knew that whatever was going on out there, I'd see the silhouette of it all from the data passed back to the casualty registries."

"I have to hand it to you, that's actually very clever."

"At the risk of sounding conceited, I know. This sort of thing *is* my whole livelihood. But the point is, there was already a List in the database for Woe Tantalum. A List thirty Solars old, from the incident that killed the planet."

"Is that unusual?"

"Not in itself, no. The colony was never sanctioned by the Empire, true, but the people who went there to start a new life were known. As were all the contractors the colonists paid to help build new infrastructure."

"So what's the problem with there being a List already?"

"The problem, Shard Caden, is that it's *wrong*."

"Wrong?"

"Yes, wrong. Some of the people on the old List are still walking about today. I've even had dealings with a few of them."

Kages stopped talking, allowing time for the significance of his words to percolate. Caden realised that a moment was passing him by slowly, that his mind was numb. He forced himself to grapple with the implications. Secret survivors, who never made themselves known to the rest of the Empire, or to their families. Were they hiding themselves deliberately? Could they be known to each other?

He put speculation to one side. His training insisted that only diagnostic questions would be of any practical value.

"How is that possible? I thought the whole planet underwent some kind of sudden, catastrophic event."

"Yes, that is indeed the official story. But when you look closer, I'm afraid the information simply does not add up."

"What do you mean?"

"After stumbling across that dramatic revelation, I dug up everything I could on the planet. Old transit logs, comms transactions, even commissions and contracts. There's a point when everything becomes chaotic all at once, then it stops entirely within the space of a few days. Then a gap of an entire Solar month before the news feeds all start to report the story of the accident."

"The way you say that, you make it sound as though you don't think there was any accident at all."

"I don't."

"What do you think happened?"

"I have no idea. But I think that during that missing month, the Empire was already isolating the planet. And I think that ultimately, they failed to keep everyone in."

"Are you absolutely certain about this?"

"In my line of work, Shard Caden, one is often obliged to double- and triple-check the identity of one's clients. I have certainly had personal contact with people who were supposed to have died on

Woe Tantalum almost three decades ago."

"How could they move around and conduct business, without being flagged as using the identities of dead people?"

"There is a way. You will not have any knowledge of it, and neither will Eyes and Ears, but believe me when I tell you there is a way."

Caden steepled his fingers, and rested his lips against them. "Kages, I was a bit preoccupied when I was at Woe Tantalum. But if you want my honest opinion, the whole planet looked to me as though it had been hit from orbit."

"I knew it."

"Given what you said before, I think whatever it was that happened to the people on Woe Tantalum, something similar might be happening around you on Aldava."

Kages managed a smile. "Not a terribly difficult connection to make, Shard Caden, but I am truly effervescent with pleasure to see that you made it. Yes, the same thought had occurred to me also."

"Which means that—"

"You have it. Which means that Aldava might soon meet with some kind of 'disaster', and have all life scoured from her surface completely."

"This is the part where you remind me that you want rescuing, isn't it?"

"That thought is foremost in my mind."

"If you want off that planet, I'm going to need something from you. Some proof that this isn't just a trick to get yourself rescued."

"I anticipated as much from a Shard, and I have a name lined up for you. Herik Pammon — he was supposedly on Woe Tantalum when the surface burned up. I am confident, Sir, that he will be all the proof you need. But I'd urge you to take me on faith, because I truly doubt there is enough time for you to track him down."

Caden noted the name, then returned his attention to the holo. "It's still a big ask. The quarantine won't be easy to get around, even if the orbital platforms aren't yet ready."

"But you're an Imperial Shard," Kages said. "If anyone can do it, that person is you. There are people wandering the Empire who should be dead, and I think you already suspect — as I do — that they are probably on the same side Medran Morlum joined so recently.

"If you don't rescue me from this moribund rock, you will never know who those people are."

Caden leaned in towards the holo. "Kages, if it means what you seem to think it means, that information could end up saving countless lives."

"Then you had best endeavour to meet my terms."

"You'd trade yourself against perhaps millions of other lives?"

"I'd rather not see other lives lost, Shard Caden, but I have to confess to harbouring a particularly special fondness for my own."

"You really are a callous shit."

"Be that as it may, this callous shit has information that you know you cannot do without. I suggest you come and retrieve it at your earliest convenience."

"How will I contact you again?"

"I doubt that will be possible. The gate's comm relays are likely to be under full lock-down within a matter of hours. Even I cannot bypass that."

"Then how will I find you?"

"My shelter is beneath the villa; straight down. I have enough food to last half a lifetime, power, air cyclers, and the water purification system from the villa feeds in here as well. I can assure you I will not be going anywhere; not with those crazy people outside and the looming threat of death from above."

"Then I guess if you see me again, you'll know what my decision was."

Caden hit the tile to close the channel just as Kages was opening his mouth to reply. The man's broad face was frozen on the holo for a moment before vanishing completely, surprise and disappointment clearly competing for ground.

Let him sweat it out, Caden thought. If that's how he wants to play it, he can sit and stew for a while.

When Kages had pointed it out, it had actually not yet occurred to Caden that Medran Morlum might have been on the same side as the people who apparently survived the Woe Tantalum disaster.

No, not disaster survivors. They were quarantine fugitives.

Medran Morlum, it had turned out, was a Rasa. If he were somehow in league with the fugitives, then they might also have been Rasas. Might *still be* Rasas.

As yet, Caden had no idea what a Rasa actually was, only what they were capable of. That small piece of knowledge was troubling enough, given that Morlum appeared to have coordinated the theft of prototype weapons from a top secret station, and that Amarist Naeb had single-handedly gutted a fortress on her way to freedom.

But worse still, somewhere in the upper echelons of the Imperial leadership, someone already knew what had really happened at Woe Tantalum all those Solars ago. They knew why. There was a good chance that they had known about the Rasas before Caden and Throam had entered Gemen Station and found Amarist Naeb, alone and out of her mind. They had left everyone else in the dark for years. They had killed an entire world of people to keep it all a secret, and they were probably getting ready to kill another.

Caden felt weak. They — whoever they were — had given the Rasas and their masters decades to prepare themselves.

His fingers clenched into fists, the tendons standing out against his forearms. Darkness bubbled around the edges of his vision, and his body seemed like a distant, foreign receptacle. Lips pressed thin, neck swollen, he stood up slowly, breathed out hard through his nose, and smashed his fists down on the desk.

"Mother*fuckers*!"

There really was no choice involved at all, and Kages knew it. Caden had to find Herik Pammon. And if that man was anything like Naeb or Morlum, then he also had to get hold of those names.

Everything is different now, he thought. Doctor Bel-Ures is the only hope I have of finding someone who's willing to talk.

○ ○ ○

Eilentes walked up and down the passageway several times before stopping outside Caden's quarters. She was not sure she wanted to do what she thought she was about to do.

"Mother*fuckers*!"

The outburst was muffled, but clear enough. It had come from his compartment.

She pressed the call panel and waited.

The hatch opened, and she was confronted by a frenzied ogre that had stolen Caden's face. The ogre snapped at her.

"What?"

"I... uh, Caden, I really need to speak with you. If it's not a bad time?"

"It's definitely a bad time," he said.

She tried her hardest, but a few small tears came anyway.

"Oh, for... I can probably squeeze you in."

He moved aside, and she walked into his quarters. The air felt like treacle, and she was trying to sit down even before she had reached the nearest chair.

Caden caught her arm, and manoeuvred her safely into a sitting position. Her kit bag dropped to the deck between her feet, but she continued to hold on to the strap.

"What the hell happened to you?"

"It's Rendir," she said. "He... tried to make me..."

"Do what?"

"He's out of his brain on something," she said. "Doesn't know what he's doing. He was trying to make me have sex with him, and I don't want to. I just don't want to do that any more. But he wouldn't listen."

"I can't believe what I'm hearing."

Caden sat down opposite her, and pressed his palms into his face.

"He's using more and more junk," Eilentes said. "He needs telling, Caden. He doesn't listen to me."

A great weight began to lift from her shoulders. It felt good to get it out there, to tell someone else.

"But you think he'll listen to me?"

"Doesn't he always?"

"Yes, I suppose he does. He can listen to me while I'm kicking the shit out of him."

"Don't," she said. "Once he comes down he'll be ashamed. He'll probably let you beat him black and blue."

"I should fucking well hope so. I don't fancy my chances if he hits back."

She laughed. Somehow, the Shard she had once called unemotional had managed to make everything a little bit better.

"Please make him see sense. I'm not exactly a delicate flower, but I can't put up with him like this; it's just not right. That could have gone really, really badly."

"Listen; there's an important conversation I need to have with Brant, then I'll get right on it. Where will you be?"

"Norskine's quarters," she said. "I'll stay with Taliam Norskine."

"Okay," he said. "I'll let you know when it's done."

○ ○ ○

Brant was confused. Caden had called him back less than twenty minutes after he broke off from their last conversation, and now it seemed that he was working to completely different priorities.

"Run that by me again."

"It's perfectly simple," Caden said. "Forget about Doctor Bel-Ures; I'll see to that myself. But you... you have a new job."

"Yes, this mission you think I'm going to go off on."

"It's absolutely critical. I can't think of anyone else I can trust to get this done, Brant."

"Really? You trust me that much?"

"We're having this conversation, aren't we?"

"We are."

"There you go then. Requisition a long-range transport or something, and get to Aldava as quickly as you can. You're looking for a man called Joarn Kages; he's the one Morlum visited. You need to get him off the surface, and — no matter what he has to say about it — hide him away."

"Is that all?"

"Oh, you poor fool. Not in the slightest."

"What's the catch?"

"The gate is probably locked out. There will likely be a military blockade. The whole planet might have been burned up. Take your pick."

Brant blanched. "You're not serious?"

"I'm totally serious."

"I'm not trained for this kind of thing," Brant said. "And like hell will I get permission."

"Simple: I'll ask your superior. Oh no wait, he's probably an enemy agent. Not to worry, I'll ask *his* superior. Oh shit — she's off on a merry adventure of her own."

"Okay, don't labour the point. I would have thought that maybe this might be a job for another Shard...?"

"No can do. I can't pass this back up the chain, because I don't know if that chain has been compromised. Kages has vital information. He could tear this thing wide open, if we can just get to him in time. There might be people who want him very dead. So no pressure."

"Shit."

"As of now, Brant, you're deputised. You're a mini-Shard. If there's any fallout from this, I'll ensure it comes back to me."

"Okay." Brant thought for a moment. "I can

probably arrange this, if I call in some favours. You want field agents to meet up with Bel-Ures anyway?"

"Yes, that's still a good idea; they can get her family to safety. And if you find time, start scouring the network for a man called Herik Pammon. But your main goal — your absolute top priority — is to find Kages."

"And Bel-Ures herself?"

"I'm going to go for Doctor Bel-Ures. If Branathes has gone to silence her, there won't be any coming back from that. Who knows what lengths he's willing to go to."

"Rather you than me."

"When you get to Barrabas Fled, don't take any chances. Avoid contact with the locals, and make sure you wear full environmental protection."

"What's the danger?"

"The people there were nuts. Whatever is causing that, we don't know yet how it spreads."

"Understood."

"I'll send you my digital seal. If you run into any serious problems, it might help to be able to show you're working for a Shard."

"You'd really do that?"

"Calm down Brant; it's just a series of numbers. Doesn't mean we're married or anything."

"Not yet. Should I take Tirrano?"

"If you think doing that will make you *safer*, sure."

"I'm just not that wild about going it alone."

Caden managed a grin. "I sort of hope you don't live to regret that decision."

"Oh thanks."

"In the nicest way possible, of course."

○ ○ ○

Caden had managed to calm himself down for the conversation with Brant. Or maybe it had been the conversation itself that calmed him down; he could not be sure. But the reprieve was now over, that much he knew for certain.

He seethed with building anger as he stomped through the maze-like passageways of *Disputer*, headed for Eilentes' quarters.

Throam was laid out across the bunk when he entered. The counterpart was face down, still wearing only his socks and his underpants. The air in the compartment tasted of stale sweat, even with the cyclers turned on.

"You'd better not be asleep, dickhead," Caden said.

Throam raised his head and squinted back at him. "Head. Pain. Shut up."

"Don't tell me to shut up, you massive idiot. What the hell have you been doing?"

"Huh? What have I done now?"

"What did you do to Eilentes?"

"What did I do?"

"Yes, what did you do. Go on; I want to hear it from *you*."

"I don't know what you're talking about."

"What do you remember?"

"Mibes, then smashing it in the gym, then waking up here with a right bastard behind my eyes."

"You massive twat."

"Will you please stop calling me names?"

"No, stupid-bollocks. I won't. Where is it?"

"Where's what?"

"What do you think? Your stash."

"Hidden from prying eyes."

"So it's under the lining of your helmet then?"

"No...?"

Caden strode across the compartment to where Throam had dumped his armour and kit, and lifted his helmet from the deck.

"Would it kill you to clean this thing?" Caden asked. "Oh man, it's all damp and cold."

He pulled out the pads of foam lining, tearing them off their velcro. A plastic bag fell to the deck, and he picked it up.

"White Thunder, I presume?"

"Come on man, that was a gift."

"A gift? You moron. You don't use this. Ever."

Caden headed towards the inner hatch.

"What are you doing?"

"This shit is getting flushed."

Throam got up off the bunk, and was between Caden and the wash enclosure in a flash.

"Don't think so," Throam said.

Caden looked up. And up, and up. Throam always looked a lot taller when he was annoyed. His body was tensed up.

"Don't think for one moment you're going to intimidate me with your pectorals and that frankly terrifying bulge. This is all going down the drain."

"I think you should hand it over."

"Bollocks to that," Caden said. He took a step back, popped the top of the bag open, and emptied it over the deck in a wide, sweeping arc.

"You *arsehole*," Throam said.

"Maybe that'll teach you not to try and force yourself on Eilentes."

"You utter cu— Wait, force what now?"

"You really don't remember? That should be the first clue that you have a problem."

"Yeah yeah, go back a page."

"You tried to fuck Eilentes when she didn't want you to," Caden yelled. "I mean, you *really* tried to make her."

Throam suddenly looked a lot shorter. He stumbled backwards to the bunk, and sat on the edge with his head in his hands, his elbows on his knees.

"What were you *thinking*? People have been court-martialled for far less. To say nothing of poor Euryce."

"Thought we just established I wasn't thinking." Throam muttered it through the gap between his forearms.

"This shit ends now, you hear me? I'm not going to tolerate it for a second longer."

"Yeah... of course. No more White Thunder for me."

"I'm not just talking about that. You're going natural, Throam. No more steroids, no more amphetamines or kickers or springs in your step. You get me?"

Throam looked wounded. "I get you... Sir."

"I can't believe you'd put yourself in this position. That you'd put *me* in this position."

"I just wanted to be better than I am. All the time, that's all I think about; being the best damned counterpart out there."

"And you think this is the way to do it?" Caden had already been shouting, but now he raged. "Pumping that shit into your body? It's not your size or your strength that make you a great counterpart, Throam. I mean yeah, that all helps, but it's not *that* that makes you the best. It's your reliability."

They both went quiet. After a while, Throam uncovered his face, and Caden saw that he looked as though he were emptied out.

"How is she?"

"I'm glad you got around to asking that. I was beginning to wonder. She's okay. Upset, of course, but okay."

"I'm so sorry, for all of this."

"Good. Now this is what you're going to say to Eilentes."

○ ○ ○

Eilentes glared across the table at Throam. Caden was sat next to him, propped up on his elbows and watching the counterpart's face.

"Captain Thande has kindly agreed to ferry us to Meccrace Prime," said Caden. "You two need to fix whatever you've managed to fuck up between you, because I need you both on fighting form."

Nobody said anything. Eilentes continued to glare at Throam, who sat and stared at the tabletop. Caden sighed to himself.

"Throam. Don't you have something you'd like to say to Eilentes?"

"Sorry Euryce," the counterpart said. His chair creaked in protest when he shifted uncomfortably on the seat.

"Good. Now tell Eilentes what 'no' means."

"No means no."

"And what's the most you'll be using from now on?"

"A nice bottle of lovely water, and some creatine monohydrate if I'm fucking lucky."

"Exactly. Now get out of my sight."

Throam stood slowly, his eyes fixed on the table. He pushed the chair back with his legs.

"Wait a moment," said Eilentes.

The counterpart paused, not sure whether to sit down again or remain standing. In the end he hovered over the space where the chair had been, halfway between both stances.

"You think you can just say 'sorry', and everything is okay?"

Throam remained silent.

"Well it's not, Rendir. It's far from okay. You could've really hurt me. You wanted to."

"I'm really, truly sorry. I was out of my head, that's all."

"That's like saying 'oh, sorry I crashed the shuttle. I was so drunk!' It just doesn't wash, Rendir. You knew what that shit would do to you when you took it, so you're responsible for everything you did afterwards."

"Euryce—" Throam began.

"No, I'm not done yet. I know you've got a lot on your mind, Ren. You miss your son, and you want to prove you left him alone for the right reasons. But we — Caden and I — we're here *now*. We should matter to you."

"You do matter."

"I don't believe you."

Eilentes crossed her arms and sat back in her chair. Her side of the conversation was over.

Throam walked out of the galley, hanging his head in shame.

"Don't batter him with it," Caden said. "He'll be beating himself up about this for ages. You don't need to do a thing."

"How did you *do* that?" Eilentes asked.

"Easy. I know his mothers."

"You should introduce me. Worlds know he never will."

"Is that something you still want to happen? It sure didn't sound that way to me."

Eilentes realised he was right.

## – 14 –
## Your Mother's Son

The news had reached the City of Peru two days before, but Rendir could still feel that same explosion of pride reverberating in his chest.

Victory!

Between the Imperial Navy and the combined MAGA forces, and the efforts of the Shards and Eyes and Ears, the Viskr Junta had been beaten into submission. The Perseus conflict was over at last.

True, the enemy had not actually conceded defeat. But they had withdrawn their forces from every front in the Perseus theatre, and that came to the same thing.

Every single level of Peru was alive with music and dancing, and like everyone else in the city Rendir let the elation wash over him.

"Come on Ren; let's dance."

Hitami grabbed both of his hands and pulled him away from the edge of the plaza. They joined the mass of people wheeling and jigging around in the public space, caught up in the rhythm of the music.

They held each other's hands, their arms crossed, and spun faster and faster as the tempo increased. She smiled at him, laughing, her dark hair flying to one side. Everything else became a blur, until all he could see was her joyful face.

He smiled back and held on, hoping the moment would never end.

The music reached its climax, then died down. The song was fading into silence.

"Let's go somewhere else," said Rendir.

"Why?" Hitami said. "This is fun."

"I'm not that into dancing."

"You did fine just then."

"That was just spinning. Anyone can spin."

"Oh come on Ren, just one more?"

"If I have to really dance you'll see what I mean. I don't want to embarrass you."

She laughed. "Okay, where do you want to go?"

"The solarium? There's a barbecue at sundown."

"I thought you didn't like going to the solarium any more," she said.

Rendir shrugged. "It's been two Solars. I guess I've got over it."

She nodded, and he took her hand and led her away. They wove through the other people in the plaza — those sober enough to move aside and those too drunk to notice them — and came to the main thoroughfare that connected all the primary zones of Level 230.

The people began to thin out. Most of those they saw were moving swiftly between one party and another, seeking the warmth of the celebrations. A few leaned heavily against walls, groaning, and Rendir could not help but laugh at the one fully grown man he saw heaving into a wall garden.

After they had passed him by, Rendir pulled

Hitami towards the wall. He held both of her hands in his.

"Ren...?"

He leaned in to kiss her.

"No, Ren," she said. She pulled her hands away from him.

"What's up?"

"I'm not... I don't feel the same way as you."

"It didn't look that way before. Why are you out with me then?"

"You're my friend, Ren," Hitami said. "But that's it. I like Josué."

"That bully? Are you serious? He's horrible. How on earth could you want to go out with him? What's wrong with me?"

"He's not the way you think he is. He's growing up, Ren. He's maturing."

"Why are you out here with me then?"

"Like I said, you're my friend."

"Where's Josué?"

"He's got some family thing on."

"Right, so I'm just keeping his seat warm am I?"

"No, that's not it at all."

"Kinda feels like it is."

"Well, you're wrong."

"I can't believe you'd choose that bully over me."

"Would you stop calling him a bully? He learned his lesson at the solarium, Ren. Some people actually change."

"What's that supposed to mean?"

"Nothing."

"No, come on. I want to know."

"Fine. Sometimes you're the most grown-up guy I know. But most of the time... well, you can be very boyish, Rendir."

"I'm fourteen," he said. *"We're* fourteen. What do you expect?"

"Next year we'll be told to make our decisions," Hitami said. "To decide our pathways. It's time to grow up."

"I can do that."

"I know you can," she said. "But I don't think our paths will be going in the same direction."

"Why not?"

"It's not going to surprise anyone when you go off to join the MAGA forces, Ren. But that's not what I want for me."

"What *do* you want?"

"I want to command a starship."

∘ ∘ ∘

It was dark by the time Rendir returned home. Lamis and Peshal were still up, both of them reading by the light of lamps.

Lamis looked up as he entered. "Hi Ren. Had a good time?"

Peshal placed an old book in her lap, and just smiled.

"Fine," he said.

"I think we should have gone out too," Lamis said.

"A full night of merry-making was quite enough for me," said Peshal.

"That's not what I meant," said Lamis. "What's wrong, Ren?"

"Just... disappointed."

"With what?"

"My friend, Hitami—"

"The pretty one?"

"Yes, the pretty one. I thought she was interested in me, and she's not."

Lamis started to smile, and turned away.

"How is that funny?"

"Sorry Ren," Lamis said. "When you get to my age, you'll think it's funny too."

"I'm not your age though, am I?"

"I suppose not."

She patted the couch, and he went to sit next to her.

"Do you think I need to grow up?"

Peshal answered first. "Little Man, I think there's plenty of time ahead of you for that."

"Yeah, that's what I thought too."

"Who told you that, anyway?"

"Hitami. She said we'll have to decide our pathways next year."

"Well, she's right. You'll be expected to choose what you want to do with your life. Assuming you're given the choice, of course. You won't be given options you aren't suited to."

"So then I *do* need to start growing up."

Lamis sighed. "Not necessarily, Ren. As long as you can do what you need to do, nobody is going to care how mature you are."

"Hitami cares."

"Hitami is just a child still."

"But she *wants* to be the captain of a starship," said Rendir. "And she'll do it too. She knows exactly where her life is going to take her."

Peshal came to sit next to Rendir on the couch. "And what do you want to be, Little Man?"

"I don't know exactly," he said. "But I've always wanted to be a soldier of some sort."

"Now Ren, we've talked about this," said Lamis. "We don't really want you leaving us to go and die on some remote world, out there in the black."

"What else am I going to do? I just don't have

the math skills to get into the Fleet. And I know what you're going to say, but I'm *not* smart enough to train as a Shard."

"There are plenty of other careers you could choose," said Lamis. "You don't have to go into the military."

"Yes, I do," said Rendir. "I've always wanted to. I need it. You *know* that."

Lamis and Peshal looked at each other.

"Maybe we should have had this conversation a bit sooner," said Lamis.

"What do you mean?"

"We know how much it means to you, Ren, but we don't really want you in the military. We'd be worried sick the whole time."

"But it's what I want."

"And it will be your choice," said Peshal. "But when the time comes to make that decision, just remember that it affects us too."

∘ ∘ ∘

*"Chim-Bo-Te! Chim-Bo-Te!"*

The chant of the home crowd drowned out everyone else, and Rendir felt his heart beating faster and faster.

Twenty seconds remained.

Coach had used a selection sacrifice to ensure it was Rendir who represented the City of Peru in this match. Coach would not be able to choose another player for the remainder of the tournament — it would have to be a blind pick in every match — and Rendir was determined that the gamble should succeed.

Ten seconds left.

He glanced to his right, and saw the Chiclayo player preparing herself to sprint towards the centre of the arena.

On his left, the player for Team Pucallpa was also preparing himself. He had both fists clenched.

The Puno player was hidden from his sight by the central hopper, directly opposite him on the other side of the arena.

Just three opponents at amateur level. It gave him hope for a reasonably strong victory.

Five seconds.

The chant was louder now, faster. Most of the crowd had come from the City of Peru; the advantage of a home game. Although the tower city was the social heart of what was once a nation, there were still major towns farther afield which held on to their regional pride. Enough pride to keep the tournaments running, Solar after Solar.

The klaxon sounded, loud even above the chanting of ten thousand voices.

Rendir launched himself forwards, running as hard as he could for the centre of the arena. He heard the *thud* of an air cannon, looked up, and saw the ball rocket straight up from the hopper.

It felt as though an age passed before the ball began to descend again, and he slowed down as he tried to work out where it would land.

Someone hit him from the side, hard. Chiclayo had tackled him.

Rendir fell sideways, her unexpected weight toppling him, and stumbled just in time to stop himself hitting the ground. He glanced up, saw the ball, and pushed her back.

She punched him in the face before she fell.

"*Chic-Lay-Oooooo!*"

The ball was coming down right on top of him.

Pucallpa was there in an instant, leaping towards Rendir to push him off balance. Rendir hopped sideways, and Pucallpa's momentum carried him past. He stopped, turned to confront Rendir, and then disappeared downwards. Chiclayo had his ankle in both of her hands.

Rendir caught the ball after it bounced off the floor in front of him, and rolled it along the ground, straight back towards the hopper that encircled the base of the cannon.

Ahead, coming from the centre of the arena, Puno was thundering towards him, and he was *big*.

Rendir chased after the ball, trying to gain ground before Puno reached it himself. He overtook the ball, ducked down at the last moment, and slammed his shoulder into Puno's stomach.

The bigger teenager fell to one side, and Rendir kicked the ball onwards.

"*Chim-Bo-TE!*"

He dashed after it, but a hand grabbed his shoulder. It was Chiclayo, trying to pull him back. Pucallpa punched her between the shoulders, and she turned to hit him.

Rendir realised he was inside the goal zone. He picked up the ball, ran for the hopper, and slammed the ball into it.

The commentator's response drowned out the cheers. "Perrrrrfect Deliverrrrry!"

Rendir raised his arms above his head, and drank in the applause of the crowds.

"*Ren-dir! Ren-dir!*"

The new chant was spreading outwards, travelling across the stands like a wave.

The cannon fired again, and the ball was back in play.

He was the farthest of them all when the ball hit the ground, and ran as hard as he could to catch up. Pucallpa and Puno were punching each other on the floor, and by the time Rendir reached the ball, Chiclayo was holding it aloft in a scoring zone. The ball glowed brightly to show she had proper custody of it.

If he took the ball from her and scored now, it would only be an imperfect delivery. But the longer she had custody in this zone, the more points she accrued.

He kneed the outside of her thigh.

She swore under her breath and glared at him, but kept the ball in the air. He grabbed her arm and bent it down, so she moved the ball from one hand to the other. The glow vanished.

Rendir grabbed for the other arm, and she pushed his face away from her. Her fingers clawed his face like talons, scraping across the sensitive, swollen cheek she had punched earlier. He gritted his teeth and bore the pain, still trying to reach her arm.

Someone grabbed his legs and pulled them from beneath him. As he fell, he saw Puno's face grinning down at him. Puno grabbed Chiclayo by the neck, threw her to the floor, and took the ball.

"*Руиииии-пппоооо!*"

"You okay?" Rendir shouted. "That was a foul."

She gasped for a second, then shouted back over the noise of the crowd. "I'm good."

Rendir got to his feet and looked around. There was no sign that the marshals were going to take any action.

The crowd roared, and he saw Puno punching the air and bellowing 'Come on!' to the crowds. He had delivered the ball back to the hopper.

Imperfect, Rendir thought. Only three points, you cheating dickhead.

The cannon fired.

Rendir was moving again, thundering across the arena. The ball was coming down on an arcing trajectory, and he was not far from where he expected it to land.

He was vaguely aware that Chiclayo was lagging behind him, and Puno had set off far too late, a victim of his own pride.

Movement to the side; Pucallpa bearing down on him.

Rendir threw out his arm as the Pucallpa player reached him, smashing it across his chest. Pucallpa's legs carried on, and he flipped onto his back, hitting the ground hard.

Rendir plucked the ball from the air, netting a few bonus points.

He glanced towards the goal — too far, and Puno was coming from that direction. There was a scoring zone just a few dozen metres away.

He hurled the ball towards the outer wall, aiming it so that it would bounce off and roll into the scoring zone. He set off at a run, making for the zone directly, knowing that any less experienced player would waste time following the ball instead of him.

Pucallpa was back on his feet, and ran for Rendir. Damn.

He reached the scoring zone just as the ball entered it, and picked it up. He jammed his thumb into the single hole, and the ball glowed with the colour of the Chimbote team.

Pucallpa was still coming, running hard. Beyond him, Rendir could see the Puno player was not far behind.

One point for every second, he thought. Make those moments count.

Pucallpa leapt at him, and Rendir grabbed one of his arms with his free hand. He yanked on it, and stamped on Pucallpa's foot at the same time. Pucallpa stumbled back, but launched forwards again immediately, grabbing for the ball.

Rendir was the taller player, but he strained to keep the ball far above Pucallpa.

Puno entered the scoring zone, lowered his head, and charged Pucallpa. When he connected, Pucallpa was thrown aside like a rag doll.

Here it comes, thought Rendir.

Puno balled his fist, advanced, and drew his arm back.

Chiclayo appeared from nowhere, and smashed her knee up between Puno's legs. The big teen collapsed on the ground.

A piercing whistle cut through the crowd's roar, and a marshal jogged over to them. Boos and hisses came from the closer stalls.

"Foul!" The marshal shouted. "Penalty against Chiclayo team."

"Are you kidding?" Rendir said. "*He* fouled *her*."

"When?"

"He grabbed her throat."

"It wasn't seen," said the marshal. "If it wasn't seen he can't be booked."

"You have got to be joking."

"Play will resume in ten seconds."

The marshal took the ball from Rendir, and tossed it carelessly across the arena. Rendir and Chiclayo looked at each other.

When the whistle blew again, only Pucallpa set off at full sprint. Rendir and Chiclayo followed as if their hearts were no longer in the game.

Puno was back on his feet by the time Pucallpa

scored, and he lumbered angrily towards the others.

The cannon fired once more.

Puno kept coming, ignoring the ball, and Rendir recognised the look on his face. He too ignored the ball, and chased down Chiclayo.

"I think you pissed him off," he yelled.

Chiclayo glanced at Puno, and yelled back. "Yep. He's got it in for me all right."

Pucallpa had the ball again, and stood holding it in a scoring zone. He looked around, confused by the lack of opposition.

With Chiclayo locked in his sights, Puno charged.

Rendir smashed a fist into his nose, as hard as he could, and down Puno went, blood splattering over his face and the floor of the arena.

The crowd fell silent.

"Oh dear," said Chiclayo.

A whistle was being blown repeatedly, and Rendir struggled to calm himself down. Adrenaline had started to flood his system the moment that first klaxon sounded, and it was difficult by this point to ignore the effects.

"You," a marshal shouted. "This is a game, not a battle."

"It's maulball; what's the difference?"

"You don't fight each other unless it's for the ball."

"He started this, not me."

"I'm finishing it. Either you substitute, or your team forfeits the match."

Rendir glared at him, seething.

"Substitute," the Chiclayo player whispered. "If someone else from your team finishes this match, your coach can stack another sacrifice later in the tournament."

Rendir looked at her, smiled a quick smile, and walked away, ignoring the marshal.

The crowd cheered him off. To a maulball audience, the only thing better than tactical violence was unwarranted violence.

"Ren, are you okay?"

Hitami called out to him, waving from the edge of the crowd that clustered around the main entrance to the stalls.

He smiled half-heartedly and waved back, then realised it was Josué who stood next to her. The smile vanished.

Josué was wearing his Navy Cadets jacket, a set of wings pinned to the lapel. His face was smug.

"You're an animal, aren't you Throam."

"Fuck off, Josué."

"Ren!"

Hitami looked shocked, and Rendir realised it was the first time he had sworn in front of her.

"Going to smash my face in too?"

"Seriously, Josué. I'm this close."

"Leave it, Jos," said Hitami. "He's all fired up from the game."

"Yeah, the game he blew for himself."

"I said leave it."

Josué turned his attention to Hitami, and looked at her as though she were a disobedient slave.

"Don't tell me what to do. You give me your opinion when I ask for it, right?"

Hitami looked even more shocked.

"Not a bully, huh?" Rendir said. "Enjoy your life together."

He walked away, and saw that Peshal was waiting for him at the exit. She joined him as he left the arena.

"Don't you start," he said.

"Rendir Throam, you don't speak to your mother that way."

"Sorry. I'm... still mad."

"I saw what happened, Little Man."

"Please, mum, stop calling me that. I'm not little any more. I've not been little for a long time."

"Okay. Sorry."

"Go on, tell me how disappointed you are."

"But I'm not."

"Aren't you going to tell me I should have bent in the wind? 'Be the reed', and all that?"

"During a maulball match? Don't be ridiculous. Metaphors have their limits, Rendir."

He was surprised. It was the sort of thing he would have expected from Lamis, not from Peshal.

"Anyway, he clearly deserved that."

Rendir smiled.

"I wanted to talk to you about this military thing," she said.

The smile faltered. "Right now? Not again. Lamis already had a go at me about it last night."

"Well, I talked with her," she said.

"And?"

"To be honest with you, I think you should do it."

He stopped walking, and his mouth dropped open. If he had been able to convince either of them, he had assumed that it would have been Lamis.

"Your mother doesn't agree with me, of course."

"But will she let me?"

"We both said a long time ago that we would

let you make your own choices when you were old enough. I told her that time has arrived."

"Why? Why now, I mean."

"Listen Ren. You're born, you grow up, and one day you have children of your own. You raise them, you nurture them, you teach them right from wrong. And if you're lucky, you get to die before they do. If you're very, very lucky — one of a tiny minority — you get to die without seeing them crushed under the weight of life."

"I don't understand."

"If we stop you being who you want to be, then we're the ones who started to crush your own life out of you."

He started walking again, with her by his side, and fell quiet as he considered what she had said. It sort of made sense, but he did not quite understand.

"I wonder... did you ever consider becoming a counterpart?"

"A counterpart?"

"Yes. If that match was anything to go by, I think you'd be rather good at it."

"You mean, the bit where I smashed someone's face in to stop him hitting someone else?"

"Yes, that bit."

"I only meant to keep her safe."

"Exactly, Rendir. That's exactly it."

"And you say I could do that as a *career*?"

She laughed. "You really are your mother's son, aren't you Rendir?"

# – 15 –
# THESE OLD SCARS

Limping, an injured lion, *Love Tap* burst from the Laearan wormhole, followed closely by the remains of his task force. The giant ship was riddled with damage, as were his companions.

Admiral Betombe paced back and forth on the auxiliary command deck, impatient to arrive at Fort Laeara. He had so much information to share, and the sooner Command knew about it the better.

What had happened at Blacktree was mystifying and edifying, both at the same time.

It was not yet clear to him exactly why, but he was beginning to suspect that the hostilities with the Viskr were a mistake. Something *else* had been out there at Blacktree; something the Viskr had committed a small fleet to fighting off, despite the fact that the Hujjur system was not even theirs to begin with.

That had set him thinking about the odd fleet deployments monitored by Eyes and Ears. They might make sense, if the Viskr border worlds were being harassed by another force. Those ship movements could have been reactive, rather than random patrols.

It was, he admitted to himself, a little too late to

be solving that puzzle — especially now that the Empire had committed dozens of battle groups to the same border systems at which the Viskr fleets were rallying.

"Ten minutes to the fortress, Admiral."

He looked up and acknowledged Commander Laselle. She stared back at him quizzically.

"Are you all right, Sir?"

"Fine, thank you."

"You're quite sure? You gave us a bit of a shock earlier."

"You're not really a proper flag officer until you've fainted on the command deck," he said.

His XO continued to look uncertain.

"Really, I'm fine. I had a long rest in sickbay, and I've been given a clean bill of health."

"If you say so, Sir. The final report on Blacktree is in your folder."

Betombe opened the report on his holo, and flipped through the various charts and tracts of text.

"Still no idea what the Viskr fired those nukes at then?"

"I'm afraid not. They worked a little too well; nothing left but a radioactive smudge."

"Damage to the colony?"

"Serious. By the time help arrived from the nearest systems, we had already moved most survivors from the danger zone. But the after-effects are going to be very damaging indeed. Some of the towns farther out will need to be evacuated, long term."

"What have we got on the unknown vessel?"

"Again, very little. It's still being analysed, but all the holos can agree on firmly is that it's a ship and not a station."

"Very helpful," he muttered.

"I've attached my own log to the report. I'm sure Command will just ask anyway if I don't provide it myself."

"Won't they just," he said.

∘ ∘ ∘

Caden walked through the hatch into Throam's quarters and looked around. The compartment was neat enough that it might never have been used.

"Cosy," he said.

Throam looked up from his kit bag, grunted, and went back to stowing his clean uniforms in the drawers of a small unit.

"You okay?" Caden said.

Throam continued to ignore him, moving things around as if he were trying to get it just the way he wanted it. Caden realised the counterpart had not spent a single moment in these quarters until now.

"You know that was totally necessary," he said. "Eilentes wasn't just going to forgive you for that."

"You showed me up," Throam said.

"It was your own fault."

"Yeah, well you could have handled it differently, that's all I'm saying."

"How exactly do you think that would have gone?"

"I don't know, like... mediation."

"Mediation? You do remember what you did, right?"

"Of course I fucking do," said Throam. "I'm not going to forget, am I?"

"I should hope not."

Throam went quiet again and began pulling the foam liners out of his helmet. He scooped them up and took them into the wash enclosure. Caden heard the sound of water sloshing around in the basin.

When the counterpart returned, he was still avoiding Caden's gaze.

"Are you going to let me talk to you about this?" Caden asked.

"Talk, talk, talk," said Throam. "All you want to do these days."

"Again, this was all your own damned fault. Stop acting like a child."

Now, Throam stopped moving around and looked at him. "Like a *child*?"

"You're sulking. That's what children do. You did something bad, got told off, and you don't like it."

"Don't tell me how I feel."

"It's not like it isn't obvious, Ren."

"Maybe for *you*."

"What's that supposed to mean?"

"You're Mister Perfect. Not a bad thought in that head of yours."

"Oh come on," said Caden.

"No wait: you're not, are you. Having me kick a man through a window? Letting Prem kill Morlum, when he was trying to help us? Going off on your own on Woe Tantalum? And always telling me you're fine when you clearly aren't, like I'm just some fucking chump you can mug off when it suits you."

" I *am* fine." Caden's voice became low and steady. "It was just a wobble."

"A wobble, sure," said Throam. "Why did I not think of that first. Maybe because it wasn't just a wobble."

"You don't know what you're talking about,"

Caden said.

"So tell me. You said you would."

Caden was aware the tables had been turned on him, that he was now the one being asked to give an explanation. But he could not bring himself to feel annoyed by that. Throam was right; he had asked Caden for them to have this talk, and Caden had agreed to it.

"I've sort of been fighting with myself. Only... only it's not me. It feels different. Like it has its own mind. Its own goals."

"Its own goals?"

"It's difficult to explain."

"You're not going crazy are you? It'll make me look bad if you go crazy."

"I certainly hope not."

"How would you know?"

It was a good question, and Caden struggled to think of a suitable answer.

"When I was a child I started burying bad feelings deep down inside. I called it the Emptiness, and its whole purpose was to be banished. Over the past couple of weeks it has been, well, struggling to get out. And then on Woe Tantalum it succeeded. I don't know how else to explain it."

"So you *are* going crazy then."

"Maybe I am. I don't really know. It was kind of intense."

"Intense how?"

"Full-on hallucinations intense."

"Such as?"

"I saw it. It was me, only... horrible."

Throam stared back at him blankly.

"And it said things. Bitter, venomous things. It wanted me to be like it is. Wanted me to do all the things I know I shouldn't do. Say the things I ought not say."

"Some of that has been getting out, hasn't it?"

"I guess it has."

"Don't need to fucking guess, Caden. You're not vindictive. You're not callous. You're fair and objective and honest. But the guy who's been running with me this past week is a first class cunt."

Caden's mouth opened, but no sound came out. He opened then clenched both hands, and had the strangest sensation that his mind had detached from his skull.

"Go on, fuck off and go bitch with Euryce."

Caden gaped, and fought to win back the power of speech.

"You listen to me," he said. "You'll do as you're told, and I'm not going to tolerate any more of this insubordination. Make that the last time you call me a cunt."

"You know damned well I'm going to say it every time I think it needs to be said."

"You do that and see where it gets you."

Throam snorted air through his nostrils, as if he thought the very idea of the threat was a joke. Caden felt his body tensing.

"I mean it, Throam. We're a couple of hours out from Meccrace Prime. I want you back in counterpart mode, with your head properly in the game."

"Yeah, and I want your head in the game too," said Throam. "None of this 'oh my childhood feelings' bullshit."

"Good." Caden managed to utter it through clenched teeth. "Guess we're on the same page then."

He turned and stormed out of the quarters, letting the argument hang in the air.

∘ ∘ ∘

Betombe shifted uncertainly in his seat. He had expected a debrief, certainly, but something was not quite right.

He looked to his side, and saw that same uncertainty mirrored in Laselle's expression.

Fleet Admiral Bel-Messari had travelled to Laeara just for this meeting. That was unheard of, even to Betombe.

Bel-Messari conferred quietly with his aides and adjuncts around the head of the large, solid wood table. Holos were being passed back and forth.

This is no debrief, Betombe thought.

"Shall we begin?" Bel-Messari said.

Those who were still standing took their seats, but Bel-Messari waited a full ten seconds more before speaking.

"Admiral Groath Betombe; you are the same officer entrusted by Commander Operations with the planning and execution of Operation Seawall. Is that correct?"

"I am, Sir," said Betombe. "You know that already, of course."

"Indeed I do." Bel-Messari gave him a smile which contained precisely no humour, affection, or good will. "However, it's a relevant fact. It needs to be reflected in the record."

Betombe felt Laselle looking at him. He could imagine what her face looked like; by this point, she too would know that this was not a debrief.

"Of course."

"Given that role, is it correct to say that you adopted full responsibility for the operational orders encompassed by Seawall?"

"That is correct, yes."

"And do you accept that Seawall was an abject

failure?"

Betombe was silent.

"No, not a failure. A disaster. A complete catastrophe. Admiral Betombe?"

"It was... not what we expected it to be."

"Are you aware that of the sixty battle groups you took to the Perseus arm, we have had recent contact with only thirty-eight?"

"No, Sir. I was not aware of that."

"How do you think that might be explained, Admiral Betombe?"

"I think the Viskr are already under attack," he said. "We found an unknown—"

"Ah yes, this mysterious ship you fought at Blacktree."

Bel-Messari touched his holo, and the raw sensor footage from *Love Tap* began to play on the room's wall displays. It showed the dark, massive bulk of the intruder fleeing from Blacktree's atmosphere, missiles and slugs slamming against it as it rose into high orbit.

"Need I say more?" Betombe said. He waved his hand at the screen opposite.

"Well, yes," said Bel-Messari. "You really should. Commander Operations would very much like to know why you made first contact in the way that you did."

"In the way that I did...?"

"We don't know who this ship belongs to. Yet you took it upon yourself to attack it with full force."

"They were already fighting with the Viskr. With our own planetary defences!"

"Did you make any attempt to contact the vessel, prior to attacking it?"

"No, I did not. But—"

"Commander Laselle. Please read out the transcript of the command logs from *Love Tap*. The time index is marked for you."

Betombe and Laselle looked at each other. He could see she was as surprised as he.

"In your own time, Commander."

Laselle looked at the holo before her, found the correct lines, and read aloud.

"Admiral Betombe: I do not intend to allow that craft to finish whatever it was doing in Blacktree's atmosphere.

"Commander Laselle: We don't even know what that was, why it's here.

"Admiral Betombe: It's clearly hostile. Blacktree's own ships were firing on it when we arrived."

"That's enough, Commander. Thank you."

Laselle pushed the holo away as if it carried a contagion.

"Admiral, did you consider at any point that the visitor might have been fired upon first?"

"No, that was not a consideration."

"Did you comply with the provisions of the Navy's first contact protocol?"

"No, I did not."

"Can you account for your various lapses in judgement, Admiral Betombe?"

There was a pause.

"Am I being asked to provide a deposition?"

"You are, yes. I think we can all agree that this discussion will likely be moving to a more formal environment. But that will be for a later date, and right now I need something to take back to Commander Operations."

"Then I respectfully decline to answer that question."

"I really think you ought to reconsider that, Betombe."

"No offence, Admiral, but I was commanding fleet operations on the Perseus arm when you were still learning your way around a helm. I don't need to explain my decisions to you."

"I'm rather afraid that you do," said Bel-Messari. "But don't worry. You can have some time to think about how you want to proceed." He pressed the comm panel in the table. "Send him in, please."

Betombe and Laselle craned their necks to look behind them as the doors opened, and in walked the corpsman from the *Love Tap* sickbay. He had the bearing of a man who wanted nothing more than to turn around immediately and leave the room again.

"Please take a seat, Doctor."

The corpsman did so, and gave Betombe an apologetic look. Betombe understood at once: the corpsman too had submitted his own report, as per regulations. And he had been a little too honest.

"Can you tell me, Doctor, what was Admiral Betombe's medical condition when *Love Tap* arrived at Blacktree?"

"Yes, Sir. He was... he was fine. Up and about, on the auxiliary command deck. Giving orders and, well, running the ship."

"And would you say he was medically fit to do that, at the time?"

"I had no reason to think otherwise."

"No reason." Bel-Messari smiled again, that same cold and humourless smile. "Please refresh my memory: why exactly did Admiral Betombe visit your sickbay?"

"We took some damage to the main bridge before leaving the Gousk system, and the admiral was injured before the deck was evacuated."

"And what was the nature of that injury?"

"He hit his head, Sir."

"He hit his head. Very unfortunate. And I understand he lost consciousness for quite some time?"

"He did, Sir, yes."

"But that wasn't the only occasion, was it?"

"No. He also lost consciousness after the battle with that... thing."

"And...?"

"And drifted off prior to entering the Hujjur system."

"During that time, did you re-examine Admiral Betombe under a scanner, to ensure he was medically fit to command the *Love Tap*?"

"No, Sir, I did not."

"Did you want to?"

The corpsman stole a sideways glance at Betombe. "Yes, Sir. I asked him, but — sorry Sir — he said no."

"In your opinion, was Admiral Betombe competent to command the *Love Tap* during the engagement with the unknown ship?"

"I can't possibly answer that," said the corpsman. "I'd need much more data."

"More than the data you had when you failed to relieve him from his duties on medical grounds?"

The corpsman stayed silent.

"I will take that as a 'yes'. Just one more question: do you think it likely that Admiral Betombe was concussed while commanding the *Love Tap* and its battle group at Blacktree?"

The corpsman shifted in his chair. "I would have to say yes."

"So: despite the fact that he probably had a concussion, Admiral Betombe's fitness for duty had not been established at the time that he resumed command of the *Love Tap*, because you — the ranking medical professional — had insufficient data."

Bel-Messari went quiet, and looked at Betombe expectantly. Betombe felt like a mouse caught in the gaze of a hawk.

"This is completely over-the-top," he said. "Command knew what information we had when the order was given to hit the border worlds."

"Let me remind you, Admiral Betombe: twenty-two battle groups unaccounted for."

"The data from the listening posts—"

"Twenty-two battle groups, still waiting to be found. One might imagine that a veteran of the Perseus conflict would have scouted the target systems before committing those units."

"Eyes and Ears assured Commander Op—"

"The conflict with the Viskr is possibly salvageable," Bel-Messari said. "But we have no idea what the consequences will be following your attack on the unknown ship at Blacktree."

"Ideally, the consequences will be that they never come back."

"And maybe they won't. But had you established meaningful communication with them, it might be that one of our colonies would not have been nuked."

Betombe was silent again.

"Do you know how many people were killed on Blacktree, Admiral?"

"No, I do not."

"Neither do we."

Betombe felt a hand on his, and looked down. Laselle had placed her hand over one of his tightly balled fists, and she squeezed gently.

"As of this moment, Admiral Betombe, your command status is rescinded. Until such time as a full hearing can be convened, you are grounded from all naval operations."

Bel-Messari gave him that dead smile once more, and Betombe could do nothing else but smile back emptily.

○ ○ ○

"Were you on Mibes?" Lau said.

"I was, yes. How did you know?"

"Because it's been all over the holos, and the capital was on fire."

"Oh, right. Yeah that was us. Sort of."

"That's why you haven't come home yet?"

"Mibes is just a small part of it, Midget. We're fighting a war on two fronts."

"Two? I thought it was the Viskr attacking us."

"It's not that simple."

"Well that's what the news said."

"Listen, I can't really tell you anything. I have a feeling it would put you in danger."

"Yeah yeah. You're not coming home, are you?"

"Afraid not. Something came up."

"Something always does."

"I want you to get out of town. Go to the countryside somewhere, both of you. Lie low, and if you see Maber Castigon skulking about, you run and you don't look back."

"Maber? What in the worlds would he be doing on Damastion?"

"He's killing Shards," said Caden. "Every one of them so far had testified against him after Ottomas. He might try to get to me through you."

"I don't think that's very likely. Anyway, if he's an ex-convict and a fugitive, surely port control wouldn't let him put down on Damastion?"

"I really don't think they'll stop him — they haven't at any of the other worlds he's killed on. And I wish you'd take this seriously; the man is deadly."

"You... you really think he'll come here?"

"I don't know, Lau. But he could."

"We can just stay with friends—"

"No, get out of the town entirely."

"You're very insistent, Ugly."

"There's something else. Something moving in the background. It might be you can't trust the people around you any more."

"What are you talking about?"

"Like I said: I can't tell you much."

"You haven't told me *anything*."

Caden reached out and touched the hologram, hoping that Lau would follow his instructions. If he ignored them, who knew if they would ever talk again.

"We're about to make our final jump," he said. "Tell her I love her. And make sure you do what I said."

o o o

*Disputer* emerged in the heart of the Meccrace system, elegant and graceful, her transition into normal space cushioned and stabilised by the local gate. She headed for Meccrace Prime, and the security of the Eighth Fleet's mustering point.

On the command deck, Captain Thande nodded along as Caden explained what he planned to do.

"How long do you expect this to take?" She

asked.

"I'm afraid I have no idea. Eyes and Ears should have moved her already, but she might not want to leave. If she doesn't, she could make this difficult."

"I'm sure you have your ways."

"None of which will work if she chooses to hide from me. Or if the enemy have got to her first."

"The enemy," Thande said. "Still not sure exactly who you're talking about."

"There are people out there who aren't what they seem," he said. "Humans, acting against the Empire. We don't know why yet."

"Like the ones you fought on Woe Tantalum? The ones we transferred to the *Vavilov*?"

"Like them, only more active. More dangerous."

"I don't like the sound of that one bit."

"You and me both. Are we in range for comms with traffic control?"

Thande repeated the question for COMOP.

"We have a channel," he said.

"Good. I need to know if a man named Gordl Branathes has reached the surface."

"Stand by... the query has been sent."

"Gordl Branathes?" Thande said.

"He's an Eyes and Ears monitor. Long story."

"Why are you looking for him?"

"He may be one of those people I mentioned."

"Response received: yes, Gordl Branathes cleared the Arrivals desk at the primary starport almost an hour ago."

"Shit. There's not much time. Captain, I'm going to need to borrow one of your shuttles for a little while."

"Help yourself."

## – 16 –
## TENEBRAE

Sayad Idiri had been giggling to himself for some time, but Borreto could hear the stress in his voice as clearly as he heard the warning bleeps from the holos. The pilot was only giddy because he was so very nervous.

He had a perfect right to be nervous.

"Worlds," said Borreto. "That one was fucking close, Sayad."

"I know," Sayad laughed. "We. Are. Going. To. *Die.*"

"Only if you let us. Get a grip."

Sayad fell silent, and nudged the *Leo Fortune* gently to starboard. A rock the size of a frigate rolled by, less than a hundred metres off their port side and just above their plane.

"How are we doing?"

Borreto twisted to look back over his shoulder, and saw Castigon was hunched in the small entryway that joined the main compartment to the cramped flight cabin. He held himself steady by gripping the edges of the bulkheads.

"Oh, fine. Lovely place you brought us to."

Castigon ignored the comment. "Any idea how long?"

"Nope," said Sayad. "Not a clue. This is harder

than I'm making it look." He giggled again.

"I'm sorry about the route we have to take," said Castigon. "But seeing as how this bucket only has second generation stealth plating, it's a necessary precaution."

Borreto chose to let the insult against the *Leo* slide, at least for now. He had a feeling that severe punishment waited patiently somewhere in Castigon's future anyway, and he was happy to leave him to it.

"Asteroid belts are not my cup of tea," he said calmly.

"They're nobody's cup of tea," said Castigon. "That's why Altakanti was installed out here."

"What exactly are you hoping to get from an Imperial listening post?" Borreto asked.

"Information of course," Castigon said.

"Yes, but about what?"

Castigon looked at him with that deathly expression he wore so often.

"Never mind. None of my business."

"Quite right."

Prayer called through from the main compartment. "You sure they won't detect us?"

"As long as Sayad only uses the manoeuvring jets, there's nothing to detect. It might take a while to get close, but as far as the folks at Altakanti are concerned we're just another rock."

"How close is close enough?" Borreto asked.

"Close enough for me to get there by EVA."

"You really are insane."

"People keep telling me that," said Castigon.

"Listen, if you go getting yourself killed, how am I going to get paid?"

"I'm not going to get killed. I've done things like this before. In fact I've done much more dangerous things than this."

"You're ex-military, aren't you?"

"The longer I know you, Captain Borreto, the less discreet you seem to become."

"I should just stop asking questions, shouldn't I?"

"Make that the last one."

Borreto fell silent. He watched Castigon propelling himself back through the main compartment, floating in the empty space, pulling himself along the hand bars with practiced ease.

Definitely a military background, he thought. This guy is a lot more dangerous than he seems, and he seems pretty fucking dangerous already.

Prayer moved around Castigon, giving him space to start pulling on the EVA suit she had taken out of storage for him. A glove floated away, and she snagged it before passing it back to him.

"Let me know when you're done," she said. "I'll check those seals for you."

He nodded, and carried on.

She moved up towards Borreto.

"You okay Boss?"

"Yeah, Prayer. I'm okay."

He could tell by her facial expression that she was sceptical, but she knew better than to ask him any more questions. He pointed briefly towards Castigon, and her eyes told him that she understood.

Captain Borreto would wait until their passenger was off the ship. Only then would it be safe for them to talk.

○ ○ ○

Brant and Tirrano pored over reports in the flight cabin of the borrowed transport vessel *Spring Eternal*. Just before she had headed out the door to join Brant in one of Fort Laeara's many hangars, Tirrano had dumped three days' worth of data onto her holo.

She had not stopped at her own work station either; she had taken information from a number of other operators' holos. When Brant had asked her about it, she had rolled her eyes and said they were already going to be up on desertion charges, so why not espionage charges as well?

Having only just got over that deeply worrying thought, Brant now sounded as though he wanted to be sick.

"Becchari, Ophriam, Lophrit, Ankhar's Star, Naruth, Guathelia, Umri Major... this is terrible."

"How many, total?"

"Thirteen systems. Seven facilities. At least twenty-six ships Command knew about as of the start of today."

"Thirteen systems," Tirrano repeated. "The gates are not responding in *thirteen systems*, and they have managed to keep a lid on it?"

Brant had paled. "I doubt they'll keep a lid on it for much longer. I mean, we found them out. It's only a matter of time before others do too. How long can you tell people a gate is down for repair, before someone gets fed up with waiting and makes an unbound jump?"

Tirrano muscled in on the holo he was working from, and swiped data tiles over each other. He leaned away to give her room to work.

"What are you doing?"

"Cross-referencing ships with systems."

"Why?"

"Look. The *Vehement* was recorded as going off the network during a training exercise. It's annotated as being due to re-appear some time in the next week. Only we know it won't, because—"

"Because its last known way-point was Guathelia, which has gone dark."

"Exactly."

"Worlds, Peras. This is just wrong. Someone needs to do something about this."

"I know what you're going to say, and I think you should not say it."

"What am I going to say?"

"That 'someone' should be us."

"What are *we* going to do about it? Why in the many worlds would I say that?"

"Because you're Mister Do-The-Right-Fucking-Thing."

"I am not."

"You bloody are. That's why your new boyfriend chose you for this suicide run."

An alert from the navigation holo interrupted them before Brant could come up with a suitable retort, and Tirrano tapped an icon to open the message.

"We're up next," she said. "Both ships ahead of us in the queue are going the same way."

"Four gates," Brant said. "Four! I really hate jumps."

"Well then; you should have found us a ship that could survive doing it in one, instead of this shitty hauler."

"It was very short notice," he said. "Worlds, do I *hate* jumps."

She watched him while he gazed out of the view port, and saw the light of the forming wormhole dancing in his eyes. He looked as though he were facing his own mortality.

"Man up, Brant," she said.

○ ○ ○

Castigon listened to the sound of his own breath inside his helmet, and the rush of blood pumping around his veins.

Aside from the small vibrations that travelled through the suit each time he shifted his feet on the *Leo*'s hull, all else was quiet.

The silence was liberating. Others found it unnerving, he had heard. But not him; Castigon loved it.

"We're bang on. Direct line between us and their rock. Nothing big will come between us for a few minutes yet."

The pilot had assured him of this before Castigon had entered the airlock. He really hoped Sayad's sensors were properly calibrated.

He looked up, arching his whole spine against the constraints of the EVA suit, and surveyed his target.

The asteroid that hosted Altakanti turned slowly in the black, one side of it ablaze in the reflected light of the local star. The other side, the side facing away from the star, was so dark that he struggled to make out where it ended.

He brought up his arm and looked down to check the wrist display. Both the air and the propellant gauges looked good.

"Here goes nothing," he said.

He unclipped the tether from his waist, and pushed off.

His body sailed away from the *Leo Fortune*, weightless and free of drag. It was better than flying; there was nothing to hold him back.

He tried to judge the distance, the trajectory. It was difficult, but he could not afford to miss. More than that: he could not afford making too many adjustments. As old as it was, the *Leo* had its stealth plates. His body had no such advantage. Any nearby object making multiple course corrections would trigger alarms on the station, even something as small as he was.

He drifted on, a tiny meat-filled bag in a vast, indifferent universe.

He watched with fascination as a tiny piece of asteroid zipped by, tumbling around its own centre of gravity. It was smaller than one of his fists.

Cute you might be, he thought, but a rock like you could crack my visor. Maybe I didn't think this through.

He checked again and judged his course to be off by a couple of degrees. A short burst from his EVA pack, and the asteroid was centred again in his view.

It loomed larger and larger, and again he found himself reconsidering his plan.

He left it until the last possible minute before he fired off the bursts that flipped him head over heels, and the smaller bursts that stopped his spin from carrying on forever.

He switched to the lower thrusters, and started to decelerate.

The asteroid grew larger with every passing second, its surface becoming the ground he was falling towards. He began to perceive a horizon, one that receded from him faster and faster.

"Come *on*," he said.

The thrusters did their job despite his misgivings. By the time his feet hit the ground, he had only to bend his knees to absorb the last of his momentum. The sudden drag of rotation nearly threw him backwards.

He tried to stand, and succeeded only in pushing himself back off into space. Between the thrusters and the weak gravity of the asteroid he managed to sink back down gently until his boots touched the rock again, and he took a few rapid steps to match the turn of the ground beneath his feet.

He walked slowly, carefully, and laboriously, towards the terminator line that separated the darkness and the light.

It took nearly half an hour before he saw the hull of the station rise over the horizon, and another twenty minutes to actually reach it. His air monitor warned him that he had passed the halfway mark, and he hoped that he would find either spare tanks or a charging point somewhere inside the station.

Of course there will be something, he told himself. They're not *that* stupid.

He found the hatch to the auxiliary airlock, right where he expected it to be, and set to work on the control panel. By the time he had managed to switch off the safeguards and alarms, his air reading was flashing one quarter.

The outer hatch opened, and he stepped inside and closed it behind him. He got to work on the panel inside the airlock. It would not help him to re-pressurise the compartment if everyone on the station knew about it immediately.

By the time the air was pumping back into the small chamber, his tank was just above the red line.

He pulled off his helmet and gasped for clean, dry air.

Castigon gave himself a few minutes before venturing deeper into the station. The automatic systems he could reprogram with relative ease; he could not reprogram a person to ignore him if he opened a hatch right into their path. If there was going to be fighting, he needed to be ready for it.

After a while, he grasped the metal wheel on the inside of the inner hatch, and turned it slowly.

The hatch opened into a quiet, still passageway.

He stepped through the aperture cautiously, checking in both directions. There were no signs of life, and he could hear only the gentle thrum of the life support systems.

He pulled his right glove off, clipped it to his belt, and slid his holo out of a storage slot in the suit. A few taps later, and he had recovered the standard layout for listening posts from its memory.

He headed towards the comms exchange centre, as stealthily as he knew how.

As he moved, the profound silence of the station began to weigh on his mind. Something was not right; a station this size would normally have a staff of twelve. Even if they had a station-wide sleep period — which listening crews never did, because they worked in four shifts — there ought to be *someone* moving around and making the noises associated with life.

He stopped to sniff the air. There was no pungency, no taint of putrefaction. So he was probably not walking around an automated tomb. That was reassuring.

He carried on, and after a while he reached the exchange centre unopposed. He placed his helmet down on one of the control desks, and looked around. The holos and servers arrayed along the wall were all in standby mode.

He resumed one of them.

"—cycle interrupted. Repeater now automatic,"

the holo blared.

Castigon leapt backwards, then slapped at the holo hurriedly, dropping the volume. Words appeared on the display.

*Dumping buffer prior to databurst.*

The words vanished and a woman appeared in their place. She stared at the camera, her face sad. She began to whisper, and he raised the volume by a few points.

"—I don't know how long I have left, or if this will even reach you. They've taken Jaesia. They've taken your father. Worlds, they're taking everybody. It's... it's like a nightmare. The sky, oh my son, they tore the sky."

He heard what sounded like a muffled explosion, from somewhere far away outside whatever building the woman was in. She looked behind her, and turned back to the camera with tears in her eyes.

"Don't come here looking for us, you hear? Do *not* come here. Ophriam is a fallen world. By the time you arrive there will be nothing left."

A burst of static washed her out of the image, then she resolved again.

"I love you son. We all do. I hope wherever you are, this message reaches you. I hope that it's safe there. I love you."

The sound of another explosion began, and then the recording cut to black. More words appeared.

*Dataset truncated unexpectedly.*

*Buffer empty.*

*Commencing emergency databurst.*

*Gate 20-308: Ophriam.*

"What the fuck was that?"

He resumed the next holo along. This one too had a recording waiting on it; the last dataset for whoever had been working at this terminal before they upped and left.

*Databurst received.*
*Relay point signature confirmed:*
*Destroyer ICS Gladius.*
*Corrupted blocks detected.*
*Attempting recovery...*

"They've taken the town. Took it from us like we weren't even here."

It was a soldier, wearing a MAGA uniform with a corporal's rank insignia. His face was streaked with grime and dried blood.

"I've never seen anything like it before. People fighting each other in the streets. Friends, neighbours! Falling on each other like animals. I've seen humans fighting alongside Viskr, against their own kind—"

This recording too was interrupted by an explosion, only the sound was closer and more defined. Dust dropped in front of the camera. The soldier flinched, ducked down for a second.

"But there's something else here. Something in the darkness and the shadows. I can... hear it in my mind. He won't stop, and... and I don't want Him to—"

A roaring, thundering crash in the distance, like the heavens falling from on high.

"What in the Deep... Oh my worlds... the song! The song is beginning again—"

Static, then a black screen.

*No further recoverable data.*
*Databurst has been archived.*

*– Relay: ICS Gladius –*
*Position: Unknown. Status: Unknown.*

Castigon stood in front of the holo and stared at the words until they were burned into his mind. He had no idea what he had just watched.

After a moment, he made a decision. He docked his own holo with each of them in turn, and duplicated the recordings before moving on to find what he had come for.

○ ○ ○

Borreto, Sayad, and Prayer floated close to each other in the main crew compartment of the *Leo Fortune*. Nobody had spoken for what seemed like an age.

"I'm not saying we should leave him behind," Borreto said at last.

"I should hope not," said Sayad. "The amount of money he's offered to pay will see us in parts and fuel for the next couple of Solars at least."

"If we get fuckin' paid," said Prayer.

"Exactly." Borreto stroked his chin. "I'm not convinced he's on the level."

"That's one hell of an understatement, Boss."

"So it's not just me then, Prayer. You see it too."

"To be honest, I was wondering why you agreed to carry him the moment he first stepped on that ramp."

"We can't just leave him here though," said Sayad. "You both know that. We won't ever find another fare in the Backwaters if we do."

"Therein lies the problem," said Borreto. "But I don't even want to know where he's going next. The guy is trouble, plain and simple."

"What if we just tell him his next destination is where we part ways?"

"It might come to that, Sayad."

"It fuckin' ought to."

"Yeah, well I'm not happy with him directing my actions either. We should have called in that situation on Lophrit, no matter what he said."

"You gonna do it Boss?"

"Not yet. The last thing we want to do is to start transmitting right next to a listening post. The minute we drop at the next gate, I'm going to let the network know."

∘ ∘ ∘

Castigon was still working at the holos, searching out the last of the messages and command dispatches he needed, when he sensed danger. There was a minute shift in the air, or maybe it was the faintest possible sound. Whatever it was, it was enough.

He raised his pistol to the doorway, quick as a flash, and his head turned after it.

"Hello again," said the woman.

He stared at her for a moment, not recognising her face. She was only small, slightly built and very short. Her features were delicate, her blonde hair immaculate, her clothing neat and clean. She seemed diminutive, non-threatening. But something about her triggered the alarms in his head, and he had always found those alarms to be reliable.

"Who might you be?"

"You don't recognise me, of course."

"Should I?" He kept his sights trained on the centre of her chest.

"It wasn't long ago, Mister Castigon. The last time you saw me, I was Herik Pammon."

His mouth opened, but no sound came out. It took him a moment to even think up possible meanings for her words.

"What are you talking about?"

"I am most grateful for your help on Serrofus Major. I had already tried to convince several locals to assist, to no avail."

Castigon's holo bleeped, alerting him that it had finished its copy. He picked it up with his free hand, keeping his eyes on the woman, and slotted it back into his suit.

"Again, who are you?"

"Why, me of course. I *am*."

"That doesn't answer my question at all."

She smiled sweetly, and he looked her up and down again. Her clothing was all wrong; she was not supposed to be here either.

"Where is the station's crew?"

"They had to go," she said.

"Go as in leave, or go as in their bodies are stuffed in a closet somewhere?"

"Just 'go'."

"What are you doing here?"

"The same as you."

"And what do you know about that?"

"This is a listening post of the First Unified Imperial Combine of Earth. There are very few reasons for people like us to come here."

He had to give her that one.

"I'm done here. I'm going to leave. Is that going to cause a problem for us?"

"Oh no, not at all. You're taking Shards out of the game. If anything you are saving me some time."

He eyed her up suspiciously, trusting her less the more she disclosed to him. She continued to smile, and stepped aside with a flourish of her arms as if urging him to carry on.

Castigon took the opportunity to leave the exchange centre, keeping his weapon trained on her. As benign as she looked, the more primitive part of his brain screamed out that she was one of the most dangerous people he had ever met.

He backed off down the passageway, and she ambled after him, her hands clasped in front of her. She hummed a tune of gentle sorrow.

"What do you mean, you *were* Herik Pammon?"

"Exactly that, and I still am. I'm sorry; it was a bit misleading. You don't seem to have a usable, conversational tense for simultaneity."

"Simultaneity?"

"Synchronicity, if you prefer?"

"What in the many worlds are you talking about?"

"You asked, so I told you."

"You're saying you are both here and on Serrofus Major?"

Her smile stretched wider than it ought to have done across that small, delicate face. "At the very least."

"Herik Pammon was a man. You aren't."

"That is very, very true."

"You're not a woman either, are you?"

"Not always. But here, and now, that's what I am."

He stopped backing away, and pointed the pistol at her face.

"Very well. *What* are you?"

The woman showed no signs at all that she was afraid of him.

"I *am*."

"You are... what?"

"Just that."

"You're fucking nuts, that's what you are."

He took a few steps back, turned, and jogged away towards the airlock.

Behind him, he heard the woman start humming again as she walked after him.

"You really want to stop following me," he said.

"I won't interfere," she replied. "In fact I would like to see you safely off this station, before the others arrive."

"What others?"

"They won't be long now."

His jog turned into a canter, and then a run. He was suddenly filled with the urge to flee from Altakanti and never look back. It was the same feeling he had experienced in the bar on Serrofus, only this time he had no reason to ignore it. No reason to stay.

She was trotting after him, managing to keep up somehow even though she looked like she was only putting in half as much effort as he did.

He reached the airlock and opened the inner hatch.

"Don't forget your air," she said.

He cursed under his breath, and looked around the airlock for a charging station. He found two together, yanked a hose out of one of them, and plugged it into the port on his suit.

"Who are the others?" He asked. His tank was charging quickly, but not quickly enough for his liking.

"They are the singers," she said. "But they do not give us the harmony. The harmony is mine."

"Fucking insane," he muttered.

"If you stay, you will know the answer. But then you might not want to continue, and I very much want you to continue."

"Continue?"

"Spare me the attention of the Shards."

"Why?"

"They will fight me to the bitter end."

His tank pinged, and he unclipped the hose.

"Hurry, Maber Castigon. Hurry away back to your crusade. They are coming."

○ ○ ○

"—repeat, come in *Leo Fortune*."

Borreto leaned past Sayad and jabbed at the comm.

"I thought we were maintaining radio silence?"

"Forget that; this place is empty. But we're going to have company."

"Company?"

"I don't know who, but someone is coming here now. Time is running out. I need you to come get me."

"There's no landing pad," the pilot said. "It'll be messy."

Borreto nodded. "Sayad says it'll be difficult to —"

"I heard. You don't need to put down, and I'm not sure there's time. Match rotation and spin; you're going to have to catch me."

"Is that possible?"

"Piece of cake," said Sayad.

"Okay, is it wise?"

"Not much choice anyway," said Castigon. "I burned a hell of a lot of propellant on the way over here, and I don't much fancy trying to hit your position with what little I have left."

"Your choice," Borreto said. "We're coming now."

"Let me know when you're in position. Out."

"You sure you can do this, Sayad?"

"No problem, Captain."

"Get us over there then, and keep an eye out for other ships."

"Roger that."

"What's happening?"

"Prayer, suit up. I'm going to need you to evacuate the cargo bay. We're going to play catch."

"Fuckin' what?"

○ ○ ○

Castigon waited, watching the woman warily. Any minute now he expected the crew of the *Leo* to let him know they were in position. The call could not come a moment too soon.

"I can't help but notice you don't have a helmet," she said.

He realised she was right, and cursed himself. He had left it in the exchange centre.

"Fuck!"

"Are you there?" It sounded like Sayad.

"Yeah... just need a few minutes. My helmet—"

"No time. Something just started moving in the belt, and it's headed this way. Don't know what it is but it's huge. It's now or never."

"But my helmet—"

"Now, or *never*."

Castigon began to panic, the first time in a long time he had experienced that sensation. He cast his gaze around fretfully, looking for any tool or resource he could adapt to ensure his survival.

Sayad was telling him they were in position outside the airlock at the same moment that inspiration struck.

"You can pop the hatch. We're ready to catch you."

"You'd better be."

He smiled at the woman, the same smile she had given him.

"You really want me to continue?"

"Very much so."

"And it's important to you?"

"I can't tell you how important."

"Then you won't mind helping me out."

He grabbed the front of her clothes, twisted them in his fist to hold her tight, and hit the emergency override with his free hand. She surprised him by not trying to struggle free.

The airlock lights began to flick on and off in a circular pattern, and an alarm sounded. A five second delay started to count down on a tiny status display.

"Why would I mind?" She said. "This is no sacrifice."

He looked at her passive, unconcerned face, and knew at once that she expected to die in keeping him alive.

He emptied his lungs just before the hatch blew, and pulled her towards him.

The station's atmosphere pushed them out of the airlock like a cork leaving a bottle. They rocketed out into the cold dark. He kept his eyes closed and hoped that Sayad was quick enough to match his trajectory.

His temples began to thump, blood roared through his skull in the deathly silence, and his lungs ached to fill again.

When he could stand it no more, Castigon pressed his mouth against the woman's lips and formed a seal. He inhaled forcefully, pulling the air out of her lungs. She didn't try to stop him.

Her body tumbled away seconds before the cargo bay of the *Leo* enveloped him.

The next thing Castigon knew, he was strapped to one of the spongy couches embedded in the bulkheads of the *Leo*'s main compartment. His head was filled with cotton wool, and it hurt to open his eyes.

Someone was doing something to his arm. He grabbed the wrist that came near him, holding it tight, and yanked it to one side.

"Ow, fuckin' stop it." It was Prayer. "It's just meds, that's all. You've been exposed to space."

He let her go, and she pressed the nozzle of a compression injector against his skin.

"Meds?"

"Anti-inflammatories, anti-radiation. Best I can do right now."

"How long was I out?"

"Few hours. You had some evaporation burns around your eyes, mouth, and nose. Took care of that, no problem. Thought you'd probably prefer to stay asleep while I thawed out your corneas."

"I feel like crap."

"You *were* partially exploded. I'd be worried if you felt okay."

"Exploded?"

"Just fuckin' around with you. You were only exposed for about thirty seconds, if that. I guess hypoxia knocked you out before you felt your blood start to fizz up."

"Yeah, I don't remember that at all."

"You emptied your lungs before the hatch popped, didn't you?"

"Yeah. About the only thing I remembered from the old safety drills: never take a lungful of air into hard vacuum."

"Probably saved your fuckin' life, that bit of advice."

"That and Sayad's positioning. Speaking of which, where are we?"

"Draydon's Folly."

"About as far from Altakanti as you can get in one jump."

"Too fuckin' right. Don't suppose you saw that thing in the belt?"

"No, I didn't."

"It was waiting for something. There when we arrived. Sensors thought it was just another asteroid until it started moving under its own power."

"Did you recognise it?"

"Nope. Like nothing I've ever seen before."

"Huh. Well, it's not our problem. My holo still in the suit?"

Prayer pushed off carefully, spinning to face away from him, and bumped against the far bulkhead. She opened the storage locker where the EVA suit lived, and tugged it until the chest was exposed. She fished Castigon's holo out of its slot.

He took it eagerly when she handed it to him, and began to flip and scroll through the data he had taken.

"What is it?" She said.

"More places to go, more people to see," he said. He glanced up at her. "I had to look up a few old friends."

"Did you find them?"

Castigon stayed silent. His eyes were fixed on the holo, and his mouth curved up slowly into a smile.

"What is it?"

"I found him," Castigon said. "That backstabbing little fuck. I know where he's going to be next."

## – 17 –
## SHAELD HRATHA

Caden stepped off the shuttle's ramp ahead of Throam, and strode out across the landing platform while Eilentes was still climbing down from the cockpit. All in all, it had been the most uncomfortably frosty twenty minutes he had ever spent in flight.

"Wait up," Throam called. "Don't rush in unprepared."

Caden stopped and turned back to face the lander. "Hurry up then."

Eilentes was already coming after him, Ambrast mag-tagged to her back. Her expression was thunderous.

"Don't let him talk to me," she said. "I'm not sure what I'll do to him if he does."

"I'm sorry, but you really need to sort that out between yourselves. I've done my part."

"Yeah, thanks," she said. "Thanks for your support."

"I think maybe that should all wait until later, anyway."

She hesitated, on the brink of saying something else, then reconsidered. "Sorry."

Throam jogged across to them, holding his rifle

across his body. "Ready."

"Coming down on the Eyes and Ears building, we probably saved ourselves a good hour," said Caden. "Branathes had at least that as lead time though, so he's probably here already. Stay sharp."

"Not being funny," said Throam, "but what kind of a threat is he going to be to us?"

"Remember Amarist Naeb? She single-handedly took out a fortress. Consider Branathes a mortal threat until he's no longer breathing."

"Shouldn't be long," said Throam.

"Stop bragging. You need to take this seriously."

"I do. I'm just not as afraid of him as you seem to be."

Caden let the insult slide. "Our links have been added to the security roster, so we should be able to get in and move around the facility without any problems. Once we're inside, our objective is the detainee holding area on level ten. That's where they're keeping her."

"Nice," said Eilentes. "Bet she's happy about that."

"Well it's only temporary. Let's go."

They double-timed it across to the edge of the landing pad, reached the open end of a tunnel spanning the roof, and before long were at the entrance to the building itself. Caden's link spoke briefly with the security console, and the doors rumbled open.

"Here we go again," said Throam.

Caden knew what he meant at once. The building was reminiscent of Gemen Station; all gently angled white walls and soft, blue emergency lighting. As soon as the doors behind them closed and shut out the damp, blustery weather, a thick quiet fell around them.

It was too much like Gemen Station, and Caden began to feel uneasy.

As if to set itself apart from the empty tomb of the Herros facility, the building echoed with a short burst of muffled gunfire. The noises stopped abruptly, a scream followed them, then all was quiet again.

"Great." Caden raised his rifle, and began to move forward cautiously. "Even better than Herros."

○ ○ ○

The *Spring Eternal* dropped out of an unbound wormhole with a rolling, lurching bump, and Brant vomited into a paper bag. He scrunched up the top, looked around, placed the bag carefully in a storage recess next to him, and wiped his mouth with a tissue.

"The thing I like about you," said Tirrano, "is that you're all man."

"Whatever." He tapped a holo on the main console. "Stealth plating engaged."

"This thing has stealth plates?"

"Why do you think I chose it?"

"I thought you'd just snagged the first ship you found."

"Yeah, well maybe I'm smarter than that."

She looked at him reproachfully. "I don't think I've ever called you stupid."

"A databurst came through with us," he said. He swiped across the comm. "Search results."

"The sweep for Herik Pammon?"

"Yep. Nothing. The man's a ghost."

"Why were you searching for him?"

"Caden didn't mention why. But if I had to guess, I'd say it was something to do with Medran

Morlum and Amarist Naeb."

"He's working with them?"

"Like I said, just guessing. But yeah, that's probably what it's about."

"Starting to pick up Navy chatter. It's pretty broken; the system nexus must be collapsing already."

"That means the gate is fully locked down," said Brant. "Any idea how we're supposed to get back?"

"This is your party. You don't have a plan for that?"

"Guess we'll be hitching a ride."

"You want to follow a ship through a wormhole? What if we get snipped?"

Brant considered this possibility. To avoid being detected they would have to stay far away from any other ships, running silent with the stealth plates on, then leap for the wormhole once the other ship or ships had passed through the aperture. There was indeed a small but significant chance the wormhole would close as they entered it.

"We'll have to think about that later," he said. "For now, let's concentrate on finding Kages."

"Laying in a course for Aldava."

"Avoid the sentry ships. We can take a wide orbit, get the planet between us and them, and go from there."

"What about the quarantine network?"

"As long as it's still under construction, we'll be fine. The platforms will be getting assembled by robots."

"What could be safer?"

He smiled at her caustically sarcastic tone.

"Landing under it when it's nearly done."

She glared at him.

○ ○ ○

"*ICS Disputer* from civilian hauler *Leo Fortune*, please respond."

Castigon watched from the main compartment while Borreto continued to try and get an answer from the Navy carrier that waited in high orbit of Meccrace Prime. He had had to argue with the captain at some length before Borreto had consented to entering the system, much less risking this approach. It had finally been worthwhile, but the cost of the trip had doubled once more.

"Civilian vessel *Leo Fortune*, we are now tracking. Please state your business."

"Urgent message for the Shard Elm Caden," said Borreto. "I understand you have him aboard?"

"Stand by," said the *Disputer* COMOP officer.

After a moment the comms holo presented a prompt, and Borreto tapped it. A man in uniform appeared, wearing the rank insignia of a Navy commander.

"I am First Officer Yuellen," he said. "I'm told you have a priority message for a passenger on this ship."

"Yes Sir," Borreto said. "Urgent communication for Shard Elm Caden."

"I'm afraid he is not currently aboard. Can I pass the message on for you?"

"I was told to deliver it to him, and him alone."

"As I said, he is not aboard."

Yuellen was matter-of-fact, and looked back at Borreto expectantly.

"Is there no way to reach him?"

The commander sighed.

"He's on the surface. If you are able to set up a

secure comm relay, you should be able to get your message through."

"We have that capability."

"Good. I'll send you the transponder ident for his shuttle. You can bounce your relay off that, and be assured it will remain private."

"Thank you very much, Commander. You have been most helpful."

Yuellen killed the connection.

"It's coming through now," said Borreto.

Castigon pulled himself through the entrance to the cockpit, and floated next to the captain.

"Excellent," he said. "Now let's triangulate that transponder."

○ ○ ○

"This is bullshit," Throam said. "No way is Branathes doing all this."

Caden was inclined to agree, only there was the inconvenient fact that the security system had not alerted them to any breaches when they themselves had entered. Whoever had attacked the building had been allowed to enter as a friend. It had certainly not been a friend who passed down this corridor before them.

There was blood on the floor and walls; some of it smeared, some of it sprayed. Bodies lay crumpled on the floor, almost all of them torn up. He saw deep lacerations, dark injuries leaking bright fluids onto paled skin.

And the walls and doors themselves; there were scratch marks in them, too.

"Something is in here with us," said Eilentes.

"Keep it together," said Caden. "These people were going about their normal day, unarmed. We're ready for a fight."

"Too fucking right," said Throam.

"We need to get downstairs. Holding is on ten, so that's only four levels."

"Elevators, two o'clock."

"They're out," said Eilentes. "Lights are all turned off."

"Must be in lock-down," Throam said. "Someone had time to throw a switch somewhere."

Caden glanced at his holo. "Stairways wind around the core of the building. We'll pass by security control on the way down."

"Can we spare the time?"

"It's the best chance we've got of finding out what we're up against. Let's move."

They hurried to the centre of the level, until the corridor opened out into a large atrium. A glass roof curved overhead, daylight streaming in above them.

"This way," said Caden. He hurried over to the edge of the empty space at the core of the building, dropped next to the wall which surrounded it, and peeked around the corner of the stairs to the next floor down.

"We're good," he signalled. They stole quietly down to the next floor, and then the next.

"Security control." Throam whispered it, and nodded towards a floor chart on the wall opposite the foot of the stairs. "It's just over there."

Caden checked the corner, beckoned to the others, and stepped out. He hurried along the corridor, quietly, following the route indicated by the chart.

Around the next corner, he saw the doorway of security control. It was wide open, and faint sounds of movement came from within.

He signalled to Throam and Eilentes to take up

flanking positions on either side of the door, and crept closer. As he approached, he edged out to get line of sight into the room.

There was — as far as he could see — only the one person in there.

"Branathes," he said.

Gordl Branathes looked up from the central console, and smiled at him.

*Something is wrong*.

"You are the Shard Elm Caden."

"That's me." He glanced around and saw that Branathes was indeed alone.

"I was wondering if you would come yourself."

"Well now you know. Step away from the console."

Branathes stayed where he was, behind the door-facing arc of the console.

"Now, Branathes. Step away."

"I am afraid you will have to make me."

Caden stepped forward. "I'm quite happy to do that."

Before Caden had time to react, Branathes slapped a button on the console. The door behind Caden slid down quickly and heavily, thudding into place. After a few seconds, he heard a soft thumping sound on the other side. Throam was probably banging his fist on it.

"Just you and me then," Caden said.

"If you say so."

*Something is wrong*.

"Whatever you want here, Branathes, you're not going to get it."

"I will. I only have to find her."

"It's over, Branathes."

"It is not over. It is barely begun."

"Look, I don't really care if you're Gordl Branathes, or some kind of enemy agent. The fact is that you've been caught."

"Kill this body; there are many more like it. I will still have the information it possesses."

"Okay... so enemy agent then. Who are you, really?"

"I *am*."

"You are what?"

"I just *am*."

The body of Gordl Branathes continued to tap at the console, no doubt trying to find the location of Doctor Bel-Ures. Caden wondered what in the many worlds he had managed to get himself involved with this time.

"I can't very well call you 'You Are', can I?"

"I have no name."

"What do people call you?"

"Too many names to choose from."

"Then I think I will just call you Voice."

Voice glanced up at him, frowned, and then went back to his work.

*Something is wrong.*

"You're not afraid of me, are you?"

"Why would I be? As I said, there are many bodies like this one."

"It would be a bit of a setback though, wouldn't it? If I popped a round through that skull? You'd have to send another body."

"You are perfectly welcome to try," said Voice. "But I do not think you will enjoy the consequences."

"Why is that?"

"They will stop you."

Caden looked around again. "There's nobody else here."

"I rarely travel alone," said Voice.

"You seem pretty much alone to me."

Voice smiled a sickly smile. "Look harder."

Caden felt the first real unease he had experienced since entering the room. Between Naeb, Morlum, the citizens of Aldava, and the denizens of Woe Tantalum, he had started to become accustomed to people acting strangely. Voice was weird, true, but he was not quite the weirdest person Caden had met recently.

But something in his tone warned Caden that he was not lying.

"Where in this empty room am I supposed to be looking?" He asked.

"Not in the room," said Voice. "*At* the room."

Caden looked around again, carefully, and took it all in.

The door was mounted in a wall of its own, one which was painted white and decorated only with some information signs and posters. Both of the two side walls adjacent to that one were lined with racks of holos and hard-copy files. The rear wall was all monitors.

*I warned you. Something is wrong.*

He tried to see without seeing, defocusing his eyes and shifting his weight from one foot to the other.

And then he saw.

Quick as a flash his rifle was knocked away from him before he could raise it fully, something soft but unyielding striking it from his grasp, and he was pushed back by the blow. The room itself moved around him.

*Let me fight with you.*

He drew a zadaqtan from its holder and hurled it at the wall in one swift movement. Its glossy, black shaft disappeared long before it should have struck the racking, right up to the handle, and it travelled sideways and down through the air. The pattern of files and holos went along with it, warping and melting and reshaping as it rippled across a shifting surface.

Movement behind him. He wheeled on one foot, and loosed another two blades.

Those two buried themselves in something that was much closer to him than it looked.

The walls aren't walls, he thought. It's camouflage!

"Shaeld Hratha!" Voice was shouting. "You cannot defeat what you never see."

Caden was moving across the room even before he knew he needed to react, his instincts launching him into cover. He ducked under something that looked like part of the ceiling but which was far too low. A not-wall lurched in front of him, hot air flowing from it, acrid and sharp. He caught the momentary glint of a dark eye, sweeping past and then rearing back.

He rolled under one side of the console, and hurled himself out under the other.

Voice laughed at his efforts.

How did I not see them before? Caden thought. They're so *big*.

He threw another zadaqtan, and the slender blade stopped just over a metre away, most of its razor-edged length vanishing into the air. The handle drew back from him quickly, as if it had struck its target in a sensitive spot. He seized the opportunity to throw himself at the far corner.

*Kill them all.*

He snatched up his rifle from the floor, rolled onto his knees, and let loose.

Holes ripped through the rippling mass of

bending décor and furnishings in front of him, and it pulled back sharply. A strange, baleful noise followed, resonating between his ears, the sensation of it thunderingly painful behind his eyes.

He kept firing, and the other one might have been hit too. He could no longer tell. The room was a whirlwind of motion and mimicry.

One of the masses pulled to the side sharply, avoiding the bursts of rounds from Caden's rifle, and Voice's head snapped back. Blood spattered against the monitors on the rear wall, and the vacant body of Gordl Branathes slumped lifelessly to the floor.

Caden was hit on one side, the blow knocking him into the wall — the real and very hard wall, he discovered instantly. He felt something sharp rake across his ribs. Warm blood began to seep through his under-layer immediately, and he glanced down to see parallel slashes in his outer armour.

He ducked to the side just in time, and something heavy thudded against the plasteel where his head had been.

He opened fire again, and—

The explosion was outside the room, but the force and sound of it still filled his world with pain. Plasteel fragments rained down everywhere, some of them seeming to bounce and roll across thin air.

He shook his head, rubbed his eyes, and saw Throam peering along his sights through a ragged hole.

Caden was through the blast hole like a shot, tossing an incendiary grenade back into the security room after him. He hit the ground, and there was another loud explosion, this one much meatier-sounding than the first.

"What the fuck just happened to you?" Said Throam.

"I think I just found out what Shaeld Hratha means," Caden said. He coughed up dust and dirt.

"And?"

"It means bring a grenade."

"Branathes?"

"Dead. Shot him. He was already gone though; Voice had him."

"Voice?"

"Whatever it is that's controlling the Rasas. I'm certain it was in the room with me."

"Holy shit."

"It didn't care about dying, either. Said it would still know what Branathes knew. But it didn't get what it came here for — I have a feeling we'll have more company soon."

∘ ∘ ∘

Brant and Tirrano hurried through the streets of Barrabas Fled, doing their best to avoid the few vacantly staring people who still stumbled this way and that.

"I don't like this," said Tirrano. "It's just wrong. And what is that *smell*?"

"Keep moving," Brant said. "We're nearly there."

"Shame we couldn't have come down right on top of the building."

"Probably wouldn't have taken the weight. That hauler might look small, but it's pretty heavy in a gravity well."

They rounded a corner, and Brant checked his view of the street against his holo.

"That one. That's it."

He pointed to a building opposite, and they ran

across the road. He found a portico entrance with wrought iron sides, and hopped up the steps. The inner doors were unlocked.

He opened one of them. "Hello?"

"Welcome, intruders, to this humble abode," a voice boomed.

Brant nearly leaped out of his skin. "It's a recording."

"Humble?" Said Tirrano.

"Before you waste your own time, know this: everything of value or significance has been removed from the premises. The authorities have been alerted to your presence."

"That might mean he's not here."

"Wait a minute," said Tirrano. "Are you a recording, or a house master?"

"I am a house master," said the voice.

"Where is the occupant?"

"Mister Kages is currently unavailable, due to the end of the world."

"We're here to rescue him from that," said Brant. "Would you please tell us where he is?"

"That request conflicts with my duty to ensure Mister Kages' privacy."

"Listen, you stupid machine," Tirrano snapped. "His life is more important than his privacy."

There was a pause while the artificial intelligence behind the walls of the house weighed up the options.

"I do not have sufficient information to authenticate your intentions."

"Okay," said Brant. "Can you tell him we're here instead? Is that possible?"

"Yes."

"Brilliant. Tell him Elm Caden sent us, and I have his digital seal to prove it."

"Please wait in the lobby while I pass the message along."

Tirrano rolled her eyes, but Brant took a seat on a marble bench. A fountain in the centre of the lobby bubbled happily to itself, strangely relaxing given the circumstances.

Long minutes passed.

"What was that?" Tirrano asked.

"What?"

"You didn't hear it? Listen."

Brant heard it the next time; a drawn-out booming noise, far in the distance. Ripples crossed from one side of the fountain's pool to the other.

"What in the worlds was that?"

There was another boom, and then another.

"Oh my... Brant, I think it's bombardment."

"Bombardment?"

"From orbit. They're glassing the surface."

"They... they wouldn't!"

Another boom, and another, and another. They were coming steadily now, at regular intervals.

"House master, hurry up."

"Please continue to wait."

"If we have to wait much longer, there will be no getting off this rock. It's under attack."

Brant began to feel the tremors through the floor.

"I'm here, I'm here," came a new voice, and he looked towards it.

The man who hurried from the hallway at the other end of the lobby looked haggard, as if he had not been sleeping. He had a civilian re-breather over his face, which gave his voice a muffled, plastic quality.

"Joarn Kages?"

"The very same, my boy. And you are?"

"Occre Brant. This is Peras Tirrano. Elm Caden sent us."

"And not a moment too soon," said Kages.

"You're telling me. We have to leave, right now."

Kages took one last look around, and followed them out of the door.

The ground was shaking by the time they reached the hauler. Every few seconds, dust and pebbles leapt into the air. Far away on the horizon, Brant could see clouds of orange-black flame erupting from the surface of the planet.

"Mestivar," said Kages. "That was the city of Mestivar."

"Let's get off the surface, before this city goes the same way."

"I heartily endorse that initiative," said Kages, and jumped onto the hauler's ramp.

They ran inside, and Tirrano hit the control to close the ship. She lost no time in getting to the cockpit.

"Running preflight," she said. "The short version."

"System overview is green," said Brant. "Go, go, go!"

The hauler lifted, and she began to put distance between them and Mestivar before the little ship started to leave the surface.

"Stealth plates engaged," said Brant.

"Oh my worlds," said Tirrano.

Brant looked over her shoulder, and saw the holo she was looking at. She had brought up the view from the aft sensor array.

Behind them, the entire horizon was ablaze.

○ ○ ○

Throam had taken point wordlessly after the encounter in the security control room, and Caden guessed that the close call with Voice and his guardians had reminded the counterpart of his primary duty.

They moved swiftly through the building, silent, checking the corners and doorways carefully but never quite stopping.

"This is it. Holding."

Caden motioned for Eilentes to take up position outside the door, and Throam raised his rifle. He nodded to Caden.

They went in together.

Inside, the entranceway was being guarded by two Eyes and Ears officers. They both carried submachine guns, and ducked down behind a reception desk the moment the doors opened.

"Don't come any closer," one shouted.

"Stand down," Caden shouted back. "I'm a Shard. We're here to extract Doctor Bel-Ures. Under the circumstances, I think it would be best if you came with us too."

"Identify," one of them called back.

Caden sent a command to his link via his holo, and after a moment he heard a chirp from one of their own holos.

"It's him all right," the second officer said.

"Where is Bel-Ures?" Caden asked. "I've killed the man who came for her, but we have no idea how many others came with him."

"She's in room six," said one of the officers. "Come this way."

Caden and Throam followed him to the rear of the room, through double doors into the corridor beyond. The officer continued, until he reached the third door on the right, knocked, and entered.

Caden followed him in.

"Doctor Bel-Ures?"

She had been pacing up and down, but stopped when he spoke. She turned to face him.

"What now?"

"I'm here to extract you, Doctor. My name is Elm Caden."

"Just you?"

"And my team. I'm a Shard."

"I see. I'm not sure if that should make me feel safer, or more afraid."

Bel-Ures was perhaps fifty, with brown hair that was streaked with grey. She was well-fed, he decided, but not fat. She had a confident air about her, moving casually but with a deliberate dignity.

"We really need to leave, right now."

"Where is my family?"

"Safe," said one of the Eyes and Ears officers. "They're at a different location. We're making arrangements to move them off-world."

"I don't suppose you would like to tell me what this is about, Shard Caden?"

She fixed him with a penetrating gaze, and Caden felt the slightest hint of hostility in it.

"We should walk and talk," he said. "Time is a factor."

"I think I would much rather wait until I know what's happening before I go anywhere with you."

"You see him" — Caden pointed through the open doorway to where Throam stood watching them — "he will carry you out of here over his shoulder if need be. I'd rather not ask him to do that."

"I can walk," she said.

Bel-Ures strode past Caden, her head held high, and stepped out into the corridor. He followed.

"You probably heard we're at war with the

Viskr again," he said.

"I did. It's all over the feeds."

"Yes, well somehow your project at Gemen Station is at the root of it all."

"You're certain of that?"

"The station was attacked. Everyone but you is unaccounted for. They took your weapons."

Bel-Ures was silent. He watched her face, her controlled expression. Her eyes twitched as she considered his words.

"Everyone?"

"Everyone."

"And the weapons too?"

"Every last one of them."

"What about Site Bravo?"

"Site Bravo?"

"You don't know." She fell silent again.

They were back at the building core, and Eilentes signalled that the staircase was still clear. They began to ascend.

"What's Site Bravo?" Caden asked.

"Those weapons you mentioned," said Bel-Ures. "They're one half of the system."

"And the other half is elsewhere?"

"Yes. As far from Herros as we could make it."

"Where is it?"

"I need to speak to Command."

Try as he might, she ignored all further questions. By the time they reached the top floor he had given up.

Throam moved ahead of them again as they left the atrium behind and headed for the corridor to the roof pad access. Eilentes dropped back, and the two officers flanked Caden and Bel-Ures, slightly ahead.

They reached the external door, passed through

it, and headed into the roof tunnel.

Caden looked at Bel-Ures. "As soon as we get back to the *Disputer*—"

His words were cut off by an explosion ahead of them, and Throam was thrown back into the mouth of the tunnel. The counterpart slid along the floor on his back, then rolled onto his knees and clambered back to his feet.

"Fall back!" Eilentes shouted.

Caden pulled Bel-Ures away before she had time to react, grabbing her wrist and tugging until she followed him back down the tunnel. He heard a shot behind him, and looked over his shoulder to see one of the Eyes and Ears officers land dead on the floor.

"Eilentes, take her," he said, and propelled Bel-Ures towards the pilot.

He turned back, hugging the wall of the tunnel, and pulled his rifle from its mag-tag.

Throam was back inside, also against the wall, sweeping the mouth of the tunnel and the landing pad beyond, peering down the sights of his rifle.

Smoke billowed from the wreckage of their shuttle's hull. So much for 'borrow'.

"Throam," Caden shouted. "We'll go another way."

"Hold up," said Throam.

"No. We go now. Stop trying to be the hero."

Throam started to step backwards, slowly at first, then turned and jogged towards Caden.

More shots followed, semi-automatic this time. Caden lingered long enough to see a dim figure stepping though the smoke and haze, a rifle aimed right at them.

"Let's get out of here."

They ran back along the tunnel, through the

door, following Eilentes, Bel-Ures and the remaining officer. Caden stopped just inside the doorway, his hand moving up to slap the control panel.

"I don't believe it," he said.

Throam followed his gaze, back the way they had come, and saw the shooter approaching the mouth of the tunnel cautiously.

"Is that—?"

"Maber fucking Castigon," said Caden. "Of all the times he could have picked."

Throam hurled himself forwards the instant he saw Caden start to move.

# – 18 –
## COMPROMISED

Bruiser was not alone in the gym compartment on *Disputer*, but he might as well have been.

With his link laying unused in his kit bag, the voices of the human crew down near the cardio machines were nothing but alien jibber-jabber; nonsense background noise drifting through the air. At any other time, his link would be constantly and indiscriminately translating the human speech it picked up. When he was training, however, Bruiser preferred not to listen. Human ideas were as numerous as human feelings, if not more-so, and both could become tiring. After a while any sensible Rodori needed a break. In any case, heavy lifting required proper concentration.

The best thing about the *Disputer*, he had rapidly discovered, was its gym. The heavy carrier must have played host to body-building enthusiasts frequently, because someone had taken the time to change the standard gym layout, emphasising the equipment that serious lifters would want to use, and putting some real experience and thought into the setting. Whoever had done it — whether it was an individual or a like-minded group of crew members — they had actually *cared* that their gym should truly serve their needs.

Much of the kit laying around had clearly been brought in after the facility was installed; crew had added bits and pieces to the various collections themselves, also cobbling together safety measures wherever the integrated systems could not accommodate unplanned additions.

At the foot of the deck-to-overhead mirrors running along one bulkhead, a steel safety cable snaked through the handles of a motley crew of kettlebells; red, black, blue and silver, some with the owners' service numbers stencilled on them, others without, all of them in order of mass, all secured by the tether that would prevent them from becoming unpredictable missiles in the event of an unexpected gravity failure.

Bruiser's greatest discovery though had been a heavy pressing bench — rated to support over fifteen hundred kilos — and the adjacent magnetic rack stocked with proper plates. They were real iron, of up to one hundred kilos each.

*Real iron!* For once, the weights were so dense he could physically fit enough of them on the bar to meet his goals. For the first time in a long time, he not only had plates which would let him hit his maximums, but a bench that could support both his body and the loaded bar without being crushed flat between their combined mass and the pull of the deck's gravity plating.

He guessed correctly that *Disputer* regularly carried members of Tanker Regiment to their assignments. Thanks, Tankers.

He was peripherally aware, as he started his first set on the bench press, that he was being watched from across the deck. The jibber-jabbering had ceased. He ignored the *Disputer* crew members, and concentrated on his form instead. Humans, it seemed, were not often treated to the spectacle of someone pressing so very many kilos, and Bruiser was well-accustomed to being stared at in their gyms.

After his first set he placed the bar carefully back on the stands and leaned over to his bag. Pulling out a huge towel, he rolled it tightly and placed it across the bench. How these people could stand to press upwards while laying with their backs completely flat was quite beyond him.

Human skeletal structure made no sense to him, no sense at all.

○ ○ ○

Captain Thande allowed herself the luxury of a cup of tea. Normally she would not take hot drinks to her station, but this was a rare moment of peace. She expected nothing more than to await Caden's return, then to leave the system with dignity and decorum.

The command deck thrummed with the gentle rhythm of power couplings and air circulation. As usual, her crew were professionally quiet, just the way she liked it.

Meccrace Prime rotated lazily at the port-side edge of the forward view port, with the large bright point that was Duraang trailing after it to the starboard-side, millions of kilometres farther out. The nearer planet must have lapped the outer one a matter of a few days ago. She knew from the helm display that Nathal was on the other side of the star right now, but even with just the two planets in view, and the star field beyond, the scene was spell-binding. Far, far too magically tranquil to be allowed to last.

Tactical shattered the serenity.

"Captain, I'm detecting a number of wormholes

opening throughout the system. They're concentrated around Meccrace Prime."

"Is the gate active?"

"Negative Ma'am."

"Close blast barriers. Sound general quarters, and signal all commands to do likewise."

"We have incoming ships," said COMOP. "Oh..."

"What is it?"

"Ma'am, they're... it's..."

Thande gave up waiting for her Communications and Operations officer to describe his readings, and craned her neck to look for herself.

"Oh my fucking worlds," she gasped.

One by one the rest of her command crew looked across, shocked by their captain's uncharacteristic outburst, and they each caught sight of the dreadful holo. Open mouths released gasps of disbelief, were covered by hands, were nonetheless betrayed by the whites of wide eyes.

The field of view of the sensor feed displayed on the holo was far too small to convey the full scale of the arrival, and yet still it awed and shook them all.

"Unknown vessels are adopting aggressive stances, Ma'am. No IFF signals as yet."

"Defensive posture," Thande said. "Back us off, maximum thrust. Do not — I repeat, *do not* — open fire. Not until we know what we're dealing with."

COMOP worked at the main battle map for a few seconds, trying to wrangle the holo into doing what he asked of it. Eventually it was convinced to pull back to a wide view combining the feeds from all forward sensor palettes, without losing the scaled-down intruders from the scene.

"This can't be happening," Thande said.

But the battle map did not lie. Across the wake of Meccrace Prime, wormholes punctured the emptiness of space. Ship after vast ship emerged, thundering silently through the dark; monstrous and predatory.

"How many?"

Tactical had turned pale. "I'm reading seven so far, Captain. But they keep coming."

"Assessment?"

"I don't like to guess," she said. "Just one of those things looks as though it'd be a match for everything we have in the system."

"I had a horrible feeling you were going to say that."

"Ten."

"COMOP. Just on the off chance they aren't looking in that direction, alert Meccrace Defence Control."

"Yes Ma'am."

"Twelve."

"Tactical, you had better not be counting ships still."

"Afraid so, Captain. Sixteen. Holding at sixteen. Wormholes appear to be attenuating, not closing fully."

"So they want a live feed between them and wherever they came from."

"That would be my bet," COMOP said.

"Santani's dreadships," Thande said, as much to herself as to anyone else. "They have to be."

"Running pre-emptive e-warfare countermeasures," said Tactical.

"Good. Prime our hard defences too. And get talking to our other commands. Coordinate a threat assessment, and work up a projection for defence of the planet."

"Yes Ma'am."

"Captain," COMOP said. "I'm... I'm seeing a number of unexpected system events across the ship."

"Explain."

"I can't. None of this makes sense. Oh! No, no, no! Bay six was just vented."

"Lock it down!" Thande snapped.

"I'm not seeing any intrusions in the comm systems," Tactical said. "This isn't interference from the outside."

"No, these are manual events."

"What in the Deep?" Thande shouted. "You're telling me someone *on this ship* just blew out a flight deck?"

The lights flickered.

"Ma'am, these events are coming from different locations across the ship."

"I've just lost main engines, and the reaction control system," said Helm. She pressed and swiped different areas of her holo experimentally, to no effect. "We're drifting."

"Internal security is compromised: cameras are down, and the firearm inhibitor system just switched off. I'm going to try rebooting it."

Thande nodded her acknowledgement at Tactical, and turned her attention back to COMOP. "Get me a location for every control interface accessed in the last few minutes, and..."

She trailed off with the dawning realisation that the gravity systems had failed.

As one, most of the crew on the command deck strapped themselves in to their stations, some having to pull themselves back down onto the seats from which their own small movements had launched them. Thande pulled her chair's restraints across herself, and snapped the buckles closed.

"Captain!"

Thande looked towards the shout to see COMOP sailing towards her through the air. No, not towards her; he would pass in front of her face. She followed his gaze, turned to her right, saw blood gurgling out of a deck officer's throat and crawling across his neck, face, and tunic, some of it bubbling off into the air. A ceramic blade, pointed straight at her, pierced the air on its way towards her own throat, a red hand and arm propelling it, and beyond that a face that was a rictus of intention purified, with no human spirit behind it whatsoever.

She saw this all in a split second; a slice of time that seemed to last forever, frosty and brittle and distant.

And then Thande's COMOP officer smashed bodily into the XO, and his momentum overcame that of the would-be assassin. They drifted back to the bulkhead, blood now crawling along his arm where the blade had glanced off him, and he grabbed at Yuellen's wrist. The XO seemed to take several seconds to realise that the situation had changed, his gaze had been locked on Thande with such grim determination. Yuellen writhed, but COMOP's grip was firm.

Thande was swamped by a sudden wave of wider awareness, and saw others coming to help, hitting the releases on their buckles and pushing themselves off from their seats to float towards the struggle.

"Tactical," she said, her voice wobbly. "Seal the command deck. Alert all security stations: we have a mutiny underway."

○ ○ ○

For a moment, Bruiser was too preoccupied to notice the change in the ship's condition. But when he brought the bar back down, and the stands took over from his arm muscles, he felt his back lift away from the bench. His feet left the floor at the same time, and he cursed loudly. No gravity meant no realistic prospect of continuing his gym session.

He rolled onto his side, and flicked the safety latches over the barbell while he waited for the gravity to resume. Allowing the bar to leave the stands under its own recognizance would be a seriously bad idea.

While he wiped himself down, he was aware that some human gibberish was being broadcast over the ship's comm system. Whatever it was it could wait. Chances were it was just some human pointing out the obvious gravity failure for the benefit of all the other humans.

The towel stayed by his side when he released it.

He found he was thirsty, and decided he might as well use the wait to refresh himself. He stood carefully, and began to propel his body along the deck in the crouching, sweeping way he had learned early on in his military career.

The lights flickered, then went out row by row. He cursed again, dragging to a stop, and waited for the emergency illumination strips to show the way.

The faint blue lights came on after what felt like an eternity, and he started moving again, then immediately stopped once more.

There was movement in the gloom ahead of

him.

He had been fairly sure that the other gym users had given up and left while he was still working — even those who were trying obviously and tragically to compete with him — and he had not noticed anyone else coming in. But then he had been concentrating on his workout to the exclusion of all else.

It did not surprise him at all that someone else might have come to start their own session, but there was something not quite right here.

Three figures now stood motionless in the dim light. Still. Silent.

One of the silhouettes moved again, and Bruiser realised with a shocking jolt that the figure was raising a rifle, aiming straight for him. The compartment echoed the plastic-sounding *twuck* of the weapon's refusal to fire aboard ship.

He was moving sideways before anything else could happen.

The figures split up, one coming straight forwards and the others moving outwards to flank him. He realised he didn't have his link, which would stop him from understanding anything they said to each other—

But then they *weren't talking*.

The observation popped into his mind, and jostled for position with all the other odd questions that the situation threw up.

The first figure reached him, and in the faint glow of the emergency lighting he saw it was a *Disputer* crewman. Without a word, the man launched himself through the air, hands contorted like bony claws, and Bruiser swung his own fist as hard as he could. The blow connected with the man's shoulder, and he sailed out to the side,

Bruiser's unstoppable force throwing him into the air.

Bruiser floated backwards slightly, the momentum exchange of the impact pushing even his huge bulk away from the collision, and his bare feet scraped across the flooring.

The man had landed awkwardly across a bench, taking the looser part of it down with him, but he was already trying to right himself, untangling his body from the equipment.

Another was coming in from the side, this one also a man. Bruiser saw the glint of a blade in one hand.

Bruiser picked up a fifty-kilo plate, swung his arm back, and hurled it as hard as he could, pushing down through his legs and feet. He floated to the overhead, and pushed off again to return to the deck.

The iron disc sliced through the air, smashing against the man's head with a wet thud. He flipped backwards, his feet lifting off the floor, and tumbled away. He hit the deck and bounced off, floating slowly towards the overhead. Bruiser had no doubt that he was dead.

The first attacker was now on his feet again, perched like some kind of feral creature atop the bench he had fallen across. He began to tense up, and Bruiser anticipated him this time. The Rodori picked up a loaded barbell, left on the stands by someone too lazy to put their weights away, and swung it with perfect timing.

The man had thrown himself through the air again, hurtling towards Bruiser with goodness knew what in mind. The end of the barbell — and the forty kilos of metal plate that went with it — crunched into his ribcage.

He folded around the weights, broken, and coughed up blood. Bruiser let go. The man and the metal tumbled away until they hit another piece of equipment, separated, and the limp body became snared.

Bruiser headed back up the deck towards the mirrors, aware that the third figure was moving in parallel with him. He reached the end of the aisle, cracking the mirror he landed against, and reached down to the metal safety cable. Hand over hand he pulled himself to the far bulkhead, and unclipped the carabiner that secured the cable.

He picked up the nearest kettlebell, and began to swing it around as fast as he could.

The third figure was opposite him, and he could see it was a woman dressed in engineering overalls. She too carried a blade.

He released the kettlebell, and it sailed off towards her. She moved casually out of its way, and began to advance as best she could.

Bruiser had to get closer to her to reach the next kettlebell.

That one too sailed far too slowly to connect, and she had ducked down long before it reached her. She didn't even stop moving.

Bruiser moved closer still, and picked up the next heaviest kettlebell. The only way this was going to work was if he used it as an over-sized knuckle-duster.

He was fine with that.

○ ○ ○

Confusion and horror competed for ground on COMOP's face, mirroring the overlapping messages that sputtered across the comm system.

"I'm getting reports from all over the ship, Captain. It's chaos."

Thande heard a distinct *pop-pop-pop* from somewhere beyond the closed blast doors. Small arms, most likely removed from one of the emergency lockers containing the spare weapons which lacked remote inhibitors.

When the gunfire had stopped, there was a pause. Then a solid object thudded heavily against the outside of the heavy security hatches, again and again.

"Get me security, now," Thande barked. "I want this shit under control."

"You'll need more than security." The XO chuckled at her. He stood, pulling against the metal restraints that bound his wrists to a safety rail. "Security is exactly the thing you don't have."

"You can fucking stand by, Mister," Thande snapped.

A metallic clanging sounded somewhere far below them, and the command deck trembled in response.

"What was that?"

"Minor hull breach below decks, Captain. We're taking fire."

"The dreadships?"

"No Ma'am. It's one of ours. *O Hallowed Morn* is firing on us!"

Commander Yuellen laughed out loud.

"Switch off the IFF recognisers," Thande said. "Tell the C-MADS turrets to shoot down anything that gets too close. Anything!"

Tactical sent the orders to the defence network, and the clanging was replaced by the familiar thumping of the turrets firing off their interceptors.

"Get me a sit-rep on the Meccrace defence fleet."

Tactical's face was ashen. "I'm seeing most of our ships listing, Captain. A handful are firing on each other."

"Worlds! There must be traitors on every damned one of them."

"I have the Master-at-Arms on the comm, Captain."

"Panovar? About fucking time. Tell him his teams are to kill anyone they see lifting a finger against the proper operation of this ship, or against any crew defending it."

COMOP relayed the order to Panovar.

"He's asking how he's meant to know the difference."

"He'll just have to do his best," Thande said. "Can't ask much more of the man."

"Ma'am, *The Last Days of Dojin* is headed right for us. Collision course."

"Do we have thrust yet?"

"Negative on that. At current speed, impact in a matter of minutes."

"Tell them to cut their engines, COMOP, or we open fire."

"They're not acknowledging, and not slowing either."

"Tactical; what do we have that will stop them?"

"Nothing short of ship-to-ship missiles will do it, Captain. They're coming at hard burn. We'll have to break up the mass."

"Shit. *Shit*."

"It's them or you," her XO said. His mouth was curled into a nasty smile.

No, not her XO. Her *ex*-XO.

"You can fuck right off." She turned her attention back to Tactical. "There has to be another way."

"There's no other way and you know it," the once-XO said. "It's them or you."

Thande looked between the traitor and the battle map. The prow of the *Dojin* was getting bigger with every passing second. With every passing second, Yuellen's sneer deepened and his crowing chuckle became more disturbing.

Them or you. Not 'us', but *you*.

Funny, she thought, the odd little things you notice during a crisis.

"Moments to go, Captain," COMOP was shouting.

"Damn it! Damn it to the darkest fucking Deep! Tactical, fire on the *Dojin*."

"Captain, I... I can't do that—"

"Nuke the damned ship!"

Tactical closed her eyes in the same moment she released the missiles, and ugly laughter filled the command deck.

○ ○ ○

Bruiser pulled himself carefully around the corner of the passageway, using the contours of the bulkhead as hand grips. Blood smeared on the white paint everywhere he touched it.

The humans in the gym had been strange; much stranger than they usually were. He was certain that they were not in their right minds, and he could not help but think back to what he had witnessed on Aldava several days before.

Those people who lived in Barrabas Fled had been insane too. Not quite so homicidal, granted, but they had definitely stepped off the same shuttle.

He had recovered his link from his gym bag, but the comm system was — for all practical purposes — strangely silent. Occasionally there was a burst of urgent noise, but nothing recognisable. Nothing his link could lock onto and translate before the sounds ended.

Red lights pulsed on the overhead, and a two-tone alarm sounded general quarters. The passageways were dim, and eerily empty. A scream came from somewhere off to his left, followed by a thud and another, shorter scream.

He reached an elevator that traversed the main decks, and pressed the call panel. It stayed dark. Above the entrance to the elevator shaft, a heavy hatch was recessed into the overhead. Less than a square metre; there was no way he was going to fit through that.

The emergency lighting faded out, bathing the passageway in the pulsing, blood-red light of the general alert. Several decks away he heard hull impacts, tearing metal, and what could have been an explosion.

As he considered where to go from there, a crew member floated swiftly around the nearest corner. She saw him, screamed in terror, and scrabbled at the bulkhead to kill her forward momentum.

"Wait—" Bruiser said, reaching out towards her. Even as he spoke, he saw she was not wearing her link. His words would have seemed threatening and utterly alien to her even if they had been standing together in a sunlit meadow.

She screamed again, pulled hard on a guide rail, and sailed back around the corner like a darting fish.

"Great. She sees a monster."

He had his link try to connect to anyone he knew who might be listening. Chun was silent, as were Daxon and Bro. Only Norskine replied.

"What's happening?" Bruiser asked.

"Mutiny," Norskine shouted. "It's a fucking mutiny, Bruiser! Don't trust anyone!"

A crashing sound in the background noise drowned her out, and he had to pull the link away from his earhole for a second.

"Are you well? Norskine?"

"Just about. Hold on," she said. Another crash. "Nearly got ourselves pinned down just then. Head for the command deck."

"I'm stuck on seven. Main lifts are out."

"Use the access hatches?"

"Too big. Too big by far."

"Guess you're stuck then."

"I know."

"Hold on... the upper engineering level is on seven. Daxon says you should go there. Pummel anything that doesn't look right."

"Copy on that," he grinned.

○ ○ ○

Silence reigned on the command deck. Thande found she had no words to share with her officers in this moment; no platitude or rousing speech that could possibly help them get past what they had just done.

What *she* had just done.

On the tactical holo, the pathetic fragments which remained of *The Last Days of Dojin* tumbled away from each other, carried by a shell of fading plasma. Some of them would reach *Disputer* soon enough, but not one of them could threaten her. Not now.

Even the XO had finally stopped laughing.

The XO!

Thande pulled against a hand-hold, turning her

body towards him, her eyes narrow and dark, her fists clenched tight.

"Who in the many worlds are you, and what are you doing on my bridge?"

"I'm your executive officer, Captain," he said. "See how I dance for you."

"Are you fuck my XO. Commander Yuellen is a good man. An honest, loyal man. Whoever or whatever you are, you're sure as hell not him."

"I can assure you, I am."

He smiled. That same smile had looked warm and sincere on Yuellen when he cared to wear it, but now it seemed nothing more than an empty taunt.

"What's going on in my ship?"

"Mutiny. Insurrection. Rebellion. Whatever you are most happy to call it. The old order falls away, you see."

"Under whose orders?"

"Orders? Oh, I don't particularly use those. They tend to get in the way."

"Don't fuck with me. Who's in charge?"

"Why, me of course. I *am*."

There was something in the way he said it that unsettled Thande. It was as if he were answering a different question. Or the same question, but answered by—

"Captain, I have Master Panovar back on the comm. He's reporting multiple hostiles throughout the ship, concentrated on the command and engineering decks."

She pulled herself away from not-Yuellen, and turned her attention to COMOP. Whatever the traitor had to say was apparently gibberish not worth hearing, and she had more important things to deal with.

"Have him concentrate his efforts on engineering; he can help restore functions from there. We'll be fine. Nobody is getting through those blast doors in a hurry."

As if to undermine her reasoning, the booming great thuds reverberating through the security hatches began to get louder.

"Of course, he might not be quite the Panovar you are used to dealing with," said not-Yuellen, with obvious satisfaction.

"What do you mean?" Thande asked.

"Until about five minutes ago you seemed fairly convinced I was your XO, and now you are positively certain that I'm not."

"Captain," said COMOP, "he's just trying to unnerve you."

"And it's working," she said. "He has a point. Can we really trust anyone outside those blast doors?"

"Ma'am, why would he risk outing one of his own?" Tactical said. "He's trying to make you think the Master-at-Arms is a mutineer because that's the best way to get you to harm your own interests."

"Can I take that chance?" Thande asked.

"You definitely should," not-Yuellen said. "Absolutely under no circumstances should you attempt to interfere with Master Panovar."

Thande closed her eyes briefly.

"Okay, Tactical. I take your point."

She drew her side-arm, and shot the still smiling not-Yuellen in the heart.

○ ○ ○

Bruiser could be stealthy when he needed to be, which was — given his lack of armaments — a fortuitous skill indeed.

He peered over the safety rail, into the deep well of the central engineering chamber. Six decks down, at least two people were moving about slowly on deck twelve. They pushed themselves over the bodies of engineers without giving them a second glance.

Intruders, he thought. Humans don't usually ignore their dead and wounded.

Silently, he pulled on the rail and lifted his body over it. His aim and speed were going to have to be absolutely correct for this to work. Looking down — which might as well have been up, but which the parts of his brain to do with his continued survival told him it definitely was not — it occurred to him that this would be a terrible moment for the gravity to be turned back on.

He pushed himself out slowly and carefully until he was clear of the edge of deck seven, directly over the well that housed the primary engineering systems. Momentum carried him up towards the overhead.

His feet bumped against the plasteel surface, and he steeled himself. This was it. In a few seconds, if he took no action, he would have rebounded so far away from the overhead that he would not be able to kick off from it.

He launched himself downwards with a good, solid jump.

The man he landed on made a horrible crunching sound, and stopped moving straight away. Almost three-hundred kilos of Rodori, accelerated towards a human body, evidently occasioned total debilitation. Bruiser almost felt sorry for him.

Understandably, the other man was taken by surprise, and he turned around to face Bruiser far too slowly. A giant fist smashed up under his jaw, and sharp fragments of his teeth popped out through his lips. His eyes rolled up into his skull and trembled. Aside from sailing towards the bulkhead and collapsing against it gracelessly, he too stopped moving.

Bruiser took a look around. There seemed to be no-one else about, but he was not going to take chances. Not without some firepower to fall back on.

He noticed a large amount of red displayed on the holos dotted around engineering. For humans, red meant danger, wrong, and limit.

"Stay where you are." The command was barked from behind him. "Raise your hands."

He did as he was told, but also turned slowly, trying as best he could to appear non-threatening.

"Who are you?" The man was holding a rifle, pointing it right at Bruiser's face. Behind him, one to each side, stood two other armed officers.

"Private Bruiser. Bravo Company, 951st."

"What have you been up to in here, eh Bruiser?"

"These are nothing to do with me," Bruiser said, nodding towards the bodies that were strewn across the deck. "Well... two of them are."

"You did this?"

"They did it," Bruiser said. "Whoever these crazy ones are. Two of them in engineering. I landed on one and smashed the other's face in."

"Back away," said the leader. He nodded to one of his companions. "Check them, would you?"

Bruiser moved away compliantly, letting his momentum carry him to a bulkhead away from the bodies. He watched as the subordinate officer pulled herself across the deck, hand over hand, examining the dead with practiced efficiency.

"Most of them were shot or stabbed," she said at last. "But like he said; this one's spine is broken in a couple of places, and that one there... his jaw has been smashed into little bits. Neck's broken too."

"Works for me," said the leader. "Name's Panovar. You probably know what I do in this shiny bucket."

"Master-at-Arms?" Bruiser asked.

"You actually read the passengers' brief," Panovar said. "You nerd."

Bruiser truly did not know how to respond to that. Sometimes his knowledge of human behaviour was simply not deep enough.

"Anyway, these creeps are all over the ship. Captain says engineering is a security priority, so let's see if we can't get it fucking secured, eh?"

○ ○ ○

The tense minutes seemed to crawl by on the command deck, but eventually they dragged into an hour. Thande sat in her chair and waited for word. Word from anyone.

Occasionally, the C-MADS turrets fired off a burst at the debris and ordnance sailing towards the hull. Outside, in the black surrounding Meccrace Prime, most of the ships of the defence fleet appeared to be coming under control. Slowly, so painfully slowly, they stopped firing at each other and regrouped.

Others were not so fortunate.

As well as the *Dojin*, Thande had seen other Imperial ships dying in the silent vacuum. The *O Hallowed Morn* had lashed out at many other ships besides *Disputer*, and eventually those still under full or partial control had joined forces to punch her full of holes. No distress beacon had been sent from the *Morn*; she drifted alone until her atmosphere bled out into the cold. Thande had then been forced to watch helplessly as *The Line is Narrow* rammed his own sister ship, *When the Walls Fell*, obliterating them both.

It was a terrible day for the Eighth Fleet. A terrible, black day for the Imperial Navy. Her heart ached.

Tactical's strained voice brought Thande back to the harsh reality of the command deck.

"Ma'am, change in condition of the unknown ships."

"Report."

"While we've been, uh, fighting, they've formed a cordon around Meccrace Prime. Some of them are going atmospheric."

"Show me."

Tactical brought up the planet on the main battle holo, and Thande peered intently at the moving ships it represented for her.

"What are they doing?" She said. "Zoom in on that one, there."

Tactical obliged.

The dreadship expanded to fill the available holographic volume. An overlay picked out features of interest, marking the functional parts the holo thought it recognised. A helical coil of rear-facing engines around the main body of the ship fired against gravity, lowering the massive craft into the atmosphere with a grace that seemed directly at odds with the vast, monstrous bulk of the vessel. Its stern reached greedily down towards the surface with sharp, black fingers.

"What in the many worlds are they *doing*?" Thande asked again.

"Panovar reports engineering is secure, Captain. Compromised systems are coming back online, and command protocols are being routed to here only; we'll have full control back shortly."

"Excellent." She continued to stare at the holographic dreadship. Its outlandish design was eerily captivating.

"It's stopped," said Tactical.

"What has?" Thande tore herself away from the holo.

"Listen. The blast doors."

"There's no more thumping," Thande realised. "Whoever was trying to get in here has given up."

"Listen!"

Though the thick plasteel barrier, a faint exchange could be heard. Muffled voices; the words blurred together, but the tone unmistakeable. In the passageway just outside the bridge, some kind of confrontation was being played out.

Thande's heart leapt into her mouth when, straining to hear, her ears were assaulted by the sharp rattle of automatic gunfire.

"Can you get the security feed back up?" She asked COMOP.

"If Panovar has restored the internals, yes," COMOP said. "I've got it. Stand by... looks like MAGA troops outside the blast doors. Those ones who came aboard with Shard Caden, I think. They've greased some of our crew."

"Mutinous ones, I hope?"

"Hard to be sure, Captain," COMOP said. "But seeing as they're all laid out across a breaching ram, I'm going to go with 'yes' on that one."

# - 19 -
# A Rock and a Hard Place

Caden's body slammed against the far wall, knocked aside effortlessly by Throam's weight.

"What the hell are you doing?" Caden shouted.

Throam had already turned on his heel, leaped towards the doorway that separated their corridor from Castigon's, and slapped his hand against the control panel. The security door slammed closed with the reassuring clang of solid metal. He was pretty sure there were no insecure controls on the other side, but Castigon was nothing if not resourceful. He locked it just to be sure.

"I said, what are you doing?"

Throam's voice was angry. "You were going to try and fight him."

"You bet your fat ass I was."

"Your orders are to extract Doctor Bel-Ures. If anyone is going to take on Castigon, it's going to be me."

"I was also ordered to kill that cunt."

"Yeah, but she takes priority. *You* have to keep her safe. I don't. I have to keep you alive. Seems to me killing Castigon is a good way to do that."

"Use your head. If you go off to fight him and he kills you, he's just going to come for me anyway, and she'll probably end up caught between us."

"So you're going to go challenge him to a duel? Are you broken? That literally couldn't make less sense."

"It did sort of make more sense when it was still inside my brain," Caden admitted.

"This is what counterparts are for, Caden. This is my whole purpose."

"I don't want you to die."

"Dying is the one thing we all turn out to be naturally good at."

There was a pause before Caden answered.

"I didn't know you ran so deep."

"I can do deep. I *read*, pal. And for your information, my ass is not fat: it's muscular and proportionate. So fuck you, right in the skinny ass."

"I love you too."

Throam turned to face the security door and rested his hand against the wall, just next to the controls.

"You need to leave," he said. "In case he's still behind this door."

"Ren—"

"You need to leave," he said again. "Now, Elm. Right now."

He kept facing the door until he was sure Caden had gone.

○ ○ ○

Even with all the weapons of the *Disputer* at her fingertips, Captain Helia Thande was powerless in the face of the dreadship incursion. While she stood helplessly on the command deck of her carrier — a ship of which she had been so proud for so long — the huge alien craft dominated the skies of Meccrace Prime, and did so with complete impunity.

Overlapping messages from the comm system echoed the feeling back to her. As each one of the Eighth Fleet's surviving ships came back under control, and broadcast their emergencies and their needs, her hope for a victory at Meccrace dwindled.

"—Captain Nahori dead, XO is now—"

"—uncontained fire: all of deck three—"

"—lost engineering. We're going to mount a counter-offensive—"

Thande gritted her teeth. It was no time to feel sorrow; there would be opportunity enough for that later. Unless they were destroyed — then, it would stop mattering.

"What word from the admiral?"

"Ma'am, the *Dawn's Early Light* has gone down," said COMOP. "The Eighth Fleet has no flagship right now."

"Who's taken command?"

"It's a real mess out there. I'm not sure anyone has."

Thande turned her back on the battle map, and returned to her station.

"What's the status of the planet?"

"Hard to tell." COMOP swept his hands through his holo, reorienting data and mapping displays. "It looks like there are plenty of transports and shuttles leaving the surface unhindered. Whatever those things are doing, they aren't stopping people from leaving."

"Well, that's one thing to be thankful for. Any word from Shard Caden?"

"No Ma'am."

She cursed under her breath.

"Send a message to all commands. I suggest

that the fleet starts taking on refugees. If those things are happy to let ships escape, hopefully they won't interfere with us."

"What about the people still on the surface?" COMOP's hands were already flying across the holo.

"There's nothing we can do about that for the moment. Signal planetary defence control for both Duraang and Nathal; if they haven't started already, they ought to begin evacuations of their own."

"Yes Ma'am. On with that now."

"As soon as you're done with that, get me a priority channel to Fleet Command. I'll pick it up in the wardroom."

"Ma'am, I'm seeing new activity. Those ships are all in the atmosphere now, and they're up to something."

"Show me."

Tactical placed her holo into the central battle map control station, and expanded the image.

"Here. This one gives the clearest view."

Thande leaned closer, peering at the dark shape. It nestled in the clouds of Meccrace Prime as if it were a vast parasite clinging to its host.

"What am I looking for?"

"Wait a moment. It happens at interval—"

"Oh! I saw. Can you replay that?"

"One moment... there."

Thande watched the holo playing back the footage frame by frame. Below the bulk of the dreadship's main hull, from amongst the sweeping, tapered protuberances on its stern, something had fallen away and accelerated towards the ground. The image was blurred, and partially hidden by cloud, but she got the impression of a long, slender shape, as dark as the craft it had parted from.

"What in the worlds was that?"

"Could be a landing craft of some sort," said Tactical. "Or a weapon."

"Ma'am," said COMOP. "When you're ready, Command is on the line."

"The situation just changed; I can't talk to them now. Just send them everything we've recorded and ask for assistance. Any and all available fleets."

"Captain, I don't really have the authority to demand—"

"You send them these sensor records, COMOP, and I guarantee you we'll be knee-deep in reinforcements within the hour."

"If you say so, Ma'am."

"Tactical, get me a structural analysis on those ships. I want to know what their weak points are."

"I've been trying, Captain. The only components that the holos and I agree on are the engines, and the point defences. Everything else is up for debate."

"We don't have time for a debate. Give me a strategy."

"Captain," COMOP said. "Fleet acknowledge receipt of our data. They're mustering a task force now."

"Oh ye of little faith," Thande said. "Any thoughts, Tactical?"

"Those engines around the main hull of the vessel look like they're holding the ship in the atmosphere. They also give the appearance of running at capacity. Knock out a few of those, the whole damned thing might de-orbit."

"Excellent. COMOP, I want you to find me a

target that isn't right over a populated area."

"Stand by... looks like most of them are aloft near to cities and major towns. Even if they drop straight down, there'll be collateral damage. It's a highly urbanised world, I'm afraid."

"Pick the ship with the smallest populations around it, and tell the local towns to evacuate."

"We'll have no way of knowing if they've got the message, much less acted on it."

"There's a ship the size of a mountain dropping things on them. I'd like to think they've got the message already."

∘ ∘ ∘

"He's moved," Throam said. "Looking for another way in. Keep an eye out."

"Understood," said Caden. Throam sounded weary over the link, but Caden knew he had a lot left to give. Rendir Throam always did.

"Gonna check the roof access points," said the counterpart.

"Listen, Throam," said Caden. "I don't want to leave you on your own like this."

"Forget it. You've got your mission; I've got mine."

Caden looked at Bel-Ures, hurrying along the corridor with Eilentes just ahead of him. He wondered how much the woman's knowledge was really worth, in units of Throam.

Probably less than one.

"I didn't mean... I don't want to leave you to face him on your own, yeah, but I meant if we have to part ways, I don't want it to be on these terms."

There was a long silence, and Caden began to wonder if the channel had dropped out.

"Kind of busy at the moment," said Throam.

"I know. But if this is going to be our last conversation—"

"Don't be stupid. I'm going to mangle him."

"He's killed pretty much everyone else he has gone after, Ren."

There was another silence.

"Thought you said I was reliable?"

Caden smiled to himself. "I did. I meant it."

"Well stop worrying then."

"But I said some things—"

"And I deserved them. Concentrate on getting her out of here."

Throam closed the channel at his end.

Caden realised when the conversation was over that he was lagging behind, and hurried to catch up with the others, bounding down the stairs two at a time. He reached the landing, where Eilentes waited with Bel-Ures and the Eyes and Ears officer, and hunkered down next to them.

"One more floor," said the officer. "Then we can leave by the level two entrance and go directly to the ground-side landing pads."

"Can you get us a ride?"

"There are usually shuttles and transports waiting in the bays. We travel to the other planets in the system regularly."

"Good. As soon as we're aboard, we'll need to place a comms call to the nearest MAGA installation. This attack cannot go unanswered. The building needs to be secured."

"I hear that," said the officer.

"Ready?" Eilentes asked.

"Ready," said Caden.

Bel-Ures nodded gravely.

"Let's move."

Eilentes set off, taking the lead this time, and

Caden brought up the rear. They moved swiftly and quietly down the stairs, and the officer pointed the way to Eilentes.

It was not long before they reached the exterior doors, and Caden motioned for Eilentes to take up a position on one side. He took the other. When the doors opened, nothing happened.

Caden peered out, scrutinising the compound that occupied the high ground at the rear of the building. More than a hundred metres away, a safe distance from the building, he could see the blink of beacons around the perimeter of a landing pad.

"Looks okay," he said.

"I'm not seeing any movement," said Eilentes. "Not much cover though."

"You want to hang back and wait for us to reach the shuttle bays?"

"Be my pleasure," she said. She hefted Ambrast, as if impatient to set him loose.

"Doctor," said Caden. "We're going to stay at a steady run until we reach the shuttle bays. Are you going to be able to do that?"

"I will manage," she said. "Not that it would appear I have much choice."

"That will do."

Caden took one last look around the compound, searching for likely ambush points, then stepped through the doors. After a few paces, he motioned for Bel-Ures and the officer to follow him, and set off at a run.

They were almost at the shuttle bays when the first splinter broke the ground behind them.

○ ○ ○

Throam hurried along one of the many identical corridors, hoping it was the right one.

After checking the rooftop, he had decided that Castigon had found another way in. There was no sign of the man anywhere, and only a single body and the smouldering debris from the *Disputer* shuttle remained as evidence that he had ever been there.

There were only a few ways to get into the building from the roof, Throam had worked out, and most of them would cause some kind of tell-tale damage.

Sure enough, looking over the roof edge to the level below, he had seen that the next floor down was bigger than the rooftop he had been standing on. There was a walkway below; a setback which formed a balcony garden for the top floor.

At one end of the balcony garden, a glass door had been forced.

He had entered carefully by the same means, moved silently through the conference room beyond, and found himself in one of the building's many identical corridors. Now, expecting that Castigon would anticipate and intercept Caden's escape route, he headed back towards the core of the building.

It turned out to be a sound prediction. He spotted Castigon ducking through a doorway, apparently unaware that he was being stalked, and decided to try to get ahead of him.

Throam sprinted down the corridor, more confident now with the layout of the building, and skidded to a near-halt at the next junction. He barrelled around the corner, sprinted again, then came to a juddering stop.

If he knew where he was going, Castigon would come through the next doorway to reach the stairwell.

Throam lay in wait, pressed up against the wall, his pistol gripped tightly in front of his chest.

After what seemed like an eternity, but which he told himself was probably a matter of minutes, the doors hissed open.

Maber Castigon was just metres away.

Throam raised his pistol and pointed it at the space in front of the doorway, ready for a chest shot.

Something skittered into the hallway, and by the time Throam realised what it was, thick, brown smoke was everywhere.

He hurled himself blindly to the opposite wall, emptying the clip as he went. Somewhere in the smoke, Castigon was firing back and also missing with every shot.

Throam's pistol gave a hollow *clunk*, and he ejected the empty magazine, grabbing another from a hip pouch. The empty dropped from the grip, fell, landed on the ground with a sharp clatter.

Something big thumped against him, and he found himself carried backwards by Castigon's full body weight. He pivoted, grabbed at the other man, and threw him to the side.

He heard Castigon hit the ground, the grunting noise he made as he landed, and the sound of a weapon sliding across the floor. His own pistol and the fresh clip had been knocked from his hands by the impact, falling into the impenetrable smoke.

Throam gave Castigon no chance to recover his weapon. Still blinded, he leapt towards the noise and reached down. His fingers found clothing, movement, and he started punching.

A hard knee was suddenly in his face, and his

head jerked back, pain shooting through his cheekbone. He grabbed for the leg, found his grip, and yanked it towards him.

Throam was beginning to get a feel for Castigon's position, and slammed a fist down hard, right where he expected Castigon's guts to be.

He heard a fast, pained exhalation, and Castigon's body folded up around him. Arms reached up to grab back at him, and suddenly Castigon was holding on to Throam's rear armour plate, his legs underneath the counterpart and his chest pinning an arm.

Throam felt a thudding against his armour, heard the sharp jab of a dagger being struck against the plates. Then suddenly a tight pinching sensation, and a pain shooting up his side. He knew what it felt like to be stabbed.

He reached around with his free arm, grabbed the back of Castigon's neck, and pulled his head back hard. His left arm freed, he smashed the back of his elbow against the murderer's face.

"That's for Ider," he said at last.

Castigon said nothing, but grabbed at Throam's arm with both of his hands. He was strong, but nowhere near strong enough to do anything of use with the arm.

Throam pushed weight down through his shoulder and strained his triceps, pressing Castigon's head and shoulders to the floor, stealing the space that he needed to strike back effectively. He brought back his right hand and punched Castigon square in the face.

"That's for Molcomb."

He heard Castigon blow blood from his mouth and laugh.

"You're gonna have to do better than that,

slave."

"Shut the fuck up. You don't get to speak to me. Ever."

Throam punched him again, then again. He could feel the fight leaving Castigon, heard his head bounce off the floor each time his big fist connected. Castigon's face was becoming slippery and sticky.

Without warning, the pain in his side burst into a white hot spear, the sensation shooting into his chest and along his right arm. Castigon had grabbed the dagger he had left in Throam's side, and pulled down on it.

Throam bellowed in agony, and without thinking about it he reared backwards, shifting his weight off Castigon. As hurt as he was, Castigon was scrabbling away immediately, and Throam could hear him climbing awkwardly to his feet.

The smoke was beginning to thin, and Throam launched himself at the vague shadow he saw moving through the veil.

He hit Castigon full on in the chest, one broad shoulder driving up under his chin, and pushed him back as hard as he could. They both went down again, sliding across the floor.

"You're going to pay for every Shard and counterpart you hurt, Castigon."

"Fucking rat," Castigon said. "You're not going to stop me. Caden is going to wish he died at birth."

Throam roared and battered and smashed, right up until the moment the sky fell through the building.

○ ○ ○

"Caden?"

Eilentes coughed, her lungs burning with the

sour tang of acrid smoke and the sharp, gritty dust that had been thrown up by the splinter. She turned this way and that, unable to see any of the others.

"Doctor Bel-Ures?"

She called out again and again, panic taking hold now that silence was returning to the compound.

There was a cough off to her right, just up ahead, and she ran towards the sound. She skidded to a halt, dropping to her knees, and found a body moving under a thin layer of rubble.

"What the fuck was that?"

Eilentes helped Caden sit upright.

"I don't know," she said. "It's... well, see for yourself."

She pointed, and Caden rubbed the dirt from his eyes. His mouth opened when he focused on the splinter, but no words came.

"I know, right?"

Eilentes had seen the splinter land with her own two eyes. She could hardly believe the size of it, and struggled to wrap her brain around the manner of its arrival.

The splinter stared back at them.

It was monolithic. A dark hull clicked and hissed as heat fled from it, and steam drifted down towards the ground. Its surface seemed to draw the light inside itself.

"I think we should get away from it," said Caden. "Whatever it is, it's bad."

"Where's the doctor?" Eilentes said. She grabbed Caden's arm, and hauled on it as he climbed to his feet.

"She was practically next to me."

"Help me."

The voice was weak, shocked, and they both moved around the splinter in the direction it came from. Bel-Ures was still on the ground.

"I think I twisted my ankle," she said.

Caden and Eilentes helped her up, each taking a side.

"The Eyes and Ears guy?" Caden asked.

"I think he's under *that*."

"Shit," said Caden. "Didn't even ask him his name."

"Too late for regrets," said Eilentes. "We have to go."

"Second the motion," said Bel-Ures. She coughed, and spat dirt on the ground.

"Listen," said Caden.

A roar was building in the sky above them, a roar accompanied by a whistling shriek. They looked up and saw white vapour billowing around a dark, slender missile, streaking towards the ground.

The second splinter hit hundreds of metres away, out beyond the perimeter. It plunged deep into the ground, sending up plumes of soil and smoke, biting into the surface of the planet and sinking until only the top half of it was visible.

"The shuttle bays," said Caden.

They half carried Bel-Ures, ignoring her moans, hurrying as best they could, and reached the end of the row of covered shuttle bays.

Above them, in the skies of Meccrace Prime, another shrieking roar was growing in volume.

"This'll do," said Eilentes.

She steered Bel-Ures into the first bay and almost dragged her to the shuttle. She released her grip on the other woman briefly, tapping her access code into the shuttle's hatch control panel. Caden swore, and she glanced back to see him struggling to take the unexpected weight of the doctor.

"Just one moment," she said.

The hatch popped and hissed open. The roar reached its climax.

"Okay, let's get her inside—"

An almighty crash shook the entire structure, sending spare parts and tools flying from the maintenance racking at the end of the bay. Eilentes stumbled, Bel-Ures falling against her, and she reached out with one arm to steady herself against the ship.

"Oh my worlds," said Caden. "That one hit the main building."

"Quickly," said Eilentes. "Let's get her inside."

"Throam..." said Caden.

"Now!" Eilentes was shouting. "We have to leave or we'll be crushed."

Caden's head snapped back towards her. He looked at Bel-Ures' pained face, and seemed to come back to the moment.

"Right. Come on then."

Between them, they managed to get her up the ramp and strap her down safely in the rear compartment.

Caden headed back towards the ramp.

"What are you doing?"

"Going back for him," said Caden.

"Don't," she said. "There's no time."

"He wouldn't leave *me* to die here."

"It's his job."

He looked at her as though she had just called him the worst names imaginable, and began to turn away. She grabbed his arm and pulled as hard as she could.

"Elm. It's his *job*."

"Let go of me."

"You can't go back. We have to leave."

"It came down on the building. For fuck's sake Euryce, he could be dead."

"Exactly."

She felt the resistance in his arm soften, and he stared at her emptily.

"That's exactly right."

For the first time since she had met Elm Caden, she saw him look broken. His eyes told her more in that moment than Rendir Throam's voice ever had done.

Caden clicked his link.

"Throam. Throam?"

The silence yawned at him.

Outside, somewhere nearby, the shrieking roar was building up again.

"THROAM!"

"I'm here."

"You're alive! Oh my worlds, you're alive. Where are you?"

"Still inside. Place is a mess. I'm sorry, Elm — I lost him. I lost him."

"Never mind that cunt. Can you get to us?"

"Everything is fucked up, Elm. I can't see a way out."

"I'm coming to get you."

"No, don't come for me. I'm not going to make it out in time. You need to get off the surface."

"Listen to him Caden," said Eilentes.

"Don't give me that fatalistic crap," said Caden. "Get out here, now."

"Elm, you're going to have to leave me."

The roar outside tore through the sky, and another splinter hit the building. The south corner sheared away, glass and stone spraying out in a violent cascade.

"Throam? You okay? Throam!"

Coughing came over the link. "Just fell through another floor."

"Don't you die on me now," Caden shouted. "Just get here. We're not going to leave without you, you hear me?"

Eilentes grabbed for Caden's arm again, but it was too late. He was already headed down the ramp. She jogged after him, back down into the bay, rounded the corner, and stopped dead.

"This is new," said Caden.

The splinter in the compound exhaled.

It was more than the steam that still evaporated from the warm surface. More than the black smoke that oozed from the burning residues on the hull. It was a thick, white, roiling fog, venting from inside the splinter itself, billowing down to the ground and rolling out in all directions, engulfing everything in the compound.

"What is it?" Eilentes said.

"Something to avoid. Back! Back to the shuttle."

They hurried back to the bay, ran up the ramp, and Eilentes slapped the control to seal the ship.

"Throam, you still with me brother?"

"Still with you. Power's out. It's dark in here."

Eilentes climbed through the access port to the cockpit, and started to run pre-flight. Green lights welcomed her; Eyes and Ears kept their shuttles in good condition.

She could still hear Caden talking, still hear Throam over the open channel.

"I... I'm sorry for the things I said to you before. You didn't deserve them. Not *all* of them."

"You were right. Tell Euryce I'm sorry. Ashamed. And you... I *was* a being child."

"No, Ren. Please listen. I have to tell you—"

"Get out of here, you idiot."

"I meant what I said, Ren. You're the most reliable person I ever met."

Eilentes hit the engine cycler, and through the deck she felt the thrum of the power relays stacking their charge.

"And you're the best counterpart I ever worked with. You really are."

"Just saying that."

"I'm not, Ren. There's a reason I stuck with you for ten Solars. You must have known that's unusual."

"Are you still here?"

"You always looked out for me, always had my back, and I never wanted to believe you would actually die to keep me alive."

This time there was no retort. Eilentes realised her hand was hovering expectantly over the launch controls.

"You do the things I can't do, Ren. You're... you're like the parts of me that are missing."

She tapped the launch tile, and the shuttle lifted gently from the ground. She nosed it out of the bay.

"I will find you," said Caden. "I will. I'll find you Ren, because—"

"Don't..." said Throam.

"—because nothing in this universe can stop me loving you."

As the shuttle lifted from the surface, climbing steadily away from the pierced planet, Euryce Eilentes wondered how it was that she had never found such words to say.

"Elm, I—"

The channel dropped out.

## – 20 –
## FEAR THE DEEP

Thande was thrown from her chair and landed heavily on the deck. She got up immediately, reseated herself, and yelled at Tactical.

"Full salvo: target Gamma. Don't stop until it blows."

*Disputer* unleashed the full fury of her forward weapons on her chosen target, battering the thick casing of a dreadship's engine mount with her munitions.

The dreadship's response was equally furious.

The carrier reeled under a hail of slugs, her C-MADS turrets almost overwhelmed by the incoming fire. Missiles wove around her streaming countermeasures, coming dangerously close to penetrating the flak curtain.

"Captain, we're losing coverage."

"Has it blown yet? I don't think it has."

The battle map swarmed with data points, the remains of the Eighth Fleet launching everything they had against their designated targets. The lone dreadship was thousands of kilometres from its nearest neighbour, and the Imperial ships harried it with only the strength of numbers on their side.

"Picking up new contacts," said COMOP. "Imperial transponders confirmed. Wait... Viskr transponders also detected. Captain, I think these are enemy reinforcements."

"Show me."

COMOP updated the battle map, and Thande stared at the flaring wormholes that the dreadships had ripped into the Meccrace system earlier on. Dozens of new indicators were spreading out from them.

"Just as Santani told us. Mark those contacts as hostile, and share that information to our ships," she said. "According to the intel Santani provided from Woe Tantalum, those vessels should be a pushover."

"Target Gamma is destroyed," Tactical said. "Orders?"

"Switch to target Epsilon."

Thande allowed herself a momentary surge of triumph, then buried the emotion before it could trap her in the treacherous grip of hope.

"Helm; those wormholes. Can you get a navigational fix from them while they're wide open?"

"One moment, Captain... yes, somewhere in the Deep Shadows. Can't get enough pulsar locks for a specific fix, I'm afraid."

"So, they're coming from the Deep," Thande murmured.

"Message *Tochi* Actual: target Theta destroyed. They're also moving on."

"Enemy ship is losing altitude," said Tactical. "It's working."

"And it's killing us to make it work," said Thande. "COMOP, time to range on the newcomers?"

"Eight minutes, give or take."

"Any word on our reinforcements?"

"Nothing so far."

"If they don't get here soon, there won't be anyone left to reinforce."

"They're flashing us again," said Tactical. "Focusing their lasers on our palettes. I can't target the engine mounts at this range, not without a sensor fix."

"They'll move on, Tactical," said Thande. "They only have so many lasers. Try and knock some of them out."

"Yes Ma'am," said Tactical. She pointed as many of the ship's gauss guns as she could in the general direction of the dreadship, and fired them off repeatedly.

"Captain, *Tochi* is reporting uncontained fires throughout their engineering section. They're withdrawing from the fight."

"Are they able to pick up refugees?"

"I'm asking the question."

Thande felt her heart sink as she watched *Leave Tochi Untouched* flee from the angry dreadship's defensive barrage. The battleship had brought a hell of a lot of guns to the fight, and it pained her to lose them now.

"The *Beckoning Horizon* is going down," said Tactical. "They're entering the atmosphere, uncontrolled."

"*Tochi* is now on rescue detail," said COMOP. "They're under half-power, but it should be enough."

"Enemy vessel has stopped firing on them. Looks like they're only targeting active threats."

"Great," said Thande. "The more ships we lose, the more ordnance comes our way."

"Afraid so, Ma'am," said Tactical.

"The gate's active," said Helm. "New wormhole forming, aft one-ten degrees."

"Identify?"

"Stand by... looks like it's ours."

"Confirmed," said COMOP. "It's the rest of the Fifth Fleet, Captain. And it looks like some of the First are with them."

Thande wanted very much to jump for joy.

"Message *Fearless* Actual, Captain. It's a holographic transmission."

"Open the channel, COMOP."

Thande's holo blinked up a new pane, and Admiral Kalabi's face replaced the systems report Thande had been keeping an eye on. The captain had never been so glad to see the other woman in her life.

"Admiral, we're very pleased you could make it."

"Captain Thande," said Kalabi. "What's the situation?"

"Incursion, Admiral. The enemy ships in the atmosphere are attacking the planet; we don't know exactly how, or even why. They have an allied fleet comprising Imperial and Viskr ships which are under their control. My COMOP is sending you the transponder idents now. We believe their support will be uncoordinated and tactically inept."

Kalabi got straight to the point. "Who is leading the response?"

"The *Dawn's Early Light* went down, Admiral."

"I see. Then I am taking command of our forces for this fight."

"Thank you, Ma'am. Our current objective is to try and take down the large unknown vessel closest to us. We're hitting its primary engine mounts."

"Stand by," said Kalabi. She leaned to one side

and exchanged quick words with her Tactical officer. "Pull back from your target, and engage the enemy reinforcements. We'll take care of this one."

"Admiral?"

"We're fitted with the prototype 'rift' weapon system. Now seems like an ideal opportunity to battle-test it."

"Rift?"

Kalabi smiled. "It'll make sense when you see it in action."

"There is one more thing, Admiral," said Thande.

"What is that?"

"When the enemy first arrived, there was a wave of mutinies aboard all our ships. I think the enemy somehow has control over some of our people. You might have the same experience."

Kalabi's eyebrows raised. "How will I be able to identify them?"

"You won't," said Thande. "Not until they start killing people and sabotaging the ship. Secure your vital systems *now*."

○ ○ ○

The shuttle streaked through the atmosphere of Meccrace Prime, headed away from the vast dreadship which hung pendulously in the sky behind them. Occasionally, briefly, the hull vibrated sharply with the turbulent detonations of nearby anti-drop ordnance.

Caden stared at Bel-Ures, a storm brewing behind his face. The resentment burned in his chest, hot and acidic. A month, a Solar, a *lifetime* ago, he would have squashed it down and soldiered on. But now... now he let it rage inside him.

Her eyes met his, and he knew in that moment that she understood.

"This is not my fault," she said.

"You and everyone else on Herros," Caden said. "Somehow, you helped this happen. I know it."

"You don't know anything about it."

"I know enough. I know you built weapons the enemy just had to have. Weapons that can kill a world, along with every man, woman and child on it."

Bel-Ures smiled, as if someone had told a joke that had soared over the Shard's head.

"Have you ever killed a child? With your own two hands?"

"Of course I haven't," he said.

"No, of course you haven't. But you've still killed children, haven't you? Because of the work you do. Now... do you think that *I* have ever killed a child, with my own two hands?"

Caden was unimpressed with the equivocation.

"You're giving the Empire the means to infect entire planets. That's very different to what I do. It raises much bigger ethical questions."

"If you think it's just the scale of it that's the issue, maybe you shouldn't be trying to lecture me on ethics."

"Don't make me laugh. Your work was about ending life on a grand scale. That's all there is to it."

"All there is to it," she said. "If only it were that simple."

"Isn't it?"

"Hardly."

"Then enlighten me."

"No," she said. "If nobody told you about Site Bravo, then you're not supposed to know."

"We're at war with the Viskr. Some kind of invasion has begun. A world of the Imperial Combine has crumbled around us in a matter of hours, and I just lost my best friend to keep you safe. We're a good way past proper clearance, don't you think?"

Bel-Ures shook her head. "You have no idea, do you?"

"I know about Woe Tantalum."

Her face froze. "What do you think you know?"

"The Empire did something to the planet, then wiped it out."

"Then you really *don't* know."

"We're about to leave the atmosphere," Eilentes said. Her voice filled the rear compartment, cutting straight through their argument. "Looks like there's a full-on battle going on up there. Be ready for some sharp manoeuvres."

○ ○ ○

"Effective range!"

Tactical's shout cut across everyone else on the command deck, and Thande was waiting for it.

"Lasers on that Viskr cruiser; gauss guns to forward ventral surface. Coordinate fire with *Pacifier* and *Fugue*."

The battle map was fast becoming a chaotic churn of icons, and Thande struggled to make sense of it. She shrank the view down to display only those ships that would have an effective firing solution on *Disputer*.

"Taking fire, three sets of incoming."

"Turrets holding."

"*Dominance* is drawing a lot of heat. They're launching drones."

"Launch our own, and have them harry the ships attacking *Dominance*."

"The *Brankfall* is moving in to assist."

"Two enemy corvettes flanking starboard, seventy-one degrees by negative forty."

"*Pacifier* has them."

"Captain," said COMOP. "The *Fearless* has engaged the dreadship."

"Show me."

COMOP flipped his holo around, and she looked away from the battle map to see exactly what it was that Kalabi had planned to do.

*Fearless* was still on approach to the dreadship Thande had been attacking, but slowing down. For a moment nothing happened, then a disc of crackling light formed in the empty space ahead of the Imperial dreadnought. It darkened, visible now only by the section of Meccrace Prime which it obscured, then began to contract.

"Is that...?"

The disc stretched, and then accelerated towards the dreadship, a twisting streamer of energy, the leading edge pulling the rest of it with a fluid elasticity.

The streamer tore into the dreadship's hull, disappearing inside the massive vessel. The dreadship showed the signs of the hit at once, tilting to one side and spewing gasses out into the high atmosphere. Fire erupted from the hole in its flank as it began to sink towards the planet.

"Worlds," said Thande. "We could have done with that earlier."

"It was... it was a free wormhole," said COMOP. "They *fired* a wormhole at it."

"About time someone came up with that," said Thande. She smiled grimly.

"Ma'am, we're still under fire."

"Yes, of course Tactical."

Thande turned her attention back to the battle

map, assessing the fight.

"What's the status of their cruiser?"

"Their defensive turrets are failing; say fifteen percent available capacity. Offensive weapon systems appear to be erratic."

"Excellent. Find us a blind spot in their remaining offensive field, and move us closer. Scramble all pilots to their fighters."

○ ○ ○

"Hold on," Eilentes shouted. "This is going to get rough."

She turned the shuttle sharply, and Caden felt his body try to throw itself sideways from his seat. The safety webbing held him in place, and he waited out the crushing sensation.

He could feel the pull of Meccrace Prime's gravity weaken as they fled the planet. It would not be long before they entered the fray completely.

"What's going on out there?" He shouted.

For a moment there was no answer, and he wondered if Eilentes could hear him over the comm.

"It's... oh my worlds. They're all around us."

"Euryce, what is it?"

"That dreadship Santani described to you. I think its extended family has turned up."

"How many?"

"Uncertain. Several are pinging our sensors from here. They're attacking the surface."

"What have we got in orbit?"

"Picking up transponders from the First, Fifth, and Eighth fleets."

"*Disputer*?"

"Yes, they're still here."

"Stealth plating, and lay in a course."

"I hear that."

○ ○ ○

"They're launching fighters of their own."

"I see it, Tactical. Barrage fire on those launch bays."

"Tracking to target... firing now."

Thande watched the points of light that represented the fighters *Disputer* had disgorged at the injured enemy cruiser. They swarmed around the bigger craft, looping back repeatedly to hit its critical systems. The data overlay on the Viskr ship showed Thande how unproductive its primary weapons had become, and she knew it would not be long before it was dead in space.

"Ma'am! Barrage failed."

"What?"

"Their turrets responded at the last second," said Tactical. "Ninety percent capacity."

"I don't understand...?"

"Their defences aren't down at all. I think it was a trap."

"Send our drones their way," Thande snapped. "Saturation fire on their command deck. Give our fighters any chance you can to pull back."

"The *Tutelar* is well-positioned to assist us, Captain," said COMOP.

"Good; request they hit the cruiser with everything they have."

"Torpedo boats on our flak curtain perimeter," Tactical said. "Port forward quarter and aft one-eighty."

"Don't let them get anything through."

"Tasking C-MADS."

"Fighters?"

"Wings Alpha and Charlie are returning. Bravo are being chewed up."

Thande pressed the back of her hand against

her mouth. She should have known better than to be drawn in by the Viskr.

But then the turncoat fleet should have been a walk in the park. Santani had *said*.

"Message *Fearless* Actual: they're starting to retreat."

"What? Get me the Admiral."

"Stand by... connection established."

Kalabi appeared on Thande's holo, her usually calm exterior obviously ruffled. She brushed hair out of her eyes.

"Captain," she said. "I'm afraid we're going to have to pull back from the planet."

"Can we assist?"

"No. The rift system is taking too long to cycle between shots. We *can* put these ships down, but they will have mobbed us long before we make a dent in their numbers."

"If we regroup, there's a good chance—"

"There's *no* chance. We've taken down two, and that was provocation enough. The others are moving to intercept us. Anyway, we have other problems to contend with over here. We can't fight both battles."

"What's happening?" Thande knew before the admiral answered.

"Fighting on my own decks," Kalabi said. "Thank you for the advance warning; you probably saved a great many lives, not to mention helped me keep control of my own ship."

"I'm afraid the intel from Santani appears to be wrong," said Thande. "The enemy ships out here are fighting smart."

"I see."

Kalabi looked down, dropping her head slightly, and went quiet for a moment.

Thande felt a knot tighten in her stomach as the admiral raised her eyes again. She knew exactly what was coming next.

"We've lost the system, Captain."

○ ○ ○

Eilentes had reacted immediately when she received the general retreat signal from *Fearless*. The irony of it did not escape her.

Turning the shuttle away from the battle, following the projected escape path that *Disputer* was turning towards, she ramped the engines up to full burn.

"What's happening?"

Caden's voice crackled across the comm, and she wondered exactly how best to put the news. Sometimes, she thought, the direct approach is the only one that will do.

"It's a general retreat. We've lost Meccrace."

"No," said Caden. "No, I have to get back down there. As soon as we drop Bel-Ures, I need to get back down to that planet."

"It's no good, Caden. The enemy has taken Meccrace Prime. The fleet is leaving."

There was silence over the comm.

"Caden?"

"Throam is still down there."

For a moment she did not know what to say. Deep inside she knew the counterpart was probably dead.

Caden must know that too, she thought. He must.

"We can't go back," she said.

The first tears oozed from her eyes, and threatened to blur her vision as they swelled and clung to her eyelashes. She wiped them away with the back of her hand, and flicked them towards the bulkhead. They bounced against each other in the zero gee, reformed, and the new globules drifted apart.

"We *have to*."

Eilentes ignored the comm, and kept her eyes fixed on *Disputer*.

∘ ∘ ∘

Thande had been silent for several minutes, her palms flat on the desk in front of her. Around her, also seated at the wardroom table, Santani, Caden, and Kalabi were similarly quiet.

They were all of them stunned.

"How did this happen?" She asked. "How did they sneak this up on us?"

Caden looked at the others. Santani was still staring at the desk, and Admiral Kalabi did not appear as if she had anything to contribute.

He sighed. "Sometimes the light dims so slowly, you don't notice the darkness until it surrounds you."

Thande nodded slowly. "Captain Santani, I owe you an apology. The dreadships are quite spectacularly real."

"I can well understand why you were so sceptical, Captain Thande."

"I'm very concerned that their support ships were so capable, so tactically aware."

"That was not my experience at Woe Tantalum. I can't explain it."

"How many people on Meccrace Prime?" Caden asked.

"Millions," said Kalabi.

"The other planets in the system?"

"I don't know. The ships evacuating them reported incursions were starting there too, just as we left Prime."

"What do we do now?" Santani said.

"I will brief Command," said Kalabi. "By the time we reach the Herses system there should be an armada ready to respond."

"But the war with the Viskr—"

Caden cut Santani off. "At this point, even Command will have to admit that that was a mistake. Sure, they will pin it on someone else, but they won't be fool enough to keep so many fleets tied up with a pointless conflict."

"I hope you're right," said Thande. "Because it will take one hell of a fight to win back Meccrace."

Caden nodded. Given the forces they would be up against, there was no way they could liberate the system with anything less than a total military commitment.

But when that day came, he vowed, his boots would be the first to touch the ground.

*I will find you.*

## – Epilogue –

From afar, on the battlement wall of Camp Camillion, the splinters of the newly formed forest had merely appeared immense. Up close, Delanka was forced to revise his assessment: they were gargantuan.

They loomed above him, reaching up into the night as though they aimed to pierce the firmament and bleed the heavens dry. They rose and rose above the layer of white fog that rolled sluggishly about their bases, towering over everything around them.

He estimated them as being a good kilometre in height. Having witnessed them falling to the surface, he knew that each splinter had buried about a half of its total length in the ground. Two klicks a piece.

What *are* you? He thought.

His helmet was complaining about the mist. Firstly it was not happy with the composition, and he could hear the respirator whirring as it cycled hurriedly. The visor display reported no known pathogens, but it insisted there was a possible organic threat of some kind. All things considered, he should have made the time back at the camp to find a suit with a self-contained air supply. The respirator might not be capable of full filtration.

The second problem was more immediately relevant. Whatever else there was floating about in the thick mist, his visor reported heat. About the temperature of a human body. There was no way he would find Suster just by using the infra-red detectors. Here, at this distance, it was not so much of a problem; the bulk of the mist was crawling around his knees and no higher. But the ground was gradually dropping away, down into a depression which the splinters' collective impacts had probably pressed into the ground. Once he went farther in, the fog would engulf him. Suster could be standing a few metres away, and Delanka would never know.

He didn't have much choice.

He walked on, into the drifting pall, and it was not long before he was surrounded by it. He became disoriented quickly, even with his visor assuring him that he was walking in a straight line. All around him was a shroud, lit softly by the faint glow of the rising moons and the shoulder lights on his armour. It was difficult to know exactly where in front of him the whiteness really was. The light faded out rapidly, and there was nothing in sight that would allow him to judge depth.

He took the journey one step at a time, one foot then the other, avoiding the rocks that had been strewn outwards by the violent landing of the splinters.

Ten minutes passed before he heard the first noise.

The helmet visor placed a pointer in his view, indicating its best guess for the direction, and he stopped dead. Turning slowly, he switched off his lights and unclipped his side-arm from its magtag. With his elbows close to his chest, he aimed the weapon steadily in that direction.

A pause, then it came again: the skitter of stones being knocked aside.

He almost soiled himself when a faint figure emerged partially from the mist, lumbering across his view.

From the size of the figure, the logical, calm part of his brain immediately solved the depth problem by estimating that if it were an average human, then it was about four metres away.

The less rational part of his brain screamed out that he should run away.

Another sound, this time behind him, and he whirled on the spot. Just visible through the vapour, he saw another figure ambling in silence.

They were heading for the splinters, in the same direction he had been walking. They also seemed to be unaware of him.

He waited for a few minutes until he was sure they were well ahead of him, then carried on, more cautiously this time.

When the first splinter began to melt through the veil, rising up endlessly above him like a dark tower, he slowed almost to a stop. He craned his neck to look at it, bending back until he was peering almost straight up. The splinter was difficult to see, but the surface, whatever it was made from, was bizarre.

There was another small noise directly ahead, and he snapped his attention back to the ground, stopping dead. Ahead of him, at intervals of a few metres, he saw a chain of motionless silhouettes.

Slowly, carefully, he dropped to one knee.

It's a perimeter, the military part of his mind yelled. The figures are standing around the splinters, in a Deep-damned defensive perimeter!

There was no way to approach farther without

being seen. He had no way of getting near the splinters without passing between the figures, and even if he came close enough to recognise Suster then they would have seen him already.

Fool! He need not have come so close in the first place; he had a link. He tried to recall if Suster had been wearing his own device the last time Delanka saw him, and could not for the life of him remember.

Why did I not try this earlier? He asked himself. Well, curiosity as much as anything. You knew damned well you'd be coming to take a look at these splinters the moment you saw the first one hit the ground.

He activated his link, and despite the airtight cocoon of his helmet he whispered the word "Suster."

The link tried to open a channel. He heard the familiar *blip* of the channel opening, then there was only silence.

"Suster?" He asked.

He had not believed that it would work, and when it came the reply made his body jerk in an involuntary spasm.

"I am here."

"I can't see you. Where are you?"

"I am here."

"You're going to have to be more specific than that, Staff. Everything looks the same. Where are you?"

"I am here. The world that was made."

Delanka paused, trying to decide if he had heard what he thought he had heard.

"What... what do you mean?"

"Harmony fills the silence," Suster said, "and eternity will dance in celebration. The song is unbroken."

"You have completely lost me," Delanka muttered.

"I am here. I *am*."

"Fuck this." Delanka closed the channel.

He was up and running the second he saw the nearest figures coming for him.

Delanka ran hard, his breathing ragged and fitful in the confines of his suddenly too-small helmet. He was acutely aware of the sound of the respirator, whirring at top speed to clear the moisture as well as feeding him clean air. He stumbled several times on rocks and in small pits and crevices, never quite going down, always bounding forward and managing to keep running.

A hand grabbed for him, glanced off his shoulder. He fell forwards and twisted around as he landed, sliding across the gravel on his back.

He brought his pistol up in a two-handed grip, firing twice into the chest of the man who had caught up with him. The man went down, falling onto Delanka's legs, and the soldier kicked out and tugged them free.

A woman appeared from the mist, her hands outstretched, face pinched in a feral, seeking expression. She saw him scrambling to get up and launched herself at him, shrieking.

Another two shots, and she went down.

Delanka did not wait for others to come towards the sounds. He ran and ran and ran.

By the time the battlement wall of Camp Camillion came into view, he felt as though his organs were about to explode. His lungs burned cold, his sides ached — more so the side where he had been wounded days before — and his leg muscles were beginning to scream at him.

He stumbled on. The sight of safety, he knew from experience, was not the same thing as safety itself.

Minutes later, he reached the plasteel module where he had left Halfre with Omin and Caela. He burst through the doorway, half expecting them to be gone.

"Junn!" Halfre's eyes were wide. "What happened?"

He released the seal grips around his neck, and lifted his helmet from his head.

"I think I found Suster."

"Where is he?"

"In a world of his own. I don't think he's Suster any more."

Halfre gawped at him, and he could see in her face that she did not understand. Worlds, he had been there in person and he could not fathom it himself.

He looked around, and saw that Omin was still secured to the support pole by a cable tie. The young man was sat on the floor, his legs either side of the pole, resting his chest and shoulder against it. His back was towards Delanka, but he could see the rhythmic rise and fall of his chest. He was still breathing, at least.

But there was something more. Tiny movements of the head and neck. Tiny, tiny movements which — in its heightened state — Delanka's brain told him were significant. He stepped towards Omin, and edged around him.

Omin's eyes were closed, but his lips were moving quickly, as if he were reciting something to himself.

Delanka leaned closer.

"What are you doing?" Halfre asked.

"Listening."

He leaned closer still. At the very edge of his hearing, he made out Omin's words.

*"Yes, yes, I feel you yes. And the song is unbroken. Forever the song."*

The words crawled on Delanka's skin like alien spores, poured out of a mouth they didn't belong in.

"What is it?" Halfre's voice was strained.

"I don't know," Delanka said.

A small voice came from behind.

"Mister?"

He turned around, and saw Caela looking out at him from an upturned supply crate.

"Mister, what's that sound?"

"I hear it too," Halfre said. "Quiet!"

Delanka listened, and his heart sank.

It was the sound of many footfalls. The sound of people running across grit and gravel, running into the camp.

They were coming.

# To Be Continued...

The story continues in
*The Ravening Deep*, available now!

The beginning of the end will arrive with
*From Shattered Stars*, due 2016!

Also watch out for two companion episodes:
— *I Dream of Damastion* —
— *The Granite Whistle* —

The Armada Wars novels are all available in paperback form, and to buy or borrow for Kindle devices and the Kindle apps.

Reviews on Amazon and Goodreads
are greatly appreciated.

**ArmadaWars.com**

# About the Author

R. Curtis Venture was born in the United Kingdom in 1978. A graduate of Applied Biology, he has previously worked in entertainment and hospitality, business development, and intelligence analysis. His first great passion was for science fiction, both in books and on the screen, and he spent his childhood years imagining far-off places.

He is currently employed full-time in the legal sector, and somehow also finds time to write.

You can find R. Curtis Venture on both Facebook and Twitter, where he welcomes interaction with readers and encourages feedback. To see what he's reading these days, follow him on Goodreads.

Made in the USA
Charleston, SC
18 September 2016